My Mother's Lovers

Also by Christopher Hope

CHRISTOPHER
HOPE
My Mother's
Lovers

McArthur & Company
Toronto

For Jasper

First published in Canada in 2006 by
McArthur & Company
322 King St. West, Suite 402
Toronto, ON
M5V 1J2
www.mcarthur-co.com

This paperback edition published in Canada in 2007 by
McArthur & Company

Library and Archives Canada Cataloguing in Publication

Hope, Christopher   My mother's lovers / Christopher Hope.
ISBN 1-55278-604-8 (bound).–ISBN 978-1-55278-680-2 (pbk.)
I. Title.
PR9369.3.H65M95 2006   823'.914   C2006-903377-3

Design by Lindsay Nash
Printed in Canada by Transcontinental Printing

10 9 8 7 6 5 4 3 2 1

'In Africa a thing is true at first light and a lie by noon.'

Ernest Hemingway

1   First Light

'They are trying to make Johannesburg respectable ... to
make us lose our sense of pride that our forebears were
a lot of roughnecks who knew nothing about culture and
who came here to look for gold.'

Herman Charles Bosman

I

I once asked my mother who my father had been.

We were shooting buffalo and, for the only time in her life, I reckon, she shot to miss. She turned her huge blue eyes on me – the rifle kicked hard, the .375 Mag H & H delivers close on forty pounds right into the shoulder – and said in her quietest voice: 'I haven't the faintest idea.' Then she handed the gun to me, her choice Holland & Holland, first made in 1912, always popular with big game hunters. She said: 'Your turn next. Remember, these beasts are tricky. Especially if you don't put him down. Captain Cornwallis Harris liked to remark that the buffalo will tramp you, kneel on you, sand-paper off your skin with his rough tongue, and then come back for another go.'

I didn't ask again.

Mind you, she told me, without my asking, that I'd been born under a thorn tree on the African plains while she had been 'with' (travelling with, sleeping with?) a white witch-doctor called Harry Huntley. He had taken her – heavily pregnant – into 'the bundu', the distant lonely veld, left her camped beneath a thorn tree and, armed only with a knife and a bag of salt, he'd gone off into the wilderness to hunt for wild bees and small game.

I always wondered: why small game, why not bloody big game? I had a very low opinion of Huntley, he seemed to me a wanker from the start.

Anyway, so her story went, it was under the thorn tree, alone, that she had given birth to her son, and he – I – might have died had her itinerant white witchdoctor not returned, and severed the umbilical cord with a whisk – get this – of his hunting knife.

My bundu birth sounded unreliable, but the bozo with the salt bag was all too typical. Africa has been chock with them. Soul-salvers, ravers, mystics, mendicants, dreamers from damp northern reaches of Europe in search of spiritual union with A-fri-ca!

Harry Huntley came directly from Leicester, and took to Africa rather as some men take to drink. He liked to go hunting elephant in Bechuanaland and his Tswana hunters apparently adored him: he went around barefoot, and lived rough in the veld on honey, roots and berries; he milked cobras which he kept in a sack; he took his water from the muddiest waterholes, and he slept at night among the roots of giant baobabs. It had been a career of feverish self-indulgence.

But, as I said, there has always been a lot of it about. You can trace a line from Harry Huntley back to David Livingstone. These guys all said the same things: they were in Africa to build railways, save souls, speed trade and/or end slavery. Popular pastimes, and useful dodges. Think of the funny hats, the odd habits, the ridiculous outfits, the bizarre wandering about in a fog of ignorance, all the while declaring they were lighting up the fucking place ... Some wanted to be white gods; others went native and became *sangomas*, or rain-makers, or born-again bushmen, or praise-singers; others set about saving souls, along with black babies, lepers and the white rhino. But all of them, the slavers, the seers, the saints, the posturing white colonials had one thing in common: they took out a patent on 'their' Africa and flogged it as the one true original.

So I don't know why Huntley turned up in Africa, and I could not explain why someone like my mother should fall for a half-naked Limey from Leicester, wearing a leather skirt. She spoke English, German, Dutch, Afrikaans and Swahili. She could fly, ride, shoot – and knit. She could also box a bit: she went three rounds with Hemingway in a Mombasa gym, though as she'd say, 'He was pretty far gone by then.'

And yet she wandered into the bush with a crazy white witchdoctor.

But was Huntley my dad?

I never got the chance to ask him. Harry Huntley decided one day to swim the Orange River. Perhaps his old European education got the better of him, and he was copying Byron when he dived into the Hellespont. Perhaps he just felt like a dip. Anyway, halfway across the river Huntley got into difficulties, and was drowned.

Which of course meant even more stories grew up around the man: that he could run down lions, that he could talk to snakes, that he was a maker of rain and a sniffer-out of witches. Over the years, any number of devotees came to talk to my mother about Harry Huntley. Hollywood took movie options on one or other of the many books about him, books with titles like *The Bee Master*, *The Man Who Loved Lions*, quasi-religious tracts found on bookstore shelves marked 'African occult', and which bore about as much relation to the real Africa as soft porn did to real sex.

As to matters of paternity, then, I hadn't a clue, and my mother wasn't saying. I knew that during the last war she had risked three attempts at marriage but each time the pilot she'd been planning to marry was killed in action. She never made much of it except to say that the life expectancy of SAAF fighter pilots in the Western Desert was counted in weeks. Any of these men might have been my father. I had no way of knowing.

My birth certificate said I was born in Johannesburg, in 1944. Then again, my mother once confided that my 'paper-work' had taken 'a lot of getting hold of'. My baptismal certificate told me I had been christened in the Church of St Mary, Orange Grove, in 1945 (why the gap of a year I cannot imagine) and I was named Alexander Ignatius Healey. I was given my mother's surname, suggesting that I was born out of wedlock, though none of it proves that Huntley was my father.

Perhaps not surprisingly, then, I have always felt like a foundling, though my mother insisted that wasn't so, and that she was my legal, biological mother.

'But, my dear boy – don't I *look* like your ma?'

Nice one, that. As if by failing to spot the lineaments of motherhood, I had somehow failed the test of filial loyalty. Of course she didn't look like my mother. Not by a bloody mile. Ours was more of a compromise: she was my mother because she said so, and I was her son because I owned up to it, though not without misgivings.

Then there was my name.

'If you'd been a girl I'd have called you Alexandra, after the township. Alexander was as close as I could get… in your case.'

'What do mean… in my case?'

'Alex is a good name, don't you reckon? I learnt to box in Alex.'

Alexandra and Sophiatown, as it happened, in the 1930s. Her sparring partners were black guys hungry to punch their way to fame and freedom.

There it was. The features of her life made up a map of somewhere she said was Africa. But to me it was more mirror than map. I had to take on trust that just behind her, or over her shoulder, I might catch sight of the place itself. But it never really happened. Whenever I looked, the mirror was filled with her face.

And what a face …

When I was a boy, she bought me comics on Saturday mornings, and I am ashamed to say I repaid her by seeing in her a faint but alarming resemblance, particularly in right profile, to Dan Dare, the swaggering desperado with the mighty jaw. Although Dan Dare had lots of sharp black stubble on his chin and my mother did not; at least, I don't think she did (though I have to say that sometimes *she seemed to*). Thus for me she summed up, though she did not mean to and he did, a kind of manliness.

Yet she was also entirely feminine, with a weakness for yellow cardigans and large leather handbags, and she loved turbans, except when she was on safari. No one, in my eyes, ever smoked a pipe so prettily, or clipped, lit and orchestrated a big cigar with such able-handed elegance. I think my ambivalent view of her was no more than a reflection of her astonishing range: she could be grave and tender, savage and subtle.

Our different ways of seeing each other went on widening all our lives and they showed in the distances between the

places where we lived. I don't mean geographically, I mean
temperamentally. We simply had very different ideas of home.
My mother had always taken the grandest view of Africa; it
was for her a shooting gallery, an endless sky, and she saw the
European searchers, the Huntleys, Livingstones and others, as
great presences, even great Africans. To me, people like
Huntley, and the others who passed through our lives, were not
mystics or miracle-workers, they were distinctly dodgy. I would
not have bought a copper bangle or a slightly foxed bible from
any of them.

I saw them as would-be actors constantly auditioning for
parts in the great romance. Pallid players in search of themselves who only made sense when you thought of them as
characters on a continent of their own scripting. Not Africa the
place, not the groaning landmass where so many have been so
betrayed by men in tunics, djellabas, and suits, who claimed to
love the place, only to unleash the usual annihilation, but
Africa the production, Africa the movie, Africa the road show.

My mother called this view banal and unworthy.

And what about her? She certainly had something of the
theatricality. Except she didn't dress up and invent a new character; she played herself.

There was also her ambition. She was never particularly
South African (that would have been far too modest), she
never exhibited that limiting self-regard that marks South
Africans, black and white, and leads them to see nothing else
as real, and no one else as interesting. My mother wasn't to be
confined to one bit of Africa, the lower leg of the continent;
she took all of it as her birthright and loved it with a passion
that was free of that yearning to merge that leads some people

to tears (though the Huntley episode shows she was suscepti-
ble to moments of 'Jock of the Bushveld' hokum).

But, in the main, she was sound.

Take, for example, her attitude to wildlife, always a good
way of telling a real African from a transplanted mythomani-
ac. Faced by the no longer teeming but still plentiful big game,
her response was straightforward: she picked up her rifle, and
shot something. Her admiration for Karen Blixen, whom she
sometimes visited when she was a girl, had nothing to do with
Blixen's love affair with the Kenyan highlands; it was more
simply based:

'My God, could that woman kill lions!'

I went hunting with her only a few times. She was a good
and patient teacher and I learnt a lot from her but it never
really took. I was simply not gifted that way. She flew us to
Livingstone in Northern Rhodesia, and then we drove into the
bush. Buffalo don't hear or see too well but their sense of smell
is exceptionally keen, and you stand more of a chance of
getting in closer when you track a single animal rather than a
herd. We stalked this single old bull most of the day, keeping
well downwind. He had huge horns and fine bosses that made
him look like some old-bufferish judge.

She was not amused by the comparison.

She was in her usual khaki shorts, and veldskoen, no socks,
and a few rounds in the top pocket of her shirt. She talked as
we walked.

'In the old days when we hunted there were lots of buffs, and
you'd stalk them at night because they like to graze then, it
being cooler. But one can't see in the dark. Problem! So what
we did was to tie a bit of white cloth to the barrel of the

Mauser – we used 9.3 by 57s at the time – and the white cloth was a night-sight and direction finder. In daylight, we hunted as a group, say five or six guns; we'd stalk the herd from different directions and when the guns opened up, the danger was always that the herd might stampede and mow you down, so you had to blast away, hope to down the lead buff heading for you, then jump on his body and use it as a kind of shooting platform.'

Though I liked her warmth and her knowledge, the business did nothing for me. I understood the danger well enough. Buffalo are very strong, and they will circle back on their tracks to attack you; they can turn amazingly fast, and they will kill you as soon as look at you.

We got to within about fifty yards of the bull and she was breathing lightly as she sighted and said: 'OK, you go. Remember, you want to do as much damage as you can with your first shot. Never go for the head or the neck. Go for the boiler room, and if you're lucky you'll hit bone. It is very, very rare that you'll bring the buff down with a single shot so prepare the second; and remember he might run, then we'll have to follow. That's tricky.'

I was lucky: my shot broke his spine and put him down. She was pleased: 'One shot hardly ever does,' she said, again.

Afterwards we made stew from the buff's kneecaps – long cooking in an iron pot over the fire – and she talked of shooting and I talked of air temperature. That's what the bush did to me, it made me itch, it made me hot, it made me bored.

'There are no bloody fans in the veld,' she said.

'No, Ma. But there are methods.'

I told her about evaporative cooling. 'You soak a sheet and hang it in the breeze. Natural air-conditioning.'

'Where on earth did you get that from?'

'I read it in a book.'

'Oh, dear me,' she said. 'Air? I really wish you wouldn't.'

I liked reading about how you altered it and treated it. How you washed it clean, controlled impurities, moved it inside an enclosed space, governed its temperature. Most of all I liked the effect of my interest – so minor, so neutral, so innocent, so light – on people in a country where beer and blood and bullets flowed so easily. My interest in air sent people up the wall. Not only did it seem perverse, it was probably downright seditious.

In the old Cassell encyclopaedia my mother kept, I found the story of John Gorrie, and he became a kind of saint to me. Gorrie was a doctor and a scientist, born in Carolina: that in itself was magic – how far away was Carolina! As far away as I cared to dream. And if that were not enough, it turned out there were two Carolinas: North and South.

Gorrie trained as a doctor in New York. Then he moved to the Gulf coast and went to work in a town called Apalachicola, in Florida. I had never heard a name so beautiful, I said it over and over. But when I mentioned it at school people were very unimpressed, their faces darkened, they frowned – even quite intelligent people – and they said, 'What's that?' On hearing it was a town in Florida, in America, they often became angry, or even sarcastic. 'Oh, is it really. Florida, hey?'

My mother was the same: 'Apala— what? Honestly, Alexander, if I'd known what use you'd make of those old books, I'd have given them away to a jumble sale.'

The uses to which I put her books and which she so deplored had nothing much to do with information in the strictest sense of the word: for me reading was much more vital, more physical, more satisfying; it showed me how to escape. It got me out of the house, and out of the country, it got me as far as Apalachicola. How it rings – that name! – still ...

In Apalachicola, John Gorrie treated malaria and yellow fever, though at the time no one could tell the difference; except that malaria began with terrible chills, shakes, and fever; it might come back again and again and sometimes it could kill. Far more mysterious was yellow fever, which only came once, and left you dead or alive. Yellow fever also began with the shivers and high temperatures, raging thirst, violent headaches, then awful pain in your back and legs. The next day you turned yellow as an old autumn leaf. Worst was the black vomit, a falling temperature and onset of the final coma.

Since it was widely believed that the terrible disease came from 'bad air' – *mal-aria* – desperate defences were thrown up to ward off the noxious effluvium: vinegar in your handkerchief, garlic on your shoes, sheets soaked in camphor, burning sulphur or gunpowder, and even firing cannons.

John Gorrie tried ice. He hung basins of the stuff over the patient's bed: cool air is heavier than hot air. It soothed, quite literally, the fevers of his patients. But ice was hard to come by – it had to be shipped in by boat from the lakes in the north – and that was when Gorrie had a revolutionary idea: he decided to build a machine to make ice.

In 1851, he applied for a patent on an ice-making machine. I knew the lines of his short application by heart and I could make my mother bellow simply by saying them out loud:

"If the air were highly compressed, it would heat up by the energy of compression. If this compressed air were run through metal pipes cooled with water, and if this air cooled to the water temperature was expanded down to atmospheric pressure again, very low temperatures could be obtained, even low enough to freeze water in pans in a refrigerator box.'"

Power for the compressor, Gorrie reckoned, could come from steam, water, wind-sails or, perhaps, horses. He got the temperature to drop by forcing gas to expand fast. Squeeze a gas and it heats up; relax the pressure and the gas expands, and as it does so it absorbs heat, and chills the space around it. Dr Gorrie's basic principle is the one most often used in refrigeration today; namely, cooling caused by the rapid expansion of gases.

He had a reverence for ice; he believed it cured fever. He was wrong about that. Mosquitoes caused malaria, not heat. But what made him a hero to me was that he wanted to alleviate the suffering of his patients, he wished to cool them, and to purify the 'bad air' that made them sick. Gorrie believed, in short, that reducing temperature would relieve suffering.

I was interested to know that, at the time, there were those who hated him, who believed that making ice was blasphemy. Gorrie had done what only God could do. He was vilified accordingly, and died young and broken-hearted.

I knew that in an important way he had been right. In my country we lived with bad air – with *mal-aria* – we had contracted the illness that was to lay all Africa low before long. We had the fevers, the sweats, the pain, the frenzy induced by infectious, highly poisonous ideas that were very much in the air: the purity of the blood, and the integrity of the tribe, group and nation. It led to madness and murder among us and it would lead to the same across Africa, as country after country came to independence. It might be called nationalism if that didn't sound too kind for a killer disease. The great disaster of our times.

My mother hadn't a trace of it, and I admired her for that. She sailed over it, she took no notice of boundaries, borders, divisions, races or tribes or nations: how could anything so stupid, so vulgar, so boring, so narrow be serious? Though she could adopt, for the moment – depending on where she was – particular people who embodied for her something of Africa. She took to Ituri pygmies, or leopard men, or even, because they had very briefly welcomed her father as one of their own, the Boers of the old South African republics. But she had no sense of clan or colour, only of friends or enemies. This was magnificent, in its way. But blind. As she saw the world, race never mattered. She simply wasn't interested in it. But as things turned out, it was interested in her.

2

I remember most clearly from the years when I could not have been more than five or six the piney tang of her flying boots, rubbed with waxy dubbin, the stuff used for saddles and holsters and gun-sleeves. I remember the smell of her pipe and the acrid bite of Boxer tobacco. Just back from somewhere, elsewhere, anywhere, she lay stretched out in her big wicker chair, the toes of her flying boots buffed to a gleam that reminded me of honey, fingering sweet shreds of tobacco from the small cotton bag with the drawstring neck, filling her pipe, black and slender, with a silver cap, clipped to a light silver chain, that snapped tight over the bowl when the tobacco glowed hot. My mother came in many versions. I sometimes thought of her as being like the sea: forever the same, forever altering. At other times I thought she looked like a man in a wig, rather like Jack Lemmon in *Some Like It Hot*. Only taller and bigger-bosomed, the recipient of a very successful sex change, with her hair in a centre parting, so it hung over her ears in a great scalloped but never entirely convincing curtain of chestnut curls.

Her long legs stuck out before her like stilts; she lay there breathing thick creamy smoke into the air, and at that point I'd be really pleased. Because she was there; because she was still, and not moving; because she was home; because we were together; because she had come back from wherever she had been: home from Mombasa or Lagos or Stanleyville. Come down from whatever altitude she'd been flying at; in Kenya or Nyasaland or South West Africa; back from whichever uncle she had been seeing just then – Uncle Hansie, Uncle Papadop or Uncle Bertie from Natal, who claimed to be a white Zulu.

Bertie had been one of the earliest of my uncles. He ran a big hotel in England; he'd made a lot of money and he believed that 'the Zulu nation' was as close as you got in modern times to the ancient Romans for 'fighting skills and stoic courage'. Why not become a white Swazi, or a white Xhosa? Well, because, for romantic hoteliers like Uncle Bertie, only certain tribes cut the mustard. One saw this whimsical fascination all over the damn place. In Kenya, it was the Masai who won hands down; in Arabia the Bedouin. For Uncle Bertie it was the Zulus.

He came out to Zululand back in the murky days of the mid-sixties when, if it wasn't bad enough living with crooks and criminals who liked to think of themselves as pioneering stock in this corner of Africa, we found ourselves groaning beneath the yoke of strait-laced puritans. We were used to dealing with rough villainy, but being ruled by guys with a sincere conviction that they were God's anointed was something we had never experienced (and have never recovered from). But of course Uncle Bertie, being from England, knew sweet fuck-all about any of this. He knew only 'Africa'. Need I say more? The guys who ran our country liked Bertie, they liked his energy, his blindness, his attempts to be reasonable and rational. They also liked his take on the tribes. Didn't they think of themselves as an African tribe, albeit the one destined by the Good Lord to kick shit out of all other tribes? Well, then, what could be better than guys like Uncle Bertie wishing to join up to the Zulus?

Uncle Bertie was created a white Zulu by King Cyprian Bhekuzulu kaSolomon. His new name was Nqobizitha, which meant 'Conquer the Enemies'. When he came to visit in Jo'burg, he did a Zulu dance on the lawn by the dahlias. A plump, bare-chested hotelier in a leather dress and leopard-skin trimmings, paws dancing on his nipples, waving a knobkerrie…

'He's an idiot,' I told my mother.

'Don't let him hear you saying that, he won't let you play with his assegais,' she said. 'And it might be one of Bertie's places we're staying in next.'

It was. He bought a game farm in Natal and my mother used to go shooting there. On the wall, next to the Queen, he hung his certificate saying he'd been inducted into the Zulu nation.

We seemed to move just about every week to some new place or other, depending on my mother's flight plans, her hunting trips, or the uncle of the moment. We lived on farms or smallholdings in the Transvaal veld; we stayed for a while in neat and stony suburban bungalows; and in broad-shouldered Jo'burg mansions where immense lawns ran down to the distant white walls, and the sun on the mesh of the tall fence burnt diamonds in the baked rouge-red sand of the tennis court.

Looking back, I can't tell them apart, and they all – these passing homes – fused into our real home, the house in which we came to rest many years later, the house in Forest Town, up the road from the Zoo. Just as all my memories fused into these pictures of my mother, when she was at home and we were together.

On this occasion I remember she had just arrived back at the Grand Central Flying Club, taxied her Stinson into the hangar and driven home in the old Land Rover. My mother flew a variety of aircraft over the years, Piper and Beechcraft, but it was a Stinson Voyager, built in Wayne, Michigan, in 1947, that she kept longest. Four places for passengers, if you put in the two back seats, and loads of room if you didn't; a strong machine, able to lift around 700 pounds easily enough.

What she generally did when she headed out into Africa was to fly on conventional landing gear until Kenya where she'd put down on the rough landing strip belonging to some uncle or other, who happened to own a convenient dam or a stretch of water. Next day she'd swap conventional landing gear for a pair of floats, it meant she could put down on a piece of water anywhere she liked. And wherever she put down was hers.

I remember that particular homecoming so well because, unusually, she hadn't brought anyone back with her: no friends from the great bush that she flew over and into; no witch-doctors, no white hunters from Gabon or Congo or Kenya. This time it was just her and me, just us. I hugged her and she smelt of elsewhere: of campfires, cordite, pipe tobacco, boot polish and aircraft oil. Then I sat and watched her, and knew that she really and truly existed, and I hoped she'd never move again. I knew she would, of course; she was only resting; her way was not to stop but to be up and off, though for the moment you would never have thought so, seeing her lying back, the liquid shine on her toecaps, the ends of a lavender scarf offset by the woolly white edging of her flying jacket.

On the bookcase behind her, with its blue-shouldered, leather-bound Cassell's *Great Stories of the World*, there sat in its carved ivory frame the photograph of her father: an alert and yearning face, with a full moustache and a bold yet bruised look to his olive-dark eyes. And photos of Dr Schweitzer and Hemingway, as well as the façade of Muthaiga Club in Nairobi and a view of Mount Kilimanjaro, and all those people and places which – never distinguishing between locations and living beings – she called 'my old mates'. And because she never saw much difference between people and places, she would attach human feelings to different countries and ascribe geographical features to people: the Congo, she said once, 'has a shy, retiring nature; it's decidedly bashful...' And Hemingway was 'landlocked; always dreaming of having his own access to the sea'. For years I thought Hemingway was a country somewhere in Africa.

'Fighting a man, you have to protect your breasts. And Hem's arms were so damn long. But he didn't watch his middle, and I got in close and pecked away. We were about the same height, over six foot, though he had a big weight advantage. I would carry my left too low and he would dab away with his left and switch to the right. Hem was strong, of course. In a brawl in a bar he'd have murdered me, but in the ring you have space to move; he'd catch me on the chest, on the shoulders, in the ribs. His timing, though, was off. I would fall back, fall back; he'd like that; he'd come after me, and I'd back away, knowing he wanted to throw his right, then I'd step in and beat him to the punch. I'd hit him on the nose or mouth. Thing with him was he knew about boxers; he knew the stance, the talk, and he believed he was good. But he was an amateur. And so was I. But I worked out years ago with people like Ezekiel Dhlamini and Slugger Ntombi; they were the real thing.'

There was her picture of Hemingway wearing only a pair of shorts, with his hair shaved, burnt almost black by the sun, carrying a spear.

'He was going through his I-am-a-Wakamba-hunter stage. He liked to show himself off, did Hem. I felt sorry for Mary. What that woman went through!'

Hemingway decided that he needed an African wife and so he had found a girl among the Wakamba.

'Was he proud of Debba! He had this dream he would live with his "light" wife Mary and his "dark" wife, Debba, in a shamba, among the Wakamba. It's like old music-hall, isn't it?'

There was her picture of Hemingway when he did a stint as an honorary game warden with some Kikuyu as his troops. He is dressed in a uniform he designed himself, a lot of khaki and his broad '*Gott Mit Uns*' belt that he said he took off a dead German soldier, and he is being saluted by the troops.

'God, he loved dressing up.'

And so did they all. Where but Africa gave white men in fancy dress more kicks, more pleasure, or power? Only in Africa did they seriously impress; not so much by their talents or their morals, though God knows they liked to think that way. No, what impressed was their firepower, their murder rate; it was all such fun, it was all so easy, it was all so brilliant. And it went to their heads. Like their hats.

Then there were her fixed points of reference:

'My old dad ...'

'My old mates ...' (Those were my uncles, or her old hunting grounds.)

'My dear boy...' (That was me.)

Frankly, I didn't give a toss about her old mates. They got between us, they took her off; they were a pain in the arse.

And if you asked me what I didn't like about them I'd say they were so fucking stagy they hurt. Like the place itself. This was heresy, I knew that but it was no good muttering the magic mantra 'Africa', as if that helped. It did not. In my experience the mention of the word was either a bloody excuse, or a threat. The place should trade in the name and start again with a new one. I heard her use it so often I learnt not to buckle under its manipulative pressure. I took the view that whenever you heard someone say 'Africa', you'd best check the gun-safe and the security arrangements because the chances were someone somewhere was planning: to (a) take you for a ride; or (b) do you in.

So my old lady's mantra did nothing for me. She was always everywhere but home where I wanted her. This was around the time when she was travelling some two weeks out of every month; when a succession of nannies arrived to look after me, and then left, because my mother had found them new jobs, as nurses or saleswomen. She thought domestic service a mug's game, could not see the point of servants, and I'd no sooner got used to the cooking, the habits, the presence of the new Betty or Blessing or Ntembi than she'd be whisked away to be trained as a nurse, a needlewoman, a scientist, and my ma was damned pleased with herself for helping them to jump ship.

It went on like this until I got to be about ten or eleven, and learnt how to look after myself, how to make myself sandwiches for school, how to boil an egg, and thank God we used no servants ever again but only a cleaning service called De Wet's Flying Dutchmen, pure white men in a white van.

Afrikaans men who cleaned the house and did the garden: tall sunburnt hairy moustachioed males in khaki shorts down on their knees, scrubbing the kitchen floor, weeding the garden and calling to each other: '*Ek sê, ou doosie, gooi ons die blerrie doek!*' ('Hey there, old cunty, toss us the rag.') It was their language which so affected Baldy, our grey parrot, and gave him his rich store of Afrikaans expletives, drawn from the household curses of those gruff male chars: Baldy loved to sing out: '*Die bliksemse seep is kak!*' ('This bloody soap is shit…') and '*My jirre, maar die blerrie Hoover is opbefok…*' ('Jesus, but this bloody Hoover is up-befucked.')

My ma's housekeeping arrangements had for years rattled the neighbours who flanked us: Mrs Terre'Blanche, Mrs Garfinkel, to the left and right; Mrs Smuts and Mrs Mason across the street. A pincer movement of fighting madams, my mother called them. But then she liked pissing off the neighbourhood. And it was pretty wild stuff, using a white male household cleaning service at a time when anyone patriotic and properly South African had two, three or four servants living in the back yard; and anyone who didn't was weird, if not downright bloody revolutionary.

She took no interest in my schooling. I was glad about that. Once she came to watch me playing cricket at school, still in her flying gear, and she leaned on the fence and lit her pipe. The other kids wondered out loud: 'Jesus Christ, who's *that*?'

For the life of me I didn't know what to say but honesty required a response and so I said she was, well, sort of… my ma.

I was met with blank disbelief.

'Naw, it can't be! You fucking liar!'

And looking at her again, they had a point. But, then, if the tall figure at the fence wasn't my mother, just who the hell was she?

This was the time of our lion park, the first in the Transvaal. I think it was my old lady's riposte to Joy Adamson, whom she absolutely loathed:

'That bloody show-off! One of those foreigners who come here and romanticise Africa. Born free, my eye! Let me tell you, dear boy, nothing and no one is born free; none of us is entitled to it; freedom's something you have to work to get and fight to keep.'

'Yes, Ma.'

'Don't you "yes, Ma" me.'

'No, Ma.'

Our lion park was to have been a money-spinner: my old lady's idea was to bring big game hunting to what she called 'the citizenry'. They were to pay twenty guineas for the guarantee of bagging a lion. She'd take the hunters out in her Landy and make sure they got what they paid for, a leonine trophy to stick on the wall right next to the flying ducks and the little wooden wall plaque that read: 'Everything I like is either immoral, illegal or fattening.'

It wasn't a bad idea. Even then, in the fifties, hunting in South Africa seldom meant big game. You needed to go north for that. Hunting more usually meant small game pursued by big men in bad shorts. My mother's idea was to make available to South Africans some of the pleasure she had on safari in Block 66 in Tanganyika, and the foothills of Mount Kilimanjaro.

She rented several thousand hectares outside Krugersdorp, already well stocked with springbuck, kudu and zebra. She talked to her pals in Arusha and shipped in half a dozen lions

– 'to test the market'. Her lions were black manes – a species long gone from South Africa – and they came from a terrain of thorn bush, colossal mats of blond grass, black lava fields and knife-edged sanseveria bushes, and she had them brought all the way down to the waving grasses of the flat highveld.

I was the gatekeeper. She dressed me in a khaki safari suit with the legend stitched in red letters on my back 'Healey's Hunts'. I sat in a plastic chair in front of the gate holding a canvas bag to collect what my ma called the 'spondulaks' from the grateful citizenry; she waited with the guns and the Land Rover. She used an old Mannlicher .256: 'nice and light for quick stuff', she said, meaning buck. For heavier stuff like buffalo and elephant, she used a .470.

What she hadn't counted on was the unwillingness, deep-set in South Africans, to pay for something they believed belonged to them. The South African hunter did not do licences, tents or sundowners or silver cups for bringing down the biggest buff. Unlike the guys in Kenya, he ate what he shot. If you wanted to shoot you went to your farm, or your several farms, or your sister's farm, and chased buck in a truck. South African hunting wasn't about safaris, or sex, or sport, or even style; the South African hunter did not mix with women, he did not use porters, and he despised those who did so. Paying to hunt was as bad as paying for sex: it was downright indecent, it was un-South African. Hunting was about guys, often in the backs of pick-ups, running down game; about being getting pissed on brandies and Coke, and throwing up under the thorn trees. It was about being proper South Africans. Proper South Africans were the last aristocrats; they owned the country. They did not pay at the gate. That sort of thing was for foreigners, faggots and females, which in the minds of the hunters in the back of the pick-up amounted to pretty much the same thing anyway.

My mother's hunting habits were different. She hunted in the Congo rainforests, in Uganda and Mozambique and Nyasaland. Her style was founded on the Kenyan model invented by rich Britons and richer Americans. Her idea of a safari had to do with blood, bullets, booze and sex: a silver service supper after a fine day at the salt lick. Good champagne whenever possible, because wines did not travel well. What she enjoyed, I suppose, were the prerogatives of birth and breeding. Her style had the marks that distinguished the old white hunters who worked in Central and East Africa: for whom hunting went with money and muscular snobbery; whose safaris starred barons, princes, presidents and film stars; who dreamt of night-time Africa in the bush as adventure: getting tiddly, or getting laid, under a fat buttery hunting moon, while beyond the circle of firelight the hyenas paced, yelping like traders on the floor of the bourse.

Thinking back, I see she wasn't wrong about bringing hunting to the citizenry but she was way ahead of her time. She set up what was to prove popular much later, what became known as canned hunts, where the victim – lion, buffalo, eland – was shepherded into the sights of some arsehole who bought a licence that guaranteed him one dead trophy. Healey's Hunts planned to offer 'salving spirits of Africa': rubdowns with aloe oil; she even talked of a line in cosmetics, 'Healey's Health and Beauty Lotions'. She foresaw the industry of 'lifestyle' lodges that would come in time to litter the South African bush. They stand there today, monuments to her idea that beat them to it by decades: 'wellness centres' and psychosomatic healing bomas, promising full-frontal African therapies like uplifting *ubuntu*, and all the attendant decor – hand-woven mosquito nets, canvas showers under the baobabs, healing baths in rooibos tea, or *buchu* brandy, along with 100 per cent genuine Zulu massage, ethnic bushveld cuisine, and all the free booze you can drink – at a mere thousand bucks a night.

Healey's Hunts folded after six weeks and was not mentioned again. I don't know what happened to our lions. But, then, I didn't know much about anything concerning my own life. Life, my life, all life, had a way of beginning in some past adventure of my mother's; and it continued like that until I went over the wall.

3

I once asked her how she came to be a flier and she said: 'I owe it all to dynamite.'

That was her stock answer to questions touching on matters she felt were too holy to be solved in a secular way. But as I pieced together the story, I got some idea of what she meant. Life was a matter of uplift. It was literally charged with propulsive power, primed to blow you sky-high and, in her case, keep you up there. Somehow, simply by being in and belonging to Africa, your adventures were legalised, and localised, and characterised by the successful use of high explosive. By blowing something up you said you owned it.

If she was used to being looked up to, it wasn't altogether surprising. Six-two in her socks – she knitted them herself – of warm grey wool. She had learnt to fly when she was eighteen, and never looked back; as a result, whenever she came back from wherever she had been, it always felt to me as if she had just dropped from the sky, which of course she had.

She always said that her old dad got her into the flying boats, and gave her a taste for altitude. I think being looked up to came naturally. She bestrode her world like the Queen of Sheba or Godzilla or Prester John: warrior queen, monster or male impersonator, who knows? And how many men loved her! Which was really odd, when you thought about it, since she always seemed to me too busy shooting things, or heading off somewhere new, to bother much about her desperate admirers, lost in the dust of her departures.

Now and then, 'just for fun', she flew me on low-level excursions over the dynamite factory at Modderfontein, on Jo'burg's eastern edge: the biggest in the world, if not the universe. She never failed to be impressed all over again by its capacity for destruction. My feeling was: so what? You fly over it, you look down, you see an expanse of roof; it was, after all, nothing more than a fucking factory.

'Why is it so important?'

'Why? How do you think we get at our gold? We drill deep shafts down through the rock; and to slice the rocky gold reef into getatable bits, we blast tunnels, or stopes, that stretch like branch lines, off the main shaft. Blasting takes lots of dynamite. Three million cases every year. Dynamite is what we do in Jo'burg. It's in our blood.'

She hoped that 'one day soon' I'd get my blasting certificate. When I said I didn't like explosives, her account of South African history, according to notable explosions, then followed:

'Eighteen ninety-six was an awful year. First came the Jameson Raid, followed by a plague of rinderpest that decimated every beast from here to the Zambezi. Then a brand-new ocean liner, the *Drummond Castle*, went down off the French coast. But most spectacular of all was the "Great Dynamite Explosion". It happened in Braamfontein on 19 February 1896. A train, loaded with fifty-five tons of dynamite, was left cooking in the highveld sun. It had been there for three days. A shunting engine happened to nudge the train and up it went, blasting a hole sixty yards wide and ninety feet deep, killed over a hundred, and injured two thousand. They had just begun to build Jo'burg, and then they blew it up. Par for the course, Alexander. Always remember how wedded we are to dynamite.'

Her idea of education, of a real qualification, was a licence to blow things up.

'My old dad got his blasting certificate when he was just sixteen. Fancy that! It was in the old Transvaal and the Kruger Volksraad passed a law that said no one but a white man could lay a stick of dynamite; only whites could load or drill or fire fuses. But this ran into the old South African problem. Blacks and Coloureds and Asians were good blasters. Coming up from the Kimberley diamond fields: hell, they could blow just as prettily as any white boy, and what's more, they blew for half the damn wage. Observe the old tableau: piety overwhelmed by greed. Why pay a stupid white boy a fiver a month to do what a clever black boy did better and cheaper? So how to stay pure while stiffing the mine owners who didn't give a toss for your race fantasies? Easy. Kruger's people lifted the race bar but they passed a law that only men with blasting tickets could use dynamite, and so ever afterwards, white men got the blasting tickets and black men carried the tools.'

I knew the lesson by heart. Getting rich was a messy business. Once upon a time, when Jo'burg was still a camp, anyone could buy some sticks, blast a hole in the reef and hope to get lucky. But singularity gave way to mass production, to control, to boredom and death.

My grandfather, Joe Healey, has come down to me in fine detail, preserved in the aspic of my mother's memories. She who forgot nothing and in whom details of the past lived on, in continual adjustment, concurrent with, and parallel to, the ongoing events of our own lives. She was a walking, talking almanac, detailing not only our family, but this country, and the mad, comic, tear-stained history of white settlement on this southern tip of Africa. Memories of the Boer War, the reef of gold, the damnable English, the bold fighting farmers of Smuts and Delarey and the talent of her dad for setting high explosives.

Joe Healey was a pioneer. Those pompous pricks forever banging on about 'the golden city' liked to say he came 'to make history'. In truth, along with all the riff-raff who swarmed on to the Rand at the end of the nineteenth century, Joe Healey came to make money, and very dodgy money at that. He came for gold and, very soon, that meant he had to pick up a gun.

'In the Boer War my old dad fought in the Irish Brigade.'

It sounded a grand name for the moustachioed ragamuffins in the picture she kept on her desk.

'My old dad blew up culverts with Major MacBride.'

She would lean on the word 'culverts' in that Jo'burg way, which lengthens the first and shortens the second syllable into a serrated knife-edge 'culll-vittz!' And then she'd add: 'Of course this was before John MacBride ever stepped out with Maude Gonne, or Willy Yeats was ever in the picture. They called my old dad "Spaghetti Joe" because when he laid a mine the explosion had the effect of knitting the railway line into tangles like spaghetti. He had the distinction of blowing up every railway culvert from Bloemfontein to the Vaal. The British' – she always spoke as if it had happened last week – 'wanted to wipe off us the face of the earth. The British saw us as barely human, cavemen, half-ape. A species headed for extinction – they wanted the heads of "Brother Boer" mounted on the clubroom wall. They came out for a spot of shooting, as if we were pheasants …'

By 'us' she meant the Boers, the taciturn, stubborn, barely literate Dutch *paysans*. These were the guys with whom she passionately identified; they were 'our people'. But she seemed to me to care with the same passion she showed for saving threatened species, like the bongo and the white rhino. She cared, too, for the theatre of it, and, of course, the shooting.

'The Khakis would turn up at a farm and give us twenty minutes to carry what we could, and then they'd torch the place. They saw us as lice, as germs! They wanted to burn us out. To get back to the clean dream of an empty land with gold under foot. As a killing machine the British Army rivalled the Black Death; it carried off people night and day.'

Even though she'd been born sixteen years after the Boer War ended, and knew about it only from those stories she got from her father, it made no difference. She had been *there*, and the fact of her substantial presence during those cruelties meant that I was there too.

It was, I later saw, very Jo'burg, this inflatable history. It was the impulse of prospectors, dirt-poor miners, to pretend that everything you could name you owned. In the beginning, vocabulary was property. Even its present somewhat rumbling moniker – Johannesburg – was an afterthought; tarting up what had been a flat piece of nothing very much, first called Ferreira's Camp.

All that mattered was that under the feet of the lean and hungry diggers of Ferreira's Camp there ran deep rivers of gold in stone. And when you considered the charge sheet drawn up against our city, my old lady had a point. Many of the punters who dollied up Jo'burg into the gilded trollop with a pistol in her purse should have been locked up for causing grievous bodily harm, being drunk in charge of a lethal weapon, for perjury, fraud and for believing in casual killing as a form of moral persuasion. To some degree, of course, you could say that that was how things were done in this country, ever since the first settler splashed ashore and began booting the locals around. And you'd be dead right. But Jo'burg did it in spades.

From the instant in 1886, when the first seekers stubbed their toes on rocks veined with gold and realised that whole rivers of bullion lay frozen beneath their feet, Jo'burg was on the rise and has been ever since. A clutch of outlaws in Ferreira's Camp talked big, talked it up, talked it into what they wanted it to be; much as later on they floated their prize fights, their horse races, their brothels with a profligacy never before seen in southern Africa. 'Eldorado-on-the-Reef' and 'California-in-the-Veld', the 'Golden City', 'Egoli', miracle metropolis in the middle of nowhere where everyone was on the take and on the make and on the money, where diggers wore hats and called themselves gents, and girls in white gloves sipped tea in Ansteys and called themselves 'madam'.

It was Paul Kruger, appalled by its whores, conmen and dusty depravity, who called the town 'Sodom and Gomorrah' . Most Jo'burgers took that as a compliment. Ferreira's Camp grew into the greatest African city south of Cairo, whose gods were two: gold and the gun. What could you expect of a town conceived by vagrant remittance men? Not even a town, in truth, but a series of dusty claims and roped-off diggings. Men in hats, with shovels and spades in hand, and gold lust in their hearts. A happy-go-lucky sort of girl who flashed her gold-spangled knickers at every passing sucker.

On the walls of my mother's many bedrooms, transferred from house to house in our travels over the years, she hung photos her dad had taken of early Johannesburg. I saw the first of the wagons that arrived after the discovery of gold on what was called Witwatenrand; the first tents that went up in a louche settlement perched upon the greatest, deepest reef of gold in the world. Gold is the barbarous metal and these were barbarous men. They stand in my grandfather's pictures with their hats aslant. They stand beside the City and Suburban Mine back in 1887, the town just one year old, and they are already full of swagger; they have blasted the rock apart and a deep crack splits the earth and over the fissure they have rigged a pulley. Lowering a bucket down into the open hole, into the auriferous rocky womb, is a black man. The white men, muscular, debonair, are watching the black man working.

In Joe Healey may be found the route and pattern later followed by so many of us. Those who lived through the Boer War never got the hang of what happened after that; they believed in some weird way that this was a normal place where they could lead grown-up lives.

Dreaming of rich shipwreck upon the golden reef, Joe Healey came to Jo'burg in 1906. A town of tents, tin and unbaked Kimberley brick, home to more than 150,000 miners – one in three were white – and next to no women. Two stone buildings, both two stories tall: Consolidated Buildings and Corner House. In the beginning the diggers traded claims and shares in the street, and so did the whores. Then when the cash came in they built themselves a bourse, and they built themselves a brothel, and most folks never could tell the difference. The bourse has been a high-rise cathouse ever since. But those who made too much of the connection missed the spiritual dimensions; because buying stock was probably the only near-religious experience most Jo'burgers have ever had.

It was in Corner House, where my grandfather went to work. A courier hauling piles of paper scrip. In and out of the brothel, the bourse, the bar, running between buyers and sellers with paper promises to be redeemed or damned.

He got the hang of things pretty fast. Jo'burg was wild, the 'Rand' was booming, and it was made of the queerest set of people yet to gather in one corner of Africa and pretend they were living somewhere else. Like England or Ireland or Estonia or Russia. For among the Barnatos, Ecksteins, Rosenthals, Rose-Inneses, Bradleys, Paulings and Goldreichs, amongst Lithuanians and Limeys and Yanks were squadrons of Chinese imported into the mines. Much as van Riebeeck, when the Dutch first arrived in the Cape, shipped in hundreds of slaves from Malaysia, on the understanding that white men were in Africa to grow rich and all others were in Africa to work.

In Ferreira's Camp on the golden reef there were plenty of black guys around, but the Chinese worked longer hours for less pay, though there were complaints about the difficulty of learning their language. Nonetheless, Joe Healey managed a smattering of Mandarin, as well as Dutch, German, French, Russian and Swahili.

The city expanded in square blocks, in straight lines laid over the memories of old farms and fountains. The broad streets were named for the desperadoes who brokered the deals and salted the mines, who built mansions on Parktown Ridge, who lied and cheated and shot their way to fame: Eloff and Pritchard, Harrison and Jeppe. Rock-crushers, shaft sinkers, surveyors, conmen and notaries. Their temples were the mining houses – De Beers, Consolidated Gold, Anglo-American – and their saints were Rhodes, Barnato, Beit and Oppenheimer, whose sacred names we learnt as children when we directed our devotions towards the Stock Exchange in prayers hot and urgent: 'Our Rand-lords, who art in Hollard Street … make us rich!'

My mother walked me through the early streets of the early town, much as she later walked me through the battlefields and concentration camps of the Boer War. Down Commissioner, the only street wide enough to turn a span of sixteen oxen, to the Turffontein races where Joe Healey, late of Kilkenny, without a farthing to his name, was soon racing his own thoroughbreds, to the Rand Club, corner of Commissioner and Market streets. The Club, along with the racecourse and cricket pitch, had been amongst the first things built: bullion, brothel, bourse, the unholy trinity that Jo'burg adored.

'The land for that bloody Rand Club, believe it or not, was given by Ikey Sonnenberg to that wicked magician, Cecil Rhodes. Given free, gratis and for nothing, in return for which, Rhodes founded the Rand Club and the Club spent the next hundred years keeping Jews out.

'Rhodes and Beit, and the other big goldbugs, bought out the small prospectors, and they built the biggest dynamite factory in the world and blasted tunnels through the rock to get to the specks of ore clutched in the rock. And let me tell you, it worked; they *were* the gold industry. But let me tell you, too, we paid for it. For every bit of ore we pulled out of the rock, a bit of brain ran out of our ears … That's how it is here.'

'Here' was always Johannesburg; the only town between the Cape and Cairo worth thinking about. Any other place was a bit of a joke; and if it wasn't a joke, it was to be pitied. Jo'burg counted; it had treasure, height, danger and speed, the risk of sudden death. And the odd thing was she felt, we all did in a way, in these dark attributes a cause for civic pride.

'History? We don't have a history, really,' I remember her telling one of my many uncles. 'Just a police record.'

Ah, that 'we': not the royal 'we', not an editorial 'we', not a warm familial pronoun. No, hers was an imperial 'we' that reached beyond family pride, to gather into its brazen possessive stockade everything that made 'ours' not just the best town in Africa, but in the entire bloody world.

I'd argue.

'London?'

'Oh, please!'

'New York?'

'Nonsense.'

'Paris?'

'Do me a favour.'

'Shanghai?'

'You must be joking.'

Soon after the Great War ended Joe Healey married Millie Brokenshaw, the daughter of a Cornish tin-miner who came out to try his luck in the Kimberley diamond mines. Millie died in childbirth and left my grandfather with a little girl to bring up. When Kathleen was about twelve he parlayed his one and only talent, an intimate knowledge of how to blow up things, into a job and, even more important in Jo'burg, into a title – he got himself appointed Chief Explosives Officer for Corner House Investments.

It was quite a change. The boy who once went to war against those hated English who plotted and murdered to rob the Transvaal of its gold, now went on to adapt himself to the peace of Vereeniging – 'that hateful, horrid surrender' (my mother's words) – with which the Boer War ended by going to work for the very bastards – the goldbugs, the Rand-lords – who 'bankrolled' (my mother again) 'that smash and grab raid on the gold and diamonds of the Boer republics'.

It turned out to be a bright move. All over Africa there was buried treasure men wished to rip out of the ground. Mines were opening on the Rand, in Ndola and the Congo, and the mining houses loved high explosives. Joe Healey could blow anything: he could stash a charge in a stope with his eyes closed. It soon brought him money, three-piece suits, a pigskin briefcase, and lots of travel in the flying boats, carrying people and mail up and down the continent.

Yes, there were problems, disconsolate ex-Boers, angry blacks and a kind of missionary greed, together with an open worship of militant stupidity, but it was the new world, and everyone was, or would be, equal. Even the Catholic Irish…

Joe Healey behaved as if, and believed, he was at home, though from the start all the indications were against it. He was in Africa and that made all the difference. He fought for the Boers who lost the war, but they won the peace. And when they came to own the entire country they had little use for Joe Healey, or for his belief in progress, in dynamite, in Johannesburg, in freedom, reason, in good sense.

'We'll sink our differences, or our differences will sink us,' said Joe Healey to his young daughter.

It sounded sensible, and modern and statesmanlike. But this was South Africa, the Boers were in charge, and such sentiments were baloney. All that the easy talk of freedom and good sense ever brought was better suits, turbans and flywhisks for the boss-men – and bigger shit for everyone else.

'We're cracked,' my mother said. 'We're the descendants of gold-crazed miners. With about as much taste or judgement as you'd expect. Everything's show. What do people want? They want a gold mine, six limos and a whacking mansion in the suburbs with an electric fence, a big pool and lots of guns. They want this from Soweto to Sandton; they all want it. Blacks and Whites and Asians and Coloureds and Chinese ... And they want it now. No one knows what he or she's supposed to be; everyone pretends like mad. One day you're a robber; next day you're a religious leader. It's not so strange. We're willing to try anything. You start off a cricketer or a drag queen, and pop up again as a traffic cop or a poet. And we don't have a problem with that. It's not strange. If you've a problem with that, you're *strange*. OK, yes?'

OK, no.

I had a problem with that. What I did, later, was a form of revolt most calculated to make my ma as mad as hell. She wanted guns and boots and the stuff that heats, detonates, goes off pop. She looked on our national predilection for hitting each other as just another way of staying in touch, and her heart softened. I wanted to throw up. So I went the other way, I went for the lightest and most insignificant and weightless of things. I came from a town where people would have had their

servants do their breathing for them, leaving them free to concentrate on masterly things, like gold, guns and talking up a
storm. I came from a place where we were ruled for ever by a
small bunch of demented bores who said they were the sons of
God, that their blood was washed in heaven and their skin
blessed by angels, and if anyone disagreed they would, happily
kick their fucking heads in, and frequently did so. Nothing
personal, just touching base.

These guys were opposed by another lot who felt that the
white guys who ran and ruined the country were so bad they
should, in the words of Louis Farrakhan, be killed and buried
and then dug up and killed all over again. And if you didn't
agree with either side, if you said what was needed was to cool
it down, not heat it up, you were nowhere. Or – as my ma said
– you had a problem.

4

Other mothers took their kids to churches or art galleries to improve their minds and souls; my ma used to fly me to the killing grounds of the Boer War. She hadn't been there but she loved fighting it all over again.

I liked flying with her; she was very calm, so calm she sometimes fell asleep. She wasn't completely asleep, more a waking doze; the plane used to climb and then descend gently, on autopilot, but it was still a weird feeling. I used to sit and watch the far-away koppies bobbing along the horizon. I didn't dare wake her and I didn't dare touch the controls.

She trained in a Gypsy Moth, when she was eighteen. She had her pilot's licence in 1938: one of the very few women in Africa to fly solo. And she wore, until quite late in life, what she called 'my old gear from the early days': a single-piece flying suit lined with quilt, and a sheepskin jacket. Her helmet and goggles became redundant, and always hung in the parlour beside the picture of Bamadodi, the Rain Queen. The helmet was lined with chamois leather and had rubber earpieces. Her goggles were of soft black leather with an elasticised headband. I used to put them on but my head never seemed big enough.

Come to think of it, that was a problem for much of my life, *vis-à-vis* my old lady. Nothing ever fitted...

When we landed in the veld she always cut thick brush and piled it around the wheels because lions and particularly hyenas had been known to chew clean through the tyres.

On my tenth birthday, for 'a special treat', we had a day on a hill called Spionkop, where the Boers had slaughtered a great many British soldiers.

We took off from Grand Central Airport at dawn, having our *padkos* in a paper bag: two chicken sandwiches, a bottle of Lemos and two oranges. In those days you dressed to fly. My mother was splendid in sheepskin jacket, leather flying helmet and shining boots. I wore my grey woollen jersey, grey shorts and grey socks, as if I were going to school. Besides, she said, the place we were visiting was practically a cemetery. We dressed up when we went to lay fresh flowers on Grandpa Joe's grave in Westpark Cemetery, didn't we? Well then …

It took around five hours to Ladysmith, and bumping over the hot air lifting off the Drakensberg Mountains always made me queasy. Then the ride in the pale green Vauxhall, borrowed from the airport manager, who met us with all his mechanics and clerks in tow, white men in safari suits gawping, astonished and embarrassed, at this woman who flew herself around the place.

We crossed the Tugela River, driving on to the ferry, and I felt car-sick so I leaned out of the window of the Vauxhall and she said: 'You'll fall in and be carried off by a croc.'

I didn't worry in the least; I always felt as if I had, long before, fallen into something just as deep and brown and roaring as the Tugela, and been carried off, and I hadn't drowned yet. Mothers were what you drowned in. The Tugela was just a river and rivers I could handle.

Spionkop was a hard hill to climb, I had short legs, and my mother, her flying goggles tied to her waist, her big boots crunching smartly up the steep hillside, marched on and on, talking as we tramped.

'This is the position the Carolina commando took, dropping like flies when the British sharpshooters got amongst them: Reinecke, De Villiers and Tottie Krige, all coughing blood; bullets in the lungs. The English were up here, they held Spionkop for a while, yes; but we held Conical Hill, and Aloe Knoll. We were well dug in, and they were not; we got our big guns on them, and then it was easy. Easy!'

She scrabbled up on to the ridge from where the far-off peaks of green Natal stood up, like men surprised.

'At the end of it all, the English were retreating and we had the hill.'

She found a trench line, the seamed and ribbed sand where the Boer spades had dug, healed over like an old flesh wound. Her face darkened. 'Louis Botha gave his condolences to the British; they were allowed to bury their dead. It was that sort of war. They deepened the trenches where the soldiers had fallen and made them into a mass grave. Strange, isn't it? You move from blowing a man's face off to talking quietly about a decent resting place.'

Her eyes were always sharp; quick to spot things I didn't see, so scuffed and battered and at one with the dust and scrub in which they lay. But they sprang back into being for her. She would press into my hands hot metal mushrooms with the delighted exclamation, 'An English water bottle, very well preserved. And what's this? A tunic button.' She spat on the small flat piece of metal and rubbed it on her leather jacket.

'King's Royal Rifles...' Sometimes she found things I regarded as more interesting treasures: small arrowheads, scrapers, tiny ostrich-shell beads, faintly stippled with ochre; bushmanware, signs of the people who had been there thousands of years before the great battle of 24 January 1900. I loved the flint blades; they were neat, light and delicate. But these trifles didn't count for her; they weren't real, like the gin bottles and the shell casings and the spent bullets; like the soldiers who fought a real battle in a real war. For her they were not ghosts, they were real men fighting, the cries and screams of the dying British troopers, the yells of defiant Boers, all of it, all of them, still loudly alive.

'They lost over fifteen hundred here on this hill, but they could afford it. We lost a fifth of that and it was too many.'

Listening to her lament as we straggled down the stony koppie was like being asked to mourn the death of someone you're told is close to you but whom you know, if at all, only as a stranger. For her it was movement, history. For me, try as I might, it seemed nothing had altered. She had a sense of belonging. She was one with the fallen Boers, and their vanished Republics. Just as, much later, she had been one with Koosie, when he was in hiding, and with the people she had flown to Mozambique or Lesotho during the long granite years of boredom and blood and racial madness, when the wild regime killed what it would not countenance. Yet her hatred for the insular lunatics who came to rule over us, and who claimed to be the descendants of just these Boers, was rooted, perversely, in the defeat of the men who fought at Spionkop.

'We' fought like lions, but 'they' were too many. 'In the end, they wore us down, burnt our farms, locked our women and children behind wire in the concentration camps and we were forced to give in.'

For her those boys who fought at Spionkop had done something worth recording. To me they were just men I didn't know, and didn't care for. But we could agree on this: they were all around us still. The English who died that day rose from the dead and were present in those who came after them, wearing exactly their moustaches, using their loud voices; soldiers no longer, but sportsmen and farmers, ruddy men with big hands, with names like Dave or Clive or Geoff, who were something in a bank, or someone on the gold mines. And the Boers they had fought were also still with us: large, square, angry men with beards and names like Dawie and Gawie and Piet, who were now something in the fucking ruling classes.

For her the Boer War mattered because it ended badly. I had the feeling that it hadn't ended at all; it seemed to me that Dave and Clive and Geoff were still locked in a fight with Dawie and Gawie and Piet. The same battle with the same fighters; and if one side was ahead now, what did it matter? I was always overwhelmed by the stupidity of the long combat. But, boy, did I know all about it, my ma saw to that. Perhaps that was her at her truest: this expert acquaintance with death. In battle, or in the bush. Describing it, she'd touch the air, picking out the scenes as if they were figures in a tapestry.

'When MacBride's Irish Brigade were sent back home at the end of the war they asked my old dad if he wanted to ride along home with them, and he told them to stick it up their jumpers! After blowing up half the Transvaal with his dynamite, he reckoned he'd made enough of an impression on the place to call it home.'

'Home!' The word hummed in the tender nasal murmur she gave it, like a hymn or a spell against the evil one. 'Home!' she'd sing, and it would echo around the house.

We had a daguerreotype showing Paul Kruger, the Boer leader, leaning on the balcony of his house overlooking Lake Geneva: it had been done by a French sympathiser, and read: '*Le vieux Président regard avec des yeux nostalgiques, la vue du Lac Léman.*'

'After the war, my old dad stayed on. Never went back to Ireland. So we had the odd happenstance that Kruger was in Switzerland, living in exile, and your Irish grandfather was in Bloemfontein, living at home …'

The daguerreotype was meant to make a person feel sad but it made me jealous. I thought Kruger a lucky bugger to be sitting beside Lac Léman. Home left me cold, but I didn't dare say so. Home was an odd place, where my mother never was; she was at home everywhere else in Africa.

We had a difference of opinion even then. I understood why she flew away; what I never quite understood was why she came back. 'Away' was so much more interesting than 'here'; that was something we could agree about. What we couldn't agree about, ever, was where it was best to be 'away'. Years later, in South East Asia, in Russia, in the old Yugoslavia, places that were home to me, I realised the difference between us: she was best 'at home', and I was at home 'away'. But I came to see that my travelling mimicked hers. We were made of the same stuff, like the earth and the moon; though our lives were worlds apart, I circled her, faintly visible but out of reach, and all our travelling – hers and mine – was really just time spent orbiting each other.

Her seductive power might be measured in the men who fell for her, though I have never had much luck in numbering my mother's lovers, or in deciding just what it was exactly that they fell for. Neither, I think, did they know themselves. After all, I was closer to her than any other man and all I can say is that she had a certain gravitational pull and when you fell, you fell towards her, crashed into her; unless, of course, you burnt up in her atmosphere, and were never heard of again.

5

When my mother was a young woman she went walking in the Magaliesberg, a range of mountains beyond Pretoria, famous for hunters, Boer rebels and ghosts. It was the summer of 1943, and she was in mourning as usual. I say 'as usual' because she had been almost married three times. She was just twenty when she got engaged to a fighter pilot; he was shot down. She tried again: her second fighter pilot went missing in action. Then she married a man who flew Lancaster bombers. It looked good for a while, then he crashed on take-off and she went from being almost married a lot to being almost widowed three times over.

She always said that nothing moderates grief like a long tramp. She climbed one of those hills so typical of the Magaliesberg, rock strewn in the afternoon sun, grey-green bush and the great silence. When she came to a village, thatched huts with mud walls painted with wavy lines, in green and blue and white, and triangles and zigzags in ochre and black, she asked for water. Though she did not know it, in that place she could not have asked for a more precious, a more sacred element.

She was taken before a proud woman with eyes like lakes of milk who sat on a wooden throne covered in lion skins; she wore a leopard-skin cloak and all around her people scuffled in the dust, and indicated that my mother should do the same. When she asked why, they were shocked at the extent of her ignorance. Didn't she know that she was in the presence of the Rain Queen of the Magaliesberg, Bamadodi vi, monarch of the mountains and ruler of the Lebalola people?

'Heavens, no! How was I supposed to know that? Boy, did I get it wrong! I asked for water, and being a rain queen she prepared to have the heavens open for me. Fancy that!'

The queens of the Lebalola had been making rain for centuries; and great chiefs like Shaka and Dingaan and Cetswayo had paid them tribute. There were other rain queens, in other parts, and they sometimes cured sickness in cattle or infertility in women. However, the Rain Queen of the Lebalola was the most ancient and the most orthodox of all the rainmakers. Bamadodi vi did one thing only: she made rain, like her mother and her grandmothers before her.

The Queen summoned her counsellors, poured beer on the ground from big black calabashes, and they proceeded to lick up the liquid.

'This was Bama's way of getting ready to make rain, all her councillors were bobbing about on their knees licking up the beer. Their six long tongues, scuffing up the liquid, reminded me of six red sausage dogs.'

'And then it poured?' I always asked.

'First she danced,' said my mother, 'then it came down in buckets.'

My mother had been carrying her knitting; she had been knitting a jersey for her dead fiancé who had been allergic to machine-knits. The Queen was intrigued by her collection of needles. Were they spears for stabbing enemies or ornaments for beautifying the body? My mother was at liberty to demonstrate the use of these small spears upon the bodies of the Queen's counsellors. The counsellors, said my mother, stopped licking up the beer for a moment and stared at her with their tongues frozen between their lips like half-posted letters.

'These needles are made not to kill; they are to create,' said my mother, who had the gift of a ringing phrase when you least expected it. She held up her huge hands. 'I have to find work for these. And there is nothing you can do so beautifully with both hands – except perhaps to play the piano – so I knit.'

The Queen was intrigued. 'Show me.'

Then the counsellors went back to lapping up the spilt beer. My mother demonstrated a row of stitches; she used two big needles on a jersey and four small swift needles on a sock. Bamadodi asked my mother to show her three daughters how it was done and so she did. On several subsequent visits my mother gave the Queen's daughters knitting lessons, and ever afterwards Queen Bamadodi and my mother were friends.

And her tribe were great knitters. I have known experts claim that knitting was something the Rain Queens of the Magaliesberg got from British missionaries who tried – and failed – to covert them from their pagan ways. That was wrong: they got knitting from my mother. They learnt everything from garter and stocking stitch to cable stich. In later years, Queen Bama sometimes wore for her crown a wonderful woollen tower of green and sugary pinks and blazing yellows.

Ever afterwards, once or twice a year Queen Bamadodi would visit us in Forest Town. She never told us when she was coming and it was always a surprise to see the royal limousine outside the garden gate. She owned a Holden motorcar and that was incredibly exotic because it came from Australia. Queen Bamadodi always sat in the back, with her praise-singer beside her, and her chair-bearer doing the driving, and her throne roped to the roof-rack and covered with an ochre blanket. The first we knew of her visit was when her praise-singer, wearing monkey skins and leg rattles and carrying a whisk of jackal skin, would come up to our gate and sing out: 'Behold the great she-lion, the mother elephant of her tribe, the rainmaker blessed by God who makes the grass grow and the cattle fat and the rivers flush and the dry veld ooze like a young girl with full breasts of milk.'

And my mother would say, 'Heavens above! It's Bama, come for tea!'

Then the royal throne-bearer would come up the garden path into the house and set down the throne of fine yellow-wood, carved with jagged bolts of lightning, and then Bama and my mother sat down in the front room. The tea-tray was placed between them, covered in finest gauze against the flies; always the best tea service, Royal Doulton, peppermint-green porcelain with golden edges, and my mother thanking the Lord she'd baked her famous date loaf.

They'd sit and sip. And tell each other tales of looming disasters; somehow they frightened and calmed one another. The Rain Queen's praise-singer lay on the grass beside the garden gate, catching what shade he could from the lemon tree that grew beside the fence. The royal chauffeur dozed behind the wheel of the Holden.

I loved her visits. I loved Bamadodi because she kept the faith and she was fun. Her singleness of purpose I found admirable. She spent her life attempting the impossible – she wished to preserve the monarchy – and she danced to make rain. I loved her for simply going on being what she was, I admired the way she got over the difficulty of keeping faith in a godless world. I loved her for all the things she simply didn't attend to. She flew in the face of common sense; she didn't care about science, and she didn't practise accountancy. Or rugby. She did not care about the price of gold. What she did was make rain.

Sometimes, by mysterious means, she made babies, and those babies were always girls because only women ruled the Lebalola people.

I was no more than about fifteen when she told me about her phantom lovers.

'My needs get seeded by spooks.'

'What sort of spooks?'

She looked at me a long time with her huge brown eyes.

'Alexander, if I knew that, they wouldn't be spooks. They wouldn't come in the night and seed my needs. And if they didn't seed my needs how would I have daughters? I don't see the spooks who call on me. I don't know who they are. It isn't important, so long as they remember their duty. The back door in the dark, and the seed. Afterwards, we do not speak of them.'

'What happens if you have boy babies?'

She lifted her huge eyebrows into her high forehead.

'We disown them.'

Queen Bama generally visited us in the summer, towards evening, a time when the highveld storms hit; and we never knew if the rain brought Bama or it was the other way around.

The neighbours were appalled. The sent a deputation to tell my mother that they hadn't settled in Johannesburg's northern suburbs to be serenaded by Johnny Witchdoctor. My mother sent back a note telling them to go and take a running jump. Other people, more dangerous, queried our Queen's credentials. They said she was a fake; said that there was only one true Rain Queen, and she lived much further north.

My mother said: 'Excuse *me*, our Bama makes rain all right. I've seen it, with my own two eyes. Besides, she's got a certificate.'

As the years passed, the Holden gave way to a succession of Toyotas. Queen Bama approved of the Japanese because though other countries boycotted us, the Japanese kept trading, and Queen Bama admired their sturdy conservatism and their freedom from moral scruple.

Very rarely, she brought her daughters whom I never knew as anything other than Princess One and Princess Two, who drank their tea with crooked little fingers and never said a word.

Sometimes Bama would bring her government certificate and, after my mother had made her usual protestations – 'Really, Bama, I don't know if I should. It's an official document' – she'd wash her hands and read it aloud:

'"This is to certify that her August Majesty, Queen Bamadodi vi, is recognised by the South African Weather Bureau as a professional meteorologist, and is qualified to practise as such within her Tribal Homeland."'

And then she'd say: 'My word, Bama, you must be so proud!'

Generally, rain interrupted tea. The sky came down like a lid. Then you heard a tentative bark of thunder a long way off, like a giant clearing his throat. The sky darkened to dead black, and bolts of lightning ripped it apart like shot silk. Each flash ended with a crack of thunder so loud it made you open and close your mouth to get your ears working again. The rain began drumming on the corrugated-iron roof. The praise-singer had run for the Holden and sat peering out of the misty window like a lost soul in the roar of water. Then, suddenly, the rain faltered and stopped, as if someone had switched it off. The sun was coming out, the heat bounced back, the grass was drying, the birds were in business, and the evening sky had turned to summer pink and gold. Only the water chugging in the storm drains and the salty, leathery aroma of the wet red dust told you the storm had been our way.

And Queen Bama sighed happily, and accepted another slice of date loaf, while the two princesses looked on with astonishment at the royal miracle.

You wanted to applaud.

6

The Stinson wasn't called the flying station wagon for nothing. It carried her guns and provisions, if she was hunting in Barotseland or with the Giriama tribesmen in the hardwood forests of Kilifi; and her evening clothes if she was planning to stop over in Nairobi at the Muthaiga Club. And since she flew with either conventional landing gear or floats, she could get to just about anywhere.

This blazing freedom to come and go on a whim and a wing. For her that was a kind of hallucinogen. The drug must be administered haphazardly if it is to lead to a sense of the strangeness of the new place that breaks down all the carefully assembled bits and pieces that make up the person you thought you were. In order to travel well, it is essential to be able to get seriously lost.

She did this brilliantly. Riding contradictions, swapping countries, roles, times made for a kind of cultural cross-dressing. On a typical day she would have got up that morning early, at home, in Johannesburg, and driven to Wemmer Pan, if she was flying on floats. Everything her eye fell on – from the traffic cop in his neo-Nazi gear, black cap, jodhpurs, glistening black leather boots, directing cars in Louis Botha Avenue, to the beggar who banged his mottled hands on her windscreen at

a stop street in Orange Grove – was familiar. At the Pan she
fired up the engine and headed north. After stopping to refuel
on a dam at a friendly uncle's place, she'd be over the Limpopo,
and several hours later, hundreds of miles north, she would put
down on Lake Nyasa.

For some years she would spend the night in a lakeside
village. Then, one day, she found out the witchdoctor had
made a replica of her little yellow Stinson, right down to its
floats, and was using it as powerful medicine. There was a
shrine to her in the village.

'It's a bit much, finding you're a goddess,' she told me. 'The
strain is tremendous. A deity is always on duty and it knocks
the hell out of you. Everyone wanting something: cures, luck,
children…No wonder the Greek gods just petered out. If
people did a little more time as gods they'd be more consider-
ate. It is a very great shock to have people always throwing
themselves on your mercy, or trying to garland you with
flowers, or bringing goats to your doorway and sacrificing them
on the spot. You want to help but there's a limit. Though your
followers don't see it that way. You're up against the believers
and they will not take no for an answer. Resigning does no
good. You stay divine. So I never went back to that village.
I didn't know where to put my face.'

In the years after the Second World War, off and on, she would
drop by the Schweitzer mission at Lambaréné in the Congo.
Some time in the late forties she put her Stinson down on the
Ogooué River, and a guy in a canoe poled her across to the
island, where the port stood amongst palm trees, and she made
her way to the tin-roofed hospital.

'I'd find Himself sitting down to supper. "Ah, Kathleen," he'd say, "I wish I'd known you were coming. I've almost run out of potassium, and sulphur and iodine ..."'

'Then we'd have supper, and then he'd play some Bach on this mangy old piano which he battled to keep in tune, and he'd tell stories; he loved telling stories, though they always had a moral in the tail. People there called him *le grand docteur*. An inferiority complex was not one of his problems.

'He told me straight: "Sometimes, I fear, Kathleen, I am just plain Mr God."

'Well, he got a touch of sympathy from me. I knew all about that, once having been a bit of a goddess myself. And I must dispel a few myths about the old boy. Fact the first: Dr A. was a crusty old paternalist; he regarded Africans as untutored savages, but let's say in his favour that he saw them as *serious* savages, admirable savages. Savage was what he liked. It was his big thing. The many, many ways that Africans found to kill each other was one of the great fascinations of his life. Whether by poison, knives or witchcraft, he felt they did it so happily, so naturally they should be left alone to get on with it. We shouldn't interfere, except to ease suffering by medical science, like cure goitres, and ulcers, sleeping sickness and elephantiasis. For the rest, leave them alone! He didn't just like the idea of the noble savages; he believed you didn't get nobility to bloom by stamping on the savagery. If there was anything wrong with these children of nature, said Dr A., it was our presence. *Us.* You and me and the so-called civilised lot. Being in contact with the likes of us led them to blow money on booze, made them forget how to carve canoes, and start lusting after our salt, our tobacco and our shoes. He got furious with them for wanting these things.' She raised her eyes in that quizzical, startled little grimace which was as close as she ever came to irony. 'As if none of this happened back home, in darling little Europe ... Anyway, he was a grand fellow – and we all have our blind spots, don't we?

'Fact the second: he was a racist with rigid ideas about discipline. He'd say about his beloved savages, he often called them that, "They must be shown that the tongue that speaks love may also lash them till they weep. *Nicht wahr*?" There was a lot of *nicht wahr*-ing in Schweitzer-talk. Mostly, in Lambaréné, he spoke French but he liked speaking German to me. Maybe because I was from South Africa, and since I said I wasn't English, therefore he assumed I must be semi-Dutch, or quasi-German, or something more or less Boer-ish.'

My mother's stories. My mother's friends ...

Great stuff. Exactly what we wanted to hear. Probably all we *can* hear. This stream of images projected on my growing consciousness. Far-away foreigners all of whom seemed destined for stardom, because character was, ultimately, celluloid. Even as substantial a figure as Albert Schweitzer, snapped on my mother's box Brownie, in his white tropical suit, solar topee and walrus moustache, smiling from the buttery bamboo frame beside her bed, under the looping letters of his inscription: 'To my dear Kathleen, aviatrix, angel!' Even '*le grand docteur*' seems a dead ringer for someone who would one day play him in some cheesy movie – the saintly healer in a domed hat – and how odd that this impersonation would seem, ever afterwards, more real than the real thing.

But, then, whoever gave a toss for the real thing? It was sometimes said that conquest, colonies, empire, money and slaves were what the white invasion of Africa was for; but that is only half the story. Looking back, the entire absurd scramble for Africa seems one long trailer for Metro-Goldwyn-Mayer. All those busy soldiers who shot their way across the dark continent, those rogues, missionaries, explorers, white hunters, the Happy Valley lot and the Bwana Brigade, Boer and Brit and the fancy French botanists, aviators, miners, entrepreneurs, fakes, remittance men, red-necked adventurers from Ealing, Chepstow, Bremen and Bruges, who came to the Congo or the Cape, to Kenya or Nyasaland, Windhoek or Djibouti, whether they said they came to get rich, or get away from home, or the bailiffs, or to get to be king of somewhere: all of them were, in fact, no more than understudies; meat for the movies.

And because they – we – always had this feeling of redundancy, our true selves eaten away by the otherness of Africa, it made us noisy and muscular. We reached violently into the emptiness around us, in order to feel we were alive, accentuating our looks, passions, hatreds, cruelties in order to convince ourselves we hadn't been rubbed away to nothing. We wrote our names on mountains and rivers, talked ourselves up; in fact, did absolutely anything to keep away the feeling that we were lost in a place that did not hate us, but simply did not notice. We called it mastery. Worse, we even called it love.

The only things white men have ever done around the place are easily noted: they have shot something, or a great number of someone, or each other; kicked a lot of folks around; or died of some indigenous disease, as if copping it from malaria was a mission statement, or perishing of black-water fever showed your heart was in the right place.

But I digress. Let me say something about the men who lived in the tropical forest and transformed themselves into leopards. It was Dr A. who first brought the leopard men to the attention of an incredulous world, and when he told my mother about them, she said: 'Let's go and meet some,' and they did. Which is pretty odd when you think about it, this scary saint from the Congo and my old lady from Jo'burg, and their mutual liking for guys in costume who sliced up their neighbours in a fashion my mother loved to recount:

'Dr A. was a fund of good info; about how they sharpened their claws of steel, and how they made their bark camouflage, and how they filed their teeth! I loved it. It was so rich! Dr A. knew lots of leopard guys: the Anyoto of the Eastern Congo, the lion men in Tanganyika. He'd been taken with these chaps ever since the thirties. In Ivory Coast, the boys come back from their initiation training in the forest and do the leopard dance in the village. And very fine it is too; a good deal of sinuosity, of arching the back, of growling. The outfits are superb, they don't go for gross realism, they go for "impressionistic renditions of what the soul of the leopard is felt to be". Quote unquote. They dress in bark, spotted black and yellow, and slink about growling and crouching and stalking and flinging themselves on their victims…' She stiffened her large hands and the red nail polish on her long sharp nails gleamed in the lamplight. 'And while the victims scream blue murder the leopard men are carving them up with bladed knives, made into claws. Some simply stalk and pounce; some, like the leopard men of Lagos, also eat their victims.'

The hairs on my neck stood to attention.

'Didn't they even cook them?'

'Never. Kill, yes, but never cook: gobbled on the spot.'

'Why?'

'Whadyamean, why? Because leopards don't cook.'

'Yes, but is it true?'

'Is *what* true?' She always came down hard on '*what*'.

'Were they really leopards – or only pretend?'

'Some of it's true; some of it's pretend. They were like all of us humans, once upon a time, in the early days when we lived close to the animals, close to real life; when we were hunters and dreamers and murderers; when we didn't know if we were men dressed as animals or animals who were also people. You could say we were ani-men.'

It was Schweitzer who took her to meet some leopard men.

'I flew him up to northern Gabon, near Oyem, where they make a religion out of a plant called eboga. It's taken from the roots of a bush found in the forest that is ground, grated or dunked in water. It looks a bit like grated turnip. The people of Oyem took us into one of their chapels, which was really a hut built to one side of the compound. Because he was '*le grand docteur*' they were happy to let us sit in on a séance.

'We sat on the floor of the chapel, watching. Then one of the chaps, his name was Emana Ola, he talked us through the ceremony, in German. It was funny hearing Dr A. and Emana Ola chattering away in Deutsch, in a village in deepest Gabon, but, then, bits of northern Gabon were once the German Cameroons, so there you go. Emana Ola told us that after eating eboga God came to him and said that all strangers approaching the village who were not of his clan were witches in disguise, and must be killed for religious reasons. Dr A. said he didn't see why you should kill people for religious reasons. Emana Ola said there was an essential difference between white and black beliefs. Christians were always eating the body of God, so as to be joined with him. That was what the missionaries taught. But the sacred meal of eboga, which was Emana Ola's communion bread, opened the door of death and took him into the very presence of God, and of the ancestors.

'Now, of course, old Dr A. was not just a medical man, he was also a biblical scholar of note. But he was a Protestant and I could see that the idea of "eating God" had about it a Catholic taint he found somewhat disagreeable. Emana Ola asked us did we want to join the cult of Bwiti, and see God? And I said yes. The Doctor said no; he wasn't eating any drugs, thanks very much. So only I was inducted; I was called a popi, which means an initiate. Two people are set to look after you and they are called your mother and father. Their job is to watch you and decide just how much eboga they can stuff you with before you pass out or throw up. They walked me down a stream with someone playing the ngombi, which is an eight-stringed harp only used when you're doing Bwiti. By this time Dr A. had stomped off in a huff to smoke his pipe. Just as well because I was stripped to the buff; then I had to confess my sins, then I ate more eboga, then the priest rubbed me down with sacred bark from twelve sacred trees, then I was dressed in white and the priest tapped me several time on the head with the parasol fruit – that looks like an enormous phallus – and people joked about it. Then more eboga. Then I had a bit of a vision, I saw my father, my dear old dad, and he said to me: "How are you doing, sweetie?" So that was a bonus; but I did not see God, as I'd hoped, and then I passed out.

'I woke up feeling pretty groggy. Dr A. had told them I wanted to meet some leopard men and he was not going till I'd met them. Emana Ola said some of his best friends were leopard men and he'd give them a shout. About a dozen blokes turned up dressed to the nines. Claws and all. They did some prowling, growling and pouncing. Next, they climbed trees but frankly I have to say they did not look like leopards. Dr A. said it was not their outer physical likeness the leopard men sought to reproduce; they were spirit leopards. Anyway, they then got down from the trees and started practising little leaps and growling some more, and showing their teeth. Humans, of course, don't have fangs or a dewclaw and that's a letdown when you're trying to be a leopard, even a spirit leopard. Now the dewclaw of the leopard will scalp a man easy as winking. Slice his face off. These guys were not quite in that class. They had made claws from knives with hooked blades: five sharp pieces of metal protruding from grips that slipped over the fingers, rather like wooden gloves. Or razor-edged knuckle-dusters.

'But I did not scoff. I found their enthusiasm very pleasing. The good doctor, too; he kept nodding and saying "*sehr interessant*", and praising what he called the consistency of their spiritual impersonations. He reckoned that even if they had to work at it, the wounds left on their victims would have been a fair approximation of the damage done by real leopards after a good mauling.

'I must say I was struck by Dr A.'s inconsistencies, and bloody impressed at how little they bothered him. Dr A. puffed a pipe himself but he hated the tobacco habit he found amongst people in Gabon. But we always took along a box of American tobacco leaves and used a leaf at a time as money. Like banknotes. He'd peel off a leaf. It was dark, strong, poisonous stuff, but people loved it. So there we were, talking to Africans who got high on psychotropic drugs, saw visions and liked to murder people. Yet Dr A. was a puritan and a man who reverenced life. He believed in the living; he did not side with the dead. The leopard men were destroyers of life, if you took them seriously. They said they were killing witches, but, in fact, they were murdering innocent pedestrians. But Dr A. went along with it all, still finding it "*sehr interessant*" because, you see, for him they were noble savages, and he far preferred indigenous drug-addicts, dressed as big cats, out on a killing spree for genuine religious reasons, to those he saw as clever savages; educated Africans whom he saw as screwed-up versions of even more screwed-up Europeans ...'

No one said anything to my mother on the day she landed at Grand Central with a passenger. A boy in the back seat and a large woman in flying goggles and a long lavender scarf, who looked like any other white madam travelling with her black servant. And besides, the boy wasn't wearing his gear, and you can't tell a leopard man just by looking at him. In the flesh he looked like any other cook or road sweeper.

When I asked her how she managed it, she said: 'Mrs Garfinkel has a gardener from Nyasaland, so why shouldn't I have a friend to stay? From Gabon?'

It seemed the guy had a yearning to see a big city. And even with Dr A.'s warnings about the poison of civilisation fresh in her mind, my mother, being in her way a sucker for rescue missions, flew him from real to urban jungle, for a taste of big city life.

He was called Nzong, and he was a lively bloke with very dark skin and beautiful hands. He lived with us in Forest Town for some weeks, and my ma got him to show me his stuff. His camouflage suit was a type of cloak made from tree bark, stippled in black and yellow paint. He tied it around his waist with a belt, and pulled it over his head to form a cowl. His tail was fixed to the belt.

We got on well, Nzong and me, even though we couldn't really speak to each other. I used to go and see him in his room in the back yard, and when I patted my tummy and chewed a bit, and he nodded, I knew he was hungry so I gave him half a loaf of bread and a Coke. He let me try on the body sheath and then he showed me how to spring like a leopard. I really liked his steel claws; and he let me wear them, though my ma said: 'For God's sake don't slash yourself, will you?' Then Nzong and I practised leopard leaps on the lawn with her looking on, and yelling: 'Arch your back, Alexander, and keep your eye on Nzong.'

He clapped his hands when I got it right, and I almost felt like a leopard. I knew that if I had a chance, in the forest, I'd also attack passers-by and tear them with my claws. It was what a decent leopard did. When Nzong was a leopard he was so good, or at least he was a good pretender. I could never be that good. I think it was because I never believed like he did.

But after a few days it palled for both of us. I didn't blame Nzong: when you get down to it, the leopard's repertoire is limited, and in a suburban garden especially so. As my ma said, for a real leopard man it was important to get in a kill fairly regularly, otherwise what was the point?

And so, by way of an outing, we took Nzong to the Zoo.

'It might make him feel at home,' said my ma.

At the Zoo, she bought us ice-cream cones and she promised us a ride on an elephant. We had a bit of trouble persuading the keeper to let Nzong up on to the elephant's back.

'No can do,' said the elephant-keeper. 'Black boys can't ride the elephant.'

My mother said: 'He's not a boy; he's a leopard man! All the way from the German Cameroons.'

The elephant-keeper took off his cap; he had a lot of blond hair and his cap, which was right by my nose, smelt of elephant. Men quite often took off their hats when they spoke to my mother.

'What's the Cameroons? I've never heard of there.'

My mother told him as if any clot knew the answer.

'It was a German colony in West Africa, on the Gulf of Guinea, extending northwards to Lake Chad. Then the British and French in the Great War won it. But some people in remote districts still went on speaking German for decades. This boy is one of them.'

'Is it, hey?' The elephant-keeper was not persuaded.

'Yes, it is.'

'Then make him say something in German.'

My mother spoke Nzong in Kwa-Swahili; and he told the keeper:

'*Dummer Barbar – verfluchter schwarzer Dummkopf – Sie niedriger Form des Lebens.*'

The elephant-keeper was intrigued now. 'What's he say, hey?'

'He called you a stupid barbarian, a bloody black *domkop*, and an inferior form of life.'

'Hell's teeth.' The elephant-keeper was impressed. 'He's the real McCoy: a genuine bloody black kraut.'

And he let us up into the little wooden seat, high on the elephant's back, and off we swayed. Afterwards, we went to see the leopards, and I remember a big cage with an old tree in the middle of a dusty floor and on the white bald branches of the tree two leopards, their tails swinging. Nzong stared at the leopards, and he smiled.

'Thank heavens, Nzong's found some friends,' said my mother.

Nzong wanted to spend the night in the Zoo but my mother wouldn't have it.

'Only real animals can spend the night in the Zoo, Nzong, humans are forbidden.'

But she must have thought twice about this because she let him do it. After all, she said, Nzong was also a leopard man and he had a perfect right to spend the night among the animals. She bought him two more ice creams and a big bottle of ginger beer, in case he was hungry in the night; and we went home alone, and worried. When we went back next morning we found him sitting outside the leopards' cage; he'd eaten the ice creams and drunk the ginger beer and looked fine. The leopards didn't seem all that knocked out but maybe that was because he wasn't wearing his gear.

But Nzong got even more broody and my ma saw things were getting difficult.

'He wants to be out and about. I do understand. It's what he does, where he comes from. If he wants to savage a passer-by, he's free to do so. Just to qualify as a leopard man you have to subsist in the forest on your own for eight weeks on whatever food you can kill yourself. But we can't have that in Forest Town. I have no idea whom he might kill and disembowel.'

She laid down restrictions: he was allowed to put on his leopard outfit only in daylight hours, only at home, on the lawn, where she could keep an eye on him. He wasn't to go into the street alone.

But she knew it was wrong and one day, without saying anything to me, she and he were gone. She flew Nzong back to the forests of Cameroon where he could pounce and slash to his heart's content.

It must have been a few months later that we went to see the film called *Tarzan and the Leopard Men* at the Lake Cinema in Parkview. In the red plush foyer there were posters everywhere, with pictures of guys in masks who leapt from trees and ate you up. There were also some pygmies. But they were fakes, like the leopard men were fakes. A poster said: 'From the Hellhole of the Congo – Come African Freaks and Marvels!'

I didn't like the film; I didn't like Tarzan, I didn't like the screaming – there was a lot of screaming – and I didn't want to watch any more so I went out and sat in the foyer, shaking a bit.

My old lady came looking for me: 'What's the matter? You scared?'

'No.'

'Well, then?'

'I don't like it.'

'Why not?'

'It's not real.'

She sat down and took my hand. 'Alexander. It's not meant to be real. This is just a film, a bioscope. Don't take it so seriously; it's only pretend.'

'I don't like pretend.'

My mother put her arms around me. 'Don't take it so personally.'

But I did take it personally. I missed Nzong. He wasn't a freak or a marvel, he was just a perfectly ordinary leopard boy who could kill and eat people, if he wanted. The actors on the screen weren't half as good, and yet everyone was supposed to go around saying how real and scary they were. Everyone but me. I didn't believe in pretend; that was my problem.

7

He would climb out of his little green Vauxhall at our gate, toddle up the slasto path to the front stoop where my mother sat cleaning her shotgun. A large bloke with a thick moustache, short brown hair, wearing a rather hairy sports jacket of biscuit-brown, with leather buttons. He was called Louis Labuschagne, known to his friends as 'Lappies', but to us he was just 'Oomie': little uncle.

He'd wink and move on. Or he'd slow down when he passed me, kneeling on the lawn, collecting snails for a penny a dozen.

'You've never seen me. Right?'

'Yes, sir.'

'I'm not here. I have never been here. Unnerstan'?'

'Yes, Oomie.'

He once told me: 'I have a very, very important job, Alex boy, only I can't tell you what it is. So when you see me, remember, I'm not here.'

Oddly enough, the man who wasn't there was to take on a lot more substance. I never thought the men who called at our place had any real life of their own; they were simply in orbit around my mother and assumed importance in relation to her. To begin with, Oomie was just another uncle and I had uncles like the garden had snails: there was Uncle Barrie, who travelled for Helena Rubinstein, and Uncle Jack, who was 'something in aluminium', Uncle Papadop from Rhodesia, and Uncle Hansie from South West Africa, any number of white hunters and one white Zulu. Each and every one of them passing strangers pretending to have real lives when what they really did was to buzz and bounce around my ma, like bees or rubber balls.

It took a long time before I could begin to see that sometimes these guys were what they said they were, men with jobs and backgrounds, lives and wives of their own, instead of being adornments my mother wore, until she wore them out. But of all my uncles I can truly say that Oomie surprised me most because I got the unexpected chance to see him in his real job. He sprang into view the way people did when they were truly alive, and not just mere blips on my personal radar that signalled heavy uncle traffic.

It was 1960, I was sixteen, and working weekends and holidays. My old lady believed in encouraging what she called 'the power of independent finance', by which she meant getting a job and looking after myself. 'See you anon', she'd say, before heading off for Kenya, Congo or Rhodesia, without leaving me any cash. She was very generous when she was flush, but paying for flying machines, she said again and again, 'costs a bomb'. So when I wasn't at school I took a variety of jobs. I did Saturday mornings selling hooch in a bottle store; I did Christmas at the OK Bazaars; I did Easter at Milner Park at the Rand Show on the instant soup stand, handing tiny scalding skinny plastic cups of the new miracle broth to passers-by. It was instant chicken noodle ... 'Brimming with goodness, made with reverence for all the old traditional farmhouse values …' said the advertising posters. 'Just add water and stir.' We had never seen its like and it proved beyond doubt that Jo'burg was flying like a rocket into the future, no matter what anyone said or thought.

Easter, and I was, once again, on the soup stand at the Rand Show. It unfolded in a great jostling mix of men, beasts and machinery, in a vast space of tractors and ploughs and irrigation piping, and dozens of free brochures touting plastic sheeting, or miracle fertilisers or combine-harvesters; great gluey wads of glossy paper that small boys carried in tottering piles, hugged to their chests, salivating at the tang of these highly desirable slabs of totally free newsprint. There were exhibition halls, cattle-pens, fairground rides, and an illuminated concrete spike marked the centre of this great bazaar and was known as the Tower of Light. It was, I suppose, not much more than a cattle fair, plus diversionary swings and roundabouts, but it was run by men who called themselves 'gentlemen' farmers, and who made believe the gathering was some sort of Royal Show.

Like many of our delusions, this pretence was vital and consoling because it allowed us to believe, briefly (and briefly was better than bugger-all) that we were not, in fact, a pathetic rump of emasculated ninnies – English, Blacks, Jews, Catholics and foreigners of whatever stripe – all impotent, all ruled by bearded, bloody-minded Boers; big-necked blokes in khaki shorts who carried sjamboks; narrow, vicious puritans, who cared only for rugby, racial purity and being right; thugs who made the word 'farmer' the sort of word drunks in bars hurled at those they wished to insult. It let us pretend that we mattered; that we were not useless and despised casualties of history.

Pretending was what we did big time in Jo'burg: pretending was not just an art form, it was a fucking industry. We didn't just make mountains out of molehills; we made mountains out of mine-dumps. We were the pretending capital of the universe. We were a mining camp posing as an Anglican parish, prostitutes playing at parsons. We were greedy, grubby bandits, forever being caught with our hands in the till, and forever trying to make it look like we were putting the money back.

The Rand Easter Show, while 'agricultural', was not for Boers, at least, not in theory. The Rand Easter Show was for our sort of farmers, jovial chaps with red cheeks and mutton-chop whiskers, who spoke English, and believed in fair play. They drove Austins and sent their sons to Oxford; Jo'burg's gentleman farmers, in hacking jackets and big red rosettes. It was our way of insisting, Look: there are English farmers, liberal farmers, too!

Things were particularly keyed up that Easter because the Show officials were preparing for a visit by the Prime Minister, Dr Hendrik Frensch Verwoerd, the man who more than any other was responsible for our deeply depraved and horribly boring obsession with racial purity and blood hygiene and religious strife.

The showgrounds at Milner Park had been named after Alfred, Lord Milner, the former High Commissioner to South Africa during the Boer War. Milner was a brutal dreamer whose visions of clean-limbed, poncy young English eunuchs ruling the world from the Thames to the Indus exceeded even those of Cecil John Rhodes in their poisonous perversion.

We had a bit of family connection, Milner and us. My grandfather, as a young bomb-maker in the Boer War, had wanted to assassinate Milner. It was 1901, the Boers gathered in Vereeniging were staring defeat in the face and had decided to sue for peace when my grandfather, who, like the rest of the Irish Brigade, violently rejected any idea of surrender to the British, came up with an idea. Lord Milner was being taken to Vereeniging by special train to discuss terms of surrender with the Boer generals, Botha, De Wet, Delarey and Jan Smuts. Well, then, why not blow his train to smithereens? My grandfather had even chosen the culvert. Alas, Jan Smuts scotched the idea with a remark that always pained my grandfather (who revered the Boer leader) for what he called 'its excess of Anglo-Saxon common sense'.

Smuts told him: 'You can't negotiate with a dead Milner.'

My grandfather was rather put out. 'And why ever not? You'll get more sense out of him dead.'

But Smuts prevailed, Milner lived, the Boers surrendered. Yet although they lost the war, ten short years later they won the country back from the British. And in 1910 they built upon the ruins of the old independent Boer republics a fantasy land in which all four provinces of the old South Africa were merged into a new Union of a new South Africa, an arrangement they called Paradise but which for just about everyone else turned into a dull and wretched prison where we would spend most of the next century.

It was to commemorate the fiftieth anniversary of that fateful union that Dr Verwoerd, evangelist of apartheid, sainted figure of segregation, was coming to speak at Milner Park. The irony of the visit – Apostle of Apartheid Addresses the English Philistines at the Poor Bastards' Invitation – had not gone unnoticed but, as usual, everyone had agreed not to make an issue of it.

I was on tea break when the loudspeakers strapped to the Tower of Light began announcing that the official opening of the Show by the Prime Minister was taking place in the Main Arena, and I wandered along to hear Verwoerd speak, moving through the crowds, feeling, as I always did at the Easter Show, that this must be what it was like to be in touch with the world, the movement and the bustle and life of it, cattle and tractors, irrigation piping and candy floss, turbines and roller-coasters, a kind of lively mess I believed made up the true world as it existed in other places, where many things happened at the same time to many people, and was not in the least like life in Johannesburg, which was a series of isolations, a Chinese box of interlocking vacuums, strong walls designed to keep out the wider world, and yet which held in precisely nothing.

Verwoerd was on a platform, with a lot of other VIPs, one hand in the pocket of his suit (double-breasted, black) plus red rosette. His cheeks were rosy and he had this lick of strong thick grey hair. The Chairman, Colonel Something-Or-Other, was thanking Verwoerd for coming, and got so carried away that when he'd finished thanking him, he thanked him again. On Verwoerd's right sat a guy I took to be just another farmer, and this guy kept putting his hand into the inside pocket of his jacket and taking it out again, as if checking his car keys or his wallet. I paid no attention to him, neither did anyone else.

What amazed me was that standing right behind Verwoerd was someone I knew very well: it was Oomie. And for a moment I couldn't for the life of me think what he was doing there.

The Prime Minister was very used to being thanked and he waited until the Colonel's speech had, at last, wound down into appreciative little smiles and winks, and then he took the mike. He began speaking in that high, rather strangled tone that always reminded me of a ventriloquist who threw his voice all right but lacked the dummy, and so his high-pitched mewl always seemed to be coming from someone else.

The farmers in hacking jackets were hoping for a miracle: to wit, that if they pretended to be good blokes, the Leader would pretend to be a civilised man and not mock and despise them as English nincompoops, silly liberals, heirs of the old enemy whom it was his duty to humiliate for starters, and then to destroy for keeps.

Verwoerd knew it was his duty to humiliate – for starters – and then to destroy – for keeps. His speech was suave; it snaked in and out between what were near-civilities and sardonic defiance. There were those, he said, who saw the 'Union' of South Africa – fifty years of it – as a triumph for 'the people'. But Union was a triumph only in so far as it had emasculated the hated British enemy. It had been a disaster for decent Boers everywhere who had inherited all the constraints and customs enforced by the old imperial enemy.

The farmers behind him on the platform looked at their brogues; trapped between deep embarrassment and furtive anger, alternately nodding and shaking their heads and trying like hell to pass both off as respectful agreement.

My eyes were on Oomie; what the hell was he doing here?

Verwoerd was getting to his brutal conclusion, his cheeks pink and white and shaking slightly with passion. His light blue eyes were blind. Fifty years of Union – his treble rose higher – under an English crown was a continuing insult to the thousands who died for the raped republics of the Transvaal and the Free State, and the sooner South Africa returned to its predestined divine status as a Nationalist Christian Boer republic run by Boers for Boers, the better ...

Then he sat down and all the farmers on the podium put on their shit-eating smiles and clapped. Good old Hendrik: he'd just kicked them in the balls yet again, and they were very, very grateful. Colonel Something got up and began to thank him all over again.

It was then that the guy who, earlier, had kept reaching into his pocket stood up and walked over to Dr Verwoerd, carrying what looked like a gun, except I knew it could not be a gun because if it was a gun, it might go off. The man called out nice and calm and polite, 'Dr Verwoerd?' as if he wanted to ask him the time, as if he wasn't quite sure if he had the right man, and then what I thought could not be a gun went off, and Dr Verwoerd sort of flinched. It was at precisely that moment that I realised why Oomie was on the platform; I knew why he never told me what he did. Oomie was a cop, a secret policeman, he was one of the Prime Minister's bodyguards.

The man with the gun then pushed it right up against Dr Verwoerd's ear, and it went off again, duller, softer this time, on account of it being right up hard against his ear, and Verwoerd fell over and began bleeding.

That was when Oomie also fell over, as if they'd rehearsed it, as if that had been the arrangement between them, and both of them lay there, and went on lying there. Except Oomie wasn't bleeding. Then Colonel Someone grabbed the pistol, other men began pulling the gunman off the stage, and when they got him down to the ground they picked him up and ran off with him because some in the crowd were obviously wanting to kill him. Sirens began screaming. So did the crowd. It was very South African now. Someone had tried to kill someone else, and a lot of other people wanted to kill someone, too. It was their turn, it was only natural, and it was only fair. The sirens got louder and then the white nose of an ambulance was pushing its way through the mêlée.

It was at this moment that Oomie, who had been lying down all the time, and who might have been dead, suddenly sat up.

He wasn't dead but it looked like Dr Verwoerd might be.

There were pistol shots that changed the world: there had been the Serb, Princip, at Sarajevo in 1914, and Lee Harvey Oswald in the Dallas Book Repository. For us there was 16 April 1960, when a man on the VIP stand at the Rand Easter Show turned politely towards the Prime Minister, and twice tried to blow his head off. And missed.

His shot echoed around Africa: it went on echoing, in the sounds of doors slamming in our faces, from the Limpopo to the Nile. From that shot onwards we would be confined to the southern tip of the continent, among our mad-as-hatters white brothers, where the master race awoke each day to bright boasts of their cleverness and innate nobility, and went to bed each night having obediently swallowed a dayful of lies. The results were not what anyone could have foreseen.

We measured the impact, or my mother did, by the refusal of the authorities to allow her to land in the Sudan. For the first time in her life she could not go as she wished in Africa; she was confined, as she put it, to bloody barracks, the white enclaves south of the Zambesi: Rhodesia, South West Africa, Portuguese East Africa. And the great journeys to Kenya; the dusty landing strips on distant farms from Dar es Salaam to the Belgian Congo; the rivers and lakes in a dozen countries where she could put down, cruising at just a few thousand feet, above the heads of hippo and the stalking lions, sunset over Lake Victoria, dawn in Khartoum: one after the other these places and pleasures were no longer open to her. I don't remember, as I grew older, that she travelled any less, but it got harder to do: she needed permissions, flight plans, papers, landing rights, bribes to fly into Central and East Africa, she couldn't drop into the Congo at will, at least not into the official aerodromes and familiar landing strips.

Though I didn't know it when I stood in the crowd that day in the Main Arena and listened to Verwoerd's speech, my mother was there, too, very close by. Between us was a throng of gentlemen farmers wearing moustaches and rosettes and looking like well-fed, well-dressed, very dead turkeys. I had thought she was in transit, in flight, in Addis Ababa or Zanzibar or Cairo.

All through my childhood I'd look up to the sky for a glimpse of my flying mother, and I pretended I could see her plane, a speeding point of energy. But I never quite got hold of her: she flew too fast for me. Later, I pictured her rather like the neutrino, a sub-atomic particle so small, so quick, so elusive that they tried to catch a glimpse of it passing right through the earth by placing measuring devices on the floor of mile-deep gold mines, and waited for a lucky strike. For years they never got so much as a sniff: the particles passed straight through whatever interceptors they used, and never left a trace. That was the way I thought of my ma, the human neutrino. She lived a life that could be predicted but not proven, and whenever you looked for her, you were too late. But eventually they got the neutrino: they saw its passing signs. It did exist. Ditto with my old lady. She sped across the continent, like some great galleon under full sail, always off somewhere, totally indifferent to the ocean of little silvery lives in the sea beneath her, or in the air above her. Living meant getting on. Getting stuck was for others, not for her.

Not being around was something for which she reproached me, after I'd left. She'd phone me, in some other world, in Hanoi or Vancouver or Siem Riep, her voice perplexed. 'Where are you, exactly? I never know where you are!' As if she did not for a moment realise that she was the model on which I based my ever-moving self.

On the day in question, 16 April 1960, I calculate that she must have been about twenty metres away, in that part of the crowd with a good view of the Prime Minister, the Chairman of the Witwatersrand Agricultural Society (how grandly silly was the title!) and Colonel Someone.

It is strange how knowledge comes to call. Mostly you get it from books, or neighbours or school; from sources more or less unexceptional. But there is an old tradition in my country that some important truths can also be delivered by bullet. Its essence goes like this: if you come across something or someone you don't like, then you shout; if that doesn't work then break something; and if the stupid bastards still refuse to be reasonable, start shooting. Gunfire-assisted learning is about as traditional down our way as rooibos tea or biltong or tsetse fly.

Certainly, this was my mother's view. I don't think she liked violence – in principle – but she was always perfectly unmoved by the amount of it that went on around her. It was all perfectly normal. It might have been bad for some, it might even have made her shiver, but she never dreamt of doing away with it because it was what people used to get things done. It was like dynamite; everyone she knew worked happily with dynamite, because this was Jo'burg, dynamite was what we did. Our family life was punctuated by explosions.

Dr Verwoerd lived; his recovery was, his doctors confirmed, amazing; it was, said his followers, miraculous. And Verwoerd now took upon himself the role of resurrected hero of his tribe, the death-defying deliverer of his people from the toils of Satan, for which read foreigners, Jews, Catholics, communists, homosexuals and, of course, the accursed 'English'. It is often thought that Verwoerd and his henchmen hated blacks: that is wrong – they hated everyone.

The would-be assassin, a certain David Pratt, was locked away in a mental home. His failure, to many, was not to have tried to kill the Prime Minister – everybody understood why he should have wanted to do that – but to get so close and then to miss twice.

South Africans have never believed, as the comforting old cliché goes, that violence changes nothing. We knew it changed everything, providing you got it right. Pratt's two bullets, fired from a .22 pistol, missed the brain. How do you shoot a man in the ear and miss his brain? Ask a South African; ask a liberal.

Then there was Oomie; he was a lot harder for us to deal with than Pratt. He presented more problems: problems of image, of race, of authority, of humour or the lack of it, of dignity and the need to keep it up, of the role of the police in what was constantly now being referred to as the 'new' South Africa, the Republic of South Africa. For the question was:

when he was supposed to be preserving the Prime Minister, had the silly mutt not perhaps simply passed out?

It was not permitted to speculate on this in public; the official line was that the Premier's bodyguard either:

1. Got down on the floor to consult with the PM on the right course of action.
2. Pulled the Prime Minister to the floor in order to protect him with his body.
3. Hit the deck as his training demanded, did the leopard roll and prepared to return fire.

No one said anything. There was nothing to be said. Whatever you felt about the cops, Oomie was a white man, and the day white men started running down white men, the end of the world was at hand.

People said power spoke to power but they did not know the half of it. In Africa power did not just speak to power, it nuzzled up and performed varieties of consensual solidarity so perverse they might be practised only by consenting tyrants.

After his fall Oomie still came to see us. I suspect we were just about the only people who would have him under their roof. He would turn up in his green Vauxhall and my mother always had a tray ready: fresh coffee and chocolate cake, because, she said, weeping sapped the energy. Oomie would take out his revolver and rehearse what had happened, showing us how he fell to the floor and did the leopard roll, as instructed at police college, swearing he had been awake every moment he'd been on the floor. Super-aware, drawing a bead on the assassin, lining him up; and my ma would soothe him while he cried softly.

'Chin up,' she'd say. 'There are worse things.'

He never asked her what the worse things were. But, then, he seemed to think she didn't have political views. He was mistaken. She loathed anything that tied her down. Everyone was free to fly. She did not just believe it: she lived for nothing else.

If Oomie never asked, I did, and she gave me short shrift: 'Pass laws, jail terms, loss of land rights, curtailment of liberties, racial insanity, lethal boredom. In a world gone as mad as ours, a man who makes a mistake is rather endearingly human. If you hunt, you know anything can happen and anyone can have a weak moment. At least his behaviour was natural. In some ways, he was the only honest man on the platform that day, was my poor old Oomie.'

8

I was sixteen when Koosie came to live with us. Koosie told me that he was 'about' the same age. There was a lot I didn't know about Koosie because there was lot he didn't know about himself. He had attached himself to my mother at the airfield, where he had been living off scraps of food he got from the pilots and airfield staff, and he earned a few bob carrying bags to the planes.

My ma brought him home, as she did when someone she liked caught her eye; and that was how we came to grow up together for the next seven or eight years. It was an unusual set-up in the sixties. He was smaller than me; very thin and he had very big eyes. He always faded from sight whenever anyone from outside looked in on our lives.

He said he'd lost his parents. He sounded like he was still looking for them, as if they might turn up. He once had a house but it 'got taken'. I marvelled at this: how did someone 'take' your house?

Koosie got kind of cross, as if I'd said he was lying.

'I did have a house and it did get taken. I remember it.'

But I couldn't get it into my head.

'Who took it?'

'They came with bulldozers and they pushed it over.'

That haunted me: 'They pushed it over. Why did they push it over?'

He shrugged. 'Don't know. Then they took us away. We were removed.'

I didn't feel much for his lost parents. I lost my mother regularly and I'd learnt to get on with it. But to have the place that made you who you were pushed over, and carted away brick by brick. Then they removed you too ...

Koosie did not live in our house but in the outside room. Instead of reducing him to some sort of servant status, it increased his standing, at least in my eyes; he was independent, he had his own roof over his own head and he was very good at looking after himself. When my ma forgot to leave enough food, Koosie picked up food at the Greek shop on the corner. I envied him, but I never felt guilty: he knew how to take care of himself and showed me, but he wore my clothes, rode my bike, read my books. Koosie taught me you could get by on half a loaf of bread and a Coke. He took me to Big Lou's place, the Golden Gate Fish Bar, for sixpence-worth of chips.

Big Lou's place was about a mile away, and we walked there. Big Lou had a round and heavy head, like a cannon-ball perched on a pyramid, a thick neck, big shoulders, he wore his white shirt open to the waist, he had lots of strong black hairs on his rocky chest, and immense hips.

He was a sight, like going to see a live volcano. Lou was always ready to blow his top. What a show he was; we could watch him for ages. Lou patting the pistol in his belt, shoved tightly among the folds of his tummy. Lou banging the chip basket on the lip of the fryer and reaching for the perforated jam tin that served as a salt cellar. Dumping the chips, glistening and steaming, on to a square bed of shiny white paper, which he had sliced with a huge carving knife. He made lovely parcels did Lou. One white sheet for the wrap, then a second slapped tight to seal. And the hot chips stung your fingertips right through the double wrap, and fumes of vinegar rose like a prayer. Sometimes he used his pistol as a paperweight, barrel pointing at the customer.

Lou with his two queues, one black one white. But only one cash register, as Koosie pointed out. Lou with his bellowing voice when some black guy stepped out of line:

'You fucking black bastards, you want fucking chips, do you? You want hot patats? Fucking hell, you bloody wait till I nod at you 'cos nodding at you means you may step forward, but only when I nod at you 'cos that means I finished serving the boss, and only after I've served the boss do you get served, you misbegotten fucking jungle bunnies, and if any of you so much as check me out the wrong way you'll get a slug in your thick fucking skull.'

And they laughed – the black queue laughed, a line of laughers – they were really and truly amused, tickled, because, well – that was Lou; because he always talked like that. He was a roadshow; he was a riot.

The white queue didn't laugh when Lou started shouting. The line of whites looked the other way. They felt it was tacky, dangerous even to talk the way Big Lou did. After all, blacks were people too; no one liked to be called names. If you wanted to say things like that, then have the decency to say them in private. Lou was a bully and a big mouth and the white queue really wished he'd shut up; the white queue wished that the black queue would stop wriggling around and grinning when

Big Lou insulted them. It wasn't right and, besides, it didn't fool anyone; no one liked to be called a troop of fucking jungle bunnies; no one liked to have guns pointed at them and told to 'wipe that fucking grin off your face, or I'll blast it off', so why were they laughing at his vile language when all it did was to make them seem pathetic and make everyone else embarrassed? But that was the thing with the black queue: it never did what it should, or what was expected. No wonder there was separation; no wonder you had to have different queues: how were you going to mix with people who didn't know better than to encourage rampant racists like Lou to insult them?

Koosie grinned across the yard of green lino that separated us. He was very easy about it all. Not me. Lou terrified me, and he diverted me, but he never amused me ... I wondered about Koosie: did he get a kick out of Lou; did he *really*? I knew what he'd say afterwards as we sat licking vinegar off our fingers: 'That's life. Lou's a gas, and the chips are good.'

When my mother landed on us, it was like a storm at sea, exciting and disturbing while it was going on, but we were always pretty relieved once it had blown over, and she'd flown out of our lives again, back to the Niger Delta, or Uganda or the Rift Valley, into the other world we called 'wherever'.

'Where's Ma?' he'd say.

'Gone to wherever,' I'd say.

Our world was the house, the garden and the easy, never-explained, never-questioned friendship between us. Behind the split-pole fence that screened the house from the cars in Jan Smuts Avenue, two teenagers, living together for seven or eight years – till Koosie went missing.

'What we eating today?'

'What we got?'

'Eggs.'

'Good, let's have scrambled eggs.'

We lived, then, two boys in a house watched over by the pictures of my mother and her friends. Here she was drinking tempo, a strong beer, with tribesmen somewhere in Kenya; there she was standing beside her plane after scouting elephant; here she smiled on the set of *Mogambo*, flanked by Clark Gable and Ava Gardner, and one or other had scrawled, in what looked like lipstick, across the pearly grey sky behind her tousled hair: 'Darling Kate – Love from Us!!'

Koosie stopped going to school, and went back to work at the airport, or he did some gardening for the neighbouring missuses. It helped with getting in more money. He could not work at the OK Bazaars; he could not work in the bottle store on Saturday mornings; he could not even get into the Rand Easter Show. None of that was allowed. I earned quite good money; he earned next to nothing.

This was all perfectly normal; it would have seemed bizarre to the two of us if things had been any other way. We were simply two guys together. But I was growing up to be a white man; he was growing up to be a garden boy. Koosie stopped being real, stopped being seen, he was my shadow; he dogged my heels. Only I was real.

Behind the split-pole fence we washed our clothes and fixed the garden. De Wet's Flying Dutchmen came once a week and cleaned the house.

Outside the fence it was different. We walked down to the Zoo Lake together though we did not sit on the same bench; we did not go to the bioscope together; we travelled on the same red and cream double-decker bus up Jan Smuts Avenue, but Koosie would take the last seat upstairs, reserved for non-whites. I went to school each day; he went now and then; I took the bus; he rode his bike close on ten miles to school in Alexandra Township.

I could not take Koosie to my school: I could not talk of him there, not even to Jake Schevitz, my best friend. It would have made no sense. Even though Schevitz came to my house, even though he saw Koosie there, even though he took a relaxed view of my mother and our habits – even then – there was no way he could have seen that Koosie was as close to being what I never had: a brother.

Schevitz was the only guy I knew who looked at Koosie and me and saw nothing too worrying. 'Odd but consistent' he called my home circumstances. He meant me, alone at home, when my mother was somewhere else. Alone that is but for Baldy, our grey parrot, and De Wet's Flying Dutchmen. And, some time later, me and Koosie, two boys, one white, one black, living in a suburban house in Johannesburg. To take such oddities calmly, quietly, sensibly was a very remarkable thing in white-demented South Africa, which at the time was not really a country, not a society, but more of an armed gang: prodigiously perverted, wildly cruel, quite horribly hilarious. A gang glued together by not just an intense admiration of, and a raging thirst for, stupidity; who took it as a divine right, as a central plank of the national consciousness, to be not just dumber than just about anyone else on the planet, but to be very, very proud of it.

Schevitz and I used to wonder aloud just who got us started on this path and we blamed it on a bloke called Jan van Riebeeck, who arrived in the Cape with the ur-gang of Dutch freebooters, in the middle of the seventeenth century. The

Dutch grew a hedge, built a fort, shot anything and everything that came their way: all the normal colonial things. In some ways they were like all invaders from Alexander the Great to Julius Caesar to the Vikings: they thought murdering the natives was pretty much in order; they laid about them with vigour.

Let's face it, there are no pretty conquerors, but give me conquistadors, or Puritans dreaming of a shining city on a hill. Give me Romans, Turks, Vikings: anyone but fucking book-keepers, ledger-clerks and smarmy parsons with guns.

Here was the trick: they were going to turn black man's sweat into white man's gold at the stroke of a whip. They set the tone. The founding fathers of white civilisation on the southern tip of Africa were going to strike it rich by doing nothing. And the Dutch did a lot of nothing: they built no roads or schools or bridges, they played no music, they composed no poems, they began no newspapers, they dreamt no dreams; instead, they sat around on their capacious rear ends and sent for slaves to do their living for them. They hadn't been in the Cape three minutes before there were more slaves than freemen. What was the Cape of Good Hope became the Cape of Slaves – you couldn't move for slaves – and that was OK because white men didn't move, that's what they had black men for. Move themselves, move the world.

Later, old van Riebeeck, a Dutch functionary hungry for gold, was canonised. He would not have known himself. He never wanted to be stuck in the Cape, at the toe of Africa, under a sawn-off mountain, surrounded by a lot of Hottentots. But they made him into this patriot. They gave him a noble brow, chestnut hair and sober mien, and put his face on the

money. There were statues. An ambitious upstart, who could-
n't wait to get the hell out to somewhere serious, stood on
prominent plinths all over the damn place.

What was the effect of this sort of monumental brazen
bloody nerve? It made you mad, yes, and sad, yes, perhaps precisely because it was sad it induced in Schevitz and me a kind
of raging hilarity. You laughed because you couldn't stand it,
really.

My mother wanted Koosie to love Africa in a way I guess
she felt I did not. That's to say: her way, her Africa. She lay
back in her chair and told us stories about how she'd been
attacked by elephants and leopards, but it was the hyena that
scared her to death. She once woke up with one in her tent,
staring down at her. She took us to shoot elephant in
Mozambique. She said she could see Koosie was a natural
hunter. She showed him how to use the big shotgun; they
tracked an old bull and had him side-on. She showed him how
to aim for a point about a third up from the belly and a little
behind the front legs. The aim being to send a bullet through
the heart and smash a leg at the same time; to kill as quickly as
possible.

He fired, he missed and the bull was gone.

'Never mind, there'll be lots of chances. Is there anything
you'd specially like to shoot, Koosie?'

He nodded.

'Lion, buffalo, eland?'

'People.' said Koosie. 'There are some people I'd like to
shoot.'

9

Just how differently Koosie and I saw things became apparent slowly. We had been on a trip with my mother to the Congo. We stayed with a small band of Efe in their village, which was called Baudouin, after the Belgian King. (This was when the Belgians ran the Congo and ordered European names for everything, before Mobutu took over and ordered African names for everything.) The Efe were very kind: they put us up in a hut in the middle of Baudouin, and all the kids came to stare at us. From the thatched roof of the hut dangled drying fish, and three thick white buffalo horns.

My mother was off all day hunting. Koosie and I saw a lot of the kids who took us into the forest and showed us how to play *mangola*, a kind of pygmy draughts, except you used dried seeds for counters, and made four rows in the red earth and moved the seeds along the little furrows. They showed us elephants' prints in the mud, and taught us to eat yellow mushrooms called *lobololo*. The Efe kids had French names – Mathieu and Lucien and Marta – which made them sound very foreign, and they sang a lot and warned us that certain orchids should never be touched or the rains would wash them away, and tree branches would tumble on their heads. They had a hundred taboos in the forest but we were safe, they said. Being *muzungu*, white men.

'I am not a bloody *muzungu*!' Koosie said. 'I am as black as you.'

But they didn't think so.

The kids sang almost all the time, and they smoked a lot of dagga; they got drunk on banana wine, they told long stories about witches. Koosie, I think, was at first bored, and then really rather cross. I didn't know why.

My mother said he was a city boy and country irritated him. I think now it was not just that they didn't see him as one of them, it was that Efe kids were incurably and utterly themselves and yet they were million miles from Koosie. That's when I felt the difference: it was seeing Africa as it looked to him and it had nothing to do with my mother or me. The pygmies failed him; they weren't the Africans he wanted them to be. They named their villages after their waterholes, when they didn't call them after Belgian kings; they ate fried manioc and chicken. The Efe had no real sense of money; their lives were one long exchange. Koosie gave up his penknife and got back smoked elephant meat and it made him throw up. He was impatient with the way the Efe leaned on the forest, like it was some sort of mixture of god and garden and guardian and lover. He was impatient with their self-defeating ways. When my mother told us that the BaBudu pygmies used nets, and nets were much more useful in hunting game, he wanted to know why the Efe stuck to their bows.

Koosie got impatient with the Efe the way the first Dutch settlers under van Riebeeck got impatient with the Hottentots for drifting here and there; and with the Bushmen for always stealing. He got impatient in the way the British got impatient with the Boers for being dogged, illiterate Calvinists. He got impatient in the way whites got impatient with blacks because they simply refused to be, well, more like us; and, when I look back now, I see he got impatient in the way that blacks were going to get impatient with us.

It was a sign but I could not read the signs.

Koosie read a lot of poetry; he read Tennyson and Charles Causley and Henty and Auden. He wanted to be a poet, but more than that: he wanted to write about flowers. Now, that was wild. Flowers? Us? He found a set of old botanical sketches amongst my mother's books.

'This is the Cape pansy, sometimes called "little bonnet", or "lion-mouth". Look, it has leaves like narrow teeth.'

He showed me his stuff; he read it to me and I can still remember lines of it:

'The white-eyed lobelia is watching me.'

It was the peacefulness and the unexpectedness of these interests I found so beguiling. In a violent land I'd never met anyone so easily taken with quiet and pretty things. I thought, imagine telling Big Lou about this. Flowers … He'd pick up his gun, he'd say, 'You're writing … what? Stay away from fucking flowers, you spastic jungle bunny, or I'll let so much daylight through you that daisies is what you'll be fucking well pushing up.'

> I look into the dark soft mouth of the petunia
> And something tells me it has only good thoughts;
> And will never betray me,
> Or dream of cutting its own throat.

That was the way it started for Koosie, with flowers and poems and amusement. That wasn't how it ended, but, then, it never is; in this country nothing ends easily. Maybe nothing ends.

Koosie was destined for resistance on a grand scale. I should have seen it when he grinned at me from the other queue in Big Lou's place. I should have seen it when he took me on those Sunday trips to the city.

The town centre at weekends was an empty tomb; the city that ran on high octane all week long dropped dead each Sunday. From Saturday lunchtime Jo'burg began to empty, and by five everyone had left. No one lived there; whites didn't want to and blacks weren't allowed to. The white guys went back to the deepest suburbs and prepared to do what they did on Sunday: nothing. They went into a coma, because that was the law; nothing moved on Sunday, and if anything did, the cops would want to know why. No trams ran, no shops opened, no one smiled if they could help it.

And the black shadows that served the white city also went home, to the dusty townships, somewhere out of sight; and the town, so wild and loud all week long, became some vast and vacant set for a movie that never got made. The streets ran like rivers of grey between the ghostly canyons. On Commissioner and Anderson, on Plein and Jeppe, what you heard wasn't just silence, it was the sigh of the dying, of life passing. Nothing moved outside the Library Gardens except a scrap of newspaper, or a single pigeon pecking at a cardboard ice-cream cup.

Sunday in Jo'burg: the day of the dead.

That's when Koosie showed me something rather special. We'd walk from our house: it took about an hour. We'd head down to somewhere central, like Commissioner Street, and then we'd wait. Not for long.

'Look,' said Koosie. 'It's a Ford Fairlane.'

The lead limo was the bridal car and it carried newly-weds from the forbidden townships. Following the Fairlane came a

Skyline in apple green with a retractable canvas roof, its white-walled tyres painted up so bright they glowed in the shadows of the skyscrapers. Studebaker Hawk, Hudson Hornet and Chev Corvette, in shades of caramel and plum, shining like heaven, filled to the brim with revellers, sitting on the bonnet and doorframes; men wearing fedoras and cuff-links, spats and buttonholes and women in tight skirts with sheeny nylon knees. Flash limos, zoot suits, spats, saucy little veils; wedding guests come to king and queen it for a few hours in the Sunday city. It was worth the walk and the wait, to sit on the pavement and watch the weddings go by, jazzing up the brain-dead city.

'You seen *Street with No Name*?' Koosie asked me.

'No.'

'Well, go.'

I did, alone of course. Koosie wasn't allowed in our cinemas. And saw Richard Widmark, alias 'Styles', in his belted overcoat, taking deep lingering sniffs from his benzedrine inhaler, and biting deep into his apple.

I reckoned they got it just about right, the showboys cruising down Harrison or Jorrissen or Jeppe in a Caddie red as cherries, red as blood, or Lincoln Continentals that looked like they were carved from whipped cream, with the hood back, ivory leather seats, silver trim. Koosie knew them all: the Russians, the Americans, the Gestapo, the Berliners; all the *tsotsi* hoods who dressed in belted macs, like Widmark, walked like Cagney, and talked like Humphrey Bogart. They were gangsters, real or aspirational, sure. But, then, who wasn't? What was crime to you was constitutional development to someone else. The guys in far-away Pretoria who ran our lives were just another gang pretending to be a government.

The township *tsotsis* floating by in their Chevys and Lincolns were in love with style and flair and angle and rhythm and irreverence; they knew – better than politicians, better than the truisms of all the parties in our lamentable land – that it was precisely *not* solidity but lightness, not uniformity but oddity and angle and colour that were the real true rebellion. The wild wedding parties jazzing up the death-grey streets were a slap in the face of the disapproving day.

I finished school; I got a job. Koosie never finished school because he never really began. He did a few things like caddying or gardening. He found it hard to get work but it didn't worry him because his work was already chosen. He was going to resist. Koosie was increasingly obsessed. And, in a strange way, increasingly dull. Koosie, the flower poet, had been so radical it took the breath away. The kid who showed me the wild carnival of limos sailing down the death-grey Sunday streets, or talked of the wise-eyed petunia – who showed in such things a bravery that stopped the heart – was subdued. The adrenalin rush of the struggle tamped down rebellion. Revolution watered no flowers. Delight gave way to seriousness, and seriousness led to obedience. Koosie did not just join the movement, he took holy orders in some sort of semi-divine congregation of heroes, a communion of latter-day saints and saviours.

I was also increasingly obsessed. I learnt that the Hungarian parliament had used ice taken from a lake as the way of cooling the building. I learnt that the Persians, as far back as 400 BC, built huge subterranean refrigerators with walls many metres thick, insulated from heat transfer with a mortar mixed from clay, goat hair and egg whites.

I can date the moment when I knew Koosie was off on some track that was not mine. He was just back from somewhere. He didn't say where, I didn't ask. We were sitting in the front parlour.

'Big Lou got drilled. Did you hear?' He laughed.

I didn't like the sound of his laugh.

'One night last week.' Koosie big eyes blinking, his voice rising. 'Lou was leaning on the counter – y'know how he leaned on one elbow – and in walked this little black guy, I mean tiny. Two bricks and a tickey high. Doesn't join a queue. Walks right up the counter. He's so short he can hardly get his nose over the counter but he's got this very big gat in his fist. He doesn't say anything. Lou says, "And what do you want, my old China?" He doesn't say anything. Lou says, "Well, if you can't find your tongue, fuck off outa here." Guy still doesn't say anything, just looks; eyes just above the counter, like croc's eyes just above the waterline; and then he drills Lou. Plumb centre. And Lou, he's heavy, so he sags to the right, so it looks like he's going for his own gun, but he's not, he's dropping under his own weight. But the little guy drills him again, this one in the chest … then he walks out. Lou was dead before he hit the floor.'

Listening to him, I heard amusement and shock, I heard anger, I heard admiration. Part of me understood the admiration – here was this little black guy who waltzes in and shoots the ogre of the Golden Gate.

Or, as Koosie put it: 'Not bad for a fucking jungle bunny.'

I was sorry, not for Lou – it was pretty amazing someone hadn't shot him years before – but because part of what we were had been blasted away. That, of course, was the whole point. After all, what had Pratt tried and failed to do when he pushed the pistol into Verwoerd's ear? Pratt fluffed it. But the magical black midget had turned in a virtuoso performance and Koosie felt good about it, and he was angry that I didn't. We no longer saw things the same way. How could we? The exigencies were so different, his anger was so great, and the times so violent.

We were hot, too hot by far.

I wanted to know why killing Lou was good but all he could tell me was that it was necessary. I thought that was old news. Koosie wanted me to stop thinking, stop remembering what we were, say nothing about the idiocy of blood certainties. His comrades were on the side 'of history'. I said history was an orgy of murder interpersed with moralising crap designed to make monsters look good.

'Your history, maybe,' said Koosie.

For me, the really interesting thing about the little guy was the novelty of his method. We did not know why he'd killed Lou. What set him apart, though, made him so different from the ham-handed guys we were, was his efficiency. He was economical, quick and deft; he preached no sermon, he started no political party, he did what he came to do and simply vanished. He was not a proto-revolutionary, not a freedom fighter; but he was perhaps an anarchist, an improviser, even an artist.

'Shooting him was the best.' Koosie came back to it often.

'For what?'

'For freedom.'

'Freedom's another fairy-tale we tell ourselves before going out and shooting someone.'

'You're soft, Alex.'

From there on out we split. It was painful, deep and permanent. Because we shared the same house it was impossible not to know what the other was doing. Koosie was deep into the revolution. I was building models of wind catchers. Wind catchers were like funnels, or V-shaped towers, mounted on the roof of a building. They might face in one direction, and drive air downward, or they might swing like a windmill. This downwash of cool air was a steady, clean form of air-conditioning. If I positioned the funnel over a basin of water, I found temperatures fell astonishingly. Koosie would stand in front of one of my beautiful creations and ask why I was wasting my time.

'Well, if you want cool clean air you can get a slave with a tree branch to wave it over your head, or you can open the back door of your cave, hut or hovel, or you can wash and dry the air we breathe.'

'Things are wild, mad, necessary … and you're blowing air …?'

So there it was. I thought history – the new one that Koosie was all for – looked dismayingly like it had last bloody time round.

The seventies saw the start of the killing years. The cops, the security agents, the spies, the strategists of the regime were very effective, and those who said or did the wrong thing got hit again and again.

It had to be said – though no one did – that Koosie's comrades were not very effective. In fact, for a liberation movement formed before the fucking Chinese Communist Party, they were amazingly duff. No one on Koosie's side ever took out a cop with the coolness of the midget killer who knocked off Big

Lou. Koosie's people, if they resembled anyone, looked alarmingly like that great double act I been lucky enough to witness at Milner Park: the Pratt and Oomie Show, who between them failed either to shoot or save Verwoerd.

That's where my ma came in. The security cops were deep inside every liberation movement: there were arrests, assassinations, betrayals, confessions, and fuck-ups, and that meant there was a queue of guys very keen to get the hell out to neighbouring havens in Lesotho or Botswana or Zambia.

Koosie made a pitch perfectly calculated to win her over. He offered her a chance to serve the cause, and his talk of it reminded me of someone who had found his family, who had signed on to salvation.

'What we need is a guy with a plane, a bloke without any tie to any political group. We need a man the cops would never dream was running people out of the country. Someone a bit odd, who is always going here or there in Africa.'

My mother didn't blink. 'Then I'm your man. I'll do it, but not for the cause, whatever that is. I'll do it for the fun.'

She would check into a posh hotel, like the Carlton, under a false name, and in the morning she would go down to the lobby, wearing a different coloured blouse, according to instructions. She would carry a copy of *Le Monde* or *La Stampa* each day for a week, and if no one showed up she would go home.

When the plan failed she'd be scathing about her handlers. 'Job's off. Waste of bloody time. This lot can't tell their arses from their elbows. I tell you the liberation movement is totally useless!'

But she kept on doing it.

When the job was on, someone, usually a woman, would walk into the lobby and sit down next to her and slip her a note with a phone number. My mother would walk to a phone booth and call the number and she'd be directed to another hotel. There she'd meet the person planning to skip the country. She would file flight plans for the Kruger Park if she was heading for Mozambique, or the Free State if it was Lesotho. Then she'd spend time in these diversionary base camps to make it look legal. On the day arranged, the customer would get to the agreed airfield and my old lady would be waiting. Once over the border, she usually put the plane down on a dirt road and ditched her passenger. She'd fly flew back to her camp in the Kruger and go game spotting for a few days. I guess she must have helped a dozen or more people to slip the net and make it to Maputo, Francistown, Addis Ababa or Lusaka.

She was pulled in twice by the cops for questioning; she was in solitary for fifty-six days, but they noted the size of her biceps, and they told themselves that anyone who went hunting in South West, made her own biltong and shook your hand so hard she crushed your fucking fingers – 'I kid you not, *ou maat*' – wasn't the type to help fucking black commie bastards jump the borders. She was a good bloke; she was the very essence of the rough, tough white pioneer.

Her cover was so good because in many ways it was so real.

They called her 'the aunty who flies'.

Koosie was the very last man my ma flew to safety. He'd been detained twice, spent 146 days in solitary confinement, and was under house arrest in Soweto when she sprang him. She flew him to Maputo.

That was the last I saw of him for a long time. I heard he went to Addis afterwards, then London. He was wedded, as they say, to 'the struggle'. As for me, well, I was wedded to wind catchers but it didn't stop me getting married twice, and divorced, in fairly quick succession.

10

It would not be true to say – well, not exactly true – that my mother sank my marriages; and yet to Benita Freeman, in the late seventies, and then to Maxine Vermeulen, in the eighties, she proved damned well fatal.

When I think back to her impact it was pretty amazing, considering that she was hardly ever there. But like the Gulf Stream, or the lunar tug, it was the effect she had. In the seventies she was flying political fugitives to Addis Ababa, or Maseru, or Francistown. In the eighties she was hunting in the Congo; but in one way or another she was always around: 'like something in the wind', as Benita once said.

Benita and her breasts go round in my head like an old song.

Benita had been a beauty queen. Miss Transvaal in 1971 and then Miss Orange Free State two years in a row, a record that has never been equalled and now never will be, names of places having changed. At twenty-seven she retired from beauty competitions, went into cosmetics as Benita Freeman Beauty and hit the jackpot. She patented a line of cosmetics called Juvenescence, and she had corporate headquarters off Oxford Road, a Bentley and a staff of thirty.

Her left breast was marginally larger than her right. Her pale, chalk-smooth complexion was enriched by a speckling of tiny auburn freckles that spread over the bridge of her nose like shapely sugar ants. I remember her use of the word 'paramour', especially the way her lip curled so prettily when she said it.

I was what I heard my mother once pretty fairly describe as a salesman of sorts. I couldn't have put it better myself. My job was desultory but my product was vital, exceptionally lightweight and widely available and, in its natural untreated state, entirely free. So a salesman of sorts summed me up pretty well.

Benita was good about my ethereal career. What she could not live with was my mother, or what my mother did. Was it my mother as hunter, pilot, explorer that she found so difficult? No, in fact, it was my old lady as bar-room brawler. Along with the broad shoulders, big muscles and huge hands that the security police had found so compelling, my ma also had – after a few drinks – the joshing manner you see when white guys get pissed in a Saturday night bar and pick fights over questions of rugby, or revolution, all of them vital male preoccupations in my home town. My mother drunk, or even slightly tipsy, had a mean streak in her.

Benita might have ignored this; our fault line was never really social, it was racial. It wasn't that she objected to Ma's views; it was my old lady's unabashed blindness that got to her. I don't think my mother distinguished between black and white. She was in no way liberal, she simply overlooked race, rather as a monarch ignored intrinsic differences of rank among her subjects. She was grandly blind.

I have to say I understood Benita's concern. If you did not know where you stood on race you did not know where you were. After all, white South Africans were trained from the womb, from the very first embryonic bundle of natal cells, to register in the minutest degree the difference that more, or less, melanin made to the complexion. So super-aware were we of racial rankings that, at every quiver on the skin-colour scale, our ultra-sensitive sensors rang out like fucking church bells.

Not so my ma. She carried on regardless, treating people as if they were like her, or would be if they were incredibly lucky. Or like everyone else, when, quite plainly, they were not. You could go to jail for thinking like that. Her blindness was not simply unusual, it was scary, it was illegal, it was offensive, it was provocative, and it was unwise.

It simply wasn't, in words Benita used a lot, 'very nice'.

Benita believed that if she tried very hard, it would be possible to live in a world that was 'quiet'. How much yearning she packed into that word. One where she could be like 'proper' people, who lived in places like Stockholm, and walked their dogs and drank their coffee in peace; instead of being trapped on a continent that bled all over the place, where at any moment some damned thing came flying in. That wasn't even a place, it was a problem that constantly challenged your right to exist, that mocked every attempt you made to impress yourself on an indifferent, endless land that by its sheer bloody otherness made you uncomfortable, continually reminding you that, actually, you had no standing, no worth, no place here! That the only way you could be seen was by standing on the shoulders of someone else. That you were even less real than some character in a novel; hell, you weren't worth the paper you were written on.

Then, too, the other difficulty was that my mother did not keep servants. It was not from her point of view a principled stand, it was plain good sense.

'I'm sorry, I've tried, but what for? What do they do? I just don't see their point.'

For Benita servants were not necessarily there to do anything in particular. They were there to stand between you and the raw life beyond; they were there so that, as a proper white person, you knew who you were: a Lord of the Universe. But the trick only worked if everyone played the game, and that meant you took up your lordly duties and they went off to clean the bath or cook dinner or mind the kids. We were superior only if they were servile. And vice versa. Anyone who didn't keep servants was letting the side down.

Benita and I led a normal life: we had a black manservant called Francis: and Benita dressed him in a white tunic and a red sash and she always rang a little brass bell to summon Francis from the kitchen where our cook, Emily, saw to things; just as, in our large green garden, two strong men, Nicodemus and Good Man, made things grow. I had never in my life used a pick, mowed a lawn, washed a dish or carried a parcel. This was all perfectly, effortlessly normal. Our lives were lived on one single premise: people like us didn't do anything; we were done unto. The only finger my wife ever lifted was to close the windows as we waited on Francis to serve the roast lamb because, as she liked to warn: 'This is Africa, and something might fly in.'

Well, my mother flew in, and kept on bloody well flying in. Wanting Benita to fly out with her, to the Congo, to Kenya; wanting to give her boxing lessons.

Then there were my uncles.

'Your mother takes lovers the way other people take hot showers,' said Benita. 'I mean, just who does she think she is?'

I hadn't the faintest idea who she was, and that was the trouble.

Benita talked casually of my ma's 'love affairs'. But I'd been exposed all my life to men who floated through our lives like motes of dust in a shaft of bright sunlight and love never seemed to be in it. Some few stayed with me – her liaisons with, say, Oomie, or Uncle Papadop – but the rest drifted away and I thought of them no more.

Benita would say: 'Surely you knew they were sleeping with her?'

And, yes, I suppose I realised in a vague way that they might have been sleeping with her; but not for the life of me could I imagine that, therefore, she was sleeping with *them*. That was to think of my mother as something other than a gale or a thunderstorm.

Benita persisted. 'If she didn't care for them, why did she do it?'

Again, I didn't know. Perhaps she did care, but not much, and not especially. At best, I think she cared for certain ways of being human – yes – but for the most part she seemed utterly careless about beings who happened to be human.

Benita was embarrassed; she said it wasn't 'nice' for someone of my mother's age to 'flaunt' strings of 'paramours'.

The reason for this delicacy wasn't natural fastidiousness, but the usual problem: race. The old and firm belief widespread in our country amongst the whites that to reveal your desires, to brandish your sexuality, to own up to your passions was, somehow, to lower yourself 'to the level of the Bantu'.

Benita never used the words 'black' or 'African', words not just politically subversive, but crass. They stirred up trouble and so sensible people preferred 'Bantu' because it gave them a way of not talking about things they knew they had to talk about but which always ended in fights and tears, thus preventing people from getting on, in life or business, as ordinary, sensible, reasonable – above all – normal, for Christ's sake, people wanted to do.

I said to her once, 'Hang on a mo', have you listened to yourself? Just listened to the bloody sound it makes? It's not just meaningless, it's silly. One Bantu, two Bantu … I'd rather be called a kaffir.'

'I have never, ever, ever …' She couldn't complete her sentence.

'Never? I've been called a white kaffir so often it doesn't touch sides.'

'When?'

'When? You mean, when not? It's the sort of thing guys say when they don't like your driving or your face or your manner, like, "Hey, what's with you? You fucking white kaffir!"'

'I have never, and I will never, use that horrible word.'

So there it was. The word was all around us, you could not escape it but you could prefer not to hear it. As South Africans we were separated not by class but by degrees of auditory embarrassment brought on by certain sounds. Sonic triggers. The long owl shriek 'oooooo' in Bantu did for me; I wanted to hide under the bloody table, I wanted to run screaming from the room. And it was the whirring, lip-shivering curl of the final 'firrrrrrr' in 'kaffir' that did it for Benita.

One day, Benita ran off with a small ginger-haired country and western singer called Frikkie La Page, the 'Boer Caruso' …

She wrote in her parting note:

'Your mother has gone native and I just don't want to be near her any more. I am very sorry, but it's her or me ...'

I tore up her note, I made myself a cup of rooibos tea, I took a hot bath, I listened to the radio, I lay in the warm water and remembered vaguely that a bath is good place to die – if you slit your wrists, death comes in a drowsy darkening of the warm water. They played an ad for chocolate milk-flavouring powder, spoken by a man with a phoney Dutch accent: he urged us to try 'Bensdorp's Chocolate Shprinkle-Shpread ...' and it seemed sad and soothing all at once.

I had some sympathy for Benita's dilemma – my mother was impossible, yes – but Benita had been wrong about the native bit. My mother did not 'go native' – that suggests a distance travelled – my mother was native from the word go. Benita wanted a kind of niceness founded upon a version of gentility, a world where native meant *Bantooo* and everything was normal. Instead, we all lived in a place, and in a way, where no one had a clue what normal was; and nothing was ever nice.

When she heard about our break my mother offered to track down Frikkie, and wallop him, and I had a lot of trouble talking her out of it. It was not something I wanted: my wife leaves me for another man and my mother beats him up!

I said: 'Thanks ma, but no.'

'Hell, I only offered because I love you.'

If Benita was 'nice', then I guess I married Maxine some years later because she wasn't. Tall, with very blue eyes. A rather wonderful forehead, broad and calm. Tiny, pink, pursed lips. Maxine taught speech and drama at the University and you might have taken her for some artsy-craftsy, airy-fairy type but you'd have been wrong: she was very tough, as I was to find out, and the finding out of it changed my life for ever.

Maxine was so far ahead of the radical academic crowd – mostly Marxists, Trots or Stalinists – that she was almost out of sight. Generally, our intellectuals lived by proxy; they were like long-range radio receivers; their inspiration, their books, their films and their language, their Marx and Fanon and Gramsci, their *New Statesman* and their *African Communist*, their pamphlets, posters, slogans and songs came from far away, picked up as faint signals mixed in with lots of static, from that great store of all that was vibrant, admirable, exciting, persuasive, the place we called 'overseas', or more often 'the outside world'. If ideas didn't come from there they were not worth knowing, and if you didn't know that then neither were you.

Maxine had a cousin who worked with a group of animal rights activists in England. They were written up in *Country Life* because they broke into mink farms, cut the fences and set the animals free. They were so radical they didn't have posters or pamphlets or books; they communicated by code. Maxine had a thing, not so much about mink but about what they stood for. She formed with some friends a radical group called Animals Against Apartheid.

When I look back now I see that Benita and Maxine, in every way different people, had this in common: both wanted the place where they were to be more like the places they dreamt about. For Benita it was somewhere careful and clean and white and quiet – like Sweden. For Maxine it was the Essex marshes, and guys in duffel-coats running about misty fields, liberating mink.

Maxine didn't keep servants, and she didn't give a damn what my mother did with other people; that was good.

It was animals that came between them.

My mother called Maxine a 'fauna freak' because Animals Against Apartheid – AAP – picketed zoos and abattoirs on the basis that animals were segregated behind wire, imprisoned and killed, much as blacks were corralled behind the wire of townships and homelands.

Maxine called my mother a murderer.

It was the trips to the Congo that got to my wife and, in particular, a group of friends among the Wambuti pygmies whom my mother visited up that way. The Wambuti and, in particular, the Efe, a people who hunt with bow and arrow, had been in the family almost as long as the bloody Boers. We'd known the Congo pygmies ever since my grandfather befriended Sir Harry Johnston, the hunter who spend a lot of time in the old Belgian Congo chasing giant gorillas and butterflies and pygmies; he believed that somewhere on the flanks of Ruwenzori, high in the Mountains of the Moon, or deep in the jungles of the Semlik valley, he would discover some extant dinosaur or specimen of early man.

Instead, what he had found was the okapi, a preposterous creature somewhere between a horse, a zebra and a buck, known to the Wambuti – though no one paid any attention – as *ndumba*, but renamed in honour of its gun-toting pursuer Sir Harry Johnston (*Ocapia Johnstonia*).

Pictures of the pygmies first came my way in a series of films given to my grandfather by T. Alexander Barnes who had filmed them on what he always called his 'kine'. His jerky grey films showed the Wambuti in the Ituri forests, wearing loin-cloths of woven leaves, smiling at the camera and tucking into their salt, which they adored. Mr Barnes referred to them as 'forest dwarfs', and he knew for a fact that the Wambuti were the missing link: 'the ape was all there, up to the hair, which was discernible in some cases over the entire body of the dwarfs ...'

My ma had been hunting okapi in the forests for years, and since no one knew the okapi better than the Wambuti, they were her guides. Her mates were a married couple from the Efe tribe, called Bara and Buti. These were their new names, taken after President Mobutu decreed in 1972 that all the old Christian and European names of the country, its towns and cities and its people, should be dropped and proper African names substituted. So the President, Joe Desiré Mobutu, became 'Mobuto Sese Seko Kuku NgBendu wa ZaBanga', which roughly translates into 'the all-powerful warrior who, because of his inflexible will to win, will go from conquest to conquest leaving fire in his wake'. A finer description, word for word, of just about every oppressive measure taken against Africans by their blasted rulers it would be difficult to invent.

And Alphonse and Desirée became Bara and Buti.

'Really good little guys,' said my mother.

Quite why it was the Congo trips that so appalled Maxine, when my mother at the time was constantly visiting Lebanese diamond merchants, Rhodesian farmers, German visionaries, white hunters in Kenya and black leopard men in Gabon, I can't say, and considering the nature of those times, you might have thought that anyone actually living among people in the Congo would have impressed the political activists as pretty bloody progressive. But, then, our radical spirits were never interested in Africa's other places; they were interested, as Maxine was, in principles. Maxine had never been anywhere in Africa but she had views.

I watched Maxine and my mother with despair. I loved my wife, and I loved my mother, but in the way you love the sea. Something you want to sit beside but prefer not to be cast adrift upon. I loved Maxine for her soft flesh and the way she cried in her sleep and the outpouring of her vulva when we made love, an almost embarrassing wetness. To be honest, I loved Maxine for her pussy; the trouble was Maxine had principles and principles won over pussy any day.

My mother had been everywhere, and she did not have views. The pygmies of the Ituri were simply friends, family, and trackers. She took strangers and rendered them into blood relatives … as if it had been meant this way, as if everyone did it.

Maxine said: 'The Congo? Sounds like a cop-out to me.'

My mother said: 'Animals Against Apartheid? More like Arseholes Against Apartheid, if you ask me.'

Maxine said sweetly: 'Tell me how it feels to be a professional killer.'

My mother raised her steely brows. 'Pretty good. I'm off tomorrow.'

It was Maxine's turn to be scornful. 'Why the Congo? What's there? The struggle's here.'

'You struggle,' said my ma. 'I'm going after okapi with the Wambuti. I may bring a few home with me.'

'Okapi?'

'Pygmies.'

'You mean you'd bring pygmies home?'

'Why not? For a bit of R&R.'

'Kathleen, that just perpetuates the pattern.'

'Pattern, what are you talking about? What pattern?'

'Hunting animals, hunting people. It exploits living beings for profit or pleasure.'

'I don't perpetuate the pattern: I'd say it perpetuates me. I've hunted with everyone from Karen Blixen to Gregory Peck and I'm proud of it. What does hunting have to do with racialism?'

'They're much the same, Kathleen. We keep our blacks the way some people keep mink.'

'I don't keep blacks. I don't keep mink either. I've never seen a mink.'

'Not you personally, and not mink *per se*. But there are people who breed mink in captivity, and kill them to make furs for stupid rich women.'

My mother was amazed. 'Where do they do this?'

'In Essex.'

'In Essex!'

Oh, the loathing, the stupefaction she put into the word.

A week later my mother called. 'Come and meet my friends.'

Maxine said: 'I'm not going. If she's got pygmies with her I'll freak. She just scoops them up and carries them off like ... groceries ...'

'Don't come, then, if it upsets you. There is always an element of provocation when she does these things.'

'Provocation! Listen, this is not provocation, this is open warfare. Of course I'm coming. I can fight, too.'

My mother was on the stoop, in a cane chair; puffing at her pipe and sitting at her feet were two small people. She reached over and tapped each in turn with her pipe stem. Her friends were tiny, around four feet tall. Above the garden walls there stretched five feet of fine wire.

'Meet Buti and Bara. They have the run of the garden.'

Buti and Bara were wearing only a few leaves around their middles, and smoking pipes stuffed with what I knew to be marijuana. Their pot bellies hung over the edges of their loin-cloths and they followed my mother everywhere, like cats. She spoke Kwa-Swahili to them and they laughed a lot, but they were very, very thin. I loved their trumpets, which they carved from ivory and wore slung over their shoulders.

Maxine had no time for trumpets.

'First you shoot what they eat, and then you collect them like dolls!'

My mother was unmoved. 'These aren't dolls, they're complete killers, these guys. Good for them, too. Killing is the thing never to be lost sight of. There is a lot of it about. The slavers did it to the tribes, the tribes did it to each other, the white settlers did it to their black servants, and their black peons did it right back to their colonial bosses, the Belgians, when they took over the Congo and chased them to hell and gone. And absolutely everyone did it to the animals, and in the forests the Wambuti get the sharp end of the stick from just about every tribe around … I'm doing them a favour. I bring them here for a bit of peace. I give them the freedom of my garden. Free chicken and all the salt they can eat. They adore salt.'

Maxine was out of her league. You don't fight whirlwinds, earthquakes, tidal waves. If you're wise you take to your heels. I was used to my mother's friends, and her finds, her prey, her passions, her memories: they were part of the way it was with us, something no one else could understand.

Maxine said: 'What is the chicken mesh for?'

'To make sure they stay in the damn garden.'

Maxine was appalled.

'It's like a chicken coop.'

'Better a coop than a bird that's flown. Without the chicken mesh these two would be over that wall in a trice and into the traffic, and they wouldn't last three minutes in the traffic.'

Maxine appealed to me. 'You've got to make her understand, Alexander. She cannot keep people locked in her garden, like ornamental peacocks.'

'These little buggers will eat anything,' said my mother, beaming at Buti and Bara. 'I have to keep a sharp eye on them. Given half a chance they might *slag* a bloody cat, or something. Think what Madams Terre'Blanche, Garfinkel, Smuts and Mason will say to that! One butchered pet on the fire.'

Instead of cats, she gave them chicken to roast over open fires and salt from a large blue can of Cerebos, which she replaced every few days. They called her 'Bibi', which amused me because it means 'the wife' or 'the married woman'; and they seemed happy to stay in the garden, eating chicken drumsticks and smoking their long pipes.

'I gave them some dagga. They can't do without it,' said my mother.

It was absolutely fine until the night someone broke into the garden and cut a great hole in the chicken wire and the Wambuti were 'liberated', according to Maxine, or 'fled for their bloody lives', if you listened to my mother.

'And,' she added grimly, 'that's what they do to mink, I believe, in Essex! Set the little bastards free to screw up the countryside.'

Bara and Buti didn't flee very far. They headed straight into the nearby and much larger gardens of Madams Terre'Blanche, Garfinkel, Mason and Smuts, and went to ground. The pygmies of the Ituri forest spend their lives in hiding; they are complete experts in vanishing. They climb, they burrow, they creep into the tiniest hiding places, and five acres of Johannesburg gardens made vanishing easy among blue gums and loquat trees and mulberries.

But if Bara and Buti stayed next to invisible, you could hear them: they hunted with music and it was the music that woke the neighbours. When they hunt at night the pygmies of the Ituri call to each other like birds, and they use their ivory trumpets to produce a sound not unlike pan pipes. It is very sweet and utterly unforgettable, a low fluting, soft and lovely in the night, and far, most beautifully far, from the usual Jo'burg symphony of dogs, screams, gunshots and sirens …

The first casualty was our old parrot, Baldy but as my ma said, you could not blame them: the Wambuti had a passion for the grey African parrot. We suspected they had slipped into the house and taken him away. We never found so much as a feather. After that, being adaptable, they made do with doves, mossies, wagtails and took their chickens live.

My mother said: 'Well, as long as it's only our stuff they poach, fine. But I have my doubts about that. If things get sticky I may have to call you.'

It didn't take long. One morning, Mrs Garfinkel was confronted by the pelt of her pet Alsatian, Domitian, swinging, salted and dry, from the branch of a mulberry tree. Luckily, she told everyone what everyone usually told everyone under these circumstances, namely that some bloody natives must have killed poor Domitian. One kept large dogs in order to savage natives, and it was inevitable that natives sometimes savaged dogs. It was in the nature of things.

My mother phoned me. 'I need you to sling some weight.'

We parked the Land Rover outside the garden gate. Then we climbed into the Garfinkels' big garden. She carried a small blowgun with a tiny flashlight strapped to the underside of the smooth bamboo barrel: an old hunting trick she used when she went after leopard at night.

She sprinkled a trail of salt from the rose bushes to the mulberry tree where she planted a fat bag of Cerebos. When Bara and Buti smelt the bait and crept towards it, she picked them off, one by one, with a brace of beautifully judged darts loaded with tranquilliser. The .04 calibre blowgun was a fine and silent weapon: the darts moved at anything up to 300 feet per second. They ran, of course, which made the drug all the more effective. We found them sleeping like babies.

'Little buggers!' said my ma, as we carried Bara and Buti to the Land Rover. 'They won't bloody stir till they're home again.'

At the airfield she sighed as we strapped them into the passenger seats.

'I do wish you'd have a word with that wife of yours, Alexander. This could have turned out very hairy.'

She taxied out and took off into the vast night sky. I watched until her lights vanished. The Voyager hit speeds of around 115 mph. She would be in Kenya by dawn, then into Stanleyville the next day. No problems.

That was the last I saw of her for a while. She stayed for several weeks in the Congo, hunting bongo.

I didn't have a word with my wife. I left people to think what they thought. Maxine believed she had freed the Wambuti from colonial oppression. Mrs Garfinkel grieved for Domitian, done to death by wandering natives. 'They probably make hats from the poor boy's fur,' she said with a shiver...

And so it was that I went away. It was a race for life. Maxine thought I had run off with someone. She was right: I went off with myself. No more mink, no mother, no more militants of any stripe. Both of them thought I was mad. Why abroad, when there was all of Africa still to see?

From then on out, I kept moving, and from then on out, my mother tracked me. It was a game, it was a hunting safari, it was a lifetime's career, seeing how far I could get before she found a way of pulling me back, trapping me, turning me round for home.

11 The Cuban Crisis

'Strange he is, my son, whom I have awaited like a lover.
Strange to me like a captive in a foreign country...'
'Monologue of a Mother', *D. H. Lawrence*

II

I had been upriver for several days on the *Mistress of Mandalay*, an old paddleboat turned steamer that plied the Irawaddy between Rangoon and Mandalay. Her owners were replacing the air-con system in her six cabins. We were heading for Bagan, once called Pagan.

Burma was special. Here was a land suspended between names: Burma/Myanmar; suspended between Buddhism and brutalism. A most unmilitary land, misruled by generals, where omnipotence resided in a bloke known as 'Secretary One', and his picture was everywhere.

In Burma you learnt to breathe the right way. In Burma you got arrested for talking, or for joking, or for no reason at all. And why not? When your existence depended entirely on the say-so, or otherwise, of the earnest bespectacled godlings whose mug-shots appeared, like men in wanted posters, on the front page of the *The New Light of Myanmar* (known to its readers as *The Nightmare of Myanmar*). The generals were shown 'vigorously' inspecting pig-slurry facilities and saluting each other frequently. Cruel, dull and preposterous; perfect specimens of the gargoyle effect of huge power upon pompous pricks.

The idea that language should be reasonable or clear or fair or gentle is a sustainable delusion only in places where the cops won't shoot you, or lock you up, for using certain words. There are signs of power madness only the victims know. Places where all words are forms of force, a means of getting your way. Where the right to talk is actually a kind of tyranny. The tongue in jackboots. Places where the boss owns the words, and you don't, and won't be getting permission to use them any time soon; and as a result people use fewer words and more signs: a sigh, a shrug, a twitch to an eyebrow has everyone telling you to keep your damn voice down. Free speech is as much a government decision as, say, free health care. In fact, in some places, and Burma was amongst the most interesting examples, keeping your voice down *was* about the only medical help on offer. Speaking out could seriously damage your health. And learning to breathe correctly – internal air-con – was the right breathing in sticky circumstances.

I loved Myanmar/Burma so much I'd almost forgotten where I came from – certainly I'd forgotten *whom* I came from. I didn't have to think about home, or her, or bloody South Africa with its poisonous insanities – I could look instead at an Asian madhouse, gentled by a Buddhist temperament, as sweet and slow-flowing as the lovely Irawaddy, with its clouds of white moths floating beside the boat, like prayers in the moonlight.

In Bagan we tied up against a muddy bank and I clambered up the steep stone steps and walked through old town, where medieval Buddhist stupas litter the baking plain like mushrooms after the monsoon. The painted figures of the guardian spirits of the town stood on either side of the ancient city gate; they were endearingly named Mrs Golden Fish and Mr Handsome. Besides the Buddha, who was supreme, and as a way complementing his perfection, imperturbable and subliminal, the Nats, more human and wilder guardians spirits of hearth and home, were also revered.

Once upon a time, in my country, people also worshipped beings called Nats, but our godlings were white, puritanical, sex-fearing bores who brought nothing to us but tears and bloodshed. This did not in any way dilute the worship of their followers who were once as numerous as the stupas upon the baking plain of Pagan, but recently they had all melted away as if they never were. A miracle!

I prayed to the Nats of Bagan: 'Mrs Golden Fish and Mr Handsome: keep me from drear dread spirits whose self-importance weighs on us all like lead. Torment the rulers of this land and infest their dreams with demons…'

In New Bagan town I tagged along behind a long caravan of well-wishers, celebrating the approaching novitiate of two small boys, about to be enrolled as monks. The rich parents led a procession of dancers, archers, handmaidens, cannons, musicians and a pantomime elephant made of black velvet with very white tusks, and bringing up the rear, someone carrying a sign: 'Video now available! Manchester United v. Arsenal.'

At the Bagan Hotel, I was handed a fax. It had been following me for almost ten days, having gone first to my suppliers in New York, from where it had been sent on to Bagan and waited for me while I was on the Irawaddy. I sat outside my room, a cold Myanmar draught beer in hand. The fax was from Jake Schevitz and, brief though it was, it crackled with his sharp dry bark.

Alexsy boy, I had your old lady round here and she has in tow this little dark bloke – with a Latin look. She must have at least half a bloody century on Don Juan. She tells

me they want to get married. Alex lad, I'm worried. You're
going to have to do something…

Yours in the bowels of Christ,
Jake S.

I liked the 'bowels of Christ' bit.

Jacob 'Jake' Schevitz always was a mordant bugger. As a Jew
at a Catholic school he learned to drive, he liked to say, on both
sides of the road. He knew all our prayers by heart; he was – his
word again – 'ambidextrous'. That had always been his edge.
He took what was known and settled and assumed and threw
it right back in your face.

Schevitz at about fourteen: ears sticking out of a sharp, foxy
face, a mind like a flick-knife. Schevitz at thirty: one of the
finest attack lawyers ever bred. Defended just about everyone
who came up against the ranters running the country. A man
with a cause. He'd reckoned the old regime to be about as close
to Nazis as we were ever going to get, and he'd fought them
tooth and nail. If you got banged up by the security cops, you
turned to Schevitz; if your kid fell out of a ten-storey window
while in police custody, you turned to Schevitz; if your friend
died in the back of cop van and they said he hit his head while
attacking an officer, and the tame police doctor confirmed it,
you turned to Schevitz. Relentlessly affable, but utterly merciless in court, he ripped police evidence to shreds and reduced
state witnesses to tears.

That was Schevitz in his glory, saving the weak from state
hooligans. Schevitz, who raised cash for black lawyers, who got
aid for detainees in solitary; who began the Legal Outreach
Bureau, who himself spent a week in solitary for refusing to

testify at Koosie's trial on explosives charges. Schevitz, whom the pundits and the prophets agreed was sure to be appointed, in some better fairer, never-again-to-care-about-skin-colour administration of a wholly new South Africa, a Supreme Court Judge or even – why not? – Minister of Justice ...

Ah, but that was then ...

There hung over Schevitz now a whiff of chagrin. More than a whiff: unhappiness seeped from him like damp. Schevitz had changed – 'evolved' was his word – from lead attack-dog in the days of the old regime to crusty critic of the new guys who governed our rainbow nation; and at the end of said many-hued illusion you were likely to find, Schevitz would growl, not a pot of gold but 'a bloody can of worms'.

Things weren't what they used to be, but Schevitz was, and it hurt. He simply couldn't come to terms with what had happened. And he wasn't alone. There were lots like him. Dismissed, disdained. And it knocked them sideways, though somewhere deep inside they all knew they shouldn't have felt quite so groggy because it wasn't the first damn time they'd been floored. They had been here before, flat on their backs, out for the count.

The fate of people like Schevitz, people like us, had been to live through two revolutions. The first happened back in 1948.

Schevitz once said to me: 'When the race-crazies won back in 1948, people, decent people – dare I say it, democrats – wrung their hands and said to them, "Gosh, chaps, this is a political reversal, isn't it?" And the new bosses said, "Fuck you, buddy. We don't do reversals; this is revolution." And we said, "For the moment. You're the government and we're the opposition ... that's democratic, isn't it? But it could change, next time round." And they said, "It's democratic, all right, that's why it won't change. There is no next time; we're here to stay. You guys think we're low-life Neanderthals who live in caves. Well, welcome to the new world. Caveman is king-pin, and you guys are seriously fucked."

'Having been seriously fucked once before,' said Schevitz, 'we should have seen it coming. But we never did. We sleep-walked into the punches, our eyes shut, our chins out. Last time round, it was race-crazies obsessed with the colour of your skin. Calvinists with chips on both shoulders; tribalists who said we were the luckiest little country on God's earth and they'd fuck up anyone who had the nerve to disagree for being left-leaning, whining, pinko-Yiddish, Commie defeatists.'

Quite so. The white regime that took over in mid-century had loathed Schevitz. Oh, what a ding-dong battle it had been! What terrific fun war can be when the bad are so proud to be so, and the angels are on your team.

Now we had new rulers, end-of-the-century revolutionaries. And they were truly good; they were so holy it ached; they weren't a political party, they were saints come down to earth to save the country. They were nationalists, true, but they were nice, caring, fair-minded, nationalists.

And yet – here was the rub – they also hated Schevitz, and for much the same reasons as the old lot. Worse, they despised him – what did he offer that they couldn't do without? A clapped-out, wishy-washy liberalism from another time and another culture. But they didn't fight him; they didn't see the point of fighting him; in fact, they didn't see the point of *him* – period.

So Schevitz was put out to grass. Retired. Kicked into touch. And everything he stood for, everything he did and loved and believed in, was suddenly old hat. He went overnight, poor

Schevvy, from radical firebrand, and hero of the struggle, to yesterday's leftovers: pale, male and past it. Worse still, in a country now more than ever obsessed with the colour of your fucking skin, he was white. Those thus colour-coded were no longer seen as living entities, but as walking footnotes or crumbling ruins. So: no more fights, no more glory; just sobriety, respect, oblivion. These were Schevitz's pickings after the years of fire.

And maybe this was what it had to get down to. Maybe Schevitz stood for those of us who, however much we may have amounted to in the past, were fatally maimed because whatever we appeared to be never really constituted our essence. Whatever camouflage we wore – and it was true some of us gave astonishingly realistic impressions of being accountants or doctors or lawyers – something was amiss.

It is true to say that we white guys are not simply proud of our ignorance, we're fiercely protective of it. Secondly, because we have been forced for so long to live at several removes from reality, encouraged at every turn to believe in our superior status, we have learnt to act out several lives at the same time, parallel lives. We have a genius, almost, for swapping individual existences for others, and taking them on more or less simultaneously, and with relief. Because it is precisely by entering into other roles, which serve as a mask for our own, that we can tell ourselves that we are not alone. Loneliness is the real horror of the people from which I come. And being other people, simultaneously, almost makes up for have no true life of our own.

What a crew: no Fausts us! We sold our souls for no great stakes. Fakes. We didn't even rise to the rank of real bastards. We just pretended to be real. Sometimes we got within millimetres of being what we said we were – bank managers, or soap salesmen or mining magnates – but we never really pulled it off. For a profoundly important reason: because the sole role assigned to white South Africans was to go around being white. Nothing else counted. Though we would have denied it angrily, we would have threatened violence had anyone persisted in saying so, yet we knew it was true: we knew it because we carried off being anything else so awkwardly. White, then, wasn't a colour, it was a destiny. A full-time occupation. It gave us status, wealth, power; it gave us cooks, gardeners, nannies … helots.

And you took it very, very seriously. That's what added *gravitas* to your dealings with the man who made your garden or the woman who cooked your food.

Yet you needed to differentiate yourself; to show you were not like the other lot – your Afrikaans compatriots who kicked people around and decided everything, from whom you might not marry, to what you could not read, to when you might hold a raffle or a jumble sale. You, *per contra*, were decent, tolerant, fair.

And indeed there was a difference but it wasn't one of morality, it was one of power. They had it; you did not. You were helplessly weak, no one cared what you said and no one asked your opinion. And so you dived ever deeper into disguise. It was necessary to keep up appearances, not only as a teacher, a doctor, a plumber; it was even more necessary to kid yourself that a niche of your own could be found, a saner world where people went to church on Sunday and called the minister Vicar, where the rule of law was taken for granted and judges handed down valid verdicts.

But we never really pulled it off; we inherited too much inhibition from our English forebears to act with the conviction that so distinguished those red-hot nationalists who ran our world. And who ran right over us.

Schevitz had been flattened, handed his redundancy papers, and he now wanted to hit back. And he reacted to his decline with a show of force – he was, after all, South African. Ask him if he got depressed at what was happening all around him in 'the new-sarth-effrica', and he would round on you, fighting mad.

'What sort of question's that, hey? You fucking crazy? Listen, I am happy, I am *very* happy. I think this is the best bloody country in the world, all right? Show me the country that doesn't have problems. Sheez, man, just because a guy points to certain problems doesn't mean he's unhappy. It just means he's got questions. What's wrong with that? Hey, hey, hey?'

And on he would go, spitting fury. 'Fucking hell! I mean, what are you saying, hey? Of course I'm bloody happy!'

So happy he wanted to hit someone in the face.

I tore up the fax. I ordered another beer. I knew my mother had done a number on Schevitz: her plan was to reach out through him to me.

I could hear his question as he looked over her latest lover. 'Does Alex know about this?'

And I heard her immediate reply.

'Certainly not, and I'll rely on you not to breathe a word.'

I remembered how, in the seventies, we used to go and see George Adamson, in the Kora National Park in Northern Kenya. He had a fine campfire trick, did George. We'd be in the middle of nowhere and he'd pull a piece of venison off the flames, douse the lights and toss the meat into the bush, then he'd turn on a torch and there were seven pairs of eyes shining back at us.

'It's a race,' said George. 'It's us they want but the meat will do.'

My mother had stared into the dark, wondered where I was, and thrown a bit of Schevitz my way.

'You're going to have to do something …' he had written.

But there was nothing to do. She was as impervious as a veld fire, as a column of army ants. This was not about sorting her out; it was about sorting me out. She was after me: the calls had been multiplying, she planned to round me up and bring me home. But she was too good a hunter to underrate her quarry. She had often talked of how her old friend, Eddie Blaine, paid for forgetting that. They were hunting up in the Masai Mara. Eddie hit a buffalo with three good shots and was sure he'd done enough damage; so when the buff turned and vanished into the bush, Eddie went in after it. When he didn't come back, my ma went looking for him and found Eddie, a mass of fraying flesh and torn clothes, with the furious buff stamping and pawing the body. She killed the buff with a shot through the brain. Then she took a good look and found that Eddie's first bullet had gone in at the shoulder but ever so slightly high, and he'd followed it with a second, marginally low. Good shooting but not near good enough. His third was a beauty: the heavy round from Eddie's .470 had gone into the head, kept moving and exited at the end of the ribcage.

'That buffalo', she said, 'was dead – but he didn't know it, and there is nothing more dangerous …'

Always in her telling of the tale there was mourning and pain for poor Eddie. I always felt for the buff. But I couldn't to say that to her. She would have taken it as a blow against her own person, against her role as a mother, a role at which she was magnificently, unforgettably bad.

I had been abroad for over twenty years, with infrequent visits home, and on my travels I had grown used to my mother's cry that echoed down the phone line across vast stretches of the globe that, I was pleased to know, safely separated us.

'You're selling air – where?'

That is what I did: I sold air. I sold the compressors, the pipes, the coolants, the fans, the pumps and the systems for putting it where you wanted it, when you wanted it, at the temperature you wanted it. I could blow hot, and I could blow cool; myself, I preferred cool. Coming from where I do, it was second nature, selling air. I did not really see it as a job. It came easily to someone who grew up where I had, where more air was routinely spent on bluster, bluff, and bombast than any place I knew. All I did was to parlay a past into a future.

Ever since I'd left Africa in the eighties, after what I think of as the 'Maxine and the pygmies' episode, I'd kept moving. I think I was in search of home, of a sort. Anyway, I'd found places where the smell of hypocrisy was so strong, the absurdity of power so wonderfully brazen, that I knew immediately where I was. Across South East Asia; in Vietnam and Laos and Cambodia, I had encountered all the old fragrances, all the things I had detested when I lived with them in my own place, and newly found, how they filled me with fierce, cold delight.

It seemed to me that the world was, roughly, divided in two. There were the settled and colder northern regions, vast oceans of air, pretty much inert air; and there were islands of turbulence where the passage of air took precedence over everything, moving through the diaphragm, over the vocal chords, out into the open in the form of shouts, screams, orders, cheers, sighs, edicts, trumpetings. Places where there were a few favoured very big, very bad wolves who got to huff and puff and blow everyone down – and there were lots of little pigs whose job it was to get eaten.

Hate, as it were, always exhaled. It was the compressed air that drove the tribe. And it was a fact everywhere to be noted that people who behaved nobly under tyranny, once free of it, often behaved as badly as their old oppressors. Indeed, it might be said that in a tyranny the victims must concentrate everything on the struggle to stay alive, and so they neglect their desires to harm those weaker or stranger than themselves; and it is only when the tyrant is removed that their natural feelings bubble to the surface and one-time victims turn out to be as cruel and stupid as the oafs who once kicked them about.

In Burma I had reached that point of stasis that good travel induces: I had nearly forgotten where I came from, and I didn't care where I was heading. The great easy swell of the Irawaddy under the boat soothed and quietened one's heart. I was no one, travelling through nowhere. I sold air, yes, but I sometimes felt, though I'd never say so, it was more than a job. It was a kind of calling.

I mean, think about it: David Livingstone wanted to bring, as he put it, commerce and Christianity to Africa, in order to alleviate the benighted lives of those he found there. So did I, in a way – my mission was put an air-conditioner in every home, to bring cool refreshment to sticky, overheated lives. I worked for two small American suppliers and we had a good relationship, based on two stipulations: I did not travel to America and I did not carry a cellphone. Fixed-line phone or e-mail was quite enough for reaching me.

One of my suppliers, a man called Hiram, once said to me: 'But if you had a cell, contact would be easier.'

And I had to explain: 'I don't want it easier.'

So then, on the news of this latest maternal caper, 'Keep moving,' I told myself. 'She's getting close.' I didn't give myself much of a chance, mind you. She was on my trail. I did what any sensible son would have done under the circumstances: I confirmed my flight for Malaysia. I had meetings in Merlaka, and I planned to be there.

Besides, I knew all about my mother's Cuban.

12

I had met him on my last visit home, a few months earlier. They were in the little parlour, just off the sitting room, over-looking the front garden, drinking tea and eating freshly baked date loaf; there was a bottle of rum on the tea tray.

It was a signal honour, to entertain him in the parlour, because no one but the Rain Queen was received there. It was a custom that went back to the early years of Queen Bama's unexpected visits. In those days, before the security walls went up, we had no front fence, and the Queen was able to keep an eye on her Holden Imperial, which would be parked outside the garden gate, with the royal chauffeur dozing behind the wheel.

He was in Queen Bama's chair, sipping rum.

My mother said: 'First things first, dear boy. I want to you to meet a very special friend of mine. This is Dr Mendoza.'

'Is pleased.' And Mendoza shook my hand.

'*Muy buen!*' My mother grinned. 'He's teaching me a bit of Spanish. He doesn't speak very much English – do you, Raoul?'

She must have had fifty years on the Cuban. In his fax, Schevitz had remarked on the discrepancy between their ages. Far more striking, when I saw them together for the first time, was the disparity in size. She loomed over him. She was so tall and solid. Mendoza was small, neat and debonair. But what struck me most was her evident delight in the man.

'Isn't he the sweetest thing?'

She smoothed his curls, and he caught her hand in his and kissed it.

'Where did you find him, Ma?'

'I got him from Papadop. He phoned a while back, and said he'd collected this Cuban, and he was in a bit of trouble and could he give him to me?'

Papadop was one of my oldest uncles. When I was a boy and my mother was still flying in and out of Africa, we used to go and stay with Papadopolous in his house in Mount Darwin, a small town north of what was then Salisbury, where he sold farm equipment from a shop under a huge jacaranda. He was a big dark man with a big square solid body, and in those days he drove a Hudson Hornet with a two tiny dachshunds dangling from the rear-view mirror. I called him Papadop and the name stuck.

He came to Africa from Athens, an orphan, a skinny, hungry boy, and like a lot of Greeks he ran a corner shop down the road in Parkview, and that's where my mother met him. But he tired of it. What was the point of being put into these straitjackets that South Africans were so crazy about? If you were Portuguese you sold vegetables, if you were Greek you ran the café on the street corner, if you were black you did hard labour and if you were a white South African you did bugger all.

'The bloody Dutchman only thinks about blacks and the English only think about games with balls. What a bunch of palookas!'

So he cleared out, went up north to Rhodesia, where folks didn't bamboozle themselves with who was, or was not, white. And he sold tractors and irrigating systems in Mount Darwin.

He became a Rhodesian; it was, he used to say, 'my middle

period'. In the life before that he had been Greek; he called this his 'primary period'. Later he became a Zimbabwean; he called it 'my final period'. He was proud of all his periods; he was proud of everything he had done in Africa. Papadop was a fierce patriot.

'Where do you keep this Cuban?' my mother wanted to know when he phoned.

'Kathleen, I'll tell you when I see you. You'll like him. He's a nice boy.'

Two days later he turned up at her place in Forest Town. Papadop arrived in his Datsun, with those skinny number-plates they go for in Zimbabwe, and he had this guy with him.

Papadop told her: 'He's called Raoul.'

My mother shook his hand. 'Will he have some tea?'

'Have you got any rum, Kathleen? They like rum, do Cubans – isn't it, my boykie?'

And the Cuban nodded, like a good dog.

Then they all sat in the little front parlour, drinking tea spiked with a slug of Blue Bay Jamaican rum, and Raoul wolfed down my mother's date loaf.

'Where did you find him?' my mother wanted to know.

'He found me.' Papadop patted the Cuban on his black curls. 'Didn't you, sonny? We are good mates.'

'How did you get him over the border?'

'I popped him in the boot and covered him with a blanket.'

'How'd he breathe, Papadop?'

'I drilled some holes.'

'Heavens above.'

'Not too many, mind. Bloody holes breed rust and my jalopy's on her last legs.'

'In the old days I could have flown him out.'

'In the old days, Kathleen, this would never have happened. Anyway, it was no sweat. The border is bloody chaos. At Beit Bridge crossing point you wait a coupla hours; they check your papers; you drive through, they don't really care. Not if you're in a car. Beit Bridge is also clogged with truckers. They wait maybe a few weeks. Then there are the guys on foot: traders, hawkers and guys on the hustle, looking to buy hard currency, or maybe smuggling drugs into SA, or they're carrying empty bags or paraffin tins or bottles, so they can fill up on the other side then go home and flog the stuff. Then there are the crooks, the *guma-guma*. These guys are seriously bad news: they'd stick a knife into you or shoot your head off, given a chance. They like to hijack motorists from down south. White patsies from the Republic are easy meat. Everyone knows most South Africans, they've never been in Africa before, they're not just wet behind the ears, they have litre bottles of the stuff swinging from their earlobes. The *guma-guma* puts on a peaked cap, pretends to be Customs, and sticks these SA tourists for whatever they got. The South Africans got cops and troops watching the *guma-guma* but no one can stop the traffic in paraffin or people or guns: they're the oil in the machine of corruption run from the top by Big Brother Bob, our beloved leader.'

My mother poured the Cuban another shot. 'Does he speak English?'

'Watch this,' Papadop lifted his teacup. 'Hey, Raoul – viva Cuba!'

'Viva Cuba.' Raoul lifted his cup.

'Viva Castro!' said Papadop.

'Viva Castro!' said Raoul, and then he added, 'Die – bastard!'

Papadop gave a shout of laughter. 'Isn't that great, Kathleen? He hates Castro. Who wouldn't? This boy arrives in Harare fresh out of Havana; first thing they do is they take away his passport, and they send him to Mount Darwin to be the doctor. But our hospital there, it's been closed for months; we have no medicines, no dressings and no light bulbs. Zilch! Raoul opens the hospital; he does what he can; he's a great doctor. Each month he's paid 300 dollars US by our great and good government. But he doesn't get to keep it. He has to take the dosh to Harare and hand it over to his embassy. Hard currency, you see. I got sorry for the guy. He'd come over to me of an evening, we'd have a drink, and I'd give him a steak and a beer. Then one day he says he's not going back. Ever. Isn't that right, Raoul?'

The Cuban nodded hard. 'I run away. I kill myself. I never go back.'

Papadop patted him on the shoulder. 'Don't you fuss, boy. I said to him, run you can't, boykie! Did you look at your shoes? You won't get far in bladdy plastic slippers. This is Africa. So I took him out to the river, where I got my fishing shack. I left him some condensed milk and corn-flakes and some oranges. He thought he was in heaven, poor little guy. Sure enough, next day the cops came by my house, looking for a Cuban. "What Cuban?" I say. Then the Cubans sent some goons from Harare to suss him out. They sniffed around town but Raoul was safe out by the river.'

I knew Papadop's fishing shack on the Musengezi River. There was more to the Musengezi than fishing. Papadop felt about the Musengezi the way Indians felt about the Ganges:

it was a holy river. He fished it, drank from it and swam in it. Though he like to remind people that it hadn't been so long ago that crocs made swimming impossible.

Papadop used to tell me the story of the first white man in Mount Darwin, a guy he called 'the Port' or that 'little Porto palooka, the priest blokie'.

This man had been a Portuguese Jesuit called Silveria, who had landed at Sofala in 1560, in what is now Mozambique.

'This guy was a go-getter. Inside no time he'd met King Monomatapa who liked the little Port and wanted to give him gold and cattle and female slaves. But Silveria said, "Thanks but no thanks, not for me." He didn't want gold or stuff like that: he was preaching the word of God. Anyway, Silveria wandered on towards what is now Zimbabwe, and he came to what is now Mount Darwin, and he met the chief of the place, who was an OK guy, except he worshipped crocodiles and sold people to the Arab slavers. Silveria tells the chief that he's way out of line in the God department: the croc is an ugly beast with lots of teeth and is not suitable for worship. But Jesus, on the other hand, is a God you can rely on. And the chief sees the light and says: "OK. No more crocs for me. Me and the wives and the tribe will shun the crocs and pray to Jesus." So it is all looking wonderful for Silveria.

'But you know how it is in Africa – always close the windows, or something flies in. Well, something flew in all right. There were these Arabs, right? The ones who sold slaves. They'd sold slaves for ever. If you stopped an Arab in Africa in those days and asked, "What d'you do?", chances are he'd have said, "I flog slaves; how many d'you want?" It was business. Anyway, all of a sudden the slavers see this Porto priest is screwing up business, telling every chief he meets, "No more slaves." Well, you can imagine what they felt about that. So they go to the chief and they tell him, "Listen, chiefie baby, this Porto priest, he's bad news, he's bad *muti*; he's a witch, a wizard. The holy crocodiles are very, very angry because you've dropped them for the Jesus god. But the crocs are prepared to do a deal: come back to your senses and they'll reward you." Anyway, the chief buys it. And when Silveria thinks everything is fine the chief gives a sign and his guys strangle the poor Port. Then they throw his body into the Musengezi to say sorry to the sacred crocodiles.

'Isn't it one of the saddest things in Africa: the bullshit local people swallow from smart-arse invaders? Yours truly included? Anyway, I kept the Cuban down in my shack on the river until the cops and the Cubans got really heavy. And then I had to get him out.'

'What will we do with him?' my mother said.

'I was hoping you'd tell me. I can't keep him. Things are not what they were up my way … you know, hey?'

When Papadop first went to Mount Darwin, in the fifties, it was a lively town. There were English farmers, there were Greek families who ran the garage and the general store, there were banks, hotels, shops and a community hall. My mother was still flying safaris north of Salisbury. Sometimes we used to stay with Papadopolous on his little farm with lots of new tractors dotted about under huge trees.

Then came Rhodesia's declaration of independence, and the bush war of the sixties and seventies. Farmers and guerrillas fought and killed each other. The community hall became the soldiers' billet where the women's association served hot soup.

After the war, Papadop stayed on. He didn't like the war, and he didn't like the bone-headed men who ran the Smith rebellion. He became a citizen of the new Zimbabwe, even joined the ruling party. He spoke perfect Shona, he was elected comrade mayor of Mount Darwin, and he took tea with Robert Mugabe – twice.

'Perfectly gentle, pleasant bloke. He didn't seem like a blasted commie at all, more like a country gentleman. He wanted to talk about cricket. Balls, balls, and more balls. I said to him: "I do not know, I do not care a bugger, about balls. But I see a lot of changes in Mount Darwin, Mr Prime Minister – and I think now is the time to consolidate."'

But the changes kept coming. The Greeks went next, then the bank, the garage, and the hospital closed. The white farmers who had once considered Mount Darwin part of Europe, and saw blacks as servants or savages, packed up and left. They were replaced by black farmers, who saw whites as a form of vermin. Papadop ran for mayor again and lost. The community centre closed, the country club became a brothel, but the ex-comrade mayor remained in his house under the jacaranda.

'I am the last white man in Mount Darwin,' Papadop liked saying, with a mixture of pride and sorrow. 'Or I was, last time I looked. Then this Cuban came along. I want to help, but I can't keep him, Kathleen.'

'So you want me to keep him?'

'The way I see it, there's a million refugees from Zim hanging out in Jo'burg. What's another one – among friends? Maybe he could ask for political asylum? What's sure is he's out, and he'd better stay out. If anyone catches him it's tickets for Raoul. They'd pack him off back to Havana, or feed him to the crocs.'

So she kept him. The Cuban with the curls wasn't someone she took as family; he was exotic. He needed special care. She found him Spanish videos and CDs; she brought home canned chilli con carne from the supermarket because she reckoned he'd like it. He didn't go out because people might be looking for him. He stayed in the house all day, watching soap operas, and my mother took care of him in her hunter's way. I'd seen it with Nzong, and with Bara and Buti. She took in not waifs or strays, she took in quarry: those she would also have been quite capable of shooting in other contexts. But even I could see there was something special about Raoul. Maybe it was just that he was the first non-African to have touched her.

Soon enough he was an obsession.

'If only I were younger I'd have driven out to Grand Central, fired up the Piper and headed for Maputo.'

But she knew in her heart that, even if she hadn't hung up her flying helmet, it was a hopeless dream. Mozambique, in the days when she'd been flying in refugees, had been a haven where they fought the regimes of white southern Africa, and dreamt of freedom.

'Now they really are free they don't want rebels.'

She also toyed with the idea of Lesotho – another bolt-hole for guys on the run, in the good-bad years – only to reject it.

'Most Sotho hate us now, ever since we invaded them and they burnt down all our banks. Poor Raoul would be picked up in two ticks.'

I told her plainly: 'You can't keep him, Ma.'

'I'll come up with a plan, you wait and see.'

13

She had driven her old Land Rover to the tall skyscraper in Commissioner Street. First trip up in the lift she didn't get out; she rode the lift all the way down again to give herself time to check the bit of paper on which she had written Koosie's African names.

He wasn't just renamed, he was relaunched was our Koosie. After the long years in exile, after the decades of struggle, he'd come home in 1993, and a year later he'd been elected a member of parliament in the democratic government. Next, he was 're-deployed' in the Black Empowerment sector, and sent to head up an outfit monitoring what was called 'transformation in the media', which meant making sure more black editors, copywriters and TV presenters made it into the mainstream.

The air was hushed when she stepped out of the lift on the twentieth floor. The large brass letters above the entrance to the executive suite read: 'The Media Marketing Council'. Through the glass walls of the reception area all of central Johannesburg showed clear: skyscrapers, mine-dumps, and in the distance the skinny Television Tower, like the strangulated hat of some minor deity.

She adjusted her tall blue turban and told the coiffed and beautiful receptionist with firm, clear confidence:

'I've come to see the Director, Mr Sithembile Nkosi.'

'*Dr* Nkosi,' the receptionist said.

'That put me in my place. This kid looked at me, in my turban and smock, as if I were something the cat had dragged in. Some mad old bird in a funny hat. And then, when she showed me into his office, I quite forgot what I was supposed to call him.' My mother gave her delightful bashful giggle, in which was contained girlish embarrassment and guilty delight. 'I said, "Hello Koosie" – and the girl looked around the room, trying to work out who the heck I was talking to.'

Koosie's new name kept pace with the new developments but, then, so too had his old name. In the old days being a black boy called Koosie was quite a smart move, a token of esteem for the Boer ruling class. In fact, Koosie's new name wasn't all that new. His name had always been Nkosi but it got Dutchified, to Koosie. In the new era it was a loser. You could not have a veteran of the fight for freedom wearing a tag that identified him an Afrikaans farm boy. So out went 'Koosie' and in came Dr Sithembile Nkosi, Director of the Media Marketing Council.

In many ways that was fair enough; all of us had been many things, impersonators from birth. All of us had led several lives. So what was one more mask? Koosie had already been a whole lot of things: orphan, domestic servant, gardener, prisoner, poet, refugee, freedom fighter, black radical and then, after the new dispensation, a man of importance.

So when Koosie and his friends came to be the Power, they went straight on pretending, the poor bastards, that the past had been mad but the future was sane and they were the future and soon – ah, very soon – true things would happen.

Koosie hadn't turned a hair when she fluffed his name; he

took her hand and drew her into the room, closed the door, sat her down, and offered her tea from a big silver teapot on a big silver tray.

And so the scene was set, a scene to be remembered or denied, cut or kept. I could see them, in the big office, with the tea tray. The big tall old woman in the blue turban; the elegant, thin ('too damn thin!') black man, our friend who-was-not-Koosie. It played out the way it always did in Africa, when white met black. It took on this quality of show and shimmer. We were shadows always dreaming of growing into real people, aching to put on flesh, to mean what we said, to feel we belonged, that we had true weight in this place, when we knew we never have had. For all you might say about the long, long misunderstanding between white and black in Africa is that neither side ever seemed to find the other.

'He was still our Koosie – but different.'

I knew what she meant. I used to see him when I was back in town and I never got used to the change either. Once he had been full of dangerous flash, lighting up the dead afternoons when he and I went to watch the weddings go by. Now that he'd become Dr Nkosi, he was slower and even a bit ponderous, and filled with what I can only call a spirit of reflective melancholy, as if he couldn't quite figure out exactly how he came to be where he was, a respected exec in a fine dark blue suit, and a red tie and a brand-new BMW. He was the very opposite of Schevitz who was sad because he never got to where he wanted to be. Koosie struck me as sad because he had arrived.

'I knew it wasn't going to be easy, but I thought of poor Raoul and I had to try,' said my mother.

•

Koosie poured tea, offered biscuits and then he asked her how he could help.

'I have this Cuban,' she said.

Koosie put down his cup. 'What sort of Cuban?'

'Well, I suppose he's just an ordinary Cuban, a common-or-garden Cuban.'

'Where does he come from, your Cuban?'

'Havana, I believe.'

'But after that?'

'From Zim.'

Koosie poured her another cup. He stirred his tea, round and round, saying nothing, till my mother lost patience.

'What difference does it make where he comes from?'

Koosie put his cup down and counted off the points on his fingers.

'One, he's here illegally: he jumped the border; he has no papers. Two, he skipped Zim while on assignment for the Cuban government. Three, he is living in your house while he's on the run.'

My mother said: 'Just a tick. Am I listening to the Koosie I know? Who used to live in my back yard? Am I sitting opposite a man who fought to be free? Who got locked up by the police? Who went into exile? Yes, my Cuban is on the run. He needs help. Like we helped each other. '

'Yes, Kathleen, we helped each other. And I'll never forget.' Koosie came round his big desk, and put his hand on her shoulder. 'But we were in the struggle then.'

'So is he.'

'We were fighting an illegal regime.'

'What do you think Raoul is doing? He's got out of Zimbabwe. One of the worst hell-holes in Africa.'

Koosie winced. 'What do you think I can do?'

'Talk to your friends in the Home Affairs Office, Koosie. Get me papers for the man.'

Koosie shook his head. 'What are you saying, Kathleen? Home Affairs has got illegal immigrants coming out of its ears. If I tell Home Affairs about your Cuban they'll have cops round at your place in two shakes of a duck's tail. They'll have you up in court for harbouring an illegal immigrant, a political defector.'

My mother put down her cup, she wiped her lips, she got up from her chair and she walked to the door.

'What would you have said if I'd quoted the law to you when the cops were on your tail?'

'I told you, that was an illegal regime.'

'So is Bob Mugabe's.'

Koosie sighed. 'That's a matter of opinion. And, anyway, it's not just Mugabe. Between you and me, I don't care a damn about Mugabe. But we've got our Cubans, too. Doctors working in the countryside. The Cubans, they loan us these medics on condition we return them – every last one of them. But these crazy guys sometimes bugger off, they fraternise, they fall in love with some local girl, and then she says I want to marry my Cuban. Next, they ask to stay here. And we can't have that.'

'Won't have it, you mean.'

'Yes. Because if we did, they'd all be doing it! We have to take a firm line.'

'What sort of firm line do you take with your Cubans?'

'If they run away, we send them home.'

'I don't believe this. Guys in fear of their lives come to you and you send them home! Why the hell do you do that?'

'Because it's the only way. Say yes to one, and who knows how many more will be queuing up?'

Koosie said he was sorry, and so did she. She called him Dr Nkosi, very pointedly, but the point was pretty damn hard to make because he *was* Dr Nkosi, or at least he was giving a pretty fine impression of being so. They were on different sides of the fence. It made her sad.

I had been noticing for some time my mother's sadness. It was new, like the walls she put up around the house, and the security gates, and the closed-circuit camera. What this sadness consisted of it was difficult to say. It was like a perfume and it changed according to the emotions, the internal temperature, of the wearer. We might be forced to choose from a very limited range of brands but we wore our particular scent of melancholy in our own way; that was why no two sad people ever smelt the same.

My mother's sadness was expressed very originally. She put it this way on one of my visits: 'There is no news any more.'

I don't know if she drew this impression from the TV or the papers. It was hardly likely to have been either. She had never taken much interest in news before the great changes. Each time I went back to Jo'burg, and that was several times each year, she'd mention the lack of news.

I asked her: what news did she mean?

She answered: 'Hah! You have no idea! If you had an inkling of what's happening …'

She'd be sitting in her blue Dralon chair, knitting on her lap. Behind her on the wall was the picture of her old friend, the Rain Queen, who still dropped by from time to time. The two women had a taste for catastrophe, yet they got on because their demons were different. Each succeeded in calming, or at least dampening down, the other's nightmares.

The Rain Queen was in trouble and it took bewildering forms. It called itself scientific and it did not like her traditional ways. It came in the form of cocky young men in baseball caps who disliked the certificate and its links to the old regime. The young men whispered words like 'a sell-out' and 'old-fashioned'. They said whatever a rain dance might once have stood for, it was not in the spirit of the new Africa.

Queen Bama had seen them off.

'I chased them away with my whip, I beat them with my knobkerrie. Fools! Africa is *desert*. Africa is *drought*! In Africa you please the gods. Do not throw out the rainmaker with the washing-up water. We must respect. Respect, Kathleen! Even the Boers knew respect. They pray for rain.'

She was in a fight for her life and it made her touchy. The modern young men were insolent; they were calling the shots now; enough of royal privilege, of floods and queens, of the rain dance. Clean, free water for all. That is what they wanted, in every house, in every village, in every life, in every pail. And they asked a question that drove her wild. What was she *for*?

Again she had reached for her stick.

'Young dogs!' she said, 'I made them run!'

My mother, so fearless in the bush, began to react to the wildness of the streets, and the kill rate. Once, she'd have ignored it. Serene and impervious. But in her eighties, she seemed to falter. It was then that she built the security wall around the house, topped it with electrified wire, and had a closed-circuit camera watching the garden gate. Now the first she knew of a royal visit was when the gate buzzer sounded and Queen Bama's liquid eyes stared at her from the TV monitor.

She and Bama had known each other so long, understood each other so well, that they sat there, drank their tea and sighed. For a long time I did not know what it was that was getting to them; then, later I began to understand. They felt sidelined: when they looked in the mirror their redundancy looked back.

Perhaps that is what happens when there has been a revolution; perhaps the markers, the patterns of everyday life, are rudely changed and everything that has fed your waking dreams dries up. Perhaps that is what my mother meant when she said there was no news any more.

Life was a very bad, very violent B-movie.

For want of news, the two friends upped their diet of catastrophe. That, at least, was a familiar staple. A story they came back to again and again was the one about the men locked in the fridge. It had happened months before: a meat truck had been hijacked. No surprise there; hijackings were not news. But this had a twist because there were six men on the truck: loaders, porters, humpers of the frozen carcasses. The hijackers drove the truck to Alexandra Township, ordered the men to offload the meat, then locked them in the huge fridge and made off.

The captives made desperate attempts to prise open the door with meat hooks. They left the gouging of their nails in the ice that caked the walls for all to see when the truck doors were opened by the police. Six men, three black and three white, froze slowly to death in the locked truck.

The symmetry horrified the two women; but something about it satisfied them, too. Since the racial mix was so perfectly weighted, the pain could be shared equally. In a time of trouble, when the world as they knew it had suddenly stopped existing, then anything, however dark, that confirmed the worst at least confirmed something. My mother saw in the murders signs of what happened when you destroyed established order. The Rain Queen saw it as an omen of what happened when jumped-up young men in baseball caps took over the country, and spat on the ancient beliefs.

My mother added drama to the tragedy by imagining what had happened, as if her feeling for the suffering men somehow made things better for her: 'Just think, Alexander, scratching your nails on the walls till your fingers bleed.' My mother emphasised her pain by feeling her way into the pain of others. 'Poor, poor men. Can't you just see it?'

Plainly, she thought I could not see it. I had disqualified myself from feeling what tragedies racked the country by living abroad.

My mother looked at her hands. 'What is happening to us, Bama?'

'Please, you tell me, Kathleen.'

My mother reached for the teapot. 'Search me, Bama. Search me.'

Then there was the dancing. Of an evening, behind windows she blacked out, in what had once been the servant's room behind the garage, Raoul taught her to mambo. Her movements were good but she was no longer quick on her feet. 'I do the stately version,' she said.

Raoul told her she did just great. '*Hecho muy bien, Kataleen!*' He would clap and snap his fingers and call out when she got going: '*Mambo, qué rico el mambo!*'

She loved it.

'Raoul says mambo is an African word meaning a conversation with the gods. It's a fusion of African rhythm and European style. Isn't that something?'

'You can't keep him, Ma.'

'I'll come up with a plan, you wait and see.'

The day I was due to fly back to Asia, she told me she had taken a volunteer's job at a home for disabled children, a place called the Sunbeam Shelter. I think she hoped it would provide cover if she were seen to be going off to work every day, while Raoul hunkered down in the old servant's room in the back yard, where she joined him after sunset, and they put on their music and mambo'd together.

'He says I move wonderfully.'

'I'm pleased, Ma. Really pleased. But what will you do with him?'

'Don't quite know – yet. But he makes me feel good. It's like old times. Before I was grounded. When I lived high on the wing.'

She laughed her old throaty rumble in the girlish way she had when she was 'tickled', the way she always sounded when she was younger and less sad, before she was unable to sail away as she chose, to any place that took her fancy. Grounded by age, by the wars that had shut off whole regions of Africa where she had flown all her life, without permission or passports, dropping the little float-plane down on any decent stretch of water. Forty or fifty years before, when Africa was wide open, and when her presence at any place of her choosing, anywhere on the continent, was something she regarded as entirely natural. When people travelled in Portuguese East and West Africa, in Nyasaland and Uganda, to Zanzibar and the Congo, South West Africa and the Spanish Sahara as easily as winking. Before South Africa severed links with its neighbours, then with reality, and retreated into an underground bunker of its own making; and before 'her' Africa went to war with itself.

I made her promise to stay in the room behind the garage when Raoul gave her mambo lessons.

'You think I'll be raided? Surely not! This is the new South Africa: the cops don't raid you any more. Don't you worry about us! I'll work out something. Something … elegant.'

'I don't want you to frighten the neighbours.'

That tickled her. She had always frightened the neighbours.

14

I was in Merlaka, staying at the New Renaissance Hotel.

Each day I started with coffee in the ornate lobby, sitting in a large leather armchair with the *New Straits Times*. The sound system would be pumping out Haydn or early rock 'n' roll. Everything came with muzak in Malaysia. I found an 'advertorial' for chicken soup, in pill form, known as Brand's Essence of Chicken, developed, it was claimed, in the kitchens of Buckingham Palace to cheer and comfort George IV. Property developers in KL were selling the rising rich luxury homes whose marble lounges contained recessed areas called 'conversation pits'; several employment agencies were offering a 'reliable maid', with a free replacement 'if she runs away'.

Malaysia was authoritarian, deeply and unprettily nationalistic. Malaysia had done what aspiring modern despotisms do: it had ensured that democracy was good for you by using it to cement the Great Leader in place, and keep him there. Running the show was a bunch of men who thought with their blood, zealots who did as they liked, while everyone else did as they were told. An empire of agitated air, noisy with menacing talk about 'the nation', 'the chosen', 'the sons of the soil': a jet stream of pomposities so super-heated you could hang-glide across the country on the thermals.

Malaysia wanted cooling off, and that was good for business. But it was odd, when I thought about it. Places like Malaysia were said, just a few years before, to be on the downside of history, to be in need of help if they were to manage to become decent liberal places in the little time left before history, already pronounced to be at an end in the West, closed down everywhere. History was hot no longer: it was very cool. Tolerance and democracy were coming to a tyranny near you; despots would retire their secret police, close up their jail cells, and pension off their hangmen. Countries once deemed 'backward' would be moving forward. Victims everywhere would flock to the polls and vote for freedom. And it would not take long because history was in a hurry to see to it that places like Malaysia sweetened up and dropped the tribalism of the favoured few.

But all that was long ago, before September 11, 2001, when those planes flew into the Towers in far-away New York. And now, instead of tight little tyrannies looking odd and old-fashioned – soon, poor dears, to catch up with the sweet enlightened, tolerant world – suddenly, tribal hatred and racial warfare looked like pretty sensible projects. Suddenly Malaysia wasn't left behind at all: not a damn, it was postively futuristic. Because in this craven new world, we were all tribalists, and that talk about tolerance turned out to be so much sentimental crap. Might was not just right, it was sensible, it was reasonable. It was progressive. Internecine wasn't nice but it was necessary when the other guys were worse. Stripped of sustaining pieties, we were our old murderous selves again. When plane came to tower, sweet talk dissolved in blood, and there was no one who wasn't happy to be twice as homicidal as the guys next door.

That's how it had always been in Merlaka. A port city, dubious, dreamy, shimmering in the hazy heat of the grey-green Malaccan Straits, where pirates waited, and on some of the islands separatist Islamists kidnapped foreigners. It used to be called Malacca, it used to be Dutch, then British, and it was always semi-Chinese, with some ex-Tamils thrown in for good measure. Now it was run by one more prevailing tribe, which, like all the others, called itself the chosen one. History hung over Merlaka like a troubled dream. Merlaka had been so many things it wasn't sure what it was supposed to be any longer.

It's odd that deeply and cruelly colonised cities, capitals built to the glory of the guys who kicked your head in, once they get their freedom, hardly ever achieve greatness. They become, instead, interesting and rather charming exercises in somewhat doubtful nostalgia, living on their memories, with occasional spurts of 'development', made in a frantic attempt to be modern. But it is done without any great sense of conviction, as if people know that what once made them important, powerful and worth fighting and dying for had gone away and wasn't coming back.

Each day I was happy getting lost; walking beside the muddy Merlaka River, or crossing into Jonker Street, where the antique dealers worked, and wandering among the old colonial shop fronts and the fine houses where the rich Chinese merchants once lived. I spent time in the shop of Mr Wah Aik. He made red silk brocade shoes for Chinese women who'd had their feet bound as children. The shoes were about three inches long. The pain, said the shoemaker, was great, at least until the bones were broken. He showed me pictures of the feet after binding, compressed to points: they looked like delicate pigs' trotters. Women did it, he told me, because men liked it, and one came out of Wah Aik's shop thinking of love, pain and tiny feet, erotic, irresistible in China for thousands of years.

I passed a doorway where there leaned an enormous billowy coffin the colour of toffee, ornamented with buttery swags of brass. The Chin Chin Longevity Shop made not coffins but kites, and the old kite maker was sitting cross-legged on the floor, splitting reeds. There were box kites and bird kites swinging in the rafters overhead; a young woman was rocking a baby in a hammock in the corner; over the road a few pallid tourists piled out of coaches marked 'Batik Tours', blinking in the immense early sun.

I made Merlaka my own with all the spurious sincerity of a traveller who really calls no place home, and so was in the habit of burrowing beneath the surface of a town and pulling it over him like a blanket, of thinking idly, happily: I could settle here – a sentiment entirely true though strongest, I noticed, just as I was about to leave.

The magic was working: I had almost forgotten where I was from. I'd stop for a beer or buy the occasional trinket, a teapot in the shape of a small boy riding a water buffalo, painted in deep bamboo greens and tans. I found a fat chuckling money Buddha sculpted, unusually, from pink resin. He leant back on his bursting sacks of golden sovereigns, his perfect paunch shining from the touch of a thousand hopeful fingers that, over the decades, had rubbed it for luck.

I had spent an afternoon walking around the old colonial town centre, a few streets painted a rusty red, woeful and uneasy amid the bustle of modern Merlaka, rather as if this slice of the past had been quarantined off. Here I found the old British Club, prim and straitened, like an elderly maiden aunt marooned in some Eastern bazaar. Christchurch Cathedral, built by the Dutch and, like so much of Merlaka, taken over by the British, was no longer a place of worship but simply a boxy building devoted to a foreign cult no one in Merlaka knew much about.

In the old Dutch Town Hall, the Stadthuys, I stopped before a portrait in oils. I looked up at it and I knew him instantly, the way you know someone whose face is on the paper money in your country. I stood looking at this burgher with his chestnut beard and his lace collar and his air of imperturbable gravity – the rock-like self-importance of these rulers was truly sublime – and I found it hard to not to break into wild laughter. There he hung: Jan van Riebeeck. He had been, in the seventeenth century, the first governor of the Cape of Good Hope and the guy Schevitz and I had decided long ago was at the root of all the rot.

You simply could not get away from the bastards.

The Cape hadn't been much of a posting at the time. A flat-topped mountain and a bay, in the back end of nowhere. Van Riebeeck planted a vegetable patch, built a fort, shot lots of natives and got the hell out. He moved 'East', said our history books. Well, now I knew where. He had gone on to become governor of Malacca from 1662 to 1665. Malacca had what the Dutch craved: it had riches, it had gold, it had the East at its feet and you could smell the spices on the breeze.

I reckoned Malacca got off pretty lightly. All that remained of van Riebeeck, in his Eastern manifestation, was this daub of paint in a dim room. We were still recovering from the damage he did in South Africa. That was the thing with national heroes: whether they were on the banknotes or the wanted posters turned out to be a matter of timing.

The room was darkening and losing the last of the afternoon light. Even the shadows seemed heavy. Dark beams overhead, dark wooden window-frames, black and white tiles on the floor, solid wooden chests ranged against the walls. I knew lugubrious rooms like this; hell, I might have been in Cape Town.

Cape Town! God, how the heart sank.

'A dowdy little madam of a town with a bloody hill slap bang in the middle,' said my mother once.

I looked at van Riebeeck and he looked at me, and I got the message. We were playing Sudden Death, that was clear. I had been put on notice; things were closing in. There is something alarming in finding that you have moved as far as the tip of Asia, only to end up facing the man whose dull but rapacious yearnings charged generations of pebble-hearted creeps with saving Africa for Western Christian civilisation. And why was it that this man, who had such crushing weight in Africa, here in this dim room seemed nothing more than a passing accident of history, just another pale, fatuous functionary on the make?

I think it had to do with power. The Portuguese, the Chinese, the Dutch, the British in Malaysia were powerful, yes, but somehow never insistent, and so the poison of their presence was less toxic than it was in Africa; from the peaks of their pride they looked down on the people of Asia but never did they assume they did not exist. In Africa they saw nothing human; they stripped it of its people, polished them off, not just with guns and germs but also by truly and honestly doubting they ever were truly alive, and so they became nothing. And once this mental genocide was done, they could populate the empty space with figments of their fancy; and shoot, collect, whip, steal and destroy as they wished. As a result,

Africa was still depopulated, vacant even today of easy, natural, ordinary people – and filled with fevered ghosts clamouring to be born again as human beings.

Africa …

For my mother it was a word she used without the least trace of embarrassment – as if she owned it, lived and was one with it. And I knew I should really feel as easily and as naturally about her. After all, wasn't that what love was? Instead, the feeling I had towards her was too hot, unbalanced and so feverish, like a bout of malaria. I felt that the word 'love' should be approached with considerable caution, in particular when coupled with Africa – keep an eye on the gun-belt all the while – because it often meant a kind of murder.

And as for being the son of my mother, well, that was an accident; maternal was not her mode. She was more like some mad aunt best kept locked in the attic, until she broke out, got drunk, took off her clothes, ran riot. She was what I loved – and also all I most wished to get away from. Whenever I thought of her, I was appalled. I think I had felt that way all my life. And I knew now, with van Riebeeck peering at me in the gloom, that the more distance I put between us, the better.

But I knew, too, it was never far enough. The further away I got, soon enough, sure as shooting, I'd find her waiting round the next corner. I'd arrive, anonymous, in some hot and torrid frontier town where no one had ever heard of me and the next thing I knew, over the hill with a warrant for my arrest and extradition, galloped the pursuing posse of my past.

But I wasn't handing myself over yet. There was an early morning express train to Kuala Lumpur and I would be on it.

15

All the way from Merlaka I shared a compartment with a cop and a prisoner in handcuffs, who was reading a book. Both were small brown quiet men. The policeman was called Bashir, his prisoner was named Affendi, and they seemed the best of friends. Affendi was handcuffed and Bashir had to pour him a glass of water, help with the sweet chilli prawn cakes we all shared, and take him down the corridor when he needed a pee.

'The poor chap is of unsound mind, and he's awaiting trial. He's been awaiting it for a few years now: ten in all. He's almost what we'd call a forgotten prisoner. I can see you're shocked but, on the other hand, if he weren't awaiting trial, he'd be in the condemned cell, waiting to be hanged. He stabbed a tourist in the Cameron Highlands some time ago. Do you know the Camerons, sir?'

I knew the Camerons. It was there that the mist came down like a veil and played games with the mock-Tudor fronts of the fake English hotels; where the Kosy Korner Teashop sold blowpipes, along with bacon and egg breakfasts, and in the pretty cottage gardens the jungle began where the well-kempt English lawn ended. It was there my friend, Jimmy Li Fu had his hotel, The Gloucester, which offered the 'Best of British

Cuisine': Beef Wellington and Spotted Dick and Bubble and Squeak; boarding-school fare transformed by Jimmy's hands into the strange and alien cuisine of inscrutable, far-away Albion.

Bashir was taking Affendi to KL, 'so this high-end mind doc can check his mental health. And, then if found to be sane, he will certainly be hanged, as soon as possible.'

He repeated this often as if it might make up for the years the prisoner had been forgotten.

Affendi was deep into a North London novel, the sort you see a lot of on the London Underground, by writers with names like that sound like suburbs – Pawnsley or Gormlee – tales of girl trouble on the Archway Road, or high jinks in Kentish Town. Affendi was reading *All My Loving* and its cover showed Buddy Holly, owlish specs shining like twin moons rising over a grainy view of Hornsey High Street.

Not perhaps the sort of thing you expect to see in the man-acled hands of a prisoner between jails and, quite possibly, on his way to the gallows. Then again, such joshing tales were, like the mock-Tudor English lodges in the jungles of the Camerons, strangely exotic, if not downright sultry, in the right place. They spoke of a world that was expensively dull, and safely grey, where no one ever starved or died of heatstroke or dengue fever, where horror never happened – and if it did, someone would demand an urgent enquiry – where the shadow of the hangman never fell.

Bashir and I played dominoes. Affendi read swiftly, eagerly, lost in romantic Hornsey, the chink of his handcuffs as he turned the pages the only sound. And the train ran on towards KL, and life or death. Outside our windows, in dusty village lanes, half-naked kids, their thin legs thudding in the dust, chased shrieking chickens, an old sport in Malaysian villages; and the hot chilli of the prawn cakes pulsed in my throat.

It was good to be moving, good to be free at times like this. The happy ache that came of knowing you were alive in a foreign place, and richly lost. Where none of your rules apply, where nothing you know is of any use.

The old Central Rail Station in the middle of KL was built by the British in the ornate, overheated style of their great cathedrals to steel and steam. It was a Moorish vision, designed by an architect who dreamt he was in Granada. The old station was all minarets and spires decked out as something from the Arabian Nights. No Disney designer could have matched it for sheer nuttiness and bloody arrogance. It took the great cartoonists of colonial times to pull it off. Birmingham dreaming it was the Alhambra. St Pancras in the middle of Asia.

The area around the station was electric with the static left behind by the great imperial star, long since exploded; it crackled with currents of an improbable past. The ghosts of the old imperialists didn't just walk around the old railway station, they held fucking demonstrations.

And it reminded me of my mother, that station, though she would have hated the comparison. She was, also, in many ways, built by the British: she was tall, she was alarmingly exotic and, when placed in the African landscape, she was a gigantic temple to strange gods. It was uncanny.

At a stall under the great roof, Affendi, Bashir and I lunched on samosas and coffee. Affendi ate, lifting both manacled hands to his mouth, but he made a bit of a mess and Bashir wiped the flakes of pastry off his upper lip, tenderly, as a mother might. We all hugged each other goodbye. I don't know why we felt so bound, so close.

Jimmy Li Fu was waiting for me. He'd parked his new Toyota next door to the cricket pitch.

'Welcome, welcome, Alex, to your hotel and then we stop at some good coffee at the First Cup.'

'What's new in KL, Jimmy?'

Jimmy smiled, his narrow brown face with its pointed nose reminding me, again, of a very elegant wasp. Despite the smile he looked slightly put out. 'Nothing – I am happy to say – nothing at all.'

I first saw Jimmy Li Fu in the teahouse of the Victoria and Albert Butterfly Farm, up in the Cameron Highlands. It was a light and spacious place because caging butterflies was a delicate thing. He was at the back of the teahouse, sitting at a long trestle table, with a very slim silent young Chinese woman, his mobile on his ear, drinking Coke. He caught my eye because the front of the room was packed with a party of Americans touring the tea plantations, and they looked heavy. It wasn't the tourists' fault but they were in the wrong place. By comparison with their solidity Jimmy was private, austere. As thin as a finger, and very brown, and we'd been – friends is too odd a word – useful allies ever since. Jimmy sometimes gave me the impression he subsisted on nothing but air and excitement.

I knew more about him now. I knew now that day at the Butterfly Farm he had been on the phone to his bookie in Singapore. I knew the woman with him was one of his 'workers'. I knew Jimmy to be of that indeterminate category best described in Asia, in neutral tones, as 'a businessman …'

If you looked at him in some sort of boring way, Jimmy was dodgy – a gambler, a brothel-keeper, a hotelier, a chef. As a boy he'd been a member of a particularly vicious Chinese triad. He had the triad emblem of red dragons tattooed on his right arm. But to bring the deadly pragmatism of the settled world to bear on Jimmy was an exercise as cruel and as stupid as chasing after the pretty, fluttering confections that looped around the plastic cages of the Victoria and Albert with a meat cleaver – and as little likely to catch the essence of the man.

Jimmy was a lost soul. He came from what I'd call the marginalities, small ethnic slivers who lived far from whatever race or country or nation or tribe or group or gene pool gave them identity, and for whom even 'lived' was a tricky word; say rather they had found a way of uneasily co-existing among much larger groups of racial purists who barely tolerated them (good); did not tolerate them (bearable); or threw them out (tricky).

Jimmy drove me to the Federal Hotel where I dumped my bag, and then we dropped in at the First Cup, a coffee shop in the B&B Plaza, slap bang in the middle of The Golden Triangle, but far enough way from the Petronas Towers to be civilised. The rich young kids of KL shopped a lot, and the B&B Plaza was a hot spot for shoppers who watched the world go by from the terrace of the First Cup.

We hadn't been there five minutes when the riots started.

Jimmy Li Fu said: 'Students. They're demonstrating against ISA, the Internal Security Act, which gets people locked up very easily, and keeps them locked up. These people don't like the government, they don't like the Prime Minister; they don't like anything.'

There were cops everywhere. They sealed off the café and the shops and the street, and began chasing the students towards big red trucks, mounted with water cannon. The metal shutters were down at Kwang's, the Authorised Money Changer. The girls at the Heavenly Massage Parlour had stopped working. The blinds were drawn in the windows of Dr Gigi and the Fong and Goh Dental Surgery. The only people out in the open were tourists in big shorts and waist-wallets.

The cops manning the water cannon tested their range by firing at the First Cup which had a deflective shield formed by the curved roof of the taxi rank across the way, which is very useful when the cops are aiming powerful jets of water at you.

Behind us, in the Plaza, the shopkeepers had visions of their customers suddenly turning into looters, so they dropped the steel grilles over the exits and if any shoppers were still inside it was too bad. Minutes earlier the rich kids had been guests at Sweet Polly's Department Store; now they were prisoners. They stuck their hands through the bars, waving and making a muffled lowing sound, like milk calves torn from the udder. Those who'd made it out of the shopping centre before the grilles came down grabbed the remaining tables, put down their Gucci bags, ordered coffee and watched the riot.

Native to each culture are the means used by the police for assaulting the citizenry. Riots have their own geography and physics, and the number of ways you may be attacked are varied and compelling. Where I came from we were chased by men with leather whips, sjamboks, made, if you were a stickler for tradition, from rhino hide, but cowhide would do. Sometimes the cops fired birdshot. This was painful but not usually fatal, and it was better than rubber bullets, or plastic rounds, or tear gas – we called it tear smoke.

The cops of KL wore black and carried long canes and when they lashed out they reminded me of the Irish Christian Brothers who schooled me. Lifting and bringing down a stick on someone's back or legs is a violent gesture: it distorts the body, starting with a flexing of the calf on the pivot of the ankle, like a golfer, a rising shoulder and a forward darting downward movement as the bamboo comes down on the flesh of the victim. You can read in the twisting body of the attacker an expression of happiness. Hitting another person – striking the target repeatedly with a fist, a foot, a stick until it runs away or falls down – has a naturalness about it that suggests it must have been one of the earliest hominid's pleasures.

The rioters, young and quick, dodged the cops by running into doorways. The cops didn't get the chance to do this often, and they were not going to be cheated. They looked around and spotted the tourists. There were lots of them. In the season of Asian slump and uncertainty, travel agents had been selling Malaysia hard. It was hot, cheap, safe, familiar enough to appeal to British and Australian travellers of a certain age: Malaysia had Worcester Sauce and Guinness, and to call the police you dialled 999.

Well, someone had dialled 999 but when the cops arrived they weren't nice English bobbies at all, they didn't smile and call you ma'am. They were nippy and vicious and wore shiny body armour that made them look like menacing beetles. The tourists were easy game. Even as they were beaten, even as they flinched when the truncheons slapped home, I could feel their outrage, their sense of shame. This was happening to them! The knowledge outstripped their pain. They'd got up that morning and had the buffet breakfast; and they expected the day to unfold as the schedule said it would. That was their right as sober, solid citizens from some of the most privileged societies the world had ever known, swathed, mothballed, counselled by state officials, whose only duty was to see they were safe, happy, pensioned, healthy. Now, without warning, they were overweight, clumsy, pale-skinned targets, ridiculous in Bermudas and money-belts, being chased by sprightly dervishes with sticks and hoses who wanted to hurt them ...

In the thick of it all, Jimmy's mobile began cheeping. He listened for a moment and then said: 'It's for you.'

I stared at him. 'Who knows where I am?'

'They know where I am – the whole of KL knows you're with Jimmy Li. Take the phone, Alexander.'

My mother's voice echoed down the line, much as it had echoed down the years of my life. The phone, in her hands, was an instrument perfectly adapted to expressing sharp emotion but giving nothing away, wearing all those verbal colours that made up her characteristic acoustic camouflage: disdain.

'What is all that noise? Where on earth are you?'

'I'm in Malaysia, Ma.'

'May-laseeeya!'

What consternation she put into the word. If I'd said I was spending the weekend in Sodom and Gomorrah she could not have sounded more offended.

'I phoned the number you gave me, and I got some hotel and they said to call this number. Are you busy right now? What's going on there?'

'How are you, Ma?'

'I'm fine – but I was fired from the Shelter.'

'Why were you fired?'

'I hugged the kids.'

'They fired you for hugging kids?'

'I couldn't help it, Alexander. I simply had to put my arms around them; I loved them. And they liked it. But the powers that be were not best pleased and they said hugging kids was not policy. They couldn't keep me. So my friend Cindy said, "Well, Kathleen, if that's the way they feel, I am going with you." And she did! Resigned on the spot, without so much as a kiss my foot. Imagine that, dear boy. And Cindy has a lot more at stake than I have, what with her own child in the Shelter.'

'Ma, what have you done with Raoul?'

'Hidden him.'

'Hidden him where?'

'Where they'll never think of looking. Tell you when I see you.'

'Ma, Jake Schevitz faxed me. He says you went to see him.'

I could hear her snort.

'Fat lot of good it did me. What a total *woes* that man has turned out to be. I had a lovely plan, but all I got from Jake was one damn reason after another why it couldn't be done. Imagine if I'd gone to him in the old days with Nelson Mandela and wanted to hide him; would Jake have told me it couldn't be done? What on earth is that noise, Alexander?'

I didn't want to tell her. I said to myself she wouldn't wish to know. If she'd phoned halfway across the globe only to find I had gone and got myself caught up in a riot, she'd have been furious. She'd have said: 'Well, really; if you must do that sort of thing, we have perfectly good riots of our own, right here in Africa. You don't have to go all the way to Malaysia.'

A boy with blood in his hair was walking in circles. A plump tourist knocked over by water cannon was sitting in the road, wiping her face with her skirt.

'So what now, Ma?'

She sighed. 'He's gone, he's safe, but I miss him. He was fun. By the way, I have to have some tests; doctor says it's important.'

Suddenly I was listening hard, as she had intended.

'What sort of tests, Ma?'

She lowered her voice. 'I've been bleeding ... I won't mention from where – not on the public phone. Anyway, I called the doctor when I discovered the you-know-what. I had a bath, I did my hair and I climbed into my old Landy and drove off to see him. Doctor says I have to go to hospital, so I am.'

'When, Ma?'

'Right now. When I put the phone down. I'm checking into Fourways Clinic, a private hospital out on the William Nicol Highway in the far northern suburbs. You wouldn't know it, darling, it was after your time. Father Phil from my parish is visiting priest there. Isn't that lucky? I don't think you know Father Phil, he was also after your time.'

The cops were driving the tourists towards the water cannon. An elderly man in short grey socks and sandals was trying to cover his head with his camera case, and the cops beat him about the buttocks. I saw three women running with their handbags flapping, then the water hit them between the breasts and knocked them down.

'I'll come home, Ma.'

'You'll do nothing of the kind! I wouldn't dream of it. I'll be out of hospital and right as rain in no time. Where did you say you were?'

When I told her again, she said: 'Well, I never! Goodbye, darling, I must go now.'

My mother hated using the telephone to say anything important, and she only phoned to communicate rage or alarm.

For her to have tracked me down was her way of being as alarming as possible. It was a rare thing, a long-distance call, it would have cost her dearly, and it meant that this trip to the hospital was a serious business. Finding me in Malaysia would have further lowered her opinion of the shocking, indeed the scandalous unreliability of the telephone: it cost a fortune and took you to very strange places where you had no wish to be.

Jimmy snapped shut his phone and dropped it with his smooth elegance into his top pocket.

'You should get one of these. People could reach you.'

'I don't want to be reached.'

'Bad news?'

'My mother: she's not well; she's on her way into hospital. I'll have to go home.'

We watched a small policeman kicking a large student who had fallen over and was trying to cover his face, but the policeman tore his hands away, wanting particularly to kick him in the mouth.

Jimmy said: 'I am shocked, Alexander. This does not happen in KL.'

What shocked him was not the boot slamming – with a sound not unlike a dry cough – into the broken mouth of the man on the ground but the riot itself. The water cannon bowled over a small clutch of tourists who fell down, like this was some fairground sport and they were having fun, and they skidded along on their haunches, screaming.

Jimmy was tutting to himself: 'Dearie me. Best to keep out of the water. It's got something chemical in it. Sticks to the skin like mad. Get a touch of that water and you're itching for days.'

·

That night we dined at the Coliseum, a reassuring shabby restaurant in old KL, a place British rubber planters once made their own and on which they had left their distinctive brand of overdone, steak-and-kidney exoticism. Jimmy presided at the bar, on the stool they reserved for him, calling for more gins. The bar was dark and warm and rich and filled with the sort of dust I think of as past particles of those who once used and loved it.

It gave him a boost to lean up against the bar and buy me gin and tonics and pretend for a while that since I spoke English he could lord it over an itinerant Brit because long ago the British had put him down for being 'a blooming chink'. Jimmy's thin face grew stony when he thought back to those times.

If it comforted him, I didn't mind. But the British were no longer the enemy and hadn't been for decades. Their influence lingered in Malaysia, where it lingered on at all, as a slightly gamy, strangely perverse, overheated kind of jungle Anglicanism. It was the Bumiputra, the regular certified pure Malays, the sons of the soil, who were the masters now and they had long ago drawn Jimmy's sting, had cut off his balls and told him, 'If you want to fill you purse, fine. But keep your mouth shut and never forget you're nobody.'

Jimmy did more than he was told, he 'loved' the Prime Minister. God help him, this sardonic, clever man had done the deal that turned his brains to soup; he had sat up and begged and in exchange he was permitted to hover around the place like the harmless house ghost, who did deals, who might loom large in the Chinese community; and he might be rich but what good was gold to ghosts? It bought influence, race-horses, whores and security. But it did not buy belonging. He was not of the tribe, he did not belong to the sons of the soil, he had influence but no power, he had cash and no substance.

'May the Prime Minister live a hundred years,' Jimmy Li Fu lifted his gin.

'Why, Jimmy, why?'

'What do you think will happen to Chinese like me, if the government falls?'

'Chinese, like me': the cry of all small communities that existed, like the Straits Chinese from which Jimmy came, on sufferance, by permission, at the pleasure of bigger, not very friendly hosts.

A perfect phrase for expressing the rights of a parasite. If you imagined the tribe as a wasps' nest, then Jimmy was a certified drone. He was allowed just one thing: to be rich, to use his influence in his narrow world but never to have the slightest say in the way his world was controlled. As long as he obeyed the rule, he might hoard as much treasure as his sharp little proboscis could carry without bursting. But if he ever so much as dreamt of stepping out of character, they would inflict on him a punishment so cruel he shivered to think of it: *they would send him home.* Home was another country where he was even more of a foreigner than he was in Malaysia. Jimmy was Straits Chinese by extraction and that meant he was generations removed from his motherland across the water.

A line of visitors stopped at our table – Chinese guys who owed him favours, then a Malay cop and his girlfriend. They paid their respects, received Jimmy's crooked yellow smile of benediction. They did not linger; they visited him the way people visit a lucky shrine, paid compliments and stored up, they hoped, good luck. Of Jimmy's slightly sinister authority there was no doubt, and I imagine he used it and enjoyed it in just about the same way he did the power that came from belonging to the triad he ran with as a boy: in much the way he saluted the Prime Minister. Politically he bought protection from whoever ran the place to keep his rackets safe. Just as we had always done.

When I was a child in the Transvaal, I visited a uranium works and was given a tiny little pellet of yellow mud they said was uranium: I kept it in a blue matchbox like a pet mouse, and took it out and looked at it from time to time. I liked the purity of the yellow, and when I think back now I wonder if it really was uranium, and thus radioactive, and dangerous. That's what Jimmy Li Fu reminded me of, and when I stopped off to see him in KL I never spent long; I didn't really want to expose myself to whatever rays he was giving off.

'So, Alex, when will you go?'

'Tomorrow, if I can get on a plane.'

'Where will you go to?'

'Johannesburg, that's home.'

'Jo-han-nes-burg? Good to know you're from somewhere.'

It was an old joke between us. He was Malaysian, I was African, but only in a manner of speaking. These alibis could be stripped away any time, and Jimmy would be turned back into a blooming Chink just like I could have my African name stripped away and turned into just another interloper from bloody Europe.

'We're from nowhere, we two,' Jimmy liked to say. 'And it will be held against us. Chinese like us.'

Now he looked at me and said slowly, carefully, like he was trying it out:

'Nel-son Man-de-la ...'

He meant well, I know it. But it didn't really touch the sides. A country that otherwise you know nothing about can sometimes be known exhaustively through one individual. One size fits all. You said the word and you were off the hook. It was like saying 'Mother Teresa' – and bingo! You're done with Calcutta. I didn't find this disconcerting. On the contrary, I liked it because it relieved me of the fatuous burden of guilt and knowledge and the even more ridiculous South African notion, once prevalent, that everyone knew all about the place: in the past, because the people there were so nasty; and nowadays because they're so nice.

Jimmy said again: 'Nel-son Man-dela.'

He did it to show that he knew and cared about where I was from. In fact, like many in South East Asia, he knew very little about South Africa, and cared not at all. African countries, all African countries, were populated by wild creatures, and South Africa's saving grace was to have strong brand recognition in this superman who had emerged by magic from the chaos and become a lucky charm, a mantra, the intoning of whose name brought calm and order and dignity to a dark place.

It was a kind gesture, offered in the hope I might like the sound of it. It made us the sort of friends that only people like us could get to be. What we were, when you got right down to it, was closer than family. We were tribe, Jimmy and me; we were joined at the fucking hip, and what connected 'Chinese like us' was this: we knew that home wasn't ever any place left behind; it was always some place you were on the way to, always somewhere ahead.

16

My Lufthansa jet entered African airspace above Morocco, then passed over Cairo and began following the Nile south over Egypt, and on to the Sudan. The 747 traced almost exactly the route that the old Empire Flying Boats, in the thirties, flew from London, across Europe, and down Africa to Durban. The great Sunderlands of Imperial Airways could fly only by day, and they kept low, like fat ducks, sitting steady at fifteen hundred feet, looking down on Africa, while Africa looked up. Lovely fun for the gorgeous few, souls gifted with the rarest of freedoms: the right to go where they pleased. Those who flew to Africa to farm or fish or run countries six times the size of England left Dover and flew over France and Switzerland and Italy, but it was when they cleared the European mainland and sailed over Africa that reality fell behind.

When Joe Healey wished to take his little daughter along for the ride, who was to object? The gold mines were rich beyond speaking. A burly Irishman in a blue suit and a panama hat, his dynamite sticks in an attaché case which 'he arranged under our seat', said my mother.

'The detonators he kept in a gunnysack. Many was the time we played blackjack using the attaché case for the table when we took the boat.'

'His job as Chief Explosives Officer took him to Northern Rhodesia, or Angola, or the Congo, and once to Egypt. I remember we put down in Wadi Halfa. You could go to places in the thirties and forties and fifties that have been off limits now for half a century.

'From Egypt the Boat flew on across the Mediterranean, towards Crete, touched Europe over Italy, the Swiss Alps, France, the Channel and then, at last, England.

'But we flew into Africa, always. Never beyond. It was … heavenly. The craft were plump, they floated in air; they were truly water creatures. Whales with wings! The captain was a qualified seaman! They also were proper boats. Ocean liners aloft. You could play a game of deck quoits – in flight! – while all of Africa unscrolled at your feet. They catered, dear boy, to those with expensive tastes.'

She recalled very exactly her old excitements: the man with a turban who rang the bell for departure in Wadi Halfa; the tartan curtains in the observation lounge; the mellow Cunard voices of the stewards; the dark green leather seats; the Blue Grass perfume, 'available in dollops, quite free in the ladies' restroom. I just helped myself…'

An Empire Flying Boat did not follow the spine of Africa. Instead, it veered east so it might begin, like a great skimming stone, to lake-hop its way down the length of the east coast. From Cairo the flight path led to Khartoum, and the plane put down at Gordon's Knee. And then on to steamy Malakal, and along the Upper Nile to Jubba in the Sudan and, if time allowed, a short detour over the Murchison Falls before touchdown at Port Bell, the big craft ploughing two hissing furrows on the dark waters of Lake Victoria and the night stop in Kampala. Next day to Mombasa, then Dar Es Salaam, and the night stop in Beira, a tawny, steamy sea-front, a taste of Portugal, prawns peri-peri and Chianti, speciality of the Imperial Airways guest-house.

The boats flew low enough for the passengers to count crocodiles on the banks of the Zambezi, low enough to spot tickbirds between a buffalo's horns. Pressing their noses to the shop window of Africa, letting their eyes fall wherever they chose. And why not? It was all theirs and it was all free.

And then the big craft dropping her nose and swooping down to hit the water, the airframe shouting and shuddering in the hissing foam as they taxied to a stop in the huge, hot, ticking silence. The obedient launch nosing out from the landing stage. On the Zambezi they sent a launch to chase away the hippos. Then the kind boatman with the strong arms helped her down, and she chugged across the water to the lodge for the night. It might be Lake Nyasa, or Livingstone in Northern Rhodesia, where the Victoria Falls raised in the sky its great fists of spray. Or the Kisumu Hotel on Lake Victoria, for a hot bath and dinner: starched napkins so stiff she cracked them open like slices of cardboard, waiters in white tunics and bright red sashes, silver service, candlelight, and Africa muttering outside the windows, a nearby lion as loud as an air-raid siren, while she tucked into roast beef and Yorkshire pudding.

Next morning, up at the crack of dawn, bound for Lourenço Marques, then into South African airspace, flying down the dark green sweltering coast of Northern Natal to Durban, over the Bluff, banking above the big hotels on South Beach for touchdown on the Indian Ocean, taxiing noisily into the Imperial Airways moorings at Congella.

'Can you feel the freedom?'

These flights across Africa were celestial board games played by people called Rodney and Felicity and Millicent and Roy, who put away the board at night, folded it up and forgot it, because terrific fun though it was to play the game, floating like gods above an exotic zoo, it wasn't real. Or rather it only became worth something when you touched down, and reality only began and ended while you were there, making the place exist by your presence.

Of course it was the nature of settlers to be cut off and to grow into mutant beings. But it seemed the destiny of these arrivistes to be the oddest mixture, assembled according to no known recipe, to be a kind of pale hallucinogenic mould or fungus that grows in the dark and thrives for unclear reasons in unlikely spots, and then vanishes.

My friend Koosie once said that the smell of defeat hung over us. And I asked who he meant – the whites, the English? – he opened his big brown eyes really wide, he stroked his tiny pointy beard, he snapped the brim of his fedora, he flicked a speck of dust off the wide blue lapel of his fancy pinstripe suit, and he said: 'Check me out. Take a deep breath, be ready for deep shock. Do I look white? Do I sound English? Listen, baby, I said "us". I meant the whole horrible crew. The most stuck, the most narrow, the most cut-off provincial palookas on the planet. You, me and everyone else is who I mean. Every man, woman and child. South Africans. That's *us*. Excuse me while I spit. Seen nothing, been nowhere, and, heee! so proud of it!'

It was the best compliment I ever got from Koosie. The nice bit was the '*us*'.

•

I had a German beside me, a big, very pink man, reading Rilke and drinking brandy and Coke. He told me he was from Namibia; his name was Dieter and he owned a big ranch near Luderitz, which the government was talking of confiscating.

'They say I'm an absentee landlord. Maybe they'll take it away. Maybe they're bluffing. Namibia is not easy farming country. *Ja*, I own a lot of land but you need more and more land for a farm that is to make money. That's the bottom line. If they want, they can give my land to poor blacks. But they will stay poor. And it's thieving. What's the good of that?'

I could see the good of that: when foreigners, aliens, incomers have robbed you blind for centuries, you want some of your own back. It's not nice but when has getting your own back ever been nice?

Dieter said: 'Do you know much about Namibia?'

I said: 'Nothing about Namibia; but I knew German South West Africa pretty well once …'

He looked faintly embarrassed. 'German South West? I haven't heard it called that for a long, long time.'

I said: 'Where do you live, Dieter?'

'I live in Hamburg.'

'Where were you born?'

'Windhoek.'

'So what does that make you?'

He was surprised. 'I'm Namibian.' He took out his passport. 'Look.'

There was something depressing about having to show your passport to prove who you were.

I said: 'I don't think you can be a Namibian.'

He took this as fighting talk. 'Why can't I?'

'Because you're not African; only Africans can be Namibians.'

He said: 'We've got a good constitution. It says anyone can be Namibian.'

I said: 'Honorary Namibian, just maybe. That's about the best you can be. Party's over, so are we.'

He was hurt, so he made the speech that began: 'But I belong here …' and went on – and on.

Large white men telling you with tears in their eyes how much they love Africa; it's a cloying, it's crap, and, worse still, they mean it. There is also usually anger buried in this claim, maybe because these lovers know that the beloved doesn't give a toss, never thinks of them, and may well loathe the sight and smell of them.

'On the other hand,' Dieter went on, 'you can't blame them for hating us. We Germans in Namibia, we don't have such a good record. They're touchy. Very touchy. I don't blame them, not at all; we have been very, very bad. In the old South West Africa, it was a killing ground. Look at what we did to the Hereros in 1904. Our troops, under General Lothar von Trotha, they shot tens of thousands of them. There, in the Waterberg. Well then, what can we expect? We killed; they died. Now they're the boss and we must pay.'

It was true. But that didn't make it, any of it, less awful, or Dieter's mewling any less sickening. He didn't need to explain who 'we' and 'they' were. Of the horrible passage of whites through Africa there was no doubt. It did not matter whether they were British or Belgians or French or Germans, the pattern was the same: contempt followed by mass murder. We had moved from the era when foreign Europeans shot locals at will to the time when white Africans spend their time apologising. Homicide to homilies, rope to repentance.

But it came too late. Worse, it came from the wrong people. Those who did the damage never felt the lash of hatred from their newly liberated serfs, never indeed ever came close to imagining that they were not wonderfully bright, kindly, superior beings appointed to rule over savage children, to correct them where possible, and shoot them when necessary. Never failing to affirm, as they caressed their whips or oiled their guns, how much they adored Africa... while Africa went on hating them, and since that hatred needed a target, we were it. What whites were left would carry the can. Like the Anglo-Irish, we had gone into other lands and stayed, settled, almost believed we were at home; and like them we were wrong: wrong people, wrong time, wrong place.

Among the pictures in my mother's knitting basket was one of her old dad. After the Boer War, and long before he had become Chief Explosives Officer for Corner House Investments, my grandfather, at a loss to know what to do next, joined the British South Africa Police. They were a kind of African Mounties. He is seen in pith helmet and puttees, carrying a Lee–Enfield, posing on the battlement of a great stone pile called Namutomi, a mock-medieval castle, with stone turrets and towers, erected in the bush by Germans with baronial delusions, dreaming of Bavaria and mad King Ludwig. The South Africans captured the castle in 1915 in the invasion of German South-West, and my grandpa is on his horse, wearing a long dust coat, and a bandolier and his high-domed solar helmet that makes him look like a smiling shuttlecock. He was there because of talk of insurrection amongst the defeated farmers whom he had fought beside all through the

Anglo-Boer war. But of course (and herein you may read the entire mad saga of the white man's walkabout in tropical Africa) under that funny hat there was a considerable killer who learned his trade in the first modern war that set the tone of conflict in our time – when peasant farmers took on the greatest army on earth.

And a story.

I believe – you could not have had a mother like mine without believing it – that nothing became the Boers as much as the way they fought to right that wrong. And nothing, before or after that event, ever breathed so much as a hint that they might be capable of such heroism. Until they chose to take on the British Empire, they had been the usual hooligans, oozing the usual bloody stupidity.

'Give us jobs, not work' was their cry. 'Proper jobs, jobs that let us do nothing but sit here feeling superior.'

But they did it: they went to war and they damn near pulled it off. Only the slow deaths of their wives and children in British concentration camps made them see at last that their enemy was prepared to wipe out the entire tribe if that was what it took, and decreed a painful surrender. And so there arrived the next 'new' South Africa. This time round, it was led by Jan Smuts, and the 'new' Boer leaders who would march us into a fairer future, at the point of a gun if it came to that. Which it did. The 'bitter-ender' Boers who had never accept-ed the new South Africa saw their chance when the Great War began, and dreamt of revolting. Last time around they had lost by a whisker. Now they would drive the hated enemy from the beloved country. And everything would be the same once more, only better!

The bitter-ender Boers had a prophet, Niklaas van Rensburg, and he took a peek into the future, and foresaw the end of the British Empire in the looming clash with Germany.

'Fight the damned khakis, kill them, and freedom is ours,' the Prophet told the rebels. 'The hated imperialists will crumble to dust and the glorious destiny of the Boers will flower once more.'

The Germans agreed with the Prophet but they took a higher tone. They told the Boer rebels that the *zeitgeist* was with them; history was working through them to destroy the oppressor.

This was their plan, so hopeless it makes me weep: while the accursed English were busy fighting the Germans, the Boer rebels would rise up and seize back their lost republics and the freedoms stolen from them. The Transvaal and the Free State would be theirs once more.

Was there ever a people with such a gift for thumping, self-destroying bullshit? It sounded terrific, until you thought it through for about a split second. The glorious destiny of the Boers, in the main, consisted of sitting on their backsides, on their distant farms, drinking coffee, bestirring themselves once in a blue moon, just enough to kick their black serfs. But now they rose in rebellion, and South West Africa became the cockpit of war. The British destroyed their free republics, robbed them of gold and diamonds. Now they would strike back. For a while raw joy surged: they had guns in their hands once more.

And everything conspired to ensure they fucked up.

This time round these farmers weren't facing the British: they were riding into war against fighters from the same tribe, they were fighting brothers, born-again modern Boers, who ran the government, the army and the country. They were fighting the 'new' South Africa.

Such was the insanity of our people that among these ruined sharecroppers, these bedraggled fighters, there were those loopy enough to believe that they could fight and win the Boer War a dozen years after it had been lost.

Although the men who ran the 'new' South Africa were not British, they were now firmly on the side of the Empire, tolerance, democracy and liberal values. They might once have been great Boer leaders but now they were determined to be statesmen; and they were not in the least sentimental about rebels. My grandfather's old comrades-in-arms, Jan Smuts and Louis Botha, were not going to dally with a bunch of bearded backwoodsmen who didn't realise that times had changed. Like all hot converts to a faith they once loathed, these New Men were more merciless than the old enemy when challenged by traitors. A rebel was a rebel, and a rebellion must be put down.

And so it was that Joe Healey went to fight the very men for whose cause he'd once blown up culverts in the veld. He may have dynamited every railway bridge in the Free State for the Boer cause, but he had no illusions about these dour, disapproving, sly, cruel, left-behind stepchildren of the trek.

Ah, South Africa... what sublime idiocy...

My mother also kept in her knitting basket, amongst the needles and balls of wool, a photo of her father with the prophet van Rensburg. The Prophet's beard is long and white; he has a blind stare and a sallow, seamed face. My grandfather is dapper; his moustache is spruce. Both men hold out stubby lengths of wood in front of their chests, each with a crosspiece, like the hilt of a sword. The two men are playing a Boer sport called *kennetjie*, using a length of broomstick as the bat, on which is balanced a small piece of wood that serves as the 'ball'. What you do in *kennetjie* is to loft the chip of wood into the air and see how far you can hammer it with your club.

That's more or less what happened to the renegade Boers of South West. This was South Africa, history did not reveal itself without a police escort, and the sort of *geist* that inhabited our *zeit* you wouldn't want to meet in a dark alley. Lives counted as little as scraps of wood, and what history did with the rebels was to toss them into the air, heft its truncheon and knock them clean out of the yard.

In the early 1950s we flew to South West Africa every week. I must have been about seven or eight, and we stayed with Uncle Hansie. Uncle Hansie built a *Schloss* in the desert, a mini-version of Namutomi, and he was the representative for Porsche in Windhoek. Though only in his thirties, Hansie was greying prematurely but elegantly. He had a silver beard, silver hair, silver suit, silver car. Uncle Hansie would accompany himself at the piano while he sang 'Die Schöne Müllerin', and my mother would be very taken, and slap him hard on the back when he finished, so that his monocle dropped from his eye like a fat, surprised tear.

Uncle Hansie was for me the closest thing to Europe I had come across, his dark oak dressers stuffed with books, gilt lettering on their blue spines – Goethe, Schiller and Thomas Mann. Uncle Hansie was the only man I knew who proudly kept, on the walls of his bedroom, a row of perhaps a dozen pictures of young women wearing no clothes at all, and seemed quite unashamed of it, and who was married to a Herero princess.

Another uncle; another airfield; another thread in the family tapestry; another ludicrous episode in the lives of the whites who went to Africa and, monumentally, got it wrong.

Did I know Namibia? Did I ever.

What do you say to those who have never been much further than Hamburg or Windhoek?

They were drawing down the blinds and putting on the movie. This was the old route of the flying boats, more or less, but we were about six miles high, in a cabin pressurised and slumberous, and outside the portholes the frozen dark rushed at us, like the future. And Dieter, the Namibian, slept, his book cradled in his lap.

The movie screens in the cabin flickered with the smiles and cries of a pretty actress pretending to be a poor unmarried *chocolatière*, with a pretty child to support; pretty girl falls in love with a pretty young man pretending to be a gypsy, on a pretty film set pretending to be France. It all had not just the gloss of artificiality – that would have been merely tiresome – but the brazen Hollywood lie that everyone will, sooner or later, simply have to believe, and beamed this one-eyed fascism into the brains of the slumbering hundreds, belted to their seats, eyes and mouths open, like dead mackerel in the blue half-light of the flying tube.

Outside my window there was nothing to see but the dark. We did not need to see where we were going. What did it matter? We knew where we were heading; it said so on our tickets – Johannesburg – and we shot towards it like a bullet.

17

Flying into Jo'burg, the swimming pools hit you first: thousands of blue eyes winking eerily out of the dun, dry veld. Then a sheaf of skyscrapers ringed by mine-dumps, yellow hills of pulverised rock that once held the gold Jo'burg hugged to its stony heart. At the outer edges of the sprawl were tell-tale smudges, so well hidden below the smoke of a thousand cooking fires that only a forensic racist – of the kind we were all raised to be – could identify them as the foot and finger and heart prints of those who built and worked this town: row upon row of tiny brick boxes that were the townships, squatter camps and shanty towns where most Johannesburgers were hidden.

We banked over Soweto, home to the heroes who fought for freedom but from where – Koosie told me – anyone who could run was leaving as fast as their pay cheques allowed, heading for the green and shaded ghettos of the northern suburbs whose names echoed the identity crises of those who told themselves how truly African they were: Killarney and Sandton, Rosebank and Morningside, Houghton, Blairgowrie and Rivonia... Once upon a time, the swanking mansions in these wooded enclaves had been exclusively home to those who called themselves 'Eur-pee-ons' or 'Wharts'...

Beside me, Dieter yawned, stretched, closed his Rilke and said, 'Af-ri-ca!' Then he went off to the bathroom, and came back wearing khaki shorts and bush jacket.

What was it about landing on the continent that addled the brain?

Af-ri-ca!

Those must be the emptiest three syllables ever coined. A menacing prayer that passed for patriotism from Cape to Cairo, the sort that said: if you love the place, reach out and hit someone.

The queue was long; the passport officers at the far-away desk were slow. Dieter yawned once more, he stretched, he smiled, and he wrapped his arms around – nothing. 'Good to be home,' he said. Again, the urge to exude, to expand, to flow outwards, to embrace the warm body of Mother Africa. It was powerful, this urge to merge – it had been like that perhaps since the first white man set the first white foot on the continent. Indeed, maybe most white life in Africa was down to footwork; white feet walked from one end of the continent to the other, stamping new names on a place that already had plenty of its own, and then white feet kicked the natives around.

In the days of the crazies, Johannesburg Airport had been one of the prime misery holes; famously, prodigiously gloomy; the departure lounge commanded by surly white officials: a place from which a thousand exiles flew out on one-way exit permits, stripped of their passports, never expecting to return.

The big thing long ago was to drive to the airport on Sundays to watch the planes taking off. Most of everything else was forbidden. It was Jo'burg's way of desecrating the Sabbath.

Guys sitting up on the airport roof for hours. Watching the big craft taxiing out for the sheer exhilaration of knowing they were going somewhere when everything else insisted we were going nowhere, and when it felt like just about everything else was banned.

Then, for a short while, after the former owners of the country retired, the airport was a joy. A new army of black officials had arisen, and blotted out the memories of the past. Black passport control, customs officers, cops: all the new people buzzed; it was utterly charming.

But the strain of autonomy got too much. Tempers shortened, the shine of the new dulled into indifference, a feeling of 'Well, if this is freedom, now what?' When it became apparent that the answer to that was 'Nothing more, just much of the same', tempers grew shorter still.

Dieter was ahead of me. At the desk he handed over his passport and the immigration officer showed how little she liked him, in the way she turned the pages, in the frown that ruffled her clear forehead, in the careful way she touched the lapels of her crisp white blouse. She scorned him and she showed it and it made him flustered. He spoke very good English but he could not understand what she was saying, or rather why she was mumbling into the air, a foot away from his right ear.

What took place between them was not just a dialogue of the deaf between a German man in khaki and a petite black woman in gold shoulder flashes, but the dance of the blind. She talked right past him; she wanted to know how long he was staying in South Africa, she wanted to see his ticket for Windhoek, and his return ticket.

Dieter kept saying, 'Zorry? Zorry?' and cupping his hand to his ear as if to capture at least a few of the words she tossed in his direction. Because he really was sorry: sorry he could not understand her accented English; sorry she was giving him uphill; sorry that a man with love in his heart and Af-ri-ca! on his lips, a farm in Namibia and a perfectly good passport should be treated in this way.

Dieter saw himself as a regular guy who paid his taxes and kept a flat in Hamburg. But to the passport officer there was so much wrong with him she barely knew where to start. He was a throwback to the bad old days. He was too sure of himself. He had property and money and had spent many years in Africa. She saw him for what his passport said he was: Namibian. Other whites who passed before the officer came from Germany and Spain and Italy: real countries, proper countries, countries they would go home to. They weren't pretending to be at home in Africa; they didn't wear safari suits and present the passports of neighbouring states; they did not belong the class of pale, aging orphans who called themselves Zimbabweans or Kenyans or Congolese but were quite clearly some inferior form of settler trash, not merely redundant but probably dead broke, adrift in a black continent. Frankly, they were an embarrassment.

There were probably further reasons for her disdain: South Africa was a hot destination for people fleeing their own fucked-up countries, guys forever trying to jump the border illegally; and that included whites from Zimbabwe and Namibia.

So she didn't like him, any more than she liked visitors from the Congo or Chad or Guinea, or any of the no-hopers from north of the Limpopo. It was pretty clear from where I was standing that she didn't like her job either.

Dieter was still saying 'Zorry? Zorry?' when, suddenly, like a gale that stops blowing, she abruptly lost interest, and waved him through with a long, lingering yawn.

He took it personally, I could see that by the way he went off reproachfully towards the luggage carousels, every so often throwing an angry look at the officer's impervious back, looking for all the world like a rejected and angry lover.

But, then, what did he expect? He'd landed in the new Jo'burg; if the old depressed the hell out of you, the new took off the top of your head. Arrive anywhere in South Africa after the granite years of racial obsession and chances are you'd step into a place recently vacated by officious lunatics.

At the luggage carousel Dieter was talking to himself. 'Fucking stupid black bitch,' he was saying as he hauled his Louis Vuitton bags off the conveyor and dumped them on a trolley.

I could see Dieter was getting the hang of it again. He was remembering where he was. I said goodbye with a lighter heart. By the time he hit Windhoek he'd be just about his old self.

I walked out into the concourse, brushing off a posse of porters, noticing how architecture and advertising have now become the way to give South African life the face-lift every-one wants to see, a kindly, 'we love each other' look. Advertising at Jo'burg International tells every new arrival how we are in this happy land where people of every shade and hue and gender, the gifted and the disabled, meet, mix, make love, drink beer and talk all day long on our cellphones; devoted to becoming caring, confident, competitive sports stars.

The girl at the Hertz desk, round, vivacious and dressed in bright yellow, like a lively lemon, opened her mouth and spoke to me in what must be one of the queerest accents in the world: pure Jo'burgundian. The tone came from the small space left when the tongue was lifted towards the back of the palate, squeezing and releasing the words with a twang that reverberated in the nasal passages in a distinctive whine that foreigners found excruciating, but which, if you were born in this town, was deeply moving.

The Hertz girl said simply: 'Hullo, howzit? And where d'you get in from, then, hey?'

'Malaysia.'

'Ma-a-la-aysheeaah!'

It was my mother, all over again, her incredulous, faintly irritable what-where-above-all-*why*? melody. It was strange how these things affected you: suddenly, I wanted to weep. Suddenly I was home.

The Hertz girl lifted her hand with the keys in it, like a benediction, and she said in her quavery singsong: 'Have a great stay, enjoy your day, take care ...'

The blessing of a car-hire company was not much to go on, but this was Jo'burg and under the circumstances I'd take anything I could get. In the shadows of the parking garage I sat for a moment in my rented red City Golf, smelling of leather, wax, plastic and, faintly, of the lavender fragrance used to wipe the dashboard, and I thought, Why move? I'd happily stay, right here, safely cocooned. It was the temptation that always accompanies the beginning of a journey, the deliciously subversive demon that whispers, 'Well, then, why not turn back now and never start at all? Climb out of the car, go back inside the airport, take a plane out of here, and never be heard of again. Get out, go back, but above all, don't go on.'

But I was back now, and I had to pretend to be part of the place. That's the traveller's paradox. When you don't belong anywhere, you're forever putting down shallow but precious roots. No one digs in as fast as true, homeless wanderers. Drop them anywhere and it's not two minutes before they're pitching a tent, setting up shop, acting like they've been there for ever. They're incorrigible settlers: they'll settle for anywhere, or for anyone, the way lost children want to tie up with any apparently benign adult who happens along.

I drove out into the sunshine, air bright with that jagged highveld glitter. I drove towards the preposterous skyline that is Jo'burg, Joeys, Jewburg, Egoli, Josi, J-town, Gauteng ... not so much names as aliases. The four-lane highway wound towards central Jo'burg. The locals called it Death Road. Lined with factories, shopping malls, rubber factories and, here and there, the hard-baked, biscuit-blond hairy shoulders of an old mine-dump. The road from the airport was littered with low-browed slit-eyed concrete bunkers, built in the seventies and eighties, when the old fascist regime and its business lackeys loved penitential office parks.

Our god, though, was not business: he was bullion, buried dark and deep, but always there when you went looking for him. My grandfather had blasted him out of the surface rock. Now you dropped nearly two miles underground in search of the plunging reef, plummeting after him: taking two lifts, dropping 11,000 feet in just eight minutes, to land in Hades, tiny passages, slime lapping your ankles, temperature up to 115 degrees, and rising, kept just about bearable by piping in miles of iced slush, and huge air-con plants. You cannot have gold without air-con: a fact that did me no harm at all in the years I sold systems to the mines. I would make the pilgrimage, rather like my granddad did except he set charges, turned up the heat to force the great god to show his face. Mine was a secular mission, I went into the underworld to cool things down. You are locked in a cramped oven, crawling on your belly, two miles of rock overhead until, in the torchlight at the end of the tunnel, a slash of red paint says, yes, hallelujah! The scream of the drills biting into the rock, the squeak of the thigh-high boots the miners wear. This stone had what you sought. Here you would set your charges, blow open the rocky tabernacle that held the sacred spirit then winch eight tons of debris to the surface, and crush it, scour it with cyanide, all to win an ounce of ore.

Every year cost more blood for less bullion: once this town mined over two-thirds of all the gold in the world; now it was down to one-fifth, and you found it where it was deeper and darker and hotter – three miles down was the latest thinking, if we could keep the air-con going and the iced water pumping.

To this deity we were fiercely loyal, and gave our souls.

When I was growing up the mine-dumps rose above the city, bright yellow hills looming above the slime dams, depositories of the cyanide sludge discarded after the gold had been pulverised from the ore-rich rock. The dumps were local landmarks; they were the only hills we had. Scrubby grass like fierce stubble grew over their crests. For decades no one gave them a second thought. Then some bright spark reckoned there must still be some gold in all that sand, tiny scraps of ore they hadn't extracted first time round, so they began carting them away and rummaging through the sand a second time.

Each time I came back, there were fewer gold mines and more casinos.

When I'd lived in Jo'burg, there had been rules to stifle anything that moved. From raffles to reproduction. Everything was off limits. Except rugby and race phobia. If you had to ask, the answer was almost certainly 'No'. We were locked inside a mad preacher's tent, called white South Africa, and what was remarkable – no, horrible! – was what happened in the tent. Nothing happened. Zilch, *nada, niks*. And no one wanted anything to happen. Happenings were subversive. Happenings happened somewhere else. Happenings were the fault of crazies, blacks, Jews, commies, pinkos.

In other places when you get too many rules you sometimes get lively disobedience. Not here. South Africa was rare in that as a country it was both dead in the head and inert below the waist. Whites were so timid, so abject, so gutted by years of the old fascist rubbish, they asked permission before passing water.

Two BMW convertibles, red and blue, left and right, came screaming past me, neck and neck, hoods back, hitting two hundred, and I swear one guy had a mobile phone glued to his ear. The Jo'burg earring. They called it 'dicing', this high-speed racing. Dicing with death. The ultimate game of chance. It was, I suppose, the new equality, this risk-taking, and whether you did it on the roulette tables or the roads, it was still very Jo'burg. In this city, playing sudden death wasn't a game, it was a serious career move. It was like playing the stock exchange; casinos just had better-looking brokers.

Jo'burg was proud of its new casinos. But, then, people who made this town have always had an identity crisis, they never knew which to build first: pleasure palaces or police stations. Were they going be screwed or arrested? Jo'burg suffered from the urban equivalent of bi-polar depression, swinging endlessly between a lust for fun and the desire to lock people up for having a good time. It resembled the greedy king who was punished for his love of gold by having molten metal poured down his throat. The difference was that the king died; Jo'burg swallowed all the gold you could pour down its gullet, but came back for more. Jo'burg did not have a destiny, it didn't have an identity; it did impersonations. For a while it got ideas about being a financial centre. It was going to be London in Africa; then, for a while, after democracy arrived, and hawkers took over the streets, it dreamt of being an African city; but Jo'burgers who had never been anywhere in Africa got to take a look at places like Lagos or Harare and the idea died: why go from gilded bordello to fly-blown wreck? But, at last, with the coming of the casinos, it believed it had discovered its true vocation: Las Vegas in the veld.

I dropped down the exit ramp into Motortown, past the old Carlton Centre. To build the place in the late sixties, they had to excavate a fifteen-acre hole. Those razzle-dazzle boys, the mining houses, put up the money and gave the place its semi-religious aura. The papers ran all the usual wanking headlines: 'SA Leads World In Big Holes' ... 'First Kimberley, Now Jo'burg!' Jo'burgers told each other they dug holes faster and deeper than anyone in the world. The Carlton hole was big enough to swallow the Empire State Building (if melted down). The tower that rose from it was fifty storeys high, the tallest concrete building in the world. It contained shops, restaurants, pavement cafés, movie houses, an ice rink and a hotel so luxurious only the super-rich could afford its silver cutlery and linen napkins.

I drove past the hulk of the Carlton, Jo'burg's own *Titanic*, sunk for years now and unable any longer to disguise its profound lumpish ugliness. All that energy, that wealth, that chutzpah reduced to an island of dereliction; the hotel shuttered; the ice rink melted; the silver cutlery sold off; and even the pistol-toting guards who used to accompany what few brave guests still came to the Carlton on daring shopping expeditions in downtown Jo'burg, long since laid off. An eerie wreck of a place: beggars, hawkers and the homeless seethed around the deserted tower. It was now just another of those tall buildings left behind when the rich moved northwards to the gated suburbs, leaving behind a shell-shocked city, all the landmarks still in place: the Standard Bank Building, City Hall, Park Station. The city centre still went through the motions, working by day, but eerily empty after hours.

Across the Queen Elizabeth Bridge and into Braamfontein, the news headlines flapping on the billboards sang old, remembered songs.

Paraplegic Kids Mugged
Corpse Applies for Pension
Puppy Milo Breathes His Last

The peculiar blend of the horrid and the humdrum, a bluesy fatalism that was very Jo'burg. The words changed, never the tunes.

I was home.

18

Fourways Clinic was large and cool and hushed, with blue-tinted windows, palms and a parking lot glossy with fancy coupés. At the desk they asked me to wait because my mother was seeing her minister.

A few minutes later I was directed down a short broad corridor smelling of beeswax. A large priest in a short cassock that showed his grey flannels was walking toward me, talking to the ward sister. He was white, dressed in black, she was black, dressed in blue, and both were round and big, like boulders. Now they rolled down the corridor towards the lifts where I sat with my back to the Coke machine. He reminded me of a wrestler. It was the way his hair was cut, the big muscles in his neck. He wore around his neck a red stole edged with gold and carried a small silver box. I guessed it had held the host, which meant he had been giving my mother the last sacrament. He was shockingly young. My mother had been a sucker for air force pilots in the war, and in later life she took to priests – maybe because they combined spiritual authority and uniforms.

He tossed the stole over his shoulder like a scarf and shook my hand.

'I know all about you. I'm an old friend, Father Phil. I'll be along again to see your mom a little later. God bless!'

The ward sister said to me, 'You're waiting to see your mother. Go along, then.'

She was in a ward with two other women, and lay propped up on two stiff white pillows, a TV monitor overhead. Her white hair spread out on the white pillow made her face stand out as if cut from stone, her chin square and firm, her blue eyes bright. The blue and the white gave her a vaguely nautical look, like some old sail-boat laid up in dry dock. She looked well – strong even – and it was really only her hands, bunched into fists, still beside her, and somehow smaller than I remembered them to be, that spoke of declining physical power and, perhaps, of pain.

A notice at the foot of the bed warned: 'Nil By Mouth'.

She blinked hard and looked at me the way she did when I showed up, pleased to see me but certain I must be in trouble or I wouldn't have been there. If I wasn't in trouble, well, I soon would be.

'Good golly. What on earth's happened?'

She raised her eyebrows at the two women on either side of her as if to say that, well, one had sons, they wandered off to some very strange places and they returned without warning and what was one to do?

I said, 'Hullo, Ma,' and bent down and kissed her.

We sat for a while, holding hands, and then she threw this daggery look at the two silent women – 'Just reminding you,' the look said, ' that this boy is capable of anything, but don't blame me, and don't say I didn't warn you.'

She said, faintly, accusingly, 'I thought you were away, some-where far away.'

'I was in Malaysia.'

She looked at her two friends and raised her eyebrows and coughed, embarrassed at this confession. The next question she did not speak, she signalled.

'Well, if you were in Malaysia, what are you doing here?'

'I was headed this way, so I stopped to see you.'

She said: 'This is Mrs Blum and Mrs van Niekerk; they have been very nice to me. This is my boy. He goes off at the drop of a hat.'

Mrs Blum's powdery skin was creamy and her hair was bright gold. Mrs van Niekerk was smooth as caramel and her hair was hidden beneath a bandage. Mrs Blum was brown and Mrs van Niekerk was white; they both wore pink nightdresses and had an air about them – something funereal. Or let's just say that they knew why they were there. I had left – left my mother and my country – and since my mother had no one of her own to watch over her, they'd taken the job and they felt slightly aggrieved that this Johnny-come-lately had turned up and claimed her, just like that, out of the blue. They had seen it all before. They knew all about vagrant children. Who didn't? All over the country were aging parents whose children had gone away to far-flung places.

Of course, this was not new, there had always been exiles. But the number had built steadily in the years I'd been travelling, and the diaspora could be divided into different layers.

There were, to begin with, what you might call the ur-exiles – most of them white guys who got the hell out in the twenties and thirties because the place was narrow, boring and distant, and legged it to Europe; lost their flat accents, turned into refined English poets or fascists or scientists or ballet dancers.

Then there were the exiles-of-shame who left in the fifties

and sixties, who had gone into such deep cover that all traces of a connection with the land they'd left had been hidden. I'd be in Bolton or Slough and – bloody hell – there was a Bloemfontein lawyer, or a Cape poet, so deeply embedded among the natives that no one guessed where they came from. And they weren't saying either: the fear of being outed as one of the new Nazis was there.

Then came the angry exiles of the seventies, guys who hung about under grey European skies: Pan-Africanists, Marxists and Nationalists, wating for the revolution to happen, who might have given up had they not been kick-started back into life and hope in the mid-seventies by the angry young kids who got out after the Soweto uprising, kids who loathed the effete old revolutionary guard, and got them off their arses.

Most of these had gone home in 1994; home to the ministerial job, the mansion and the Merc.

But oddly enough when the old regime collapsed, a wave of new migration began. Young men. Being pale and male in the new South Africa was a loser's ticket. You were not wanted on the voyage. But abroad was cool: better dough, bigger cars, more fun, zero guilt and no one hitting on you for your colour.

Most of those leaving were professionals: doctors, lawyers, engineers, nurses, and teachers. Entire snowy towns in Canada were serviced by Afrikaans medics on the run, who worshipped at their own Dutch Reformed Church and said 'Jislaik!' when surprised, and ate *melktert* after the *braaivleis* – even when the mercury dropped to 30 below. Others settled in colonies in Australia, around cities like Perth, occasionally pining for cold Castle beer and dreaming of Mrs Ball's Chutney. London and the Home Counties were thick with them; they colonised entire neighbourhoods, implanted *boerewors* in deepest

England, and Tassenburg wine; sticks of black biltong swung like fly papers in butchers' windows in Chiswick and Ealing.

These new expats were intensely patriotic, and unlikely ever to return. The flowing green of the new national flag flashed from their car bumpers, and medallions bearing the face of Nelson Mandela swung from their car keys. They talked loudly on the Tube, alarmed the locals by going barefoot in public places, and became misty-eyed when they heard '*Nkosi Sikelel'y i Afrika*'.

One thing drew them back home, unexpectedly, briefly, from Birmingham and Boston and Azerbaijan, blinking in the dazzling highveld sun, slightly sheepish, slightly guilty, slightly – let's face it – foreign. They came back when a mother sickened, or a father died; they came back *in extremis*. For a last-in-a-lifetime visit.

So, no, it wasn't Mrs van Niekerk and Mrs Blum who were the angels of death; it was people like me.

Mrs van Niekerk put her hand on my arm. 'I want to tell you how very, very proud we are of your mom. There is a dreadful nursing sister who thinks she's the bally bee's knees; doesn't she, Kathleen? She's been awful to us. But your mom told her where to get off.'

'And she called your mom a stupid white bitch,' said Mrs Blum.

'I thought she was going to take a swing at Kathleen, she was so cross!' said Mrs van Niekerk.

'We are proud of your mom,' said Mrs Blum. 'Kathleen is a person we have got to know very well.'

My mother had that light in her eyes that told me she had been making waves somewhere and it had done her good. But before I could ask her what it was, a nurse arrived and I caught sight of the trolley outside the door. This time it was a white nurse and the air was heavy with a sense of what had gone before.

'Time for theatre, Mrs Healey,' said the nurse in soft tones that were kind and apologetic.

My mother nodded, then she sighed. We all waited, uncomfortably. At such moments the predominant mood was one of fear mixed in with embarrassment at all that could not be said. Just as I was wondering if I'd ever talk to her again, she found her voice.

'Just a tick.' She gave her old smile of hellish delight. 'D'you remember my wig?'

'Yes, Ma, I remember. From Monrovia.'

'Yes. Well, one day I may want you to give that wig to Koosie. Would you do that?'

'Of course.'

'He's been phoning me: wanting to make amends, I think. Or to save me from jail. I guess I scared the daylights out of him.'

'You did the same to Jake Schevitz.'

My mother sniffed slowly. The degree of disdain in that long intake of breath was deep.

'Poor old Schevitz. What a fall was there: a burnt-out firebrand. A wet, a *woes*, a schlemiel! I wanted something very simple, very elegant. You would have thought I'd asked for the earth.'

She looked straight at Mrs van Niekerk and Mrs Blum and said simply: 'I wanted to get married, to a young doctor. From Havana.'

Perhaps then it began to dawn on these new friends that Kathleen was, after all, not someone they knew at all.

She had us all now, even the nurse.

'We bought a ring, my Cuban boy and I. We took it with us when we went to see Schevitz. But instead of helping, he read me the riot act. Can you imagine? Fat lot of good he was. If I'd wanted a sermon, Alexander, I'd have gone to see Father Phil.'

She turned on the nurse. 'Now, my dear, I am ready.' She gave her pantomime aunt pout. 'Into thy capable hands does this old biddy commend her ridiculous body.'

I sat in the waiting room, an open space at the end of a corridor, between the lifts and the Coke machine, and studied the notice-board to which was pinned a tourism poster that used a montage of zebras, Zulus and Table Mountain to push the line: 'South Africa – the World in One Country'.

To the left of the lift doors someone had stuck a handwritten notice ending in a line of formal capitals: 'It has come to our attention that certain staff are failing to meet their roster times. If this continues, fines will be levied on latecomers. YOU WILL PAY THESE FINES!'

I wondered about those capitals, the tone of the warning. It sounded like bluster, couched in new words which made everyone equal: no sex, no colour, please – we're new South Africans ... But I knew who was talking to whom. The writer of this warning wasn't at all sure that 'they' would pay the fines. Maybe 'they'd' tell him to bugger off. And there was nothing anyone was going to do about it because these days 'they' ran the show.

Of course, there were always some who bored on about common sense and logic. Who decided – God save us – to be sensible; who said some things would stay the same because they had to; who insisted that there were facts, and facts would not yield to political manipulation; that two and two always made four, and germs spread disease. These methodical madmen said that if you ran a hospital you ensured the staff turned up on time, made the beds, washed the patients, opened the operating theatre punctually.

Plain facts, inexorable logic. Such rules stood to reason, and they had nothing whatever to do with skin colour and they would be followed. But this was South Africa: nothing followed and *everything* had to do with skin colour. If you were black or Asian or mixed race or white, you brought with you your colour, your historical baggage, yourself.

I guess about two hours passed in these reflections, then, suddenly, the matron in crisp blue and white came in and asked me to see the surgeon.

There is comfort in quiet professionalism. The surgeon was a small shy man who managed to communicate his helpless distress at knowing the facts but being unable to do more. He did not waste time, he did not equivocate.

'The cancer is very large, very aggressive. All we can really do is to make her comfortable. We're putting her in a private ward. You can see her when she wakes.'

I knew she was dying and he left it open to me to say so or to ask him to confirm it, and he would have done so. But I didn't need to ask.

The matron walked me back to the waiting room and I asked her about the trouble between my mother and one of her nurses.

She did not flinch. 'One of our nurses was changing your mother's dressings and your mother called her "my girl", and told her not to be clumsy. The nurse responded in an unprofessional manner.'

'What did she say?'

'She said she wasn't a servant. If your mother spoke to her like that she could change her dressings herself. At least, that was the gist of it.'

Not quite. I could hear her. 'Can't you be a bit more careful, you silly woman!'

And the silly woman would have said, 'Who are you to talk to me like that? You stupid white bitch.'

I never knew my mother pay a smidgen of attention to skin colour, but she didn't pull her punches, and she never hesitated to attack. And my ma would have said: 'If I wasn't feeling bad, I'd knock you over, my girl.'

She wouldn't have been bluffing either.

The matron said carefully, 'I want to apologise for the behaviour of the nurse.'

'I'm sorry, too. My mother can be sharp.'

'Your mother is ill, she's our patient. The nurse was rude. Your mother is in our care; it's a question of being professional. We do not allow rudeness to patients.'

We looked at each other. We were speaking for the people we came from. We were, at the same time, putting aside the fact that she was black and I was white. We didn't believe saying sorry changed anything, but we apologised anyway. The situation required smoothing falsities. Nurses shall be professional at all times no matter what the provocation. Put that in capitals and pin it to the notice-board beside the lifts, and it still rang false. Then again, knowing something wasn't true generally meant we had to start believing it.

19

It was towards early evening that she began coming round. She didn't open her eyes but she suddenly said: 'Give me your mitt.'

We sat there for a long time, holding hands. She'd try to say something but the anaesthetic kept knocking her back. Her breathing was heavy, her hand easily covered mine, and I saw in the V between her thumb and forefinger a vein pulsing fiercely. A transparent bag filled with clear liquid was suspended over the bed; a tube ran into her arm and skipped to the tune of her pulse.

Then she seemed to wake because she said, suddenly, clearly, with this fine smile: '*Hecho muy bien, Kataleen!*' And I knew she was dancing in the back room to Raoul's mambo music ...

I put my lips close to her ear. 'What did you do with him, Ma?'

She opened her eyes and looked at me as if she wasn't really sure who I was.

I said: 'It's me, Ma.'

'Yes,' she said, 'I think it is.' But she didn't sound too sure.

'Where is the Cuban, Ma?'

She opened her eyes wide and her grip on my hand was strong. Then she began to talk, slowly, clearly, with such pleasure, interrupting herself now and then to shake her head or laugh or sigh. But mostly to laugh. It wasn't so much that she was telling me: she was telling herself the story because it thrilled her.

'When Koosie turned me down, I was flummoxed. Then I had a thought, a tiny thought. I remembered something Papadop said when he brought Raoul to me. He said there were millions of Zimbos around Jo'burg without proper papers. And there were lots more who had the correct stuff. So I asked myself where in Jo'burg a person might get hold of the correct stuff and the answer had to be Hillbrow, because you can get just about anything else you want in Hillbrow: girls, guns, gold. So I got in the car, and in Kotze Street, outside a chicken roastery, I saw this guy. He had about four cellphones round his neck as well as a lot of gold chains, and red trainers, and a white shell suit, and he was leaning up against the wall. I just had a feeling about him so I asked him where I could buy some ID papers for a friend. Just like that, straight to the point, no beating about the bush. I didn't even bother to keep my voice down.

'Such a charming guy, even if his clothes were a bit odd. He told me his name was Chinaza – it means "God answers my prayer" in Igbo – how about that! He came from a place called Ogbelle in the Niger Delta. What a surprise. I've flown that Delta more times than I can remember. Snails the size of soup plates, and lots of red snapper. Big fish eaters, the Delta people. They call it bush up there but it's really rainforest; waterways, swamps; sometimes the mangroves can hang two hundred feet above the floor of forest: they're like cliffs on either side of the wings when you drop down to land. It was a tricky thing, putting down on water. I liked to sight on the fishermen in their dugouts for depth reference but I often landed a bit long and had to use reverse pitch to pull up.

'Chinaza told me that fish was not what most people lived off today in the Delta. It was all oil up there now; big orange flares burning day and night, helicopters and oilrigs. Lashings of money in the Delta but no work. So he came south, and hit Joeys. He explained he didn't actually do identities. He did stimulants and substances. Any kind of powder I cared to purchase. But if I was after paper, not powder, I needed a paper man.

'Chinaza took me to a house in Yeoville, to another Nigerian, with lovely brown eyes. He was a top paper man. And so courteous. "Your wish is my delight," he told me. He had helped hundreds of people. All I had to decide was did I want to borrow or marry? Or did I want a "Newborn"? If I borrowed, that meant I got the use of the personal particulars of a living person. He'd arrange to marry Raoul off to some genuine South African without, of course, her knowing the first thing about it. Or, if I liked, he could give him a new name, a new life, and make him a Newborn.

'Well, I didn't want to borrow, and I didn't like the idea of Raoul being married, even if his wife would never know. So I went for the Newborn option. But I also wanted him to stay a doctor. This country needs doctors. No problem, says the paper man. I can make him whatever you like: doctor, lawyer, professor, whatever the client wants. He needed four passport photographs, five grand in small denominations, notes no bigger than fifty bucks, a new name and date of birth. And if I told him which medical school I'd like my friend to have attended he'd throw in a perfectly good diploma, ready framed ...

'Such service!' She squeezed my hand. 'Don't you love free enterprise, don't you love the energy of immigrants?'

She photographed Raoul, stuffed the cash into an envelope, and went back to Yeoville. One week later, her Cuban had his papers: his driving licence, his birth certificate and his passport. Raoul Mendoza vanished into plain view. She had turned her Cuban medic into a new South African, with a very traditional name, an Afrikaans name. He became Dr Cornelius du Toit.

'His friends will call him Connie, you can be sure of that. Letting him go wasn't easy but it was best, for him. He's free. I opened the cage and let him fly.'

And he had flown to freedom, like many thousands of others – Armenians, Russians, Thais, Mozambicans, Zimbabweans, Congolese, Syrians, Chinese, Arabs – all busily buying, acquiring, assuming, stealing or borrowing. In a word, achieving citizenship. It was only right, when you thought about it. It was really the fulfilment of a very great lack. After all, there had never been any true South Africans: right from the starting whistle the term was no more than a convenient form of shorthand, when it had not been a sentence of exclusion. It was a nationality so baggy, so amorphous, and so phoney, it was ready made to fit just about anyone who tried it on. It was made to be stolen, or borrowed.

I reckoned Raoul would be OK. How could he fail? These Newborns, so recently transformed into South Africans, were likely to wear their new identities with more assurance and authority, ease and enjoyment than any of the bloody indigenes – white or black – who really hadn't the first idea what it meant to be anything.

I was pleased, though, she had made him Afrikaans. To turn him into one of the former racial rulers was a master stroke. If she was going to give him a start in life in the new South Africa, the last thing a decent Cuban needed was a whole lot of liberal angst and ineffectual grief. We – this dwindling band of fugitives – were leftovers from the silly idea that parts of the world were improved by mere Anglo-Saxon presence. This had been not only sentimental but shortsighted. What counted was what always counted for all invaders, settlers and colonists, if they were not to be wiped away for ever like some invasion of pubic lice – firepower: it secured their presence and their loot and their legitimacy.

But of all the invaders our lot seemed to have been the scrapings. Not for us the clear directive: 'Tell you what, go out to X, exterminate the natives, inherit the land like the Yanks, or the Ozzies, and you'll be laughing.'

No, for us it was more like, 'You lot are bloody useless, can't find work, can't feed yourselves, can't cross the street unaided. So here's a free passage to Africa – where you can pretend to be important.'

So we off we went, and the rest was history. We became marooned ex-sailors or failed farmers in a place where we were not prepared to work, or kill, with sufficient energy. We were never even a tribe: the best we managed was a kind of B-team. The sort of people who'd rather be murdered in our beds than make them ourselves.

The story of Raoul's transformation into Connie had tired her. Her eyes were still closed, and she hummed a snatch of a tune I recognised as '*La Faroana*'.

'Promise me something, dear boy.' She was twisting the sheet with her free hand.

'What is it, Ma?' I took her other hand.

'I've fixed things.'

'What things?'

'All my things. Everything's fixed — but you make sure. Will you?' Her grip on my hand was urgent, almost frantic.

'Make sure of what, Ma?'

'I need you to find them.'

Her breathing was ragged. I did not know who 'they' were so I said, hoping to make her feel easier, 'I'll find them.'

It seemed to be the right thing because she let go my hand, tried — and failed — to snap her fingers, and then said softly: '*Mambo, qué rico el mambo!*'

Her breathing was more and more difficult. She seemed to be choking. I wanted to tell someone, so I stood up very quietly and had got almost to the door when she suddenly opened her eyes and looked at me, as if this was the first time she'd seen me.

'I thought you were in … Malaysia?'

I went back to her. I tried to sound easy, 'I was, Ma, but I had to pass this way so I stopped in to see you.'

This time I knew it was me she saw. But her surprise sprang, I rather think, not from my sudden turning up — she was pleased, yes — but from her own success.

She was fighting to speak and yet I heard the contentment in her reaction.

'Lordy, Lordy, how you get about!'

I found the duty nurse and told her abut the choking and she asked me to wait in the corridor. The faint nightlights ran like blue glowing mushrooms down the passages; the doors to the wards opened and closed with a swish. I studied the patient lists pasted to the glass windows of the night matron's cubicle. The VIPs were identified by initials only: Prince X from Zululand was in post-op; His Excellency, President of Y, and

His Excellency, Prime Minister of X, were to have nil by mouth; a Lebanese named Khoury, a diamond dealer described as Zairean, was in for observation; and his bodyguard had requested vegetarian meals; my mother was listed as Ms Healey – Kathleen, PILOT. I liked that.

When I was allowed back into her room she was deeply asleep and they had put an oxygen mask on her. The bag above her bed began to turn pink. When the night sister put her head around the door I pointed to it.

She said softly, gently: 'It's blood; it means her kidneys are failing.'

The oxygen eased her breathing. She seemed almost fine. Her size, her solid bulk under the blankets, the peace of her sleep, all of it flew in the face of what I knew. The bag above the bed was a warning flag, darkening all the time. From the road outside came the rush of traffic and, further off, police sirens; familiar Jo'burg night music. Her breathing was steady. I leaned back in the chair and closed my eyes for what I thought was no more than a moment, and when I opened them, her eyes were open, too. It was very quiet in the room and the bag was filled with deepest red.

I called the night nurse, who came and checked her pulse and sighed and said: 'You've been very good; I am so sorry.'

I looked down at the bed and saw my mother, unchanged. But what I saw, too, was the gap, the place where she no longer was, and it was immense. It ran not just from one end of my life to the other, it reached from the tip of Africa to Egypt, from Zanzibar to Mombasa. It was as hard to think of her as dead as it was to think of clouds passing away, or of dead air. It was like seeing Gulliver pinned to earth. Pinned down only at the edges, like some enormous kite, or the pelt of some great animal, pegged to the far corners of the continent where she touched ground; at those points where her friends, her quarrels, her landing strips pulled her to earth. But mostly she stayed aloft, her life was spent high, the billowing spread of her sailing overhead.

The night sister said: 'This is painful, but I am going to do something now.'

She lifted my mother's hands and slid the rings from her fingers. Then she opened the drawer of her bedside table and took out her glasses, her purse, two strings of pearls and a prayer book, and gave them to me.

'We prefer not to leave these here. I think you should take them with you, keep them safe.'

It was one of those things I heard often enough. A belief expressed rarely in public, perhaps only in deepest privacy, or *in extremis*. A statement that both speaker and audience understood would be absolutely denied if reported or challenged. The night nurse, who was black, spoke to me as a professional, telling me in the code of the place that if the rings, the cash, the pearls remained when the staff came for my mother's body, when they took her down to the morgue, these things might vanish. This was another truth she was sad about but there it was. People were not well paid and it was best not to leave temptation in their way. Her statement answered the question I did not ask: did that mean they would rob the dead? Damn right they would. Hatred and anger, poverty and a lack of power, the arrogance of rich white bastards who ran the world and ruined the continent conferred the right to rob them blind, alive or dead. The old advertising slogan beloved of South

African tourism that boasted of South Africa – 'The world in one country' – was just a word short of being dead right: we were the world war in one country.

III   Last Rites

'Life is life and fun is fun but it's all so quiet
when the goldfish die.'

Bror Blixen

20

I drove home as dawn was breaking slow and pink over the East Rand, a sky of crisp highveld colours so delicate that you do not so much see them but taste them, running your tongue over the cool grey edge of the early breeze and the damp red earth. In this quiet time, the city glinted like dodgy jewels in an outstretched palm, or those fake watches hawkers flashed on crowded streets. Like all the contraband that made this town.

I swung up past Sandton Centre, through Illovo, then Rosebank. On the pavements, in wooden hutches, night sentries were knocking off, stamping on their fires, shaking out their blankets at the foot of the high walls that hid the houses from the world. No town had built more walls or built them better. Tall, beautiful walls of brick, terracotta, plaster, of dressed stone and steel; tipped with spikes or high-voltage wire, studded with closed-circuit cameras, bright with the hoardings of rapid response teams, flying paramedics, neighbourhood watch and guard dog patrols ...

The roads were empty, briefly free at this early hour from the anxieties of the armed hijack. Usually, this was a matter of pistol-toting thugs demanding the keys to your car. And then shooting you, lest you identify them. This was not only callous but unnecessary as the inability of the police to catch hijackers was almost as legendary as the robberies themselves. Hijacking happened so often that only celebrity victims made news: a well-known chef shot and paralysed; a neurosurgeon abducted and murdered. The boss of a gold mining company gunned down and left to free-wheel down the road till his Merc hit an overhead bridge, and someone reported what looked like an accident.

The early headlines were on the lampposts, singing the songs that made the music of the place: that morning it was a real lulu ...

'School Hall Stolen'.

I drove up Jan Smuts Avenue and turned into Forest Town. It took me some time to locate the right keys in the bunch I had found in her purse. The house was quiet and dark. I walked in through the porch where my mother used to have tea with the Rain Queen. In the sitting room, on the old stinkwood desk, sat the collection, in blue leather covers and gilt letters, of Cassell's *Great Stories of the World.* There were three small snaps of me as a child of about two, sitting in a small car, my hair done up in a kiss-curl; at ten, I was pointing a toy rifle at the sky. At around twelve I was seen with my first kill: a gemsbok in the Kalahari. My foot rests proudly on the dead buck's skull much as a boy might rest his foot on a ball. There were no other hunting pictures of me; I lost interest after that. I preferred Cassell's *Great Stories* and I grew up in other lands, on other terms. That never pleased her much; she had little patience with bookish people.

'Africa', she liked to declare, 'does not need readers.'

I went over to the map of Livingstone's journeys, traced in

rashes of red stipple which always reminded her of 'a lost ant stumbling round several big drops of water'. The big drops of water were the Great Lakes, a favourite destination when she was still flying: Lake Victoria, Lake Albert, Lake Edward.

Below the lakes were these lines from Livingstone's journals, copied out in green ink in my mother's looping script: 'There is no law of nations here. The weakest goes to the wall.'

On the floor beside her desk was a wooden box: about nine inches wide, and a foot deep. Someone had addressed the box in bold black ink:

> *To: Prof. R.A. Dart*
> *Dept of Anatomy,*
> *Medical School,*
> *Hospital Hill,*
> *Johannesburg.*
> *Contents: Skull*

The other sides of the box carried a warning:

> *Contents Very Fragile*
> *Handle With Care*
> *Stow Away From Boilers*

She told me that this was the very box that once held the skull of Mrs Ples, 'an Australopithecus lady who lived near Jo'burg about two and a half million years ago, probably a close relative, far closer to us than the apes.'

The box she used for housing her collection of Congolese stabbing spears.

On her desk was a letter from her old friend from the Kenya hunts, 'Testa' the Argentinian. Testalozzi had been such a hit with the women in Nairobi, and had hunted more of Africa than any man. Testa hunted the two Rhodesias, Kenya, the Sudan, Bechuanaland and Barotseland, where he specialised in black-maned lions. He married an Italian contessa, only to witness his mother-in-law taken by a croc in the Zambezi, and he finally cleared out when rebels in Chad hit his camps and killed his trackers, his dogs and his wife. He now ran an African safari park in the American west and wrote long sweet letters of which this was the last:

'Africa has stolen my heart and buried it in the African bush as surely as Livingstone's was – except that Livingstone was dead before it happened and mine was buried still beating ...'

Bamadodi, the Rain Queen, proud on a wooden throne, in one of her wildly coloured knitted crowns, bright zigzags of pink and green. The photo was inscribed: 'To Kathleen, from her friend Bama.' Hemingway with a shotgun; Schweitzer in a pith helmet; various smiling moustachioed pilots standing beside Hurricanes and Spitfires and Lancasters; and assorted uncles: Uncle Hansie from South West and Uncle Dickie from Kenya, Uncle Bertie with assegai, Uncle Papadop, Uncle Manny from Nyasaland; and the twin uncles Ronald and Rupert from Uganda; my mother in flying helmet and goggles and scarf at the controls of her Stinson, somewhere over Africa.

And the many pictures of a hunting life, taken in the 1940s and 1950s. Each location had been noted and ranged from the Kalahari to the Congo. My mother beside a buffalo, elephant, bongo, duiker or lion she had just shot. Her face grave and reposed she sat astride a huge croc, a river behind her, rifle across her knees. Or fording a river with a string of porters.

Here she was towering beside a tiny pygmy in the Ituri forest ...

There was something haunting about these pictures of the kill, something primal but also absurd: the small live hunter, the big dead beast; and to stand, as she did, looking neither greedy nor silly nor bloody, but simply sedate, required a degree of unselfconsciousness that the world had long ago lost.

My mother after a kill is a being in a state of happy repose. She is no longer thinking of the hunt, she is happy to have done what she planned and now she is ready to be off again. Somewhere, out of the picture, her plane waits to lift her up and away. She cares utterly, passionately for the sport of the moment, but when the hunt's over she will not give it another thought.

Grainy, creased, fading snapshots, yet I could see quite easily the muscle of her forearm. She was colossal but feminine to a fault, a wisp of dark hair blown free of her pith helmet, which she would not tuck back but kept out of her eyes by every so often giving it a little puff of air, which made it fly up on to her scalp and lie for a while before beginning to fall once more.

And from the locations of these safaris you could have drawn another map, which would have said as much about my mother's Africa as her map of Livingstone's ant-like wanderings around the Great Lakes. He was propelled further and deeper – into what? For Livingstone, said rational people later, looking back at his feverish wandering, the goals were Christian conversion, commercial opportunity and potential colonies for England. But, really, to me his travels seemed the wanderings of a lost man, grimly going mad.

What propelled my old lady, I rather think, must have been the feeling of immense space. Venturing into it, crossing it, looking down on it, spotting game from the air or simply finding a suitable landing strip or a sufficiently long stretch of water to land a float-plane. Above all and everything the feeling that it was empty and all of it belonged to her. Every one of the countries she had felt at home in was something else now, and all the people in the pictures were dead or displaced. And the space had never been empty. One had to allow for the possibility that her travels had been an even greater folly than Livingstone's.

Maybe white incomers were condemned to redraw the map of Africa in their own likenesses; the punishment for having it all their way was the obligation to reinvent it. From their very first arrival some demon blinded them to the real place and made them believe in their empty maps. Africa for them was, literally, Africa *à la carte*. Perhaps that was why, when asked where she was at home, my mother puzzled over the question. She knew what she was: she was a South African from the Witwatersrand, the daughter of a settler. She regarded Jo'burg as her city and the greatest metropolis south of Cairo. But all her life it seemed to me she resisted the suffocating trap of that identity. Resisted, yes, but I did not believe she escaped it, because where we came from identity was destiny.

In one of the few formal photographs on the wall she sat in front of a group of women dressed in white robes with green sashes. Everyone is smiling, but stiffly posed, like a class photo. These were the Zoo Lake Zionists, a local choir. Back in the bad old days, the black choir had not been permitted to sing in the Zoo Lake grounds since they were reserved for whites only, and so the ladies rehearsed in our back garden on Sunday after-noons, and elected my mother their life-long patron for letting them do so – until the cops closed us down after an anonymous complaint. Anonymous, though everyone in the street knew it came from our neighbours, Mrs Terre'Blanche, Garfinkel, Smuts and Mason, in the form of an unsigned note pushed under the door of Parkview police station.

The note read: 'Mrs Healey's got a bunch of Bantus in her garden – every Sunday – yelling their heads off…'

She received an official summons, a fussy piece of creamy paper commanding her to appear in court for 'for disturbing the peace by permitting a Bantu Vocal Assembly to foregather on suburban premises in contravention of the health and safety regulations of the City of Johannesburg'.

She had it framed. This document was a beautiful case of the bullshit that passed in those days for meaning. If you translated 'foregather', it meant in Jo'burgese 'a fucking bunch of fucking blacks is fucking cluttering up the fucking back yard and fucking yelling their fucking heads off'. But 'foregather' went down on paper because no one ever wrote the way they talked, any more than they ever said what they meant. The phrase 'health and safety' was another flashy number meant to pump up self-esteem, but it had nothing to do with hygiene or security: it referred to the divine right which not only permitted but encouraged whites to use any means – boots, guns, dogs, jails – to keep blacks down and out of sight. As for the 'City of Johannesburg', that fatuity rang oddly in a mining town recently descended from a mess of threadbare diggers' tents and vermin-ridden shanties inhabited by hucksters, whores and highwaymen. But, then, the actual words Jo'burgers used, when they used words at all, were so curt, so ball-breakingly stupid, so in thrall to muscle and might, that no one has ever had the heart or the guts to reproduce the few dozen grunts, cuffs and bellows that passed for the everyday patois of this town, preferring instead the florid lies and airy legalese of my mother's creamy summons.

The signs of her departure a few days earlier, after she had phoned me in Kuala Lumpur, were evident: her bedroom neat with its water-colour of Stanleyville, the masks from Guinea and the kudu skin on the polished Oregon pine floor. And in the bathroom, her nylons hung neatly to drip-dry over the bath. Everything of her was there but herself.

My bedroom was untouched. She must have known I'd come home: the bed was made. Someone had been working in the house and garden, I could see that. Life is so sad that sometimes you can't help smiling. What option did you have?

I made myself a cup of coffee and went back to the living room and sat down in the blue rocker, facing the blank TV. Her chair. The house empty made an even stronger statement than it had done when my mother was alive, when she'd be sitting in her blue Dralon chair, with her knitting on her lap. On the wall, the Rain Queen watched me with dark and beautiful eyes.

And on a hook, right next to the Queen – a fall of bright orange foam – she had hung the wig. You might say she died dreaming of wigs. Not your normal hairpiece, the sort of thing you would see in some hairdresser's salon or theatre, but a Day-Glo blood-orange fright-wig of the sort kids wear at Hallowe'en. This one had belonged to a kid – with an AK 47 almost as tall as he was, who fought in Liberia, in the children's army of a man called Prince Johnson. His picture was on the wall next to the wig. He leans on his gun, like a staff. He is about fourteen, perhaps, and his eyes are red-rimmed, and it's not camera flash. Oddest of all, he is wearing a wedding dress.

I was in Hanoi at the time the picture had been taken. It was 1991 – June – and very hot. I was staying at a hotel called Le Colonial, not far from Hoan Kiem Lake, and I had been spending time at the Ho Chi Minh Mausoleum where they were thinking of renewing the air-con in the chamber of the little mummy who lay there, his wispy beard making him look rather like a blanched prawn.

One day when I got back to my hotel, the desk clerk gave me a message, scribbled on a piece of hotel notepaper.

'Off to rainforest – back soon – Ma.'

She didn't say which rainforest; I thought, at first, she must have meant the Congo because I knew she was particularly concerned about her friends. In the early 1990s the civil war in eastern sections of Zaire had got bad, and some soldiers, convinced the pygmies were magical non-humans, had taken to eating them.

Rainforests are not easy places and yet I knew she would have gone alone. She was by then at least seventy-five, and the news was alarming.

That was the idea.

Did I do anything about it? Certainly not: there was nothing I could do when my mother reached out towards that visionary destination she called 'Africa'. This sort of thing happened increasingly as she got older and I roamed further. But this was one of the most compelling of her messages I received, as I kept moving around the world.

My mother's hunting techniques were based on shooting large game. She was at heart an elephant hunter and elephants are sociable beasts and move in groups, usually an old bull and plenty of females. African elephants stand some thirteen feet high and weigh anything up to six tons. They don't see too well but they have a very acute sense of smell and fine hearing. So keeping downwind is essential; the slightest deviation will mean they get your scent, even up to half a mile away. They are also very smart; perhaps, with the exception of ourselves, the most intelligent animals we hunt. Elephants will come to each other's aid: most hunters killed by an elephant are killed not by the animal they're hunting but by an ally who has waded into the fight. It is always dangerous. You also need to get up close: forty yards or less.

The classic kill of an elephant is the brain shot but it is difficult and best left to professionals. Always take your first few elephants with a heart shot was my mother's advice.

The brain of the elephant, though about twice the size of a human's, is deeply buried in bone and spongy protective cartilage anywhere up to two feet thick, and a shot from a small-bore rifle that misses will simply result in the elephant bolting, not much the worse for wear. The wound will heal pretty quickly, too. There is also the risk that if you're using a high-velocity gun, say a .375 or a .404, your bullet, instead of travelling straight along its ordained path, may strike some obstruction and alter direction and hit something, or someone, on the far side of your target.

As my mother liked to remind me: 'I've seen men shot, fifty yards on the far side of the elephant, by a bullet that changed its mind ...'

She also liked to point out that bulls are particularly tricky. Because even when well hit, they can stay on their feet. 'I once put three .700 nitro bullets into a big bull up in Northern

Rhodesia, and they were damn good shots, and he still wouldn't go down.'

Quite so.

When on my trail, and within range, she alternated shooting strategies: sometimes she tried for the brain; sometimes she went for the heart. The rainforest caper, when I was in Hanoi, was a head shot. She knew it would intrigue me. Even more than it worried me. She knew I'd want to know why she was in a rainforest, and which one she was in. She wanted me to care, she wanted me to share her excitement, her sense of adventure, her hunting talents; she wanted me to be *there*.

I wasn't. I resisted and rejected it. I thought her love of the place, of Africa, was absolutely, inextricably tied to various forms of murder, large and small, and I did not see it as a sacred vision, a cause, or a victim to be saved. Neither did I see all of it as a natural extension of my own back yard. And I thought of those who did as willing collaborators in the killing game.

This scepticism led to differences between us, which were not resolved. It has been suggested to me that the succession of lovers my mother took over the years was an attempt to make up for the love she never had from me. There might be something in that. But what we get back to, as always, is this: you've only to look at the direction of the links between my mother and her lovers to know that they needed her, not the other way around.

And this was the case with the boy who was to become the youngest of her far-flung adorers. Was there anyone not bowled over? Because she loomed so large, she felt so close. It was an optical and an emotional illusion. Her lovers longed to cross the gulf of their own yearning. Distance was essential to admiration.

As it turned out, it wasn't the Congo, or the pygmies, that had taken her off. It was the Liberian rainforest she had in mind, and she got there via Sierra Leone. In the old days she'd have flown herself but this time she took a commercial flight to Freetown and then rented a four-wheel drive and headed over the border into the Guinean rainforest and on to Sinoe County, South Eastern Liberia.

But when I learnt this it didn't much help because I knew she no longer hunted. At seventy-five she could not be sure of her aim.

'Always shoot for the spot – never at the whole animal – as any professional will tell you. And I don't see too clearly, and my hands shake.'

What then took her to Sinoe?

I guess it was the preservationist in her. Like many hunters, she believed passionately in shooting animals, and she believed just as strongly in seeing animals prosper: it's a difficult position to maintain but one she held with her usual equanimity, as she did with positions that had what she felt were real African dimensions.

Sinoe was where she'd once hunted bongo and elephant back in the fifties and sixties, when she'd known the late President Tubman, of whom she had fond memories.

'He was a crook, but he was a gentleman crook. When he died, things fell apart. Liberia was founded by freed slaves from America, who had no sooner been freed than they enslaved every local Liberian they could find. Naturally the locals rebelled.'

I'll say.

President Tubman died in hospital, and after that things went downhill fast. His successor, President Tolbert, was murdered by Master Sergeant Samuel Doe, who became President until Prince Johnson killed him. And from then on, everyone tried to kill everyone else.

It was into this mess that my mother had stepped. Her concern for wildlife in Sinoe was misplaced. At that time Liberians were so given over to human slaughter that the animals came off OK. But the fighting was another matter, and she had to leave the rainforest, only to find there was no way back into Sierra Leone. So she pushed on towards the capital, Monrovia, on roads choked with refugees and corpses and soldiers hopped out of their minds on whatever they could find. She was planning to get a ship out.

It was outside Monrovia, a place called Chocolate City, that she met the Small Boys' Unit headed by a kid called Washington. Roosevelt Washington was about fourteen, or so he thought. Two-Ton Terror was his *nom de guerre* and he was dressed in shorts, a filthy Bob Marley T-shirt and a bright orange wig. He carried the usual AK 47 slung over his shoulders in the manner of a broomstick or a spear.

'Always approach an AK butt side on,' said my mother, in one of those pieces of advice I hoped never to need.

Washington and his 'battalion' of skinny, highly armed, hungry kids mobbed my mother when they saw she had a camera.

'Take me, take me,' they kept yelling.

Washington's nails were painted ivory and worn long.

'Why ivory?' she asked.

'Because it goes with my dress,' said Washington.

'You wear a dress?'

'Yes ma'am, I fight in a dress.'

He went off and came back wearing a wedding dress and his orange wig; he also carried a small handbag.

And that was how she photographed him.

'They were smashed,' she recalled later. 'They had been drinking cane powder, which is fermented sugarcane juice spiked with gunpowder.'

That's what accounted for the red-eye in the boy in her picture.

The boys were fighting for Prince Johnson and they were commanded by a guy known as the Bare-Assed Brigadier because all he wore were sneakers when he led the boys into action.

'When I met the Brigadier he was properly dressed, and quite open about this methods. He told me: "Before leading my troops into battle, we would get drunk and drugged up, sacrifice a local teenager, drink their blood, then strip down to our shoes and go into battle wearing colourful wigs and carrying dainty purses we'd looted from civilians. We'd slaughter anyone we saw, chop their heads off and use them as soccer balls. We were nude, fearless, drunk and homicidal. We killed hundreds of people, so many I lost count."

'It took some getting used to, dear boy. I read somewhere that he became a preacher later, did Brigadier Bare Ass.'

When Prince Johnson killed President Doe he had the events videoed. Copies were being hawked by the boys on the road to Monrovia, and Washington said it was known locally as 'With or Without Pepper Sauce'. Did she want to buy one? All proceeds to the Small Boys' Unit.

The video came home, along with the fright-wig. It makes difficult viewing.

Doe is naked to the waist. Tied up and badly beaten, he begs Prince to loosen the ropes. Prince Johnson sits back while his face is mopped by a female aide and pulls at his beer. Then one of Doe's ears is hacked off.

In the video you see Johnson expanding in importance. Heating up. Whoever wants power must fill space and grow heavy and important and obtuse. He puts on suits and turbans, tunics and swords, and then rolls over and crushes the poor sods beneath him ...

In Africa, it wasn't that the emperor had no clothes; quite the contrary: he was the only one wearing any.

Prince Johnson always denied he'd actually murdered Doe. He told a journalist who approached him later, with all the right degree of reverence and horror modern political power demands:

'I captured the late President Doe and held him until he was pronounced dead. I still say he committed suicide.'

The terrifying respect that rode on the title 'the late President Doe' was one of the most grisly features of failed leadership across Africa. The 'late Pres' in this case having been captured and tortured, remained a man to respect, and talk of with care, even when you had cut off his ears and eaten them. Or did Prince Johnson force Doe to eat his own ears, and his balls – as Washington insisted – 'with or without pepper sauce'? That was the question the red-eyed troops of the Small Boys' Units of Chocolate City asked, and to which there was no answer. But, of course, to look for answers in the execution of the late President Doe was to mistake its purpose.

I saw later just how far ahead of its time that film was. It looked ahead to when we would become consumers of cruelty. Once again, Africa has showed the way. From the first hominid sucking marrow from the splintered tibia of his neighbour to the latest reality TV. It was not about providing answers; it was about providing a new form of entertainment: murdering a real man in real time in front of the cameras. And where Liberia led, the world sooner or later was sure to follow. Earless Samuel Doe, bleeding everywhere, and dying on camera, told us that the gap between showing and doing, between cinematography and killing, was shrinking fast, and the day was coming when the murder and the movie would be much the same thing, with or without pepper sauce.

She had left the back yard as it was, overgrown and remote, but there under a loquat tree, in what used to be called a servant's room, I came across him.

He said: ' My name is Noddy, sir, and you are Mr Alex.'

Clarity is helpful when you're mourning. Death is a loss, yes, but it is very confusing: you're cut off from someone you relied upon; the anchor has gone and you drift. You are the one who is lost.

His name was really Uthlabati, and it meant 'Man of Red Earth', but he preferred his other name.

He said: 'I work for the madams, sir. I am Noddy of the Five Madams. Madams Healey, Terr'Blanche, Garfinkel, Smuts and Mason. I do their gardens and I live at your house.'

I hadn't heard the term 'madam' for some time. It was a throwback to the old days and that, too, was comforting. He would have been Noddy of the Five Madams only when my mother was alive.

'She isn't here any more. She passed away this morning.'

'I know, sir.'

It was an expression of sympathy; it was also, I rather felt, a declaration of firm intent.

'Madam said you would want me to work for you.'

When I was a child, in one of many, many houses where we camped, we found a man living in the garage, and my mother kept him on.

'What else could I do? He came with the house.'

Now her house was mine. And so was the man under the loquat tree, and he turned out to be one of her revolutionary bequests that were to change so many lives. She had gone but I had taken her place. That made me the fifth madam.

Strange how things turn round: we become like our parents when we get older but we don't get older till they're dead.

21

The funeral was set for three, on a Wednesday afternoon, blue, and shining, and I was early. Rosebank Catholic
Church, on the corner of Tyrwhitt and Keyes avenues, was a
broad blond building with a soaring façade, and a police station
across the road. There was a sex shop on the corner: Lucky
Lovers, 'Everyone's Favourite Adult Entertainment
Emporium'. It sold inflatable Miss South Africas (in 'all shades
of our randy rainbow nation') and genuine rhino-hide whips
('taste the sting of Africa!'). A small thicket of penis enhancers
decorated the window.

I parked outside the police station. Close by I could hear the
girls of the Convent of Mercy singing the *Salve Regina*, much
as my mother would once have done long ago in her convent in
Boksburg, where her old dad had installed her when his trips
to distant parts of the continent took him away for weeks at a
time, and he couldn't keep a sharp eye on her.

On the hot tarmac yard of the cop-shop, a sergeant was
briefing a line of rookies on the art of shooting to kill. Several
ladies of the Zoo Lake Zionists' Choir, in black skirts and
white blouses and silver stars, were sitting patiently on the
kerb. I hugged Nandi and Rebecca and Makania and Grace.
Someone put his arm around my shoulder. It was Schevitz,
wearing a dark blue suit and a red tie.

No more than a month had passed since I'd picked up his fax in Bagan, and everything had altered: the Cuban was gone, so was my mother, and I could see from his face that he felt he'd failed her when she came to see him with her marriage proposal. His mouth, always slightly droopy, worked in a way that suggested grief but came out as rage.

'I'm sorry, Alex, boy.'

'Me, too.'

'I wanted to say: she came to see me just last week. Said nothing about our little falling out, and asked me to fix up her will. I didn't need to do much. It was all down on paper, neat as a pin. I shoved in the legal bits, had it witnessed and registered. Being your old lady, it has, let's call them "aspects". I'll explain when I hand it over. Can I drop by?'

'Any time.'

'I should've helped her with the Cuban crisis, and I didn't.'

'Don't take it hard. She saved him herself in her own crazy way.'

He wasn't hearing me. What came next was what always came next: fighting talk.

'I got it wrong, or I started out from the wrong place: thinking what was right for the law. I should've remembered it's humans that count in this place, the law is just rubbish, man! She knew that; I forgot that. She was on the side of human beings. Just because things have changed doesn't mean we forget who we were, and what we believed, and become other people. They say we should be reasonable and sensible and adapt; they say we must fit in with the latest dictates of the latest bunch of gonzos who've taken over this country. That isn't just shameful – horribly shameful – it's plain wrong. "We" won: that's their argument. So we're supposed to roll over and die. So what if they won! Does it make them right? Did it make the Bolsheviks right? Or the ayatollahs in Iran? It doesn't make them right! I'm pleased you're home, Alex, because I want to talk to you about the politics of power in our country.'

I didn't really want to talk about anything of the sort at my mother's funeral. I was glad when Father Phil came over, a Nike bag slung over his shoulders.

'Will you speak today?'

'I wouldn't know what to say.'

'If you don't mind, I'd like to say something. Your mom was …noble.' He held up his Nike bag. 'Now, I'd better shuffle along to the vestry and change into my togs.'

A small pale lady with a vague look came over and shook my hand.

'I'm Miss Dewar, your organist.'

She was calm and comforting, a professional who had done these things many times.

'I take it you'd want a mix of music, in the main?'

'Yes, please.'

'Your mother was a wonder. Such carriage. Shall we say a Catholic hymn or two? Some Bach? And something African? The Zionist ladies are going to do "Swing Low, Sweet Chariot" and "By the Rivers of Babylon".'

'Thank you.'

'Come along, ladies,' trilled Miss Dewar to the Zoo Lake Zionists, who stood up, brushed down their skirts and followed her into the church.

'Carriage', 'noble': good words, if a trifle ponderous. They missed, somehow, her essence. There was something about the way my mother held herself. Always tall, always straight. If I were to add another term it would be imperious, almost, but not quite, to the point of being overweening: it was a matter of bearing. Like some great schooner she skimmed over life, over lovers, over family, over Africa.

I would also add that she had no maternal instinct I ever saw. Now she was gone I faced a puzzle. I had to do my best to live up to the expectations of being, as it were, my mother's sole surviving child. But I felt a fraud. I didn't truly connect myself with the woman we had come to bury: Kathleen Mary Healey. I carried her name, she had brought me up, she called herself my mother, and allowed the world to believe so. And yet there was something lacking between us. Even assuming that DNA tests confirmed that I was her son, it was also, and nonetheless, a learnt connection, a role I had had to grow into. I loved her, in a helpless headlong way, as did the elderly men now turning up in numbers outside the church, some in berets and some in wheelchairs and some on the arms of nurses. The truth was I hadn't the faintest idea who she was. She pretended to be my mother and I pretended to be her son. In the end we both believed it, sort of.

Being lifted now with gentle care from the back of a new Mercedes SUV with Namibian plates was Uncle Hansie; and doing the heavy lifting was a tall Herero woman in tribal costume, and a diamond bracelet, and what looked like Gucci bag and shoes, who said to me: 'I am Veseveete. Please accept my condolences on your great loss.'

Uncle Hansie, more silvered than ever by the decades, smiled as Veseveete strapped him into his wheelchair. 'She speaks English, German and Herero, and it shocks the hell out of our political masters that she lives with me. Because we Germans once massacred Hereros, they believe it's wrong for blacks to speak our language. Alexander, the world is filled with fools. Veseveete is my last mistress. My last duchess. D'you know what Veseveete means in Herero? It means "Let them die for the good of the liberation ..." It commemorates the guerrilla war when parents gave their kids warrior names. Good revolutionaries always toss their kids into the bonfire of their good intentions. There is no crueller parent than a loving revolutionary. When Veseveete was five she was flown to a camp in East Germany to be trained as a little guerrilla. Then the Berlin Wall collapsed and, suddenly, in the old East Germany no one liked blackies any more. So they packed teenagers like her on a plane and flew her back to Windhoek. After ten years away they couldn't find her parents so there was a sort of auction for these unclaimed kids, and I bid for her. She was sixteen. Let me be honest: I liked her breasts, she liked my castle.'

'How is the castle, Uncle Hansie?'

He laughed. 'I am invited by the government to consider selling it to them. Willing seller, willing buyer. The invitation was delivered by five policemen with AK 47s.'

'Come on now, Hansie,' said the splendid Veseveete. 'You know that sort of talk will only upset you.' And she pushed him into the church.

'Goodbye, dear boy,' called Uncle Hansie. 'Your mother was a wonder. God bless her!'

Papadop was just pulling up in his old Datsun. Like him the car looked tired, out of date, out of luck. What struck me again and again about the whites of Africa, those still there, was how they'd aged, how little glamour was left. Once Africa was a doddle: now it was a mug's game.

He wept a little when he hugged me. 'I'm just this minute down from Zim. I miss her, boy. She was one of the best fellows I ever met.' Stooping close to my ear he whispered: 'D'you know what she did with our Cuban?'

'I do, Papadop. It was brilliant. Tell you later.'

'What's the seating plan?'

'You're in the front pew; it's for family.'

I watched him shuffle, sighing, into the church. The loss of good friends robs us of life.

I looked out for the Rain Queen; I was sure Bamadodi would come. Of my mother's feelings towards men I knew very little, but I knew she loved Queen Bama.

A hearse was turning at the corner of Tyrwhitt and Keyes, passing Lucky Lovers. The white-winged emblem was stark on the waxed black doors of the slinky limo: 'Doves' it said. It was one of my mother's old jokes: 'Storks brought you into the world; let Doves take you out.' The coffin was barely visible, lost under a foaming mound of flowers rising to the roof of the car.

I had run funeral notices in the *Star* and the *Sowetan*, asking that friends consider making a donation to Sunbeam Shelter, rather than send flowers. This had been done with malice aforethought: it seemed to me that by pelting those unimaginative creeps with unsolicited cash, I might piss them off as much as my mother's habit of hugging kids had done. My reasoning was this: an excessive and unexpected outflow of generosity was something they found hard to handle; fine, let them choke on unsolicited dough. But looking at the mountain of wreaths in the back of the hearse, it seemed no one had taken any notice.

Two black undertakers in morning suits were climbing out of the hearse.

'Excuse me, sir. You are the bereaved?'

'I am.'

'Mrs Kathleen Healey, late of Forest Town, she was your mom?'

'She was.'

'Thank you, sir; we must check.'

They began unpacking the great hill of flowers covering the casket and putting them on the roof.

'Sorry, sir. They're supposed to go on the roof to begin with. But we can't put them on the roof. Not while we're driving,' said the first undertaker.

'Why not?'

He seemed surprised at my question.

'Then what happens when we stop at the lights?'

'What happens?'

'We lose them. They can strip a car inside a few minutes.'

'People steal flowers from a *hearse*?'

'Sir, they'd steal the brass handles off the coffin, if you gave them a chance. *Eish*! This is Jo'burg.'

The second undertaker nodded hard. 'That's right. Over in Alex, sometimes they steal the coffin from the grave. They dig them up, and sell them second-hand.' He lifted up to his chin a huge bunch of lily of the valley: his face peered over the wall of waxy purity like some clerical imp in a dog-collar. 'You don't know about the slimmer's scam?'

'I don't.'

The convent choir in the school next to the church began singing the *Salve Regina* in high treble voices that sent shivers down my spine. Across the road in the yard of the police station the instructor teaching rookies how to shoot to kill was yelling at his men: ' Nummer wan! Never go into a crime scene without back-up. Nummer twooo! Remember: body shot beats brain shot, hands down!'

And so it was: while the police sergeant talked body shots and the convent girls praised the Queen of Heaven, the men from Doves told me of the slimmer's scam, and they were not mocking, not cynical, but carefully explanatory; they took me for a foreigner, and they wanted to talk about their city, about its habits and customs.

'What happens, sir, is like this: you find someone with slimmer's, right?' Undertaker One measured between his open hands, so close the palms almost touched. 'Someone thin, thin, thin. Like this, but who's got a bit of time to go, right? If they're too thin, then it's no good.'

'Unless you put them in a fat suit,' said Undertaker Two. 'And not everyone's got a fat suit; fat suits don't grow on trees.'

'This is how they do it,' Undertaker One continued, having allowed the point about fat suits to sink in. 'You take your slimmer to the hairdresser and you buy her new clothes and get her to look almost OK. And then you send her on a shopping spree to buy everything, everything, everything you tell her. On credit. Furniture, TV, you name it. And when it's delivered, you pack it in a lorry, pay her good bucks for food money, beer money, fun money – whatever – and you tell her: "Have a good time, enjoy yourself" and then off you go and you flog the stuff chop-chop. When the shops send in the bailiffs to repossess, it's all gone, it's walked: fridge, carpets, Hoover ... all gone.'

'So has the slimmer,' said Undertaker Two. '*Eish!*' He laughed in praise, in admiration, in disbelief. 'No one to arrest, no one to blame. That's the slimmer's scam.'

Into their voices there crept that note of astonished horrified pride this town inspired in its citizens.

The undertaker's men assembled a little trolley. 'We're taking Mom inside now, sir. Can you please stand here and watch the florals?'

I was watching the florals when a woman came over to me, with the controlled totter of a woman on very high heels, in a very tight skirt. She was somewhere in her late twenties, I reckoned, with dark hair and a complexion of pure honey. Her eyes were green and her fingers ringless. She was dressed more for a wedding than a funeral. A low-slung pink blouse, a very frilly hat. She rested one hand on the head of a boy of about seven. He had fairish hair and a flattish nose and a flattish face and I knew before I saw the slanting eyes that this was a Down's child. He carried a tennis racket, which he swished from side to side, and she had to watch him carefully, or he might have swatted a number of mourners.

'I'm Cindy,' she said. 'I worked with your mom at Sunbeam Shelter. This is Benny.'

The boy had the biggest smile I ever saw and he held on to my fingers after we'd finished shaking hands and he said: 'You play tennis?'

'I do.'

'Oh, let's!' Benny tugged my hand.

'Not now, darling,' said his mother. 'First, we're going to say goodbye to Kathleen.'

'Where's Kathleen gone?' asked Benny

'To Heaven,' said his mother firmly. 'Accompanied by clouds of angels.'

'Don't you mean crowds?' asked the second undertaker, loading wreaths on to the trolley.

'No, I mean clouds,' said Cindy with the air of a woman who knows her own mind. 'Kathleen hated crowds. Look at all the lovely flowers!'

'I asked people not to send flowers. I asked them to make donations to the Shelter. Looks like no one paid attention.'

She looked at me kindly. 'I'm sure they paid attention. Maybe they also wanted to give flowers.'

'I thought donations were best, even though they fired her.'

'I know. I worked there, too.'

'Yes. And when she was fired, she told me that you went, too.'

'I had to. She was my friend and what they did was bad.'

'Why did they fire her?'

Cindy screwed up her nose and shook her head. She had a beautifully balanced head, sitting on a shaft of neck. Very, very neat was Cindy.

'I think she had this effect on the kids. I think the management did not know what to make of it. Voluntary helpers had special tasks – like washing the kids, drawing, singing, painting – but your mom didn't do any of that. She'd start OK but inside two minutes there'd be this love-fest going on. They'd sit on her lap and cry or laugh or just sit, and she'd tell them stories. The permanent staff couldn't deal with it.'

'Why? What was so bad about it that they got rid of her? I simply don't get it. Actually, the whole business baffles me. I don't know why she did it anyway. My mother was not the sort to go around hugging anyone.'

'Perhaps she felt she had to. I don't know what the chemistry was, but you'd find her and some kid hugging the life out of each other. It happened all the time. It was like she never had any babies of her own and these kids had never had a mother.'

She looked at me reflectively, as if somehow along the road I had failed to provide my mother with the sort of huggable heaven she'd found in Sunbeam Shelter.

A chauffeur-driven BMW was pulling up and out of it got my old friend, Koosie. He looked elegant, if very thin. His tie was dark blue, his suit black, his chauffeur was white.

'Sad day, Alex.'

I said to Cindy, 'This is my friend, Koosie, Dr Nkosi, as he now is. I can't get used to it.'

Koosie shook her hand and said, as much to her as to me: 'There's a lot he can't get used to. It's something that maybe runs in the family.'

'I have a philosophical problem', I said, 'with forced change.'

Koosie said to Cindy: 'He means a political problem. About freedom.'

We stood there; it wasn't the time to quibble. Koosie and I fell out because he took a view of the world that I rejected. He was in power now, or close to it, and that messed things up. Worst of all was what it did to words. The big talk that followed liberation played hell with all the good old words. People talked of freedom when they really meant power. Power was what counted. And hot air.

Koosie said: 'I went into politics; Alex went into air-con.'

It was just as well the undertakers came back then with the empty trolley.

'We'll take the florals now. Thanks, sir.'

Koosie said: 'I'm sure your ma told you about our meeting.'

'She did.'

'What did she do with the Cuban?'

'He's fine.'

'I won't ask what that means. You tell me about it some time?'

'Sure.'

'Come and see me.'

'I don't feel good in government offices.'

'I'm not working right now. See me at home. In Soweto.'

'I've never been to Soweto,' said Cindy.

Koosie shrugged. 'That's OK. It's normal. About ninety per cent of people have never been to a township. But Alex here, he was named after one. Ask him to tell you about it. No – better – get him to bring you when you come to see me.'

'Can we please go and see Kathleen now?' Benny asked.

Cindy and Benny and I walked down the aisle towards the coffin, which was set on the third step of the altar, banked with flowers and patrolled by Father Phil in his emerald-green togs looking like a kind of holy scrum-half.

The organist was playing '*Panis Angelicus*', 'Bread of Angels', a curiously appropriate hymn. The outer skin of Rosebank Church was a golden biscuit colour but inside it was a lime-green meringue; the light filtering through the stained-glass windows was filled with motes of dust that seemed to sway in time to the organ. The Zoo Lake Zionists took over from the organist and gave us 'Swing Low, Sweet Chariot'.

'Where's Kathleen?' asked Benny.

Cindy didn't answer.

'Is she in the box?'

'Yes, Benny,' said his mother. He didn't look like he believed her and I didn't blame him.

Benny was right to be sceptical. My mother had been an escape artist. The coffin on the altar under its weight of cellophane, crêpe bows, notes, ribbons, lilies and orchids was like the pillow stuffed under the blankets by the prisoner who has fled his cell: a decoy designed to buy time.

My grandfather once said about her:

'Kathleen was like the wind. Tie her down with baling wire and she'd slip the knot like a lubricated rabbit.'

'Lubricated', I said, 'means drunk.'

He said, 'It does, when used of me. Then it means drunk, plastered, slammed. When used of your mother, it means slippery, gone in a flash, like greased lightning.'

From first to last my mother proved him right; and now, one more time, she'd slipped the knot. She was off and she didn't know where she was going. Neither did I: she hadn't filed a flight plan.

Benny said: 'Why's she in that box?'

'Don't point,' said his mother.

'Why?'

'It's rude. Look at these pretty flowers. Shall we look at the flowers?' said Cindy.

There were wreaths from the ANC: 'With deep appreciation ... Kathleen – Who Flew Many Comrades to Safety'. There were flowers sent via Interflora by uncles in Kenya and Umhlanga Rocks and America and Scotland. There were wreaths signed Siegfried and Llewellyn and Boetie, from men who wrote their messages in shaky ballpoint: 'Gone but Never Forgotten' and 'Flying High In My Heart' and '*Rus in Vrede Ouus*' and '*Hamba gahle*'. There were also tributes signed with the sorts of names people used when they wrote letters to the papers, denouncing the rape of babies and/or the lousy pronunciation of radio announcers: pseudonyms like 'Zulu Warrior', 'Lover-Boy' and 'Oscar–Romeo'.

I said, to myself really: 'Why don't they sign their names?'

Cindy raised an eyebrow. 'Secret admirers? Could be, hey?'

'But pen names on funeral wreaths?'

'*Ja*, well, no. But this isn't the sort of place anyone just comes out and says what they think. For ages no one signed his name to anything if he could avoid it. Where, if you asked the President a question at an election meeting, he sent the secret police round. Even today, when the President hears that rivals want his job, he calls in the secret service to suss them out. Not long ago, even reading things could be tricky. Everyone's been hiding for so long it's like a habit.'

'It still strikes me as pretty odd. A grown man signs himself "Love-Lorn of Cyrildene" on a bunch of lily of the valley, which he sends to a dead woman, and everyone nods and says, oh *ja*, that's how it is.'

Cindy shrugged. 'That is how it is.'

When I saw the ring of white roses with the simple message '*Hey Mambo!*', and I knew the Cuban had seen the funeral notice.

Even in her absence, there was more to my mother than most people dreamt of: she was large, she opened spaces, and the sheer range of mourners in Rosebank Church that day testified to a most unSouth-African breadth. In the front pew reserved for family I sat with Koosie and Jake Schevitz, Uncle Hansie and his mistress, Cindy and Benny, Papadop, who wept easily and quietly, and Noddy, the gardener, who came in last of all, and carried a Tyrolean hat with a rainbow feather.

And that mix was a pretty faint selection of the sort of wild richness she had relished all her life: a politician from Soweto, a Jewish lawyer, a German aristocrat, his Herero mistress, as well as an ex-Greek, a Jo'burg dolly-bird, with a sweet and ruffled-looking boy who kept pointing up to the dust floating through the candy-coloured light from the stained glass windows and saying: 'Look, it's clouds of angels!'

Behind us sat Mozambicans, Zimbabweans, Kenyans and Malawians; blokes who once farmed in Africa, then took the gap and headed 'Down South', leaving behind the ranches and fisheries, safaris, mission schools, forests and farms they once called their own, and loved to distraction.

How many of her friends found their way that day! There were even a few of the last old white hunters still in Africa, those who hadn't gone off to the States to open safari parks, where African buffalo and white rhino wandered under the American sun. There was 'Scrubber' Atkinson, who had once killed a leopard with a knife and had half of his face ripped off by the leopard's dewclaw and now wore a kind of highway-man's mask over his mouth which he lifted only to eat and drink; and old 'Slapper' Dewey, the gypsy hunter who, in his teens during the thirties, went hunting with the Prince of Wales; and 'Tick-Bite' Tallinger, who was said to have had an affair with Grace Kelly when she came out to film with Clark Gable; and Big Bill Bruma, who shot his brother by mistake when the bullet carried straight through the lion and out the other side.

Old friends from Stanleyville, and Salisbury, and Lourenço Marques; wraiths and shadows of their once huge selves, from town and countries that were, like them, sad phantoms. Once so sure of themselves, so secure, so effortlessly superior, so rich, so ruddy, so stolid it seemed nothing would ever shift them.

When I was a kid my mother used to take me the Muthaiga Club in Nairobi. I would sit in front of the fireplace and eat oxtail soup and listen to the hunting talk. The words: '*Na Kupa Hati M'Zuri*' were carved above the fireplace.

MAY GOOD FORTUNE FIND YOU ALWAYS ...

The high-pitched, reedy, lisping English voices calling for more champagne, talking guns.

'I was out near Makindu station, with Frenchy Du Preez. I had my .375 and I went for a brainer. Hit the buff well, but a touch high because he came at us like a bloody locomotive. Next thing: blam! Frenchy's big .500 blasts, right next to my ear, and the buff goes down like an oak, not two feet from me.

'Careless, Alfie, very careless ...' was all that bloody Frog said. Talk about *sang* bloody *froid*!'

My mother once pointed out that, before independence, whites hunted widely across Africa; after independence, whites were widely hunted, and often shot. Odd how many died violently.

And she'd reel them off: John Alexander, Dian Fossey, George and Joy Adamson ...

And she'd say: 'At least they're dead, and not living on, like Beryl.'

She meant Beryl Markham whom she'd met when she was a girl and kept up with during all those years, after Karen and Bror Blixen and that world faded. She used to drop in on Beryl in Nairobi, now an old woman in a small concrete house, drinking gin and orange at a terrific rate, and trying to remember the places where she'd once flown; taking out a rusted tin box with her flight maps, and the bush air strips, to chart the great solo flight she'd once made across the Atlantic.

'Beryl keeps being robbed. The last time landed her in hospital with a cracked skull. Alone, you see, and old. But all she wanted to know was had I flown recently to Mara-Mara or to Oloitokitok?'

Among the mourners, too, that day, were some who still lived where they'd always lived, and had flown down to Jo'burg for her funeral: the Africa lovers, the big talkers, the 'I am devoted to the continent and I'll fucking knock your head off if you don't love it too' brigade. There was Rex Thistledown from the Kenyan Highlands, one of the few white ranchers still going in Kikuyuland, son of old Nicky Thistledown who used to hunt with my mother, drink with Hemingway and whore with Bror Blixen. Rex, the poor bastard, was what so many once wild and improper white settlers had been reduced to: good causes and keeping quiet. Rex was into ecology now, saving elephants on his 50,000 highland acres, and saving his acres from the Kikuyu tribesmen who persisted in believing his land belonged to them, and had started invading it, waving pictures of Robert Gabriel Mugabe, a continental hero ever since he'd started booting white settlers out of Zim. In the fifties, Rex's dad, Sir Nicky, known as the nabob of Nairobi, once rode his horse into the club with a naked blonde over the saddle and drank a stirrup-cup to the cheers of assembled diners. By contrast, Rex drove an old Range Rover, didn't drink and, like lots of Kenyans, he kept a farm in South Africa, as a kind of insurance against the day the Kikuyu finally won, and kicked him off the land.

Behind us there was a row of ancient chaps in their blue blazers, their rheumy eyes blinking back tears, all of them lovers of my mother, all of them lost in an Africa they had not bargained for, narrowed and angry and young and hostile. But one person who didn't pitch that day – and it surprised me – was Queen Bama.

Father Phil was in the pulpit.

'We come to say goodbye to Kathleen, a towering woman who changed lives, who flew and fished and hunted; who did not just aim for the stars, she was one. Conservationist, Africanist, a woman with the poise of a fashion model. A woman whose innate warmth was like some great and good campfire; a woman from this town who was made of the treasure of this town, a heart of gold ... a mother who had children reaching out to her; and hunters toasting her around the campfire. I am sad she is not here; I miss her deeply. She shone so brightly that to mourn her too deeply, to grieve too greatly, is natural enough, but I for one would rather celebrate her amazing life.'

It was rum. Very. Here was a man dressed like a Christmas tree and speaking by common consent, rather well. Cindy was weeping. It was exactly what we always do at such times, run the fancy stuff alongside the real stuff. Standing up in the pulpit, in his Erin-green togs, talking nonsense about my mother, was one of the last of her lovers. The priestly role in Africa was about as odd as the ruffian's, the entrepreneur's and the explorer's. The same love of dressing up, the do-goodery; the desire Africa inflicts on otherwise intelligent people to go around succouring the weak, saving the sick, and alternately seducing and savaging the same. All in the name of 'love'.

Next to me, Papadop shifted and wept. Papadop, who used to tell me about Father Silverio, the poor little Porto palooka four centuries before, who sat by the waters of the Musengezi River, just as Papadop had done, as the Cuban did, as I had done. Silveria was the first white man in Mount Darwin, just as poor Papadop, a thoroughly fucked by now ex-Greek ex-South African, ex-Zimbabwean ex-everything, was today the last.

It was amazing how these things connected up. Everything joined and converged: Father Phil, the sad figure of Papadop slumped in the pew, the Cuban's wreath. The Cuban whom Papadop hid in his hut beside the Musengezi, the river into which the first white man in Mount Darwin had been tossed to appease the crocodile gods.

My mother had never recognised this Africa. She had simply sailed over the top of it, and so made good her escape. Believing you could be who you were, disdaining even to regard colour; she did Africa without doing race. But those she left behind were finding that option wasn't available any more, despite the lies, the sweet talk, the high hopes: we were saddled with the skin we wore.

Amazing and terrible to face it, after half a century of thinking of nothing but colour, tribe, blood and race; and swearing that whatever happened in the future, we would never do it again. Not only were we doing it again; it was the only game in town.

When I left the church, I found Queen Bamadodi's praise-singer waiting for me across the road, outside the sex shop. He was in full regalia and he was shifting from leg to leg. Maybe he figured the shop offered a neutral backdrop. Clearly, he didn't feel too relaxed, turning up in knee-rattles and monkey tails at a Christian funeral.

He had not come in the royal limo; he was there by taxi, a packed minibus waiting for him across the road. He was wearing a Swatch and for some reason this troubled me. A modish Swiss timepiece on the wrist of an old royal retainer who has to use a taxi … Things must be bad for Queen Bama.

Only his greeting still had the rich old ring.

'I bring you blessings from the great cloud of plenitude, she who makes the rivers run and waters the world. She without whom all would be desert and dust. The great udder of heaven embraces the son of Kathleen and asks him to visit her in the Great Place.'

I felt sorry for him. He had to get a cab back home to the Magaliesberg, and he knew he'd better arrive with news the Rain Queen wanted to hear. I understood and appreciated the honour I was being accorded yet I did not want to go. It made no sense. The Rain Queen did not entertain men, she did not have sons, she did not care for husbands and, whichever way you looked at it, I was a man, and a white man to boot.

But she was part of my family.

The praise-singer was anxious to be off; his taxi hooted.

I said I'd come.

He was relieved: 'There will be feasting and rejoicing in the Queen's Great Place.' Then he thought it over, and said, carefully: 'There will be rejoicing. Look, I have marked the way.' And he gave me a tourist map, which read: 'Welcome to the Magical Magaliesberg, in the Platinum Province. A Bird Watchers' Paradise.'

Then he consulted his Swatch, and shoved off.

iv Golden City Blues

'I am not defenceless; I have a Lüger in my locker.'
West with the Night, Beryl Markham

22

I saw no one for some weeks after the funeral except for the gardener. In the time I lived in my mother's house in Forest Town I had no better friend or companion than the Red Earth Man. Nothing I said persuaded him that Noddy was a poor substitute for his real name. He was Noddy – Noddy of the Five Madams – and it did not bother him one bit.

In the afternoons I'd walk in the Zoo. When I was little my mother took me riding on the elephant, swaying in the wooden seat, high up on his back. She held tight to the brass bar. She said the world looked better from an elephant's back. Afterwards, we visited the lions and she'd point and say, 'Golly, just *look* at those teeth.' Then we'd wander over to the monkey cages and watch people feeding peanuts to the chimps. People would be yelling and throwing and pointing and jigging up and down; sometimes they threw orange peel, which the monkeys caught and could not eat.

'Honestly, how cruel can you get?' my mother said. 'I really can't tell which side of the bars the monkeys are on, can you?'

You need time and some space to mourn.

There had been changes at the Zoo. The elephants still took kids for rides and the lions were as yellow as ever. But the cages had gone. The animals lived in enclosures dotted about with trees and veld grass and waterholes. A deep trench kept people further away from the chimps, so they couldn't throw nuts at the chimps. Down the road a bit, across a moat filled with clean green water, lived a gorilla.

Things take you in strange ways when you're grieving. I began hanging around the gorilla. I felt the way neglected kids feel: they cling to the nearest friendly stranger. It's not real love. It's replacement therapy. They don't want you really; they want their mothers. You aren't her and they know you aren't, but you'll do to hang on to till what they've lost comes back.

They didn't have a gorilla in the old days but my mother would have liked him. She had a great sense of wonder, and a fine sense of fear. The two went together, which is why she thrilled to see the lions' teeth. The gorilla had a whole environment to play in; he had trees with old car tyres swinging from their branches, and a hill built of fake rocks with a little cave halfway up where he could rest from the hot sun. A ramp led up the back of the fake hill and entered the gorilla's cave. This was the keeper's entrance. The gorilla's name was written on a big sign over his enclosure: 'Rwandan Gorilla, Origin Kigali'. Just that: pretty bald, pretty lonely, take-it-or-leave-it sort of stuff.

One day Noddy asked if he could come with me to the Zoo and it became a regular outing, two guys taking a walk. He showed me pictures of his wife. She looked young, perhaps twenty-five, with that burnished glow of young Matabele women.

'She is called Beauty, Mr Alex, and I have two kids with her. My sons are Joshua and Sipho and they are at school and the fees must be paid each month.'

He showed me pictures of Joshua and Sipho. Bright and shining faces, in school ties and crisp white shirts. His sons were happy at the school. It was run by a good principal, 'one of our best men'. He said this with unusual force, as if I was going to argue with him.

'My wife, she works in the school. Some days each week, in the office of the principal himself. He's a first-class fellow.'

Like many migrant workers, Noddy had no papers. If he was picked up he'd be jailed and deported. I couldn't see it happening because I couldn't see Noddy in jail; it was hard to think of Noddy doing anything that warranted it. He was simply too decent a man, too responsible, too caring of his wife Beauty and his two boys. He was so solid that, next to him, I felt like a vagrant, a gypsy.

'Jo'burg people don't like immigrants, they don't like me. I am not from here, sir. I am foreign from Matabeleland, I go there twice a year. Where are you foreign from?'

'I am foreign from South Africa.'

'But where is your home?'

I tapped the ground with my toe. 'This is my home.'

He thought about that and I saw he got my drift. Not all of us feel at home at home.

'It is hard to be a traveller.'

'Why is that, Noddy?'

'A traveller loses all he leaves behind.'

He was homesick, like all of us. He had left home and headed down to Jo'burg for the same reason that anyone ever came to Jo'burg: for the loot. He did piece-work in five gardens six days a week; it paid a fair cash wage and he sent most of it home to his family in Matabeleland.

If I liked anything in particular about Noddy it was his wide range. He was many things. Travel, distance, other places, other worlds, and other ways: these things are very hard for

Johannesburgers to live with. They take offence. Jo'burgers believe their city to be the very hub, the navel of the world. They think it is like New York or Chicago. It's not, of course. If it is like any American city, in its sprawl, its smog, its money, its drive-by shootings, then it is remotely like Los Angeles. But tell people that and they think you're putting them down. Very few of them have even been to these American cities but that never stopped a Jo'burger knowing what was what. And telling you.

Noddy didn't like the government of Zimbabwe. He talked politics with me, he talked easily, he didn't have any of the brittle concern about sounding the right way that so gets to people down South.

'They sent the Korean killers, the Fifth Brigade, they murdered our people and threw their bodies down old mine-shafts.'

Noddy noticed how the clothes of the people killed in those shafts were mingled with bits of bone.

'It's a miracle, Mr Alex. Our clothes last longer than our bodies. Ha, it makes me sad.'

When I think back now I know we were useful to each other. Without him, I would have been even more lonely. I was back in a city that had been my own and I found I wasn't really there any more. I felt like one of those shades in the under-world, anxious, plaintive, always wanting news of the real world. So the flesh-and-blood guy I found in the back-yard room was a gift. We had more in common with each other than we did with those we should have been closest to. I got his company, and in exchange he got a free room; that was very important to him, the room. Without it, he would have been forced to rent a room in Alexandra Township, a tiny shed carved out of someone's garage. And having to pay through the nose for the privilege. He wrinkled his forehead; Alex was too bad, too dangerous, too much drink, too many guns. He would get lost in Alex.

I see now that Noddy was very kind to me. He knew I was adrift, he knew I was lost. He knew that too many years on the road had addled my brains; and, especially, he knew I was hurting. We were foreign natives in a strange city and foreign natives had to look out for each other. He had travelled, he knew a man can live in more than one place, and if he does he will be more than one person. And that's all right.

Back home in Matabeleland Noddy was a landowner: he had his own farm, he raised cattle and goats, he had peach and apricot orchards. He was in every sense a man of substance, a fact very hard to square with the piece-work gardener in his grey trousers and his T-shirt. He had about him weightiness, a gravitas quite out of keeping with his size, his little hands and his neat feet. Solid, reliable, these were the things that struck you about Noddy, even if he was barely five feet tall and so fragile he looked as if the wind would knock him over. He had standards, ideals; a man of quality, he did all the things you're supposed to do to get on. In another, better world he would have been helping to run his country.

We were two foreign natives talking about China and Iceland and Montenegro and he liked that because it made him not seem too far away from all he knew and loved, his farm with its fruit trees, his wife Beauty, his boys.

For day-to-day work in the garden Noddy wore grey flannels and a white T-shirt. The T-shirt showed an Alp and the Swiss flag, and read 'Gstaad, my Love'. On Sundays he went to the Methodist church over in Parktown North; he wore a dark blue pinstripe suit and black shoes, and his hat, a beautiful dark brown shapely confection with a generous brim and a black hatband. Riding athwart the hatband was a brilliant pheasant feather – a jaunty cockade. What we had in common was that home lay behind us. What I got from him was a sense of relief that things did not have to be the same, always and everywhere – which is what death insists on. He gave me other ways of being, he stood out against death, he was good in bereavement. Death is monotone, unalterable, it reduces us to bone and bits of clothing. It is the ultimate application of force. Death is radical that way, it threatens your own life and so you seek reassurance. Noddy reassured me because there were so many versions of the man. He was never monotone, he was many-sided. He was versatile. Noddy in the week, Noddy on Sundays, grandest of all, Noddy, country squire.

Only the feather in his hat pointed to some other life that was garish, noisy, fast and loose. It is not too much to say that when he wore that hat both lives were on show: one down-to-earth, dependable; the other floating and brash.

He liked fine feathers. And he loved the costume museum across the road that had been created by the Bernberg sisters. I could still remember when I was a boy seeing the sisters walking out in the afternoons to catch the bus to dancing classes. They wore white stockings and ballet pumps and must have been in their seventies. My mother watched them with scorn. 'What do they think they look like?', she would say. 'Who do they think they are?'

The tiny Bernberg sisters always dressed to kill. Sometimes they were 1920s flappers; sometimes vamps, in short black skirts and white stockings and flat shoes and berets or cloche hats. When they held hands at the bus stop, which was right outside their house, they looked like very old little girls dressed up for a party. They were a splash of colour in an otherwise dull street, dancing birds of paradise in Forest Town.

When the sisters died they left their house and their fashion collection to the city of Johannesburg. The rooms were filled with costumes of the eighteenth, nineteenth and twentieth centuries. The models stood in glass showcases wearing Voortrekker shawls, or slinky cocktail numbers from the 1930s. There were national costumes from a dozen countries. There were even examples of the great Parisian couturiers like Coco Chanel. The Bernbergs had cherished what in Jo'burg did not rate: the pretty, the delicate and the foreign.

Noddy liked it that I knew nothing about gardens and he decided to teach me odd things from time to time. 'Removing the buds on your dahlias gives better blooms, Mr Alex.' He set the tines of two sharp garden forks at the neck of a dahlia plant so that they locked around its throat like fingers.

'Dahlia tubers should be lifted from the ground – like this. It stops you breaking their necks.'

I didn't much care for dahlias, but there it was. I didn't plan to learn to raise dahlia tubers without breaking their necks.

Now and then, so strongly it shook me, I felt that Noddy was the key to something vital, if only I could see it. He could not tell me; he could only hope I saw it. I did not. I fell into the worst sort of provincialism; he was the country I could never quite grasp the reality of, so I doubted its reality. I tried to understand him by referring only to myself.

Noddy saved his money in the Natal Building Society and his book was fat and neat and shiny and tied with two elastic bands in a red rubber cross. He showed it to me, cupping it in the cradle of his fingers, rather in the way the tines of the two forks intermeshed when he lifted the dahlia tubers. Here were his wages; here was the monthly sum he sent home to his wife.

We talked of climate and customs and politics. Was it very cold in England, or very dangerous in America? Did they also hate foreigners in other countries?

Noddy would stand at the great apes' enclosure and read off the description: 'Rwandan Gorilla, Origin Kigali'. There was an air of grief about that gorilla. So it felt to us. He came from many miles north, from mountains and forest, to this penitentiary beside the war museum that is the Jo'burg Zoo.

'He is also a foreign native, Mr Alex.'

Sometimes he sighed and I knew he was thinking of his boys who went to school at St Aloysius where his wife Beauty worked in the office of the principal who was a first-class fellow.

Jake Schevitz eased himself into the blue Dralon chair, and he gave me the crooked smile I knew so well. Behind his head was Livingstone's water-colour sketch of Victoria Falls; the path that snaked up to the Falls was inked in royal blue and it seemed, from where I sat, to grow out of Schevitz's left ear.

'It must be strange, to be here without her.'

'It's the emptiness. It feels like I've been living all my life next to some huge engine. A turbine. Or a waterfall. A bloody Victoria Falls so loud, so monstrous, I couldn't hear myself think. And now suddenly it has been switched off; and the silence is harder to deal with.'

Schevitz got up and came over and put his arm around my shoulders.

'You going to stay on?'

'Yes. At least until I make sure everyone gets what she left them. I promised her that.'

'Well, don't be a stranger. Give me a bell, we'll hit a few pubs.'

I said I would but I could see he didn't really believe me, and I could see, too, that he was relieved. Jake Schevitz might have been an old friend, but I had been away a long time and he no longer knew what to say to me. I wasn't who I had been. My being-awayness had emptied me of the stuff that made recognisable South Africans: brawn, blood, beer, BMWs, ballistics, balls, as well as any amount of passionate bullshit. It had ruined me for flesh-and-blood company. I was living in my mother's house but to Schevitz I was more ethereal than she was. She might be dead but I was the real ghost.

Jake handed me a heavy buff envelope. On the envelope was typed in capitals: 'LAST WILL AND TESTAMENT OF KATHLEEN MARY HEALEY'.

'Keep your head down, Alexsy boy. It's loaded. Hand-grenades from heaven. She had a helluvuh sense of humour, your old lady. She's parcelled out her stuff in such a way that it's either exactly what you might have liked, or the last thing you'd ever want. For instance, I get her Spanish dictionary and grammar books and *Spanish for Early Learners*. Lest I forget I stood between her and happy marriage to a toy-boy defector half a century younger than her.

I began to see what she had meant in those last moments when she had extracted from me the promise to see to all her 'things'. Her bequests had been chosen with a certain Olympian piquancy. The pairing of gift and recipient calculated to keep her smiling in the after-life. Schevitz got the Spanish dictionaries; I got Noddy, the house and garden.

And that was just the start.

23

Cindy September inherited her flying jacket, boots, leather helmet and goggles. I phoned her and she explained, as one might a visitor from another planet, where she lived.

'D'you know Sheerhaven?'

I did not.

'Well, for sure you know Lonehill?'

Cindy's sonic history vibrated down the phone line. Her long 'a's deepening into '*j-a-a-r*'; her short 'a's fading into flat – 'flet'– 'e's. Her constant use of 'ut' to express surprise or solidarity: 'Uzzzut, hey?' Each note a marker, a flag, an identity. The places out of which we evolved had been scratched on the way we spoke, in much the way slave-shackles rubbed raw the wrists of the prisoners they encumbered. We were what we sounded, until we sounded different.

She was incredulous when I said no again, but she was game.

'Y'know Halfway House?'

'I do.'

'OK. *Ja* … Let's see then. *Ut's* easy to find … if you know how to get on to the William Nicol Highway. That's where your mom was in the clinic. OK? Get on the William Nicol, and just keep going. Don't branch right for Halfway House when you hit Buffalo Belle's.'

'What's that?'

She laughed, short and, I thought, slightly bitter. 'You don't know *thet* either? Everyone knows Buffalo Belle's. You can't miss *ut*. Anyway, you don't want to stop there, that's for bloody sure. Aim for Monte Casino.'

'Monte Casino?'

'A ginormous bloody place, like an Eyetalian town. Couple of k's after *thet*, make a left and you're there. Big gates; lotsaguards. You'll see a Woolworth's smack bang opposite the gate. If you see a Checkers opposite the gate, you're at the wrong gate. Woollie's *uz* the smart end. Ask for me when you get to the gate. See you now-now.'

When I met Cindy at my mother's funeral I'd have said she was probably from somewhere down in the Cape. Mixed race, 'Coloured'. But listening to her on the phone, I'd have put her down as white Jo'burgundian, northern suburbs, possibly Jewish.

Wrong on both counts.

I was driving out into the flat veld of the northern reaches, where the names of walled, gated and guarded suburbs – Fourways, Lonehill, Halfway House – spoke up for what they were: border outposts on Jo'burg's long march north, its rush to leave behind its other older self among abandoned skyscrapers and shrinking mine-dumps. Jo'burg was on the move and it was taking the city with it. Shiny shopping malls stood shoulder to shoulder with glossy auto show-windows stuffed with mouth-watering new models, glinting and winking at the drivers stuck in the endless traffic jams in much the way whores patrolled for trade on street corners: hoiking their skirts and flashing their pants at passing punters.

Do it with product; do it with pussy. Same difference, as they said around here.

I kept hearing Cindy's voice as I drove. 'Woollie's *uz* the smart end…'

Somehow, the entire fucking history of the country was lodged in that phrase.

I'd grown up in what I believed was the 'real' Johannesburg of years gone by, when there was nothing north of Sandton and Fourways on the map, it simply didn't rate: a stretch of nothing between Krugersdorp and Pretoria. Well, it wasn't nothing any more.

The flat stretches north of Johannesburg were pullulating with intense termitic activity. I was in a solid line of very slow-moving traffic; expensive traffic: 4x4s and Mercs and BMWs, stuck in a jam tailing back all the way to the outskirts of the old Jo'burg. There was new world fervour, giant cranes and tiny workers swarming over the rising walls and roofs of what were becoming estates, stockaded cluster suburbs. Pinned to the walls of these gated refuges 'For Sale' signs showed grainy photographs of estate agents, etched on the metal: Evaleigh and Trompie and Charlotta were happy to flog you the padded cell of your dreams in the happy lives, the lonely townships, where everyone lived safe, certified lives.

The melancholy faces reminded me of something I could not for the moment quite identify.

Everywhere bulldozers rolled forward on great rubber knees, preparing the ground for yet more temples anointed with the names of faint yet still magical European memory: Mon Plaisir and Ma Provence, La Capri, Tuscan Heights, Tuscany Towers, Casa Tuscana, Linga Longa, Le Mistral, Verona Heights and Aquitainia…

Then, rising out of the flat veld, I saw it: a russet fortress with turrets and battlements. Monte Cassino. I remembered there had been a famous battle fought by South African troops against the Germans in a place of that name but I did not imagine for a moment that whoever built this giant gambling joint, masquerading as a castle in Italy, had in mind a far-off battle in a war no one remembered. No, this piece of mountainous kitsch was about the new South Africa, increasingly, also, a giant casino and clip joint that totted up its assets in poker chips.

Next thing I saw was a ranch house, an arch of entangled cowboy hats and lariats, surmounted by a pair of big neon horns, and the legend: 'Buffalo Belle's – Love's Our Life-Style!' Cindy had been right. You couldn't miss it.

A few minutes on and I came to a set of steel gates, a guard-house and, yes, Woolworth's across the road. I'd hit Sheerhaven; the smart end. The double wall that looped around the estate reminded me of the old barrier between East and West Berlin, fifteen feet high and topped with electric fencing.

A discreet notice at the front gate advised: 'Attention. There is enough power in this fence to cause fatal injury.'

The CCTV cameras looked me over; the guards asked my name and business, then they signed me in and phoned Cindy who said: 'Oh, hi, Alex. Glad you found *ut*. Just tell the gate you want Beauchamp Drive.'

Beauchamp Drive lay on the other side of Hampstead Ponds and below Berkshire Meadows. Cindy's house was a three-storey villa, all columns and colonnades, with windows above the huge portico that reminded me of the White House. Two life-sized copper cranes stood on the lawn; a pink Porsche was parked out front; the garden walls were painted in Ndebele zigzags of green and black.

Cindy wore white jeans and a top of gilded silk and her dark hair was piled high. It was good to see her.

Sheerhaven was built around the golf course, and it was, Cindy told me matter-of-factly, metre for metre, the priciest real estate in town, and the most closely guarded. There were armed patrols and a lethal fence; infra-red sensors were buried below the wall to stop anyone thinking of tunnelling, and there was constant TV surveillance. There was no crime in Sheerhaven, no robbery, no rape, no riots. There were also no shops, no bank, no restaurants, in fact no hustle or bustle at all. I got the feeling nothing moved, except by arrangement.

Cindy said, 'Dead right. No one is in this place who should not be in here.'

'What if you need stuff?'

'We've got Woollie's. Anything else we want gets brought in. Don't smile, I'm serious.'

'It's unreal.'

'Maybe. But we don't want reality here; we pay big bucks to make sure it doesn't come near us.'

It was my first experience of paradox in Cindy: she was sharp, quick, shrewd, unsentimental and unimpressed by much of the tinsel that so excites Jo'burgers. And yet she loved every last tacky bit of it.

She took my hand. 'Like to look around a fairy-tale house that goes with a fairy-tale life? Come see.'

She was open, affectionate, and I found her deeply appealing. In half an hour I had felt the temperature of the water in her coral-pink pool, I had seen her bedroom, with its little pathway made of resin cobbles with roses buried inside the cobbles; I had reviewed pink fairy-lights that twinkled from the plastic bough that leaned over her heart-shaped bed. I had admired her pink and green Venetian mirror that made the two of us look like mischievous leprechauns in her candy-floss cavern. I had approved of the lamps built of clunky African bracelets, and the tall African pots, and the two stressed yellowwood giraffes standing a metre tall, supporting on their heads a shelf displaying big books about the Masai, Jackie Kennedy and the latest hottest designer game lodges in Kenya.

'OK. Now we can make a little tour of Sheerhaven. It might be interesting for someone like you ...' she gave me a sideways grin I was soon to know as a sign of Cindy entering sardonic mode '... who's never seen our premier lifestyle suburb.'

We went walking, and Cindy reminded me just how rare this was. The sun shone bright on Waverley Villas and Tunbridge, on Wessex Weald and the Devonshire Downs. A long, rather graceful silver pipe, lifted high on great silver stanchions, a conduit I took to be some sort of viaduct, ran high above our heads, the fairway, the river and the rooftops. Sheerhaven's villas ranged across the architectural spectrum, from African Zen to Spanish haciendas, to French Provincial to New England; each bulking large on surprisingly small plots of land. The owners built right up to the edges of their allotted space, creating a strained and almost stifled look, at odds with the broad empty streets and the landscaped public spaces. What passing traffic I saw was made up of small, politely painted vans dashing hither and thither: 'The Flower Fairy', 'Darling Domestics', 'Hephzibah's Antiques' ... For the rest the streets were eerily empty but for the occasional black maid pushing a stroller and young kids piloting electric golf carts. On a low hill overlooking the golf course stood a large and tumbling shanty town of corrugated-iron huts and wooden hovels. Cindy saw me looking at it and she was amused.

'Our sister settlement, our face in the mirror, that's Donkergat, "Dark Hole", the squatter camp, or "informal settlement", they call it. Close by, isn't it, hey? Right in our faces. Reminds us we're related.' She was truly delighted. 'Very Jo'burg. Lest we forget.'

'Related, but behind your wall.'

'Sure. Related, but not terrorised. That's what all this is for. We live in Sheerhaven the way people used to live: with our doors open, and our kids safe, and the sun in our faces. But you only get as much of paradise as you pay for.'

Nowadays, the colour of your money was what counted; and the quality of your security. Jo'burg had gone back to core values. Whoever could stump up the bucks was welcome in the sated, gated suburbs, where road-booms shut out intruders and algae-sucking hoses called Kreepy-Krawlies chugged across the swimming-pool floor; where the high-voltage current humming in the razor wire that topped the beautiful walls sang the song of safety. A world of Lamborghinis, gunfire and sirens, where the panic button brought you instant armed response patrols and the hotline got you the 24/7 Medivac chopper. And where, even if God wasn't in his heaven, at least the sentry was on the gate. Where – on paper at least – life was perfect. On paper. But, then, perfection in this town was always paper-based, and paper-thin, and papered over with dummy shares, fake title deeds, IOUs and dodgy treasure maps.

That was Cindy's take on locking yourself away in a fortress in the veld. You bolted the doors, paid the guards, unleashed the dogs and called it heaven. Wellness within the walls: phoney, but blissful. Cindy knew that in no far-off blessed time did anyone live safe with the sun in their faces and their kids free to come and go. Time, in our terms, being measured from the moment van Riebeeck's boot hit the beach in the Cape and he began shooting Hottentots. The war had gone on since then with peace talks that lasted just long enough for the belligerents to reload. But so what? You proceeded by proclamation; you said things were bloody marvellous even when they terrified you because our terror was more bloody marvellous than the mundanity of others; and you locked up, or duffed up, anyone who disagreed. You invested time and energy creating a past that led flawlessly up to the present creation of yourself. Declared it to be the real true you; and then did it all over again. Everyone did it but no one did it better than Jo'burgers. You might have thought, if you didn't understand the enormous benefits of self-invention, that ours was a patch of veld where murder was as common as dirt; rape was rife, where the poor starved and women were attacked, often fatally, by their partners, more often than anywhere else on the planet. Cindy knew that but ignored it. A bit of steadfast denial and it was easily fixed. You just slapped in a tall wall, an electric fence, an armed patrol and – bingo – welcome to Sheerhaven, welcome to the premier lifestyle!

I rubbed it in a little. 'In what you call "the old days", people also built a Berlin wall around the bedroom. Everyone lived in daily expectation that the servants were swiping the booze, and gangs of burglars lurked in the sanitary lanes that ran between the houses, or plotted in the servants' rooms behind the houses, waiting to hit your place and clear you out of soap and silver. Everyone compared designs of burglar bars. Did you use grilles or slats or mesh? And in your choice of domestic chain mail, did you like circles or rectangles or graceful art nouveau flourishes? Did you rivet them, weld them, or bolt them? Did they spread like a grille across the space or did they spring free of the wall in wavy lines? Did they come in tasteful shades of pastel to match the face brick? These were hot questions, even then, and the pistol sat in the sock drawer, just as it does now, except now they have his and hers. What's the difference, at heart?'

She grinned. 'Something pretty crucial. We take anyone at all into the stockade. In the old days they ran a fence between people. We don't.'

'You do walls.'

'Honey, this is Jo'burg: everyone does walls between us and the outside. But inside Sheerhaven, we're totally open to anyone at all. Black, white, pink: anyone who can fork out several million bucks. The new black billionaires are really just Jo'burgers at heart: they don't want to be revolutionaries; they want to be Rand-lords...stinking rich and safe as houses. That's how it was, that's how it is. Shall we go home and have a drink?'

She carried a tray of drinks into the back garden that ran down to a stream with its view of the main fairway, off to our right. The great silver pipe soared overhead, catching the sun rather beautifully, and we sat there and drank gins and tonics.

'What's that for? Does it carry water?'

'*Thet*,' said Cindy almost proudly, 'is a sewage pipe. Weird, hey?' She clearly enjoyed my surprise. 'It takes ours, and it takes theirs, from Donkergat next door. It's our link with the outside world: our only link.'

It was quite a thought, the stuff flushed down the costly Italian-tiled toilets of Sheerhaven merging with the sewage from the even more prized – because rare – plumbed-in lava-tories of Donkergat (which made do for the most part with the old bucket system). A wondrous, characteristic twinning, signified in an elegant viaduct that shimmered in the heavens above Highgate Ponds and Hampstead Heath, Cheltenham Close and Cheam Crescent, sweeping over the green fairway and the bowling club: a pipe in the sky so rich and elegant and really rather lovely, and full of shit.

'I have something my mother gave to you.'

I fetched the stuff from my car. As I was handing them over I was uncomfortably aware what a sad bundle other people's old clothes can be.

'Her pilot's gear.'

I had wrapped the flying boots and helmet and goggles in the sheepskin jacket. 'Don't look like much but they were hers and she left them to you in her will.'

Cindy held up the flying jacket; it was much too big for her. Then she picked up the flying boots. They did what boots do when made of soft leather – they buckled, and caved in.

She hugged me, and then she hugged me again, and she said, 'Thank you, thank you! Dear, dear Kathleen. I loved your mom.'

Cindy in her tenderness and her reverence made me feel sad and pleased and somehow wanting. I felt she knew more about my mother than I did; but, then, who didn't?

Cindy said: 'I've been thinking about your question: why did Kathleen hug the kids? I'd have to say it was unqualified love.'

'I'm sorry but I don't think so. Love isn't something she knew about, not love for people, at any rate. She was commanding, stubborn, arrogant, successful, passionate and because of, or maybe despite of, this, there were people who loved her. Fine. But I'm not sure if she ever loved any of them.'

She gave me the close look she'd given me at the funeral.

'It's maybe an obvious thing to say, but I think that what love is depends on what you want, or need. She was getting something when she worked with the kids. If you get what you need from someone, that's a kind of love. Even if they don't know they're giving it to you.'

'That's double Dutch.'

She shook her head. 'It isn't. You can feel love even if the person you're aiming at isn't consciously giving it to you.'

'But where is it coming from?'

'From here.' She touched her chest. 'You get it precisely because you're the one giving it. There isn't any perfect love. Something is love if it's love to you.'

'What is it to you?'

'Something that gets me out of a hole. Two people have done it for me: my mom, and my husband. Ex-husband, I mean. Bloody useful, let me tell you, if you come from where I do. No one – repeat, no one – would want to get stuck where I was. So I ask myself, what hole did it get your mom out of, loving the kids? I don't know but maybe it was something she never had from anyone else? And if you turn the question around and ask, what did the kids get from your mom? I can tell you some of it: warmth. You should've seen her with the kids; they adored her. My Benny thought she was the best thing ever. He'd climb into her lap, she'd fold him in her arms and they'd sit there, rocking … just that, no more.'

'Where is Benny now?'

'At the Shelter. When I quit, I just couldn't take him out. He loves it so much. He spends the day and I collect him around five. Want to ride with me later to fetch him?'

24

Cindy drove a Porsche, bubblegum pink, with black leather seats, which reminded me strongly of some sort of lingerie, a silly, sexy, powerful car that seemed absolutely right. It went with the territory, the extraordinary world of Cindy September.

'I sell property in these.' Cindy waved a hand at the fortified, look-alike, cluster communities that dotted the veld for as far as I could see. 'They're wannabe Sheerhavens. Only they don't cost the earth. But then again, they don't do paradise quite so well. I'll show you.'

She drove into Tuscany Towers, flashing her pass at the guard at the gate. It was a tight conglomeration of small ochre townhouses, each with a square of lawn and a braai area. 'Here's where the youngies start. Bladdy small. No privacy whatever. You can hear a fly land on the roof; but very, very popular with the first-homers. Not *too* pricey but you still get your gates, your walls, your guards, your instant armed response service, your peace of mind. Just because it has an Eyetalian name doesn't mean you're limited. Styles are what we call African-eclectic, which basically means French Provincial, African fusion and African Zen, as well as ethnic bush style – bush means thatch. But Tuscan is tops. Tuscan is over everything like a rash. I flog teeny little hutlets as "Genuine Tuscan-

African" – Tuscany isn't a country, it's a lifestyle. The youngies love it for a few years and then they go.'

'Where do they go?'

She blinked her surprise at me. 'Into bigger clusters. I told you, we're not selling houses, we're selling lifestyle. It's secure, it's comfortable. It's all the rage. As opposed …' she giggled '… to death style. They get the clubhouse, the braai area, the pool, floodlit tennis court, kids' playground and giant TV, so everyone can get together on weekends and watch the rugby.'

'Don't they ever go out?'

'You mean to work?'

'No, just for the hell of it.'

'Not if they can help it. Out is where they work; out is the world. Out is what you want to forget at the end of the day and over the weekends. Out is dangerous. They don't want out; they want in. Maybe they'll drive to the gym for a workout, or the shopping centre. But mostly they have it all here: some of the blocks have eateries, laundrettes. And there are plenty of pizza places outside the walls that'll deliver.'

'Do they walk?'

'Good God!' As if for reassurance, Cindy opened the glove compartment, reached inside and touched the pearl-handled butt of her pistol.

'No one, but no one in their right minds walks in Jo'burg.'

We left behind the thousands of little hutch-homes; the great crowded emptiness of Fourways and Lonehill and drove back to the city, the skyline where worlds met and collided and the minibus taxis darted, stopped, cut in, stalled and never stopped hooting.

'Rather hooting than shooting,' Cindy said. 'We have taxi wars here. I've ducked for cover in this road more than once.'

Cindy had a delightful way of emphasising disaster, leaning back and placing her fingers under her chin, which had the effect of lifting her almost perfect nose. I wondered briefly if she had had plastic surgery. The sharp corners of her dark hair would swing down till they brushed the tips of her ear lobes. Her green eyes were bright when she said terrible things. In her laugh there was a mix of pride and helpless delight at the unique terrors of her home town.

'When women got together in the old days, they used to ask, "Who's your gynae?"'

She looked at me to see if I was impressed, amused, shocked. I wasn't any of these – but I enjoyed the music, an old familiar tune; dark, bluesy and very Jo'burg, I could hear the rising tones, up and up the voice would go till it hit the long 'e' in 'gyneee', and in the sudden silence that followed I'd see those last 'ee's hanging in the air. The Jo'burg twang knows no modulation; it takes off and keeps climbing until it peaks and there it hangs like a naked trapeze artist – *ee-ee-ee...*

'And now?'

'Now they'll say: "What calibre you carrying, doll?" It's got worse since freedom. It seems another world where, once upon a time, people slept with their windows open because they liked feeling the wind in their faces. Democratic freedom has brought personal terror. One person, one prison.'

Keeping out of harm's way was as old as the city but listening to Cindy I got the impression it had become an entire career. It consumed, exasperated and exhausted her; strategies for survival filled her waking hours. I had already had pointed out to me my lack of qualifications for saying anything about Jo'burg. I lived elsewhere, wherever that was. She asked in passing about Hanoi, Laos, Thailand, Siberia, America, but always with a slight scepticism, as if either she had trouble believing they existed, or she could not quite understand why anyone should bother to be there. It was a scepticism like my mother's: it did not doubt the existence of these unseen foreign places but it was quizzical about what made them interesting when, fuck *ut* – as Cindy would say – all around you was the real thing. This city, this weird, made-over mining camp, treasure trove, killing ground … ripped-up town of demented rip-off artists.

'*Lissen*,' said Cindy. 'Crime's so bad, even Rwandan refugees are leaving …'

Like a lot of Jo'burgers, she felt that if you left town for long enough, you lost all recollection of the unique textures that made the place so terrifyingly special. In my experience, just the opposite took place: it was amongst those who had lived in Jo'burg and never left that the returning traveller found real amnesia. Johannesburgers had no sense of the past, perhaps because if they kept on remembering they would go mad, perhaps because the present is so all-absorbingly wild. Or, when they do remember things, it is often because they wish to highlight, with perverse pleasure, what a falling-off there has been. The outside world and its crises are irrelevant – meaningless wars and quarrels. The only questions that matter run along the old parallel black and white lines, despite all the talk of love and unity. From the hungry majority: 'How do I get fed?' From the lucky minority: 'How do I not get shot?'

OK. But what I didn't understand was – if it had always been a bit like that, what made it so different now?

Cindy nibbled her fingernail. 'I guess I'd say: murder. More of it. People are into it in a big way. Anyone, at any time. All of us, any of us. That's why I'm bloody glad I live in Sheerhaven.

And so would you, so would anyone be if they came from where I come from.'

As we drove, she told me a depressing, unexceptional tale, common from coast to coast. She'd been born in a place called Blaukrans, a dirt-poor settlement out among the slime dams, in the shadow of the mine-dumps; a ghetto for despised, in-between, neither white nor black people, who were at home nowhere and loved by no one. Everyone else – blacks, whites, Asians – at least knew, as Cindy put it, 'who the hell they were, even if they didn't have a bloody clue where they came from. But us, we were no one and nowhere.'

The Coloureds of Blaukrans, descendants of Malay slaves or German mercenaries, Dutch sailors and English renegades, or Khoi people or San Bushmen, or all of them, were disparaged by their Indian neighbours, loathed by their black neighbours and ignored by their white overlords.

So far, so utterly ordinary. She came from not just the other side of the tracks, but the other side of the universe. She told me about herself with that steely enjoyment with which so many people have learnt to disguise the considerable pain of growing up another colour in another world.

'We were so far from being anyone we were outa sight! We were called Coloureds or Browns or Mixed Race people or Hottentots or Kleurling or Klonkies or Goffles, or whatever name got fixed to us. But, in the beginning, when we arrived in the Cape, I think we were slaves. September was a slave name. I could have been October or November or December. Same difference, isn't *ut*?'

I nodded. 'The guys who ran the Cape were not exactly bursting with ideas. They called their slaves by whatever name came to mind. Months were an old standby. Days of the week. Monday to Friday.'

She laughed. 'Cindy … Friday: I like that!'

Leaving the Cape for the Reef and heading up to Jo'burg, that had been the one bit of good fortune her mom ever had. In Jo'burg she met the man who became Cindy's father, and it was downhill all the way after that. The Septembers lived at number 24 Paradise Street. Her old man had hawked vegetables and hit the bottle as well as his wife and his kids. She had two brothers: one fell into the cooking fire and was burnt to death; the other peddled dagga, and was killed by the cops.

Her mother had been the one to resist: her mother remembered; she hankered back to the Cape, which became, in retrospect, a great, good place. It was not surprising. In the hard Transvaal, where all that counted was the gun, the whip and the boot, the Cape took on aspects of paradise.

'It was balls, when you think about it,' Cindy said, 'but I don't blame my mom. Longing to be back home. In the Cape she'd been to college, she qualified as a bookkeeper. Her big stroke of luck was to land a job keeping the books in the local Dutch Reformed Church in our township. Coloured branch, of course, but what the hell, it was a job. My mom kept us going. My mom got me to school, and after school she got me a job in Motortown. It was my mom who made me. It was 1989, I was sixteen. "Take your wages, rent a room in Hillbrow," said my ma. She cried but she made me promise: "Never come back." And I promised, and so I never did.'

'Never?'

'Never. Later, I heard that she died and I felt bad but I said to myself she'd have died glad. She got me out of there. I had that job in Motortown, it was a new life, a new me: I was out in the world. By the nineties, the old ways were breaking down. They didn't, like, hold your colour against you. They never noticed mine much anyway. You know what they called "trying for white"? Well, I didn't even have to try. I just was.'

It was familiar, and amazing. I thought of myself, of Koosie, of Noddy, of Bama, all of us marked by the places we came from. Maybe we escaped them. But we never denied what made us. Cindy had to unmake her home and she didn't have bulldozers to knock it down, like Koosie's place was knocked down in Sophiatown. She had to demolish her old life herself and start again.

'Would you do something for me? Would you show me where you grew up?'

She was astonished. 'I've known guys who wanted to go to bed with me. But no one ever asked me to show him where I come from.'

'It depends what excites you.'

'You are weird. But sure, we can go; we're in no rush. Benny won't be out till five.'

The city lulled and infuriated. We were in Orange Grove. No oranges, no grove. Small yellow-brick villas behind broad-bellied burglar bars, old cars rusting among the weeds in the front yards. Cindy's small, square, confident hands on the wheel of the Porsche ...

I got more reading the walls than I ever did from the papers. Parables, sermons, eye-candy ... 'Booze Brothers', 'Geffin and Garfunkel – Attorneys', 'Mtshali and van der Merwe', 'Tuxedo Tavern', 'Tombstone Memorials – Lifetime Guarantee', 'Ace

Guns and Acme Gold'. Then we were passing 'Nussbaum's Kosher Butcher', 'The Doll House Road House', 'Zuma's Teeth Whitening Clinic', 'Harry's Hair Relaxation Parlour'. And across the road from a yeshiva: 'Kalashnikov Security', on whose white-washed wall some street-wise physician had scrawled a prescription for our paranoia: 'One settler – one Prozac'.

'Like it?' Cindy asked.

'I love it. I grew up right here; this is one of the many parts of town where we lived. I went to school down the road.'

She looked like she didn't believe me. As if someone who spent so much time so far away couldn't really come from here.

We picked up the elevated motorway that curved around the city, like a lariat, and headed south into the smudgy edges of the great sprawl. Where no one ever went if they could help it.

25

Number 24 Paradise Street turned out to be a building of yellow face brick. Left to gather damp on the tired lawn, old mattresses sprouted mould like huge cabbages. You might have thought there was not much to steal and yet the sun was bright on the burglar bars behind the broken window-panes. Cindy was horrified. Three black guys in woolly Rasta hats sat on the low wall: great colours, lovely needlework, my mother and Bama would have loved them, but they did not look very friendly. One of them slowly lifted his arm, sighted and made to pull the trigger.

Cindy said: 'Oh, great! So much for freedom.'

'It is a long way you've come. Out as a clerk, back in a Porsche.'

She responded by gunning the engine. 'Yeah. I made it. I'm a target now, like everyone else. That's what is making me nervous. This car is begging to be done over. Seen enough?'

I nodded.

'Good. Let's go.'

We screeched out of Paradise Street, swung hard into the main avenue, only to be stopped by a red light. Three beggars surrounded us, their reflections swirling in the high gloss of the Porsche's bonnet. One guy was the colour of rust, and wore an old grey hat without a crown that was kept up by his ears, and he carried a piece of brown cardboard on which there was written in green chalk: 'White, poor, honest and hungry. No food for family. Please help.' There was a cripple, who made an attempt to clean our windscreen with one hand, rubbing with his sleeve until it was really smeary. In the other hand he held a cellphone. The third beggar was a child; he stood just at Cindy's window and stared at her. She said, 'Fuck this! Fuck it! Why do they do this? I work! You work! Why should I run the gauntlet? Bastards or billionaires, that's all we seem to produce … What a fucking country!'

The light flashed green, she put her foot down, and the cripple fell away. The child leaned forward and withdrew, like a bullfighter making a particularly dangerous pass, as close as he could get to the razor point of the bull's horn as the wing-mirror passed within millimetres of his nose.

On the highway she sighed. 'I'm sorry, but they freak me out. We've got enough stress around here. I just have to look at street people and I do my nut. I want to get out of the car and injure someone! Isn't that awful? But I do, because I'm think-ing it's me or them. D'you know what my nightmare is? Listen, this is it. Right? I'm stopped at a robot, and some guy sticks a gun in my eye and throws me out of the car and drives off with Benny still in the back. It's happened, you know. A mother gets hijacked, and her baby starts crying and the hijacker throws it out. Now, let's go fetch Benny, and let's drive the long way round and I'll talk to you like a Dutch auntie. Do you wanna hear Cindy's rules for staying alive? They're on the internet.' And as if this conferred sacred status, she chanted them for me like a poem, or a prayer:

1. Be alert and save yourself from murder, rape, assault, robbery and hijacking.

2. Be especially careful at night, at stop streets, at red lights, in heavy traffic, at tollgates on all national roads.

3. If stopped by the police, where possible do not stop but drive to a police station or phone 10111. Hijackers like to play at being cops.

4. If you break down, do not stop, never leave the car, drive on your tyre rims to somewhere safe.

5. If you see someone in distress beside the road, *do not stop*.

6. On arriving home, drive slowly past your house, go round the block, twice, especially at night.

7. Kill the radio before driving into your house. Listen hard. Look carefully.

8. If hijacked or held up, do not make any sudden movements.

9. Undo your safety belt before driving into your driveway in case you are held up, and loosen your safety belt in case a sudden movement makes the hijacker think you have a weapon.

10. At such moments, do not reach for your cellphone.

11. Keep looking your hijacker in the eye. It soothes him. Try to remember what he looks like.

12. Co-operate or die.

'That's it. Remember them: they may save your life. Why're you smiling?'

'It's thinking about you on Paradise Street. It's something about the unconscious poetry of names.'

'Poetry! Do me a favour!'

She didn't have to add what I began to learn was her usual signifier: 'This is Jo'burg.' I heard it in her voice. Life was too fierce, too fast, too deadly for poetry. In general, I was to discover, Cindy was withering about anything that distracted from the one serious question: how to stay alive? She was particularly scathing about 'artsy-fartsy stuff', which she regarded as little more than a dishonest diversion from the acid of 'real' life. Artsy-fartsy stuff, said Cindy, was 'unreal', even 'sickmaking'. I'd never heard it put like that before; the accepted view was that art was for faggots or foreigners or women. Cindy seemed to feel it was also bad for your health.

I asked what was wrong with painting or poetry or ballet.

'There's just something in the air that's against it. Don't ask me why; there just is. Something won't let it be a natural thing. I guess it's OK in, like, other places. But here, not. This isn't Mozart country; this is murder and robbery country. *Ut*'s ball games, big talk and beating-people-up country. People who go arty go down; they fall into little cliques; they go around sniffing each other's droppings. It's kind of grubby.'

'And murder and robbery are clean and up-front?'

She shrugged. 'You come from overseas. It's not the same there.'

'Cindy, I come from here. I lived in this town longer than you.'

'I don't say I approve of murder, I just say it comes naturally: lots of people do it. It's in the air. But, yes, you're right. When I see Paradise Street I know I have come a long way and, like I said, I owe it to my mom first of all, and after that I suppose I owe it to Andy. That's my ex. Andy Andreotti. I was a receptionist in Motortown, and he came in to buy a new Alfa

Romeo. He seemed pretty geared up. He was manager at the Bank of Naples. Soon we were going out. He never asked where I came from, he never asked to see Paradise Street, he never imagined for a moment that I wasn't what he thought I was: a nice girl from the northern suburbs. And that was fine by me. He was pretty crazy about me but, even better, he seemed to think I was, like, perfectly normal.' She gave her high, quick, disbelieving laugh. 'I remember thinking, I've made it! I thought my mom would have been really proud.

'Andy took me to Sun City, and that's where he asked me to marry him and, of course, I said yes. And so that's how I got to be the other half of a classy Jo'burg couple. We had a house in Fourways, a Jacuzzi, armed response, his and hers pistols – the whole bladdy tutti. We drove matching Alfas; we bought a farm in the Lowveld; we sailed on the Vaal. I did the lot: the book club, the BMW, lunches at Baldassar's in Rosebank or Carlucci's in Hyde Park. My friends were called Melissa and Sharon. Not bad, hey. It's amazing how quickly you pick it up. I ended up as Mrs Andy Andreotti in Fourways. A *twenny-four* carat, genuine Jo'burg princess. Isn't that absolutely fucking amazing?'

It was, and I said so.

'Even more amazing is this.' Again she laughed at her luck but also at some genuine discovery she'd made. 'When I think of Andy now, I realise that people like me are more fashionable than people like him. Isn't *ut*, hey? D'you know what I mean?'

'I don't think I do.'

'Well, people like Andy, whole gangs of them, are such utter dorks. I mean, now. They weren't then but they are now. Sort of out of date. Anyway, did Andy fuck up! Did he ever. But I can say, really, honestly, *troooly* I'm grateful to Andy, like I'm grateful to my mom; except my mom was a saint and a martyr, while Andy was an arsehole from the start. From when Benny was just born. You could see straight away Benny was different. He was slow to move, slow to crawl: he's not co-ordinated. All Andy could think of saying was, "But he won't be a sports-man …" That's Andy for you. That's my luck.'

It didn't sound like luck to me.

'But it is, it is! If he hadn't been such an arsehole, I'd still be married to him. And then where'd I be? Probably where he is.'

'Where's that?'

'He's in jail right now. Ten years.'

'Gosh.'

'Yes, well, like I said: he's an arsehole. But then again, don't feel sorry for him. Andy thought ten years was cheap at the price.'

'What was the price?'

'Everything he had, and then some. It was around about 1998, the new age, the age of freedom. We'd been married around three years. Buffalo Belle's had just opened. It was a brothel, right? Except they didn't call it that. Libido Lounge, they said. A parking lot the size of a rugby pitch, gaming tables, six bars burnished in brass and chrome, big screens showing reruns of old rugby matches, water-features, mud-baths, saunas, massage. They had Japanese koi in the pond; they had private suites named after the big five, the trophy game you always hoped to see in the wild, these suites with names like Buffalo Bay, Elephant's Walk, Lion's Den. All the other game-park crap.

'But it was a whorehouse, purpose-built for guys looking for a bit of fun after a lifetime in government-issue concrete cod-pieces. At long last, white men could fuck for freedom. Andy started going there. The girls waited at the bar. Prices went as high as a thousand bucks a trick. They shipped the girls in. They had Cambodians and Romanians and Russians and Thais. As it happens, the cops are after those girls right now. They're illegal immigrants. The papers are full of it. Foreign competition. The local sex workers bitch that they're losing out to cheap imports. Part of me thinks they should leave the girls alone. If enough dickheads want to get screwed by foreign fluff, so what?

'Anyway, that's where Andy met Mona-Lize. She wore a white negligee over a white G-string, and long white boots. They checked into the Leopard's Lair and he found to his amazement that she was priced at the lower end of the scale: 500 a trick. Andy wasn't only surprised, he was really angry: Mona-Lize with her blonde hair, blue eyes, white negligee, was the most beautiful woman he'd ever seen. How could she price herself so low?

'Mona-Lize liked that. She liked Andy for seeing it, and for saying so. For being understanding. She said it was cheap labour, it was immigrants, it was globalisation, and it was all those tarts from Taiwan, Estonia and Prague ... But she was local and local was – as they say – "lekker".

'And Andy lapped it up. He wasn't just a dork, he was a patriotic dork. In fact, Mona-Lize was more local than Andy knew. In real life, as if anyone gives a monkey's about real life, her name was Mary, from Blairgowrie. She was married to a Romanian called Mimicu, had two kids by him and then thought she deserved better, so she decided to up her household allowance by working a night-time shift at Buffalo Belle's ... So Mary Mimicu from Blairgowrie got to be Mona-Lize of the Leopard's Lair.

'He didn't just love her. He wanted to make up to her for the stupidity of all South African men who paid to fuck tarts from overseas. He wanted her to have what she needed, and Mona-Lize needed a lot. For starters Andy bought her a diamond ring, a BMW, an entire fucking tank of Japanese koi. Mona-Lize loved it; she said Andy was a born hunter.

'That's when I heard about it. He just told me one day there was someone else and he wanted a divorce. It was pretty horrible; I had Benny to think of. Anyway, we got a divorce, I got a settlement, I kept the house and Andy went back to Mona-Lize.

'The divorce cost him a bomb; suddenly Andy was short and Mona-Lize didn't like men who were short. So what did my ex-dork do? He began lifting large amounts from the trust accounts at the Bank of Naples. Then he set about making up for being short. He bought her a mansion in Wendywood for a million, a Rolex gold watch, he got through another quarter of a million in pretty trinkets, he paid for her to have her face lifted and her boobs done. In six months he blew three million bucks.

'But Andy, remember, was an arsehole. Worse, he began to have, well, pangs. He was not a thief by nature. It weighed on him, taking the money from the Bank of Naples, and he did something you do not do in Jo'burg: he began to fret. He told Mona-Lize how unhappy he was and why he was unhappy. Mona-Lize became very unhappy, too. She had always thought it had been his money. Now here he was, telling her that the money he'd spent on her was stolen. How was she supposed to feel about that? How could he do this to her? What right did he have to feel bad about it? What about what she was feeling? All right, then, if he was going to feel bad about it, then he should give back the money. Andy said he couldn't do that: he'd taken too much. Well, then, said Mona-Lize, do the decent thing, go tell the Bank of Naples what you've done ...

'Andy said he wanted to do the decent thing but he didn't want to go to jail. So you know what? Mona-Lize did the decent thing for him. She got into her BMW and went along to the Bank of Naples and told them what Andy had done. He was arrested; he got ten years.'

'Did the bank get its cash back?'

'Some of it. They got back the house in Wendywood. But how do you reclaim on a face-lift and a boob job? In court it turned out that Mona-Lize had begun to suss out that Andy might be a diminishing asset long before he did. So she had begun to diversify. On the nights she wasn't seeing Andy, she was running ads in the personal column of the *Star*: "Sex Kitten Seeks Lions and Tigers for Rough and Tumble. Strictest Confidence; all Major Credit Cards Accepted."'

Cindy laughed aloud. 'What a woman! Wasted in a knocking shop. She should have run a gold mine. Maybe she did, when you think how much cash Andy shovelled her way. Anyway, she did me a favour, too. Andy went to jail. I was free and I went into real estate. Thank you, Mona-Lize!'

What a town! The headlines wired to the lampposts sang out the edgy, bitter, banal news of the day, so familiar, so wild:

Raped Baby's Mother Arrested
Toddler Shot Dead in Bed
Two Burn in Shack
Boks Crush Aussies

'Your eyes are all glazed,' said Cindy. 'Are you on some-thing?'

'Yeah. I get high on home.'

'Well, sober up, buddy, I need you: I didn't just bring you along for the ride. Fetching the kids has got harder since guys began mugging the moms who came to fetch them.'

'You're not serious. In broad daylight?'

Again I saw on her face that look of horrified pride. 'Sure. Daylight never stopped anyone. Nice, hey? You're pretty encumbered with a kid who can't walk, or something. So they wait here … Smart thinking.'

'Bloody hell!'

'Welcome to Jo'burg.'

Sunbeam Shelter was once the home of a great and rich Rand-lord – a red-tiled fortress up on Parktown Ridge, built of hand-cut yellow Jo'burg stone, and big lawns running down to the electric fence. I watched Cindy teetering across the road in her snakeskin backless high heels to join the knot of mothers, and nannies in crisp white tunics, and kids in wheelchairs, kids in leg-irons.

She came back with Benny. His round face, the full skin, made him look younger than his eight years.

Cindy told him: 'You remember Alex. He's Kathleen's son.'

Benny looked at me as if I was much too old to be anyone's son.

'Where's Kathleen?'

'Kathleen's in heaven, Benny, darling. Remember, we said goodbye to Kathleen in Rosebank,' Cindy told him.

'When's she coming back?'

She looked at me. 'What do I say to that?'

'She's not coming back, Benny,' I said.

'Why?'

'Because she likes it where she is.'

Benny looked a little crestfallen but he took it well enough. He said: 'Will you stay and play tennis with me?'

Cindy looked at me. 'Would you?'

'Sure.'

She turned to the boy. 'OK. But just for a bit and then it's bath-time for you, my fellow.'

Playing tennis with Benny meant batting the ball to and fro, but he'd only use his backhand. He was obsessive about certain movements, certain ways of standing. All the time we played he sang: 'One man went to mow, went to mow a meadow.'

It was very relaxing. Cindy came out to watch. 'Try your forehand,' she said.

'No, I won't,' he said.

'He gets, like, fixated,' she said by way of apologising.

'Don't worry, so do I.'

I watched her bathing him. He took particular pleasure in kicking, long sinuous thrusts of his stubby legs, as if he were pushing them into stirrups or silk pyjamas, or soft leather riding boots. It was beautiful. Benny, so ungainly in the air, was so easy in water. He loved, I think, the sudden lightness of his cumbersome body which was too solid in air; he liked having something to kick against, he liked the feeling of getting some-where because for Benny getting anywhere was pretty hard going. It was different in water: then he might go somewhere as a fish. He was made for life underwater, a mer-boy, sen-tenced to live in another medium.

Driving home that evening I saw again the pale faces on the estate agents' signboards outside the walled townships and I knew what they had reminded me of. In Serbia, during the tribal wars that followed the end of Tito's reign, I spent time in a town called Pec, fixing air-con in the local Offices for Security and Co-operation in Europe. A very hopeful sign it was, too, in a town on the brink of war, filled with Serbs and ethnic Albanians who loathed each other. But, then, installing air-con is always a serene thing to do: it supposes calm; it assumes life will be stable for a while; it promises that there is a world in which simple things like comfort win out over killing. But that didn't happen in Pec. People didn't want to be cool; they wanted to kill.

In Serbia, the dead were remembered in photographs on lampposts or tacked to trees. Flimsy memorials to the departed. The faces of the estate agents on the 'For Sale' signs outside Sheerhaven and its sister stockades reminded me of those guides to the land of the lately deceased.

I knew such refuges were the future, they were what everyone wanted. It was a very South African way of cheating those who wished to end your life. You checked into one of these electrified mausoleums and pretended to be dead.

What had Cindy said? 'One person, one prison ...'

Once, it had been the state that had locked us away in the narrow cells of skin colour. Now we were free and we didn't need anyone to lock us up. Give us the bars and we'd do it ourselves.

Later that night Noddy knocked on my door. He had been weeping. I thought the cops had picked him up. Looking back now, I should have known something like that would not have rattled Noddy. Arrest, however awkward, was social, it went together with the benefits of a civil society, with rules and lawyers and bail and law courts, things that Noddy – the farmer, the landowner, the man of property – approved and supported. Arrest would have not done this to him. The man on my doorstep was going to pieces.

We went through to the dining room and sat down at the table. I waited for him to tell me what he had come to talk to me about but it soon became clear that he wasn't going to do that; he reached over to the pot of snapdragons on the window-sill and began pulling the drooping heads off the flowers.

'This is snapdragon wilt, Mr Alex. There is no cure.'

Then from his back pocket he took a letter, opened it and gave it to me. It was written in pencil on a sheet of lined paper and it was very short and it had all the ornate flourish of a letter penned by a scribe.

'Greetings, my brother,' it began, 'I have to inform you that your wife and mother of your children, Beauty, has been found to be carrying the child of another – to wit the principal of St Aloysius School, and I write to ask you, my brother, to take such steps as are necessary without the least delay. I am, my brother, your brother, Johnson.'

Noddy looked at me. 'A woman who does this thing, who carries the child of another man – when she is married – must not stay any more under her husband's roof.'

'Where does she go?'

'She must be sent back to her father's house. It is our custom. My brother says she cannot be my wife. I do not know what is best. I asked the others, "Tell me what I must do." The others have said their thoughts to me.'

He had been canvassing his madams. Pulling out the letter, watching them as they read it. Just as he was watching me.

I thought it was mad and wrong to go round from house to house, asking other people to decide the fate of his wife and family. I gave him back his letter.

'Noddy, where will Beauty go?'

'My madams all say the same thing. "Take her back," they say. "Forgive her," they say. "Shame, poor woman," they say. "Think of your sons, Noddy."' He sighed and he pushed the letter back into his pocket. 'I hear what my madams say. All women say the same. But my brother says: make her go. It is our custom. What do you say?'

'What about your boys? How will Joshua and Sipho managed if their mother is gone?'

He didn't want questions, he wanted answers. He said again, hopelessly: 'It is our custom. I must go there. I will go by train.'

'I'll get you the ticket.'

He inclined his head. Like someone accepting a jail sentence.

I have never made travel arrangements with less joy. We could not talk about where he was going because it wasn't travel in the sense that we knew it; duty and sadness took him back to Matabeleland. He packed his brown suitcase with the brass clasps, he wore his best Sunday suit, and his hat. Set for disaster, or joy, we look the same. I drove him to Park Station and he waved goodbye to me from the train window, as if he were going on holiday.

26

Her guns went to Oomie: the .505 Gibb, her favourite elephant gun; the .416 Rigby; the .375 Magnum Holland & Holland; and a Mannlicher .256 that she preferred for lighter game.

But Oomie had vanished without trace. Just as he had 'gone to ground' (my mother's kindly phrase) when the shots from David Pratt's pistol rang out forty years before, now he seemed to have done it again. I had to consider that he might be dead, but somehow I reckoned my old lady must have had a shrewd idea that he was still around when she left him her guns.

I tried the Johannesburg Central Police Station, from where, in the old days, when it was called John Vorster Square, Oomie and his mates had made their prisoners beg for mercy or concocted ingenious accidents whereby they died, after slipping on bars of soap in the showers, or falling from high windows. But this was the new South Africa and, apart from looking at me rather strangely, the new cops had no note or memory of the former secret policeman who had once been assigned to guard the one-time Prime Minister and who hit the deck with such alacrity at the Rand Easter Show all those years before.

They weren't covering up for the guy. I don't think their memories went back to the sixties. If anyone was responsible for expunging all traces of the former detective sergeant, in the secret detail assigned to guard the Premier, it had been Oomie's old colleagues who simply had not known what to do with the strange case of the recumbent bodyguard. (How instantly he'd dropped to the floor that day!) How embarrassing, how ridiculous … Faced by unpalatable facts, they did what they had done when faced by unpalatable people: they abolished them.

I ran ads in the *Star*, the *Cape Times*, the *Natal Mercury* …

> *If Mr Louis 'Lappies' Labuschagne, formerly of the South African Police Service, and a friend of the late Mrs Kathleen Healey of Forest Town, Johannesburg, would contact her son, at the address or phone number given below, he may hear something to his advantage.*

A few days later I got a letter, special delivery, from the Nelson Mandela Retirement Village, Umbilo, Durban.

> *Dear Mr Alex Healey,*
>
> *I am the man you are looking for. I am the old friend of your mom's. I am in a home in Durban. If you would phone me some time we could arrange to a get-together.*
>
> *Yours sincerely,*
> *Louis Labuschagne (Det-Sergeant, SAPS – Retd)*

The Nelson Mandela Retirement Village and Frail Care Facility – 'Celebrating Our Diversity' – was a complex of neat sturdy thatched rondavels, with only slightly less security fencing than Sheerhaven. I had taken the precaution of parking the Land Rover around the corner. I didn't want to have to explain to the armed guards at the gate why I was carrying enough firepower to start a small war.

Once inside the grounds I realised that the difference between Cindy's golden citadel, or the neo-Tuscan barracks where the 'youngies' spent their lives, and this modest old-age home was minimal. All such retreats represented the final destination for those who had once reigned supreme in South Africa; a supremacy that had some just claim to be called the most stupid in history, but no matter. All were heading for what looked, and felt, like early retirement.

The man who came to meet me at the reception desk was wearing white shorts and a matching belted tunic, buttoned down the middle, reaching below the hips. It was that old standby, the safari suit. Where had all the safari suits gone? One upon a time, entire phalanxes of servants ironed late into the night to keep regiments of men in crisply creased uniform, a uniform they wore with brisk aggression, like a badge of honour. The safari suit came in white, slate-grey, electric blue and khaki, a favourite shade. The tunic was worn open at the neck in a deep V, showing a patch of chest hair. The knees were exposed, and below them you wore long thick woollen socks and brothel creepers, if you were English, or veldskoen, if you were Afrikaans. There was always more of the pharmacy than the veld about the safari suit. Something strangely antiseptic, the perfect costume for shaven-headed fascists.

He patted me on the back. 'Alex, man, it's good to see you again!'

There seemed no comparison whatever between the dark, restless, taciturn Oomie who used once to call on my ma and this rather gentle old gnome. Small, fine-featured, with a sweet, rather sleepy smile. White hair, white beard, white eyebrows, his skin smoothly milky. Even Oomie's safari suit was cream and for some reason I found that rather moving. Strange how these things take you.

'We'll go sit in the lounge,' said Oomie. 'Have some coffee.'

The lounge was a large room with parquet flooring and lots of green leather armchairs, with a picture of Mandela on the wall, smiling down on us. At a couple of tables, people were playing cards. Other people were sitting staring ahead of them. Every so often a nurse would come in and turn them round a bit, or coax them to have a cup of tea. A couple of elderly ladies were ranged in front of an enormous TV, which was running a very violent American gangster movie. One guy kept smashing his gun into another guy's face. The old ladies watching did not move. When I was growing up TV was forbidden, like everything else that might frighten the voters. Then when TV finally arrived in 1976, someone made a bulk buy of B-grade stuff, and every set showed what seemed to be the same clip over and over again, for ever after. In bars, hotels, filling stations and corner shops you saw some guy who kept smashing his gun into someone else's face. It is very standard stuff. Hitting had always been our way of staying in touch.

Oomie sat me down in one of the green leather chairs and offered me coffee and fruit cake. I said no; to eat was somehow to take part in the submarine gloom of the room. Give him the stuff, I thought, and get the hell out.

But Oomie wasn't to be rushed. He seemed strangely comfortable, as if he felt good inside his skin, as if he'd made peace with whomever there was to make peace with.

'Sorry your mom passed away. She was a wonderful, wonderful woman.'

I said, 'Listen, Oomie, she wanted you to have something.

That's why I tracked you down. It's not money, or anything, it's
—' I stopped. How did I describe a personal armoury? 'It's
more ... personal.'

'*Ag* no,' he said. 'I'm very, very touched Kathleen remembered me.'

'She remembered everyone. I'm just not sure if she remembered them the way they wanted to be remembered.'

'Your mom had a hellavah sense of humour.'

'Did she? Sometimes I wished I knew my mother the way
others did.'

'*Ja*, she used to say to me, "Oomie, we must laugh at our
little peccadilloes, there will be time later to be saints." Only
your mom would call them peccadilloes.'

She had been very forgiving of Oomie's little lapse, his
failure of timing. In fact, it had endeared her to him far more
than it would have done had he blasted back at Pratt the
instant the silly fellow let fly at Verwoerd. But at the same time
I couldn't help feeling that coming from someone who had
never, so far as I knew, failed to shoot when the moment
demanded, or the target offered itself, there was something
especially perverse in her bequest to Oomie, something faintly
ominous. A man who couldn't handle a gun gets left her entire
arsenal.

Oomie said again: 'A wonderful woman. You must be very
proud, Alex.'

He had tears in his eyes. I never did know what to do with
what felt to me like excessive emotion. It frightened me, this
welling liquid. And it didn't feel right. My ma died as she had
lived, doing exactly what she wanted. There was nothing sad
about her; there was much that seemed to me shocking, outra-
geous and even cruel.

I said: 'So what you been doing, Oomie?'

'Long story, Alex. After the SAPS, I couldn't get no work, *ja*. But then I got a break: I heard they was looking for security people over at Sheba Sands. So I goes along and I meets this guy, Barrie Gluhnik. You know him?'

Who didn't? Gluhnik was a typical white South African; that's to say his family came from somewhere else, from Poland or Russia or Argentina or England, no one was quite sure, and it didn't matter. The family Gluhnik had come to this country, like many before them, hoping to get very rich, kick a lot of black ass and never work again.

But it hadn't panned out. Gluhnik had grown up poor in the southern suburbs of Jo'burg; he'd been in his time a wrestler, a bouncer, a water-diviner; he was burly, quick-witted and barely literate. Like many whites, if men like Gluhnik thought there was anything wrong with apartheid, it was that there wasn't a whole fucking lot more of it... But successful entrepreneurs soon learnt that backing the status quo never stopped you making a buck by beating the system. And Gluhnik found a way to do it.

Gluhnik saw that the price white guys were obliged to pay for a guarantee of lifelong superiority plus servants was large amounts of boredom. They sold their right to excitement (except on the rugby field or the rifle range) to a clique of rabid fundamentalists who branded any form of sexual expression theologically unsound because it offended God, or politically seditious because it offended them. In short, Gluhnik saw that most whites signed up to the dictum: 'A normal South African is a neutered South African.'

Barrie Gluhnik's first breakthrough was to see that, although they may have signed up to it, they didn't exactly like it. Having sworn off gambling, illicit sex and inter-racial mingling, there was a real itch for gambling, illicit sex and inter-racial mingling. His moment of illumination he summed up in a phrase: 'If you want an orgasm, go abroad.' So Gluhnik, in the 1960s, started an outfit called Pussycat Tours. Each week a planeload of punters took off from Jo'burg for Amsterdam and its red-light district, to Las Vegas and its gaming tables, to Hamburg and the girls in the Reeperbahn.

Pussycat Tours was a smash hit. But a planeload of blokes in safari suits does not make a very big market. If only Germany and Holland and Las Vegas were not so far away, if only abroad was closer to home …

I recalled reading an interview with Gluhnik who told of the moment when the answer came to him. 'It had been', Gluhnik told this interviewer, 'like a flash, like a vision. Like that doll had at Lourdes. Or St Paul, when he was heading down Damascus way on his camel, and blam! Know what I mean?'

His idea was simple. Why fly clients halfway round the world to do what they could do in our own back yard? South Africa was, in fact, littered with foreign countries. We had more foreign countries than we knew what to do with. All over the damn place the regime had created black homelands, with their own flags and presidents.

'OK,' said Gluhnik, 'if they are sovereign countries, why can't they have sovereign casinos, and sovereign bordellos, and sovereign striptease?'

That's when Gluhnik knew he had it made. He would create pleasure palaces in the bare veld where red-blooded South Africans could do whatever they did abroad – without leaving home. In the country down the road, or next door. Or over the hill. Sheba's Secret was the first of the great pleasure domes;

then the Solomon Sands, then the Monomatapo Majestic rose like mirages in the bone-dry veld of dirt-poor black reserves. They offered golf, girls, fruit machines and chorus lines, flown in from London and Vegas. There was striptease, mud wrestling and books, movies and musicals banned in South Africa. Sex across the colour bar was as easy as calling room service. And all just a couple of hours' drive from the gloomy Calvinist dungeon-state of white South Africa.

I said: 'Of course I know who he is.'

'Well,' says Lappies, 'Barrie Gluhnik looked over my CV and he says to me, "OK, Detective Sergeant, I'll tell you what. I see from your CV that you were security for Dr Verwoerd, and I remember from the papers there was, let's say, a little falling-out when the nutter Pratt took a pot-shot at the PM. I also know there's some that say you took a dive. But I say I think you did a good thing: you took cover, so as better to think about your next move. Now, I like a guy who thinks, Lappies, because the world is going more and more towards blokes what can use their heads. The days of goons is gone. There's always room for shooting, I got nothing against shooting, Lappies. There will always be shooting. But these are not the sixties any more, these are the seventies. The country's changing. We got a thinking Prime Minister now. We're gonna need *thinking* security. I've had the privilege of meeting Mr John Vorster and I want to tell you he's a true gent. Between you, me and the gatepost, I never liked Verwoerd. Too rigid. And a fucking immigrant to boot. But Vorster's different. He's gonna press ahead with these homelands, where blacks can stay blacks, but he wants them to be happy blacks. He wants them to love their homelands and I, Barry Gluhnik, help them to do just that: they work in my palaces as security, maids, caddies, guides, cleaners. People who never had a job before. The PM is very appreciative of that. Very. Let me tell you, I believe one day John Vorster will play golf with Gary Player on one of my championship courses. At the Solomon Sands, or the Sheba. How about that?"

'He must have seen the look on my face, 'cause he said: "I know, I know, you're thinking this guy's loony! The Prime Minister's never going to come to the Solomon Sands when the Soloman Sands is just one big casino and knocking shop, where everybody watches dirty shows, and sleeps with black girls, like they cannot do back home. Well, let me tell you, Lappies, I have a dream, just like that bladdy Martin Luther whatever he's called, over there in the States. I'll tell you my dream, Lappies. My palaces are just the start. One day, instead of people having to leave home to do what they want, they're gonna be able to do it at home! And when that happens everyone will see that Barrie Gluhnik wasn't just about gambling and girlie-shows and golf. Barrie Gluhnik was about freedom! He saw that when everyone is free to gamble all day, screw whoever they like and at the end of the day have a round of golf – and do it at home! – then we'll have a new South Africa. That's when they'll put up statues to me, like Winston Churchill, or Simon Bolivar. It'll be 'Barrie Gluhnik, Liberator'! What do you think, Lappies?"

'And I said: "Sorry, Mr Gluhnik, but as you're asking me, I think you're fucking crazy. It'll never happen."

'And he said, "You look after security, Lappies, and leave the vision stuff to me."

'So I did. I worked for Mr Gluhnik till I retired.'

Again, the watering of the eyes. 'And, you know, he was right. Today, we are like that. You don't need to go to the Solomon

Sands any more; you don't need to drive to the country next door to be free: you can be free, and do whatever you like, right here, at home.' Lappies looked up at the picture of Mandela. 'Mr Gluhnik saw it coming. The new South Africa. Hell, I'd put him right up there with Madiba.'

You had to hand it to these guys. From security cop ready to kill to weepy Mandela devotee. At the drop of a hat. I had no doubt he meant it. He would have hung Gluhnik next to Mandela, just as once he would have put Verwoerd there. Hell, he would have put Attila the Hun up there, if it kept the gods happy.

Across the room a nurse was feeding an old woman. The woman was thin and her skin was like silk tightly stretched, so smooth and shining. She had trouble chewing so the nurse was moving her jaws up and down. But she could barely swallow, so the nurse, who was big and black and young, massaged her neck after helping her to masticate, rubbing her neck the way a farmer will massage a goose's neck when he pours grain down its throat to enlarge its liver, from which one day he will make good *foie gras* ... Feeding the patient like this was the nurse's professional duty; but it was also a contest of wills. The old lady did not want to eat. I could see her trying to break free from the fingers clamped around her jaw, but the nurse was not going to relax her grip until the patient opened her mouth and took another bite. She did. Then the massaging of the neck began again and the old lady swallowed painfully, the nurse nodded and smiled, brightly, encouragingly, and implacably.

'You will eat your biscuit; you will swallow your food ...'

I remembered my mother in hospital. I remembered the warning to errant staff who had broken the rules:

'You will pay these fines ...'

My mother had died fighting the nurse, and the nurse had kicked back. For all the sweet talk about racial amity, there was a war going on, and it had hotted up since the end of hostilities had been proclaimed. In truth, there was no peace, there wasn't even a ceasefire. There was more anger, more killing and more hatred. We pretended more desperately. We lied to ourselves more fiercely. Like Oomie, we mutated.

Oomie looked so peaceful, so relieved, because he had made the leap of faith and ceased to think. His brain had turned to a watery mush. Verwoerd, Vorster, Gluhnik, Mandela ...

The place gave me the creeps. All the elderly residents were white; all the staff were black, and young. And it seemed to me that this was the way most whites were heading, straight into old-age homes, with smiling leaders, any leader, looking down benignly upon their last days. Out of the frying pan and into frail care; and pretty damn good riddance most of the country, the young country, would say.

Oomie saw me looking at Mandela and he said: 'A great man.'

'Yeah. That's why he had to be locked up all that time.'

'We didn't know.'

'Didn't know what, Oomie?'

'What was going on.'

'Balls. Everyone knew what was going on. It wasn't possible not to know. Everyone knew about it. People dying, being shot, vanishing, being kicked to death, thrown in jail, being assassinated, shadowed, spied on and blown to bits by parcel bombs. It was in the air, it was in the papers, day after day.'

'In the English papers,' said Oomie, 'but for us that was all just propaganda.'

'Come on, Oomie, be serious. You were amongst the guys who made sure what was going on kept going on.'

'Not me,' he said with complete conviction.

'But you were at the heart of the machine that made this happen.'

'How so?'

'Because you were there.'

'I never killed anyone, I never beat people to death, I never tortured them, or shot them and burnt them and buried them in the veld.'

I was wasting my time. You could travel the country and never find anyone who had loved and supported the old regime, the old gang, the old ways. It was a fucking miracle. Everyone had turned into Oomie. Or maybe Oomie had turned into everyone.

Just as bad was the suspicion that maybe this was the way to go. It wasn't just expediency, it was good sense, reasonable, necessary, even − God help us − kind.

'Shall we go get the stuff from my car?'

In the street he seemed nervous. 'You left your car outside, in the street? You're bladdy lucky you haven't been robbed.'

I opened the boot and we looked down at the guns. 'That's why I parked out here. I didn't know what the guards would say to this lot.'

'Jissss,' said Oomie, the air hissing between his teeth. 'There's a bladdy lot of them, isn't it?'

'She was a professional hunter; she needed a lot of guns. Heavy, medium and light gauge.'

'Hell, man, what'd she think I was going to do with all that?' *Go down shooting?*

I didn't say it. Why hit Oomie where maybe it still hurt?

And, yes, her armoury was impressive. But then again, when you thought about it, my mother had done a lot of shooting, a lot of killing. In fact, she was, in her way, a big-hearted mass murderer. That was, in a profound way, her *point*.

'Look, if the guns are a problem, tell me, and I'll just close the boot and take them back.'

'No, I'll keep them. They're from Kathleen. She wanted me to have them. It's just that I don't know how we'll get them inside, to my room. We can't just like walk past the desk carrying a load of shotguns. Maybe I could ask a favour? You drive around the corner, where you can't be seen from the desk, and you take out the guns and pass them over the wall. I'll be on the other side and I'll stick them behind the flowers. Then you come inside and help me get them to my room. How's that?'

That's what we did. I lifted the guns over the wall. Oomie hid them behind the dahlias, and then we collected them and took them to his room. It was a modest room with a cupboard, a table, a single bed with a blue candlewick counterpane. On the table was a picture of Oomie and Barrie Gluhnik. The cupboard was too small for the guns so we stowed them under his bed.

Oomie fetched a bottle of Klipdrift brandy from the bathroom.

'Can I give you one for the road?'

'Sure.'

He poured two shots of brandy and lifted his glass. 'Here's to your mom, God rest her soul.'

Again, his eyes filled with tears. What was it about Durban that induced these displays of emotion? I reckoned Alan Paton started the rot with *Cry, the Beloved Country*. Ever since then people have gone weepy each time someone remembered how bloody awful we had been. It has never done a blind bit of good. Oomie wept for my mother, but he also wept for himself. It was a powerful magic and I wished very much that some of it might touch me but it never had. I didn't in my heart feel in the least sorry for my mother. I felt sad that she was gone. I felt unsettled and abandoned, too. Her going had been, like all her departures, on her own terms and at her own pace, and in her own way.

No, if I did feel sympathy for anyone, it was for Oomie. He had been at a loss when he looked at the weapons. He felt uncomfortable to be faced by this gift – enough firepower to blow away a dozen prime ministers …

'What'll you do with the guns?'

He drained the last of his brandy. 'Hell, I don't know. But I'll think of something. Suppose I could always blow my brains out. Isn't it, hey?'

Still, maybe he'd been right about Gluhnik. Because of all those who'd been sure they knew how things would be in the new South Africa, when peace came and the future arrived, if you took a punt on Alan Paton or Gandhi, or Jan Smuts, or Hendrik Verwoerd, or Nelson Mandela, I think you'd have to say Barrie Gluhnik came in an easy winner.

Noddy turned up in Forest Town one night, dressed as he had been when I saw him off: Sunday best, the feather rampant. I put my arm around his shoulders, took his case and told him how glad I was to see him.

He couldn't say anything. He went to his room, hung up his suit and put away his hat. Next morning he was in the garden wearing his old pants and his T-shirt, and the day after that he was back with his other madams. I couldn't pull out the *Times*

Atlas and get him to show me exactly where he had been, and make him feel better about being someone who lived a lot of the time away from home, just as he had helped me to feel better about being a gypsy.

He seemed to be walking in his sleep. He'd been home and home had crumbled to dust. He was bereft. But I could do nothing to help him in his bereavement the way he'd helped me in mine. I knew he had listened to his brother, he had told Beauty to go. Joshua and Sipho could not go back to St Aloysius and the headmaster who had impregnated their mother. That was not possible. And they could not stay at home without a mother while he worked down south. So he had boarded the boys at his brother's place. They went now to a farm school three days a week. A bad school.

Maybe I should have said something that night he'd asked me about Beauty. But how could I advise a man whether or not to put away his wife? And what difference would it have made? Which way would I have gone? I had added my voice to those of his other madams and told him to be kind, to forgive. But I reckoned that in his shoes I was much more likely to have done what he did.

Anyway, it was eating him up.

He bought a blue overall with the legend: 'Executive Horticultural Assistant' in red stitching across the back. In place of his sober blue church suit, he bought himself as flashy a number as I'd ever seen. It was cream silk. It had golden buttons; it had a certain elegance; the vents of the jacket were lovely to look at; the turn-ups fell beautifully on his new brown and white golf shoes.

He had always been a tiny, dainty man but now he seemed to be shrinking, drying up from the inside. It was as if he had decided to be everything he hated before, as if his gravitas, the responsibility that he'd worked so hard for, was horrible to him now and he was going to squander it, ruin it, and ruin himself. Before he was always sober, now he was forever tanked; before he was solid, now he was flighty. Before he was Noddy, the farmer from Matabeleland; now he was wrecked. But showy.

He kept nothing of his old self. Certainly nothing of our friendship. Gone was the steady measured life in his back-yard room. We didn't talk or walk. He didn't come with me to the Zoo, or the costume museum. He didn't attempt to remedy my deficiencies in the garden. Gone was the sober suit on Sundays; gone was weekly trip to bank his wages, carrying the building society book, so comforting and fat in its red rubber bands. It was cash now for everything.

He had a new friend, one of the guys who worked down the road. His name was Jake and he lived in Alexandra and I didn't like him much. On Friday nights, Jake took Noddy to the she-beens in Alex, both in their sharpest suits. He'd be back much later completely smashed. Saturdays they'd wander down to the bottle store and come back with paper bags full of bottles and sit in Noddy's room and sink the stuff like there was no tomorrow.

Everyone was changing but Noddy wasn't built for it. Anyway, he was more interesting when still in his original form. And the least interesting of all was to evolve into a Jo'burg boykie, dress in his cream suit and hit the shebeens with Jake; everything dedicated to reflecting the brilliance, the cock and strut, the shimmer of the feather in his hat.

Noddy was undergoing some kind of internal collapse: a decline from the solid man from Matabeleland, who had weight and substance and reality, to the small, brittle made-up Jo'burg wise guy.

It was closer to self-mutilation. It was not natural organic change but obligatory metamorphosis, a kind of plastic surgery of the soul. The only question was: did you do it to yourself, or did it happen anyway? Let's call it identity trauma in an age of change.

Where does a whale keep its heart?

That was the question my mother asked me once.

I'd been about thirteen and we were walking along the beach in Durban, where we were spending a week's holiday, and we came across two Southern Right whales stranded high on the sand. It appeared that several attempts had been made to pull them back into the sea. Harnesses had been draped over their enormous bodies and, here and there, the ropes had cut deep into skin and blubber.

Near them, in a deck chair, there was posted a skinny white guy, burnt mahogany by the Durban sun, a tiny tennis visor on his mottled bald head and a big box of Westminster 50s in his breast pocket. He was there to keep out blacks, Indians and Coloureds who might have had the nerve to try sitting on sand assigned to others. He was angry now, as only a white functionary could be who suddenly had to deal with the unexpected, and improvise.

'Fucken,' said the deck-chair man.

'Fucken what?' asked my mother, helpfully.

He was not happy, the deck-chair man. In reply he jerked his tennis visor towards the whales.

I saw some kids playing on the whales, scampering up a black and shining shoulder, skipping around the encrusted barnacles, then sliding down again, as if the whales were giant beach toys, huge, inflated inner tyres.

'Fucken people, that's what.'

Such were the crowds of the curious that however often he shooed them away, as one might clouds of flies, the next thing they were back.

Worse, they were 'mixed'. What contributed to the anarchy was the fact that, although people knew they were not permitted on beaches other than those colour-coded to their racial grouping, there was nothing in the law that said you could not go down to the sea and look at two beached whales. The whales were bigger than the beach laws. Besides, the sightseers were not swimming or sunbathing or eating ice creams – all expressly forbidden – they were gawping at two giant fish.

'I got coolies, kaffirs and klonkies ... I got bladdy liquorice all-sorts ... Now, I don't give a toss about these bladdy whales, but that's not nice, is it? Using them as a kids' playground? Taking rides? Some people, they come with knives and cut off whole pieces!'

'It's horrible. They should be put out of their misery,' my mother said.

'Sure thing, lady. But what d'you want me to do? Hit them on the head? I spend the whole bladdy day keeping the fucken people off the bladdy whales. I didn't ask to do it. I get paid to see to the chairs, and the chairs is all I get paid to see to. And keeping the wrong people off the beach. Not off the whales.'

My mother said as we walked away: 'Why didn't I bring my rifles?'

'Do you know how to shoot a whale?'

'I'd find out.'

'Where would you shoot a whale?'

'Head. I suppose. That's where I'd shoot an elephant. I don't know about a heart shot. Where does a whale keep its heart?'

I considered that. The whale had a very large head and so, I assumed, a very large brain. But I did not know where whales kept their hearts. How many shots would you need?

'Ma, I don't think you could just walk on the beach and shoot those whales. They harpoon whales, don't they?'

'What does it matter how you do it? To leave them lying here is a crime.'

The next day the word went out that the authorities had a plan for the humane disposal of the whales. We went down to the beach, and found hundreds already waiting. The deck-chair man seemed to have given up and gone home. The sand had already banked up on the seaward side of the creatures and the smell was strong. They had trucks, a crane and a man in a white coat and lots of municipal workers. There were cops with loudhailers and we were pushed back some fifty yards or more from the whales.

Supervised by the guy in the white coat, workers cut into the heads of the whales with flensing knives. Then small charges of dynamite were set into the cranial spaces and, with a meaty boom, their brains were blown out. My mother could not resist nudging me. 'See? Head shot.' The cranes lifted the mighty remains on to flat-bed trucks and the headless bodies were taken away to be turned, it was said, into animal feed.

'Next time, save the whales – and blow up the bystanders,' muttered my mother.

Looking back now, through the long lens of memory, I saw her and Queen Bama, sitting in the little parlour, sipping tea and shuddering at the world. Far away and fading fast. And I thought of those whales. Washed up and waiting for someone to come along and dynamite them to kingdom come.

I did not know where Noddy was going, but he was off somewhere, that was sure, and I missed him already. He was one of the few friends I had made since coming home.

Except maybe for Cindy, and so I phoned her and asked her to come over. I had a problem, I said, a problem with staff.

27

Noddy was forking over the sweet-pea patch, wearing his blue overall with its 'Executive Horticultural Assistant' tag, when I took her over to him.

'Noddy, I want you to meet Cindy; she's a friend of mine.'

He stopped digging and gave her his shy smile. 'Hello, madam.' Then, spitting on his hands, he picked up the big garden fork and went back to his work.

We went inside. Through the windows we could see him working with a furious concentration that made me sad.

Cindy said: 'Noddy? Is that really his name?'

'Noddy of the Five Madams. He insists. But his real name is Uthlabati, which means "Red Earth Man".'

'Where did you find him?'

'He was here when I came. He has the back-yard room.'

Cindy watched him 'He's not a happy bunny.'

'No.'

'Live-in staff are bad news. Very. Most people use the agencies now. You don't need live-in. You ship in who you want; ship 'em out end of the day. No drama that way.'

'But don't lots of people still have live-in staff?'

'Yeah, but mostly old-school types. Or they're just plain lonely. The kids have left for Detroit, or Calgary, or wherever.

The house is too big, too empty. So they cling to their staff. Bribe them, pet them, cosy up to them, buy them cars, send them on holidays, even adopt their kids – anything to keep them sweet. It can be useful. You pass it off as proof of what a great rainbow person you are, but it hides the truth: you're shit scared of being left alone so paying the maid's kid to study medicine or rocket science looks good. And maybe it'll keep you safe from burglars, rapists and guys keen to bop you over the head one dark night.'

'Does it?'

'Sometimes. And then again, sometimes it's your staff that does the bopping. You like the guy, don't you?'

'He's from somewhere else. He's like me: a traveller.'

'Yes. But there must be more.'

'I like him, and I let him down. He came to me for help when his wife ran off with some guy and I didn't help. He's been really torn up by it.'

Her pretty face softened for a moment. 'I can relate to that. Happened to me with Andy. Happened to you with your mom.'

'Please, don't give me the Oedipal stuff.'

'Your mom always felt you ran off; she spent her life trying to get you back. She told me so.'

'Listen, she ran off with an entire regiment of guys. She ran off with a bloody continent. She went her way and I went mine.'

'She ached for you to come back, Alex. She wept for you.'

'Are we talking about the same person?' I didn't recognise my mother in the woman she was talking about.

'Yes, she said you only understood things looking back.'

Maybe that was right. Maybe that was what I was lacking.

I couldn't see how to go about making myself into the sort of person who would be recognised here, in Africa, or who could see what others really were. But there was no 'really', just as there was no 'nice'. Only constant refashioning, method-acting your new role until you became what you played.

As I took from the house, one after the next, those things my mother wished her inheritors to have, as I saw the house emptying, I'd hoped to get closer to doing the sensible thing: to sell up and head out. Once I'd tracked down the last of the beneficiaries, I'd be off. That's what I told myself. But I had the uncomfortable feeling that I was lying to myself and it wasn't just unfinished business that kept me stuck in Forest Town: it was something in me. I wasn't finished.

For reasons I could not explain, Noddy was important even as he went down the tubes. There was something about his transformation that I failed to understand and bitterly regretted. Uthlabati, the man of red earth, the man of quality, was on his way to becoming a parody of a flash guy around town. And yet maybe precisely because he was altering so disastrously it meant he got closer to the way to be than I ever had. I kept feeling there was something he was trying to tell me, something my old lady had in mind when she left him to me, along with the house.

'So what do I do about him?'

She gave a little shrug. 'Why don't you fire him?'

'It's too late: he's fired me, that's my problem.'

She put her hand on my arm, then she put her arm around my shoulders and like that we walked to her car. I could feel Noddy behind us, watching, forking over the earth, driving the shining tines deep into the dark red earth.

Cindy said: 'Listen. There's a big bash, Saturday night, at the Prester John's Palace, in Sandton. Fourways Rotary is giving a dinner in aid of Sunbeam Shelter. Not my usual thing, but it's a duty, really. Would you like to come with?'

'With?'

'With me. As, like, my partner.'

'It's been a while since anyone asked me to a party.'

She looked at me steadily. 'Does that mean yes?'

'Thank you. It does.'

She gave her dazzling smile. 'Nothing to thank me for, you may hate it. It may be very, very ordinary. Pick you up around seven.'

She was dead on time, wearing an off-the-shoulder black dress with a neckline whose diving descent between her breasts reminded me of a fast ski run. Her hands were deft on the wheel and she talked and laughed and did her Jo'burg riff as we drove, stabbing the air with her forefinger, a perfect pink nail driving downward as if to tear the air apart and make it bleed. Always this immense emphasis. Noddy had used the same force to drive the garden fork into the sweet-pea patch. I lived in a world of agitated air. Angry interrogation, pronouncement, edict, threat: these were the ways the country talked to itself. What a perfect opportunity for the missionary who wished to teach easier breathing.

But it would have been silly to try. They did not want it; there was no discussion, there was declamation: you shouted, or took a shot at something …

The evening headlines were on the street; blocky black capitals on shiny white posters, wired to the lampposts:

Racism Row Hits Rugby

100-Year-Old Granny Eats Baby

Motorist, Hijacker Die in Shootout

Residents Stone Rapist

Rand Lurches Lower

Cindy was talking hold-ups with the same happy passion with which she'd taught me her rules for staying alive.

'Armed heists, cash-in-transits: they're so bloody well organised, so frequent, you wonder why these gangs aren't running the country.'

'Maybe they are.'

'Yah, and if they aren't maybe they should ... hey? If you're going to be ruled by gangsters, at least let them be pros. Better all round.'

One of my mother's delights had been flying over the Serengeti, skimming so low she could hear the drumming hooves of the stampeding zebra. Cindy got high enumerating the advantages of the secure parking. She gave a rave to the facilities offered by Prester John's Palace and Casino.

'I mean, it's essential. Izzzuntut?'

'Is it?'

'Sure. Who'd go out otherwise? It's like sex, hey? If you're not relaxed, you can't perform. Isn't it? If you don't feel safe, you can't spend. If you're not happy, you won't come. Given the schlep of just getting there, Christ almighty, the last thing some hotel or shopping mall or casino wants is for you to be shot dead in the parking lot. It pays to keep the punter alive. Know what I mean?'

I knew what she meant but marvelled all the same.

'You'll see how good it is at this place we're going to tonight. You're out of your car and into the lobby without looking over your shoulder. Mind you, they learnt the hard way. At the start Prester John's had this idea of transparency, right? When they built the place everything was see-through. Crystal, glass, Perspex: desk, walls, shop fronts, the works. That way they thought nobody could sneak up on them. You could see right through the lobby into the shopping mall on the other side. But the morning after it opened an armoured car drives smack through the plate-glass doors and into the lobby. Four guys with machine-guns jump out, shoot the desk clerk and rob every single shop in about thirty minutes flat. Nobody could do anything but watch. They called it "the see-through heist". The place hadn't been open twenty-four hours and they got hit. It set some sort of record.

'Boy, have we or have we not got talent? These gangs have a structure. On the ground they use "spotters" to case the joint before the hit. Then there are stealers, who hijack the get-away vehicles used for the heist. Then drivers. And then the shoot-ers, who do the hit. They use heavy stuff, often AK 47s, and wear body armour, and send a lot of lead around the place and scare the shit out of everyone. Even if you've got big security. Even if the cops arrive in minutes, what are they going to do? Shoot back and kill passers-by? Anyway, half the time the cops are outgunned. In the effective armed heist we lead the world. One person, one vote, one AK 47. What a town!'

She laughed that high trill in which were mixed pain and pride; true amusement with a sharp edge of hysteria. Could you be proud to be scared? You could if you were Cindy.

That was one of the best things the town did to those who

lived there. When they got to the other side of all the big talk and the bullshit, people took a dark delight in being sinner, shyster, seducer; in being down so deep they had nowhere left to go but up. And how were you going to con everyone else if you couldn't do a pretty good job on yourself? But after telling yourself things had never been better, bigger, richer, safer, fairer, then came the flash of honesty that grubbed in the dirt and the dark, like moles, and came up with what you said was gold. But moles were blind, weren't they?

The Prester John's Palace was a cliff-face of bland stone glittering with glass and marble trimmings, standing in a grid of streets with women's names like Alice and Maud. Within its brightly lit cells, people ceaselessly shopped. The tower held within it the Prester John. We turned into the parking lot and dropped steeply down into the basement, our tyres squealing softly as we descended.

Four levels down, a flunkey dressed in powdered wig and white silk stockings stepped forward, as if expecting us. Cindy handed him her keys, and he all but kissed her hand. We walked out of the garage and into the hotel lobby set about with fountains, finished in black and pink marble. The whole place was hung with banners and posters shaped like hearts, each one pierced by a thorny arrow and inset with the photograph of a child.

'Prester John Loves Sunbeams', said the banners floating in the vast lobby.

'Our Little Angels', said the posters.

The staff wore golden 'Sunbeam' halos with jagged edges.

'Well, what do you reckon?' said Cindy. 'Nicely over the top, or what?'

'I'm impressed.'

'That's the spirit,' said Cindy. 'This just might be fun.'

We stepped into the glass lift and drifted skywards. The lift shaft had been lined in thick pink plush. It felt as if we were travelling up through a very deep throat, fleshy and gleaming. We passed lounge after lounge where thick-necked men in smooth, costly suits sat over drinks in spaces so large they shrank to the size of lonely midgets. The fountains reached roofwards like watery palm trees.

The African Renaissance Room was a domed penthouse built to evoke a giant beehive, or traditional tribal hut, in vaguely Zulu manner. The expansive floor area was broken here and there by rectangles of neatly raked pebbles, and Japanese paper screens. It was a style, Cindy told me, known on the cluster estates as 'Neo-Fusion' or 'Afro-Zen'. The great windows looked down to the highway far below where long lines of Saturday night thrill-hunters, each car chained to the next by the bright links of its headlights, headed for the fruit machines and gaming tables in clubs called The Erogenous Zone and Flagrante Delicto, for an evening of lap-dancing and karoake. In the middle of the dance floor, a raised canvas square with roped borders was rather puzzling.

Cindy looked at it. 'What do you reckon?'

'Of the dance floor? I've been here before.'

Oh, had I ever been there before! What I felt was the shock of the deeply familiar. Laid out before me, in the Renaissance Room of the Prester John's Palace, was an event I knew deep in my marrow. This was, with small variations, what I'd known thirty years before. Maybe it was *foie gras* and not chicken in a basket, maybe it was twenty-year-old Chivas Regal and not brandy and Coke, Martinis and not port and lemon, maybe it was black tie and five hundred bucks, and it wasn't in the church hall, it was a high in the glassy eaves of the Prester John's Palace, corner of Alice and Maud Streets, Sandton – but it was the same damn thing come back to haunt me. I had one foot planted in Vegas and the other buried in the back yard. Thirty years after I left Jo'burg I was back at a fucking dinner dance.

Moving on.

People in this town were continually kidding themselves they had moved on. In fact, what we, our tribe, the last pale speakers of English in Africa, did not do – *ever* – was move on. What we did was to sink into retirement, obscurity. The young in New Zealand, the old on Zimmer frames or taking refuge on residential golfing estates, checking share prices, cruising to the Maldives, or fixing nostalgic school reunions where men called Harry ask for news of Merle, last seen in Rhodesia in 1954, and before that head girl at Parktown High…

Not moving but drowning.

We inhabited a universe whose essence could be summed up in the single word 'more'. We went to bed dreaming of more Mercedes, and woke up dreaming of more mansions on the coast. Our former serfs seemed to have hit on a way of destroying their old tormentors by giving them what they wanted – *more* – opening their mouths and pouring it in, making sure they swallowed it, like the nurse did, her fingers massaging the throat of the old woman in Oomie's retirement home. More! Shovelling down our gullets the treasure that would choke us.

'No, not the dance floor,' said Cindy. 'I meant the ring.'

•

'I don't know. That, I must say, is new. Kickboxing? Mud wrestling?'

She gave her helpless, happy, despairing laugh. 'Oh, my God! Let's find our table. Whatever it's for, I'd like to be sitting down when I find out.'

Large round tables covered in creamy linen were liquid with silver and crystal. Our table was beside the dance floor. There were flowers and pink place cards and a crowd of people hitting the scotch. Our table companions were reasonably tanked, and talked about themselves with the openness of Jo'burgers meeting for the first time. In a few minutes you knew where they worked, what they believed and where they played golf.

To my right sat Sharalee and Duane, who were in advertising and marketing. To Cindy's left sat Lindiwe and Tembi, in matching gold and black tunics. Lindiwe was with the Ministry of Health; Tembi headed up a black empowerment outfit called Afri-One.

Sitting opposite them was a merchant banker called Jacobus; he sold what he called 'financial instruments'. His wife, Monique, helped small businesses to cross the divide between the old, cold South Africa and the new, warm fiefdom of the future.

Beside them sat Rupert and Petronella, a couple of leathery throwbacks. Rupert once headed up the Farmers Bank. Petronella, solid as steel under her green silk gown, her face sitting high and proud of her immense bosom, was a lifelong trustee of Sunbeam Shelter. The sunburnt folds of their faces were stitched into smooth seams rather like crocodile-skin handbags. They embodied a type: ruddy-faced men; women with rasping voices who had once had it all for the taking –

sun, smoke, whisky. Their coterie had once run state banks and nationalised industries. They'd got out when the former regime collapsed, fortunes intact, and now did very little: some charity work, a lot of golf. They'd washed up in comfortable retirement, wrecked but rich.

Also there – corn-blond hair, and a rumbustious manner – was Willem. And on the other side of Cindy a guy called Dikene. Their wives, Nicoleen, white, slim and svelte, and Tanzi in black, ebony and ivory, like two piano keys. They talked babies. Willem and Dikene talked money. Willem was in construction. Dikene had been a youth leader in 'a local party structure' until, said Willem, 'as CEO, I decided to bring him on board'. In doing so he had made Dikene a millionaire. In return, Dikene had sweetened Willem's image among the new masters of the universe by altering his alias from what Willem happily described as 'exploiter, racist and Boer bastard' into what Dikene called 'a forward-looking element within the new democratic structures'.

It was hard to think of Willem, so exuberantly what he had always been – a noisy bully with a big bank balance – as an 'element' in the ' structures' of anything except his sport-bound world. But words were the paint needed to tart up old models, and words came cheap and were mutually advantageous. The cosy swap Willem and Dikene had pulled off had nothing new in it. The pattern had been fine-honed over the decades by the Dutch, then by the British, then by the Boers, then by Afrikaner nationalists so recently departed. In those days, heavy men like Willem (except then he would have been among the supplicatory classes and spoken English) with interests in cement, or steel, or gold, would have palled up with men just like Dikene (he would have been an Afrikaans power-broker) and cut a deal.

It was called 'mutual co-operation' then; it was called 'transformation' now; but whichever you named it, everyone agreed that this time round it was genuinely new. There had never been anything like it before. Right? Forget the past, forget what the world was, or you were. Embrace forgetfulness, dissolve your doubts, and don't listen to anyone who said things were not a thousand times better. Forgetfulness wasn't just useful, it was patriotic. Denial wasn't a fault, it was a career move.

For this was our destiny, we the pale ones, we the ridiculous ones, who had neither the gall of our old masters, who knew that murder was better than prevarication and power was more perfect than any principle, nor the authenticity of our new rulers because they can say what we never could, except when lying through our many pieces of fatuous headgear. They can say they know who they are. We never even get close.

Those around our table, huddling close to what they hoped were the new renewable forms of power, skimmed across a glittering surface, gold ring on one ear, cellphone tacked to the other, telling themselves, 'We've changed, we've changed, we've changed, we're moving on, we are new, we are free, a liberated, tolerant tribe, with DVDs in our BMWs, anti-hijack satellite trackers in our 4x4s, winners in the racial rainbow stakes ...'

It looked like being quite an evening.

Supper was served. There was smoked salmon and venison. The wines were good. The waitresses, in short black skirts, white aprons and mob-caps, moved between the tables, but I had the feeling some moved very slowly, unsurely, and others held hands. And their eyes were strangely still.

Cindy whispered, 'Do you think those girls are what I think they are? The ones that bump about a bit between the tables?'

I said – not quite believing it myself – that I thought they were.

Cindy let out a long breath and raised her eyes to heaven. 'God Almighty.'

Petronella, across the table, caught her look. 'You noticed, hey?'

Cindy nodded sweetly. 'You're using blind girls as waitresses?'

'Not all. Some of them can see a bit. Each unsighted girl has a helper, like her seeing eyes. At first we thought they could use their dogs but Prester John's management said no dogs in the dining area. So we got in seeing girls, too. There are eighteen waitresses altogether. Nine from St Thomas's School for the Blind and nine from the Orange Grove Orphanage,' said Petronella briskly. 'Fourways Rotary believes very strongly in helping the disabled.'

'*Ag*, shame!' said Nicoleen. 'Blind girls, and girls who got no moms or dads. Working for kids in Sunbeam Shelter. That's so cute.'

In a way they were. Most of them in their teens, peachy-fresh in their maids' outfits, flushed and nervous as they reached to clear plates and glasses and serve fresh courses.

Lindiwe from the Health Ministry was talking about ramps. 'Government wants to improve access for everyone: the handicapped, as well as women, and kids, too. Government says participation at all levels is the aim.' She took a large bite of venison. 'That means more ramps!'

'Ramps?' asked Jacobus.

'Lots more ramps,' said Lindiwe. 'Government has a national plan to install ramps outside all government buildings and to make a plan to employ quotas of disabled people in all government departments. But government can't do it all. Government looks to private enterprise. Government hopes all stakeholders will come to the party.'

'I think it's wonderful, letting people participate,' said Monique, who helped people bridge the transition between old and new South Africa. 'I think it's fabulous. It's just a pity that those who make change happen in our country don't get the recognition they deserve.'

At about ten o'clock, over coffee and liqueurs, the lights in the Renaissance Room dimmed and bright spots flooded the boxing ring, which had small flickering neon hearts hanging from the ropes. A girl in a golden cloak dipped under the ropes and stood in corner of the ring. A man in a silver cloak took up a position in the opposite corner. A second woman in silver and second man in gold now entered the ring: four cloaked figures in the four corners of the ring, where the pink neon hearts flicked on and off. Ravel's *Boléro* started up and with a simultaneous flourish, rather like that which waiters use to lift the lids of silver salvers, all four people in the ring removed their cloaks and stood there, wearing nothing but a coating of oil, brief thongs and ballet slippers.

A man and woman moved now to the centre of the ring, grappled, and began to mime, in detail, positions from the Kama Sutra, while the other couple waited at the end of their ropes. It was something between tag wrestling and a live sex show.

This beat the hell out of anything I might have imagined. Judging by the way Cindy reached for my hand and squeezed it, I think even she was pretty shaken. This was, after all, as I kept trying remind myself, a fundraiser run by solid citizens on behalf of a school for kids with special needs. But, then, as Cindy never tired of telling me, this was also Jo'burg.

The Renaissance Room was very quiet. I guessed that even old hands were pretty awed by what was playing out in the ring. The only sounds were the occasional chink of glasses when one of the sighted waitresses blundered into something. To the blind waitressess the dark was no problem, but it made things hard for their orphan helpers.

In the spotlit ring each dancer, or partner, replaced the other until, in a loud finale, all four people joined in a palpitating foursome of backs, bottoms and body oil, a choreographed group orgy, and everyone clapped and whistled.

There was pistachio ice cream for dessert with a lychee sauce. I sat there in a little buzz of happiness. I had just seen simulated sex in a boxing ring in front of a room full of Rotarians.

I could admit it now, Cindy had me on toast. I thought I knew Jo'burg. I was wrong. I understood then her helpless awe when confronted by the inventiveness and grotesquery of local life. A-1 kooks; alpha lunatics. You couldn't have told anyone about what I'd just seen: they would not have believed it. I struggled to believe it myself.

A waitress squeezed her way past the back of Rupert's chair and he turned appreciatively and said in a clear voice, 'Nice little backsides they got, hey?'

Petronella spoke to him from on high, as if she were some ocean liner hailing an errant leisure craft: 'Rupert, man, don't let's have any nonsense, hey!'

'*Ag* man, I'm just looking.'

'Looking never stops there,' said his wife.

And it didn't stop there, with the pistachio ice cream and people back on the dance floor, because, what with the wine and the floor-show sending a charge though the crowded room, things got hotter, and it was the waitresses who felt it first. A hand lay lightly on a passing hip; at the next table a big man with a beard pulled a girl on to his lap. Somewhere someone was crying. At our table, Duane planted a kiss on the nape of a waitress who had bent to clear his plate, and a small blonde girl who made the mistake of reaching past the old leathery crocodile straightened suddenly with a little scream, and ran away, tripping as she did so and sending her tray crashing to the floor. And all around me women were saying, loudly, accusingly: '*Ag* shame, man!'

Someone took the mike then and said he had a 'Very Important Announcement', but wild cheers drowned him. 'Please, folks, please, folks,' he kept saying, until at last they let him speak. 'We're getting reports of some folks preventing the girls from approaching the tables.' (Applause) 'Now, it's been a lovely evening, guys.' (Cries of 'Yes! Yes!') 'Let's not spoil it. Play the ball, not the man.' (Laughter) 'Our waitresses have done a sterling job here tonight and they want to get home to bed.' (Laughter/cheers) 'So folks, may I ask you to take your partners for a last dance ...'

They all danced, and then they all sang the national anthem. It sounded pretty good, too, and quite covered up the sound of the sobbing that went on softly somewhere out of sight.

•

In the car Cindy said: 'Well?'

'A complete triumph.'

She glanced across at me and said in the straight way of hers, 'Do you want me to take you back?'

I thought about it, about the empty house, about Noddy, brooding in the back-yard room.

'I don't have much to go back to.'

'That's what I reckoned,' she said, and swung the car towards Midrand and Sheerhaven. It was past midnight, the traffic had thinned, and the pavements were deserted. Only the lost, the dangerous and homeless walked after dark.

We stopped at the lights where Sandton Drive hit William Nicol; the headlines read: 'Ten Shot Dead in Bed.'

A huge triangular neon sign mounted on a traffic island flashed its message in the night: 'Say Hello to Safe Sex or Say Goodbye to Life.'

Later, she lay back with her eyes closed, her dark hair spread on the snowy pillow, the tip of her nose pointed directly at the angel blowing a trumpet which she had painted on the ceiling, a blonde angel with flesh like butter, borrowed from Rubens, and a pretty face borrowed from her son, Benny.

With her clothes off, stretched out, there was something entrancing about her symmetries, the way she lay perfectly horizontally, and pointed: her nose at the angel, her nipples at the overhead light, a fluffy affair of pink satin; her toes, smoothed with a soft nail varnish, aiming at the mirror on the wall opposite the bed, a scalloped mirror of gold frame and bevelled glass in which, for the past hour, Cindy had been riding. Making love, for her, was rather like making off on some far trip. She worked softly, slowly, with little circular movements of her pelvis, her eyes shut, a lock of hair over her eyes, a look of peaceful intense concentration. The mirror gave back its brazen view, her firm brown breasts rising and falling above my softer, older body as she built and built and rode herself to climax.

Then there was Cindy ridden, someone else again: stretched out, letting her head fall back over the base of the bed, her strong brown to my pale, mothy white. Her dark hair trailing, her eyes open, expectant, as if I should take her somewhere; as if, by watching and hoping, by some miracle, she should not end up where she had started.

v   Mutant Strains

'*Wapiganapo tembo nyasi huumia.*'
'When elephants fight the grass gets hurt.'
Swahili proverb

28

Cindy and I had a thing going, though precisely what it was neither of us knew, or much cared. I asked her, just once, what she saw in me.

'I see your mother in you.' Enjoying my bewilderment, she added, 'And, for that matter, so does Benny.'

She was so clear about it that all I could manage was 'Really?'

'Sure. That's why he likes you.'

Cindy took me as one takes a trip, a slug of booze, a whack of something mind-bending: for respite, relief, escape, recreation; yes, in order, for a while, to think of something else, to be someone else.

Her hair, cut to a point over each cheekbone, reminded me of the tips of black palm fronds. Her short, sturdy body, her short perfect shirt, her high backless heels, her slightly chunky calves, big leather bag, her poise on those high heels, her air of someone always being perfectly turned out even though she also always seemed to have thrown her clothes on at the last moment, always in a hurry, always late. Yet all of her always arrived together.

Cindy was the most accomplished actress and make-up artist. It was her ability to become the woman she played that fascinated me. I had been in awe of Maxine, and her passion, but she was, in our terms, very familiar. Cindy came trailing all sorts of recognisable signs that tied her to this place, to Africa, yet so much of her was strange and new. I'd never met anyone so fiercely original. I think I fell in love with her in much the way uncounted uncles had fallen in love with my mother, and for very similar reasons. The intensity of her vision of herself and her city and her life. My mother escaped skywards, reaching across the continent from Cape to Cairo, but that had been in another era when the rulers of all had automatic overflying rights. You could say my mother never had her feet on the ground (she would have been the first to agree). Her feeling about Africa was that it actually encouraged her to leap over it in her seven-league boots. A version, indeed, of the boots she had left to Cindy. They were far too big, that was clear from the start, and the contrast in the way they saw their worlds was also vastly different. Kathleen Healey's was the view from the clouds. Her Africa was airy, free, and endless.

Cindy was an insider. Her country a was a tightly guarded stockade, a Tuscan villa set in an English close; copper storks on the lawn, fat golfers shuffling over the fairway, electric fencing and infra-red sensors buried deep in the earth to stop the tunnellers; it was a pink Porsche, sudden death at the traffic lights. It was, at the same time, utterly of the place; and about as far away from 'Africa' as she could get. It was about being somewhere else.

Cindy, too, like my former wife, Benita, had never in her life met or mixed with Africans. Cindy lived among millions of darker-skinned people but it did not mean she saw them, knew them or credited them with any sort of existence except as a

shadowy presence: benevolent when it washed ⟨
when it erupted in fury and kicked someone's ⟨

To some degree they both shared a view ⟨
island, midway between mundanity and ma⟩
Dutch have reclaimed precious land from the sea, p⟩
South Africans have turned back the tides of Africa by building dykes, beautiful walls, fences, barricades, built them not
just of bricks and razor wire but of strategic ignorance.

The differences between Cindy and Benita became terribly
clear when you knew where they came from. Benita was once
vaguely 'British'. Cindy would have been called 'Coloured', or
'mixed race', 'brown Afrikaner', mulatto, or some other ugly
designation. In the recent, even more cracked terminology of
our new times, some insisted she be called 'black'. But in truth,
and in life, she was as far from being black or African or native,
as Benita was from being British. Benita believed or imagined
that she possessed a real provenance: she came from somewhere and, much more importantly, she come from *someone*;
she belonged to a long and honourable line of Anglo-Saxon
adventurers who had headed off for foreign parts and called
them home. Or so she said. But people like Benita were ghosts.
She called herself 'African' but it never convinced anyone; not
even her, I think. People like Benita had to pretend to belong,
pretend to be normal, pretend to be alive.

Cindy didn't know who her progenitors had been and, for a
long time, if she had known she wouldn't have said a word about
it. She knew, so ran the common wisdom, that people like her
did not exist till Dutch settlers slept with slaves, or Hottentots,
or anyone else in convenient chains, and then, appalled by their
own faces in the mirror, denied any resemblance. People like

dy were walking warnings of what happened when you crossed the racial borders marked out by our rulers from the very first moment white met black in Southern Africa, and unbuckled his belt or reached for his rifle.

But while all claims to identity had been a boast, or a lie, it had been the 'Coloureds' who were forced to live out the cruellest fictions.

Cindy was a ghost, pretending to be a Jo'burg princess. The one-time 'Coloured' girl from a dusty township was now the mistress of Sheerhaven, with her Porsche and her Gucci bag and her stunning impersonation of a Jo'burg dolly-bird, as svelte as they come this side of Sandton, living in a sphincter-tight security in a villa in Beauchamp Drive, in what she called '*absolute bladdy luxury*'.

You'd have sworn she was straight out of Parkview and Saxonwold and Sandton, Sandhurst and Rivonia. A good school, followed by a couple of years on a fine arts degree. She was the epitome of the Jo'burg 'kugel', those warrior matrons, or Armani maidens, named for round doughy sweetmeats, so delicious and so dangerous, stuffed with raisins, and razor-blades.

Every stroke of this portrait was made up as she went along. And she didn't pretend it was anything else, she was proud to be what she'd turned herself into. That was the advantage of being forced to lead many lives: sometimes you hit one that suited you, one you could pass off as your very own. She was a lovely creation, and she'd done it all herself: a true queen in a camp full of con artists.

What I did not realise – not for a while – was that she might decide to do it all over again.

The only time Cindy showed any sympathy for her ex-husband was when she told me that Benny was not just a Down's boy, he was also slightly autistic.

'That really finished off Andy. He used to say he could deal with the other things because we knew what to expect. I mean how Benny looked, the rounder face, and the fact that he was slow, that he didn't grow as fast as other kids, and the way he had a smaller mouth and the way his tongue stuck out. It still does. Maybe he could have taken that. But then there were Benny's fixations. He will only sit on a special chair in one place at one time. He switches every light in the room on and off exactly six times. He carries the tennis racket with him everywhere. It's a toy and a friend and security blanket. He goes to bed with that racket. When I changed my car from the Porsche to a Merc, he went bananas. I had to go get the old car back.'

Benny was her joy and her terror. He was, I suppose, not only her child but also the child in her. Because of his slow and dreamy way, because of his fixations – with small round objects, golf balls, plum tomatoes, marbles, which he would twirl between finger and thumb for hours at a time, and his distant but affectionate way of hugging her, or me, or the cushions on the settee, or the table leg, with equal passion – he had an unearthly remoteness you simply could not penetrate. He would, occasionally, abruptly, affectionately, reach out to you; but you could not reach into him.

Watching Benny was like watching a creature in a perpetual state of preparing to be, to come out into the world. And though he always seemed on the brink of doing so, Benny never emerged: he was away in his own space, and love might look in, but it could not step inside. It pained her terribly; she tried but she could not reach into him. He was sometimes perfectly loving, but only on his own terms. He hugged and kissed her, but he hugged and kissed me, too, and anything else that took not his heart but his inner eye – he tried to hug the Porsche – his love simply went equally in all directions.

'Oh, hi, Alex,' was all he said one morning, when he found me in bed with his mother. 'Have you seen my golf ball?'

'You left it in the fridge, with the tomatoes,' said Cindy.

Benny nodded. 'Good, it keeps fresher that way, doesn't it?' And climbed into bed with us.

He said to his mother, 'Why have you got no pyjamas on?'

'Because I'm as warm as toast.'

Benny drew back the sheets and looked hard at her naked body. 'You do not look like toast to me. You look like … an orange …'

'Why an orange?'

'Because you got all little grooves in your skin, just like an orange.'

'Those are goose-bumps,' said his mother, who found Benny's dreamy stare, so deep and yet so blind, very disconcerting.

'Why did you got them?'

'Because I'm cold.'

'You said you was warm as toast.'

She firmly drew the sheets around her. 'I was, until you took the blankets off.'

'An orange,' Benny repeated, 'a blood orange.' He turned to me. 'And you look like a clothes peg.'

'Now we know what we look like and it's quite a combo,' said Cindy, 'the blood orange and the clothes peg.'

·

It might have been worse. We were a peculiar couple. Perhaps alliance better described us. No: on balance, 'act' is the better word. A fine double act. She played the Jo'burg princess; I was the visiting hick from abroad. Our oddity came not just from the difference in our ages but also from many oceans of otherness between her past and mine. It didn't matter because we pretended so. That was not hard to do. We had been many other people, in many other places, before landing the parts we were playing now.

To her friends she introduced me as, 'This is Alex; he's from overseas.'

It was the best disguise I could have had. They talked, her friends – Dean and Sharon, Lindalee and Tristram, Lionel and Hephzibah, Izzie and Bopi – above and around and across me. Sometimes they asked me what I did and I said I travelled and sold air-con, and that did what it always did: my profession faded immediately as a topic of conversation. How many times had I been grateful for its vanishing qualities.

Travel: that got them more interested.

'Where to?' they asked.

'Cambodia, Burma. Malaysia …'

They nodded vaguely, their faces relaxed; lands of no importance.

'It's just so hard to get a handle on, being in those places,' said Cindy.

That was fine by me. It was like those near-death experiences where the patient, apparently unconscious, hears and sees what is going on around him, while doctors and nurses talk about him as if he wasn't there. It was like being Lazarus; except that people actually saw Lazarus when he came out of the tomb, restored to life. I was more like one of the ghosts in

Virgil's Hades, pale and bloodless and not merely ethereal but clueless. I said something of the sort once, and Sharon wanted to know where Hades was.

'It's where souls go after we die. It's what the Greeks and Romans called the underworld.'

'I knew it couldn't be northern suburbs, or I'd have heard of it,' she said.

29

To Koosie went my mother's old flight plans, escape routes and Washington's fright-wig. The routes she flew were detailed in her large round hand on yellowing pages of lined foolscap and preserved in plastic envelopes. An aerial diary of desperate, often dangerous escapes; fake flight plans she'd filed with the authorities, as well as the real routes flown; dozens of risky trips to remote bush strips and secret airfields in Zambia, Lesotho and Tanzania. Notes of mechanical problems: 'compression down/cylinder/50 over 80 psi…' A fat dossier of charts, diagrams, fuel estimates, weather forecasts, times of arrival, payloads.

When I told Cindy I was going to Soweto to see Koosie, she remembered him instantly.

'The thin guy in the limo at Kathleen's funeral? Can I come? He said I could. Only… what do I wear?'

'Whatever you feel comfortable in.'

'One thing's for sure: I won't feel comfortable in whatever I feel comfortable in.'

On a bright blue Thursday morning, I picked her up in my old lady's Land Rover. Not that I reckoned her pink Porsche wasn't just the job for Soweto, but it simply wasn't the sort of car I'd have felt comfortable in.

She wore a white T-shirt, a pair of denim jeans so snug they seemed painted on, a broad belt of fake snakeskin with a silver buckle the size of a soup plate. Between her breasts, reminiscent of presidential heads carved into Mount Rushmore, smiled the bearded, slightly podgy face of the young Nelson Mandela, bought, I guessed, from the hot boutique in Rosebank where Steve Biko and Bram Fischer and Hector Pieterson had moved from being martyrs to fashion idols, from torture cells to T-shirts, for a generation unborn when they died.

'Whadya think?' she asked me. 'Here I am, armed to the teeth. Do I have what it takes?'

'You look wonderful.'

'But do I look right?'

'Who knows what's right for Soweto; I'd say you're perfect-ly pitched. I'd say you're exactly on the money, I'd say that's remarkable, for someone who has never been there. Must be osmosis.'

'Os-*what?*'

'Never mind. You look great.'

Cindy had also dressed with certain anxiety and I sympa-thised. What do you wear when you're heading off the planet, into intergalactic space; how will the aliens receive you? But her instincts, as always, were sound, because Soweto was as much an invention as she was. The journey alone that we made that morning, from Sheerhaven to Soweto, was at once so wild and so humdrum that only the paranoid could take it in their stride. We moved, in a forty-minute drive, from the gilded northern ghettos to the smoky dormitory town, south-west of the city. We'd traversed galaxies.

Soweto was a puzzle. What it was depended on who was asking the question. Sometimes it was Jo'burg's sister city, sometimes a revolutionary bastion. Its real name, South Western Townships, spoke of banal anonymity lurking just below the sexy acronym. It was never planned as more than a dumping ground for those kicked out of real places. It was, and it wasn't, a city. It was Jo'burg's guilty secret, where the city walled off its workers and told them they were in heaven. Miles of brick bungalows in the spreading veld, under the cooling towers of the power station which, so the legend went, supplied electricity only to Johannesburg. Just as Soweto existed only to supply workers to the city of gold. Even the numbers of those who lived in Soweto was subject to doubt and manipulation; was it one, two or three million? The answer varied, depending upon whom you asked. But since the riots of 1976, followed by the shootings, riots and sieges of the eighties, and the election of 1994 that brought Mandela to power, everything had changed. People said so in the strangled way that warned you not to ask what had changed, or they'd take a poke at you.

After 1994, increasingly, those who could, got the hell out, headed for the other places, for the real 'suburbs' in the 'real' Jo'burg. Places like Houghton and Morningside for those with the bucks; high-rise slums like Hillbrow and Yeoville for the stragglers.

I hadn't been back for years. Last time I'd seen Soweto my mother had been flying blokes out of the country; there had been armoured cars on the dirt roads and blood in the dust. Soweto, when I knew it, had been a dusty dormitory of modest brick houses roofed in corrugated iron, stretching away for miles, with some pockets of conspicuous affluence. As far as I could see, so it was still. The cops and the armoured cars had gone, but it seemed Soweto had been asleep for decades. I knew it wasn't so: the country had been turned upside down.

But everything I saw and heard and smelt was so the way it had been that it was hard not to feel shocked by the unchanging familiar blur of it.

Koosie was still in the small house in Diepkloof where he'd always lived, only the black Mercedes under the blue striped awning was a sign of status.

He opened the door himself. 'Hey, Alex, good to see you back here again after all these years.' He gave me a hug. 'Hey, that's good. It's been too long.' He felt thin, frail almost, his bones small under the good blue wool.

'You remember Cindy?'

'Sure? Kathleen's funeral. Don't be shy, Cindy. Come in, come in! Welcome to Soweto. I like your shirt, and that belt.'

She melted; you could see it. That they took to each other was not surprising. They were the made-over people, the changelings: Dr Sithembile Nkosi and Ms Cindy September, in their starring roles. I was a fly on the wall and, probably, in the ointment, the man from nowhere. Just as Cindy had dressed for Koosie and the township, he had dressed for her, the rich blue suit, the careful cuffs; dressed for his status as an arrived man, but dressed also, I had the odd feeling, for disguise, to stabilise himself before meeting us.

'Let's have coffee, or a drink, or something, and then I'll take you on Dr Nkosi's Eyeball-to-Eyeball Tour. Show you over the place, top to bottom. You'll like Soweto; and Soweto will like you.'

Cindy said: 'That'd be fabulous … If doesn't take too much of your time.'

'I got time,' Koosie said carefully. 'I haven't been into the office in months. In fact, in fact, not since your ma came to see me. I've been on sick leave.'

I said: 'Nothing serious?'

'Bit of this, bit of that. I'm much better. Got a new doctor who isn't trying to kill me.'

He laughed, and we laughed, as if it was natural that your doctor should try to kill you. As if killing you was what doctors did.

I gave him the flight plans and the maps in the big plastic envelope.

'Kathleen left these to you in her will.'

Koosie took the envelope. 'Escape routes. That says it in one, doesn't it? Your mom always had a sharp sense of humour, isn't it, hey?' He turned to Cindy. 'Kathleen used to fly people out of the country. She was wonderful. She was a true friend.'

He put the envelope down as if he wasn't quite sure what to do with it, then he smiled his thin, clever smile.

'What's the wig?'

'It's a fright-wig. It belonged to a boy soldier called Washington, up in Liberia. A souvenir of a friendship.'

Koosie shook his head. 'Boy soldier! Your ma never missed a trick, did she? That guy, where did she hide him, finally?'

Cindy said: 'What guy?'

Koosie said: 'She was hiding a Cuban doctor who skipped from Zim.'

'Was she?' Cindy shook her head in affectionate admiration at the oddity of her friend. 'She was truly something else, your mom. What did she do with him?'

I said: 'Mambo, among other things. He was teaching her.'

'Oh, my God, to mambo!' She was laughing helplessly and shaking her head and half crying all at once. 'Where's he now, this guy who was teaching her to … mambo?'

'All I can tell you is that she went out and got him a new

identity. Bought it. Apparently, it isn't difficult to do, if you know the right people. There's an army of new South Africans and my old lady's Cuban joined the ranks. Apparently, it's a fucking growth industry.'

Koosie told Cindy: 'She came to see me about her Cuban. She wanted me to help and I turned her down.' He tapped the plastic package. 'That's why I got left this: evidence of our old adventures. It says she helped others. And me. Then I let her down. And the wig says it, too; I was a boy soldier once. But I had forgotten it. That's what all these presents mean. That I forget I was a rebel. Except it wasn't like that.'

I said: 'Wasn't it?'

'I tried to tell your mom: those days are gone! I didn't forget, I just grew up. What we did then we can't do now.'

'For God's sake, Koosie. The guy was a refugee from Castro's Cuba. Castro locks people up. Castro's a creep. But for you Castro's legal because he's a socialist brother.'

'Alex, the guy was on the run. He had absconded from a country where he was contracted to work. He was in South Africa illegally.'

'What's this legal shit, Koosie? Fact is, legal is what you decide it is. Legal is what suits, when you say it suits. Once upon a time you guys legged it across the border, and that was good and legal. But a Cuban medic who goes AWOL, he's a criminal and should be locked up. Even though he's running from the despot on our own doorstep, Bob Mugabe. But Mugabe's legal, hey? Because he's an African brother. So your party props him up, just like the old regime propped up the old white Rhodesia. For the same reasons.'

'I find it damn offensive for you to compare our democratic

government with the old apartheid regime. If it wasn't for our revolution, you would not be free.'

'Koosie, let's be straight. There was no revolution. As a liberation movement your lot were complete bloody wankers, from start to finish. What actually happened was that your people and the last lot cut a deal. The guys with the guns, and the guys with even more guns, they carved up power between them. That left people like me, and the Cuban, and anyone who wasn't one of your guys or their guys, absolutely bloody nowhere.'

Koosie was angry. 'If it hadn't been that we were so damn magnanimous, you lot would have been in the dock for war crimes. Like the Nazis at Nuremberg.'

'Guys, guys, guys,' said Cindy, taking our arms and leading us out to the car. 'Where's that tour you promised me?'

We took his car. Cindy sat next to Koosie who began an expert, loving, funny, sometimes scathing, and altogether riveting performance, emphasising his points with wide sweeps of his arm, like a conductor encouraging an orchestra to deepen and enrich the sound, painting his town in all its moods and all its originality.

Koosie giving his eyeball-to-eyeball tour was Koosie at his best. None of the earnest moralising that seemed to have become the other side of his nature, nothing of Koosie the party loyalist. He was sardonic, sharp, unsentimental. And he loved the place the way you love a dangerous kid. He told us house prices were on the up; and guys no longer got thrown out of trains on their way to work; and crazy folks didn't open fire from the windows of Zulu hostels, well, they hadn't for a while.

Touch wood. And the taxi wars had quietened down so he did not wake to the sound of AK 47s ... And with each deadpan line he'd glance to see if he got the reaction he wanted; and he did. Cindy's face mirrored all the joy and terror and delicious awe of the first-time visitor to a legendary scary place. He was, for a while, the old Koosie, the guy who took to me to downtown Jo'burg on Saturdays to watch the weddings go by. The boy I grew up with, my brother, and my friend.

'This suburb where I live is called Diepkloof. It comes in two versions. Like a lot of things. The Diepkloof you see here is a bunch of little houses, each with a shack or a garage or lean-to in the tiny back yard, and this gets rented out. The lodgers in the back room get no water or light. Rents are *very* expensive but people will take anything ... because they can't get any place to live. Only in Soweto do you get middle classes who are pretty poor, but who're also slum landlords at the same time.'

The houses began to expand now into mini-mansions, bulky, brick palaces with front gardens and real garages, and no shacks in the back yard.

'Here is the other Diepkloof, where you find our upper classes. Mostly bank managers, drug dealers, and so on. They keep BMWs in their garages, not tenants. You'll notice there are no burglar bars or watchdogs. Or walls. This is a low-crime area. No one steals. Because if you do, you're dead.'

We passed the hospital. 'This is the Chris Hani Baragwanath Hospital. Biggest hospital in the southern hemisphere. Hani was a friend of mine. Poor Chris, leader of our army, fighter and communist, gunned in his suburban driveway by two white fanatics just before the 1994 election. The hospital can be dicey sometimes. Doctors hijacked, even gunned down as they left work. Couldn't have that. Bad for morale. It's safer now than a few months back. They've beefed up security at the front gates.'

Cindy swallowed hard. She was hooked; Koosie's delivery kept the concentration level high.

Next up was the lost car pound, where hundreds of vehicles waited like stray pets behind the wire for owners to reclaim them. Recovered from hijacks and hold-ups; retrieved before they could be driven over the borders, into Mozambique or Zimbabwe, or disappeared into a local chop-shop, a kind of oxyacetylene abattoir, where a few deft strokes of the welder's torch reduced desirable models to their lucrative body parts.

'If you lose your car,' said Koosie to Cindy, 'come look for it here … or right next door, at the cop-shop. Sometimes the cops bring them here.'

'Good.' It was the first word Cindy had spoken since we set off.

'Not really. It can be unlucky.' He smiled. 'Our cops do a big trade in spares. You might get your car back, missing just about everything.'

Past the school, where a couple of men had shot a teacher the week before; and on to the great taxi rank, where hundreds of mini-vans waited, rumbling and steaming, ready to run to anywhere in Africa, from downtown Jo'burg to Lusaka, or Cairo.

'It's a long wait, so the drivers grab some sleep, or they do a bit of dagga. No wonder when they hit the road at three in the morning they're not always in a good mood.'

The real pleasure of his tour was in Koosie's performance; and Cindy's face.

She said: 'How poor are really poor people?'

Koosie touched Cindy's sleeve. 'Let's go to Mandela Village.'

Mandela Village was a slum of small wooden and plastic and tin shacks, with rutted dirt paths between the houses. We met Daisy, who had four small kids and a husband in town, looking for work. The shack was small and clean and terribly empty of everything but babies' blankets and cooking pots. The floor was hard earth. The walls were papered with Sunlight soap wrappers and looked wildly bright. It had been home to Daisy for eight years. The whole impression was of order and patience, and Daisy herself exuded a dignified despair.

'I hope things get better for you,' Cindy told her.

Daisy simply sighed and shook her head, too polite to contradict.

Outside on the street, Cindy said: 'I'd like to go back and give her something. But I feel bad about giving her money.'

'Go back and do it,' Koosie said. 'She has no electricity, no running water except a stand tap or two, no job. Daisy is the sort of person we promised to help, nearly ten years ago, but the cheque's still in the post. Then we'll go on to the "shrine".'

This was a granite circle and a large parking area: the Hector Pieterson Memorial. Within the granite circle there was reproduced in all its grainy horror the image of the dying boy being carried by another boy, like a sacrifice, an offering, into the guns of the police. The boy seen carrying Pieterson that day was called Mbuyisa Makhulu, and he disappeared after that march and was never seen again. He almost certainly died at one of the camps where cops like Oomie had been based.

'The shrine,' said Koosie. 'Remember the day – 16 June 1976 – when schoolchildren with no weapons of any kind took on the state.'

What made the 16 June uprising so remarkable was its single-minded simplicity. Kids still in school were ordered to learn Afrikaans. Being ruled, beaten, mocked, used and hated by murderous and stupid persecutors was something they had withstood as best they could for what must have seemed like for ever. But this was too much: they would not be forced to speak the tongue of the enemy. They said no, and they marched into the guns.

The children's revolt belonged to them: it had nothing to do with the liberation movements. A true rebellion, so amazing it was still not fully comprehended and was now increasingly hard to recall in all its blood and bitterness. Now it was patchily commemorated in a public holiday, and served as an occasion for self-serving speeches by tired functionaries and rambling monologues far removed from the spirit of that spontaneous, leaderless revolt.

As the spirit diminished, the shrine deteriorated.

We struggled to find parking; the big coaches were depositing French, German and British tourists. It had always been foreigners who went to Soweto, to see it for themselves, to visit the memorial to Hector Pieterson and the schoolchildren's revolt.

'We have a way of turning tragedy into a tourist trap.'

Koosie waved his hands to embrace the touts waiting around the flower-beds: hawkers of bad American rap and elderly editions of African verse, cellphones clipped to their belts.

'These guys like passing themselves off to foreign visitors as the heirs of the children's revolt.' Koosie shook his head. 'It doesn't work: foreigners know racist American rap when they hear it.'

I said: 'Mark a place as sacred, elevate it into a site of pilgrimage and you get touts and hawkers making a quick buck. Selling the saint's dandruff. The virgin's sacred unicorn. It happens at Lenin's tomb in Moscow; it happens in Bernadette's grotto in Lourdes. It never stays pristine.'

'Why not? Why the crap?' Koosie asked. 'Why not some… respect?'

'It doesn't stay pure because, probably, it was never pure in the first place. It's getting towards thirty years since this boy was shot. He's a hero; but he's also a draw. Maybe it's a sign of normality. Messy, meaningless, commercial normality.'

'Then I don't want it; it's too soon.'

'I know what you mean,' said Cindy. 'You want things to stay, like, pure. Pristine.'

'I do. That's the word, "pristine".'

'Like it ought to be,' said Cindy.

I said: 'Making things like they ought to be is what did the damage. To us. To the country. I hate it. It's brought us nothing but blood.'

'Alex doesn't understand,' said Koosie kindly, with an edge of mockery in his affection.

'That's what I tell him,' said Cindy.

Koosie and Cindy smiled the smile of fellow conspirators who knew at a deeper level than visitors, than strangers, what constituted reality because they lived in a place they have never left, a place called 'home'; who felt they knew it, loved it, fought for it, owned it. Who made their personal geography into morality? Who believed that if things were not right they must be made so?

'Keep telling him,' said Koosie.

I left it there: it was enough that they got on; enough that Koosie talked more easily to her than to me; enough that Cindy was beside herself with pleasure. I got this shiver at the back of the neck, this hollow in my middle, this terrible falling feeling, because those who will do anything to keep things 'pristine' generally mean what they say. All forms of perfection seemed to cost a lot of lives.

We pulled up next at a very ordinary little villa and Koosie said:

'Nelson Mandela's old house. It is not so very remarkable, is it? Do you want to see inside?'

'Yes, please,' said Cindy.

'I'll stay here,' I said. 'You go with Koosie.'

Cindy said, upset, even a little shocked: 'You don't want to see Mandela's house?'

'It's a fake.'

'I don't believe it. It can't beeee,' Cindy wailed.

'Well, not a fake, exactly. More a reconstruction,' said Koosie delicately. 'The original house, that was destroyed.'

'Who by, the police?'

Koosie paused carefully. 'No. It was the neighbours.'

'Why did they do that?' She was appalled.

'When Mandela was in jail on Robben Island, Winnie lived here; this is where she kept her football team. You know, the kids she sent to mess up people. This is where those kids got locked up at night and some of them didn't come out again. The stories out of this place were not good. They were disturbing for the neighbours. Maybe the screams, too. One day the neighbours here, they burnt the house down.'

Cindy didn't say anything.

Koosie took her arm. 'It's called a Museum of the Revolution now, and it will cost us a couple of bucks at the door.'

I watched them go in. He held her arm and she looked up at him. Teacher and pupil. Koosie was good, he was sound, but there was something not right with him. Cindy's ignorance was deep and sincere . She knew no history, of her own, of her country, of its past. Didn't know, didn't want to know. The kids who'd been held in the Mandela house had been guilty of not being as they ought to be. Not pristine. The fatal flaw. But Cindy didn't know a damn thing about what had happened to them. The nature of what she did not know was embarrassing, and normal, and even, perhaps, admirable. After all, Cindy was emphatically part of the new; and part of that was not needing to know about the past. She knew where to shop, what to do to protect herself against robbery, rape, hijacking … what more did she need? And if she did need to know, then someone would supply. Koosie was showing her Soweto, much as the poor schmuck, her husband, Andy Andreotti, had shown her Sun City. Come to think of it, though they served very different purposes in the wild cavalcade of South African life, each place was as horrendous and as unreal as the other.

When they came out, Cindy was crying. I thought it must be that she was so moved by what she'd seen in the house, and what she'd learnt of the tragic struggle of Sowetans. Though a moment's thought would have told me that Cindy did not cry over politics. And politics would not explain why she kept putting her arms around Koosie and hugging him. He looked abashed, uneasy at all this attention, as if he hadn't meant to stir up this emotion.

We drove back to his place without speaking. Cindy was behind us and she had trouble stifling her sobs.

When we got back to his place Koosie didn't ask us in. He thanked me again for my mother's gift to him. Standing outside his house, in his blue suit, the sun glinting on his gold cuff-links, he waved us goodbye with the big plastic envelope that held her old flight plans and the escape routes, upon which, in another age, many lives had depended.

We were back in northern Jo'burg, riding through streets lined with tall walls, razor wire and sentry boxes, when she said:

'I'm sorry I made a fuss back there. But it really got to me.'

'Soweto?'

'No, not Soweto. I liked Soweto.'

I must have looked blank because she said: 'I got an inkling inside five minutes of meeting him. It isn't just that he's thin, it's the look. There is a definite look, and once you know it, you don't mistake it. I've seen it before. And then, when we went for our little walk around the Mandela house, he told me. Straight out. He made it a bit of a joke; he said he couldn't tell you because it took a South African to understand.'

'Understand what?'

'Six months ago he tested positive for HIV.'

I did not know what to say.

'When he was diagnosed he was with a private doctor who prescribed ARVs. Antiretrovirals. He was lucky. Most people don't get them. He started taking the ARVs, but then he stopped.'

'Why did he stop?'

'He says Aids is a syndrome and a syndrome isn't a disease. He said his problem might be due to a whole lot of factors. Diet, genetics, spiritual malfunction. There are other treatments, other solutions. And he is exploring them: his phrase again.'

'But he knows he's ill.'

'He says he hasn't been well. He does not say he has Aids. And even if he did, he takes the line taken by a lot of powerful people here, right up to the President, that antiretrovirals don't help with Aids. That is, like, the party line. Official. Aids is not Aids, it's something else. It's TB, bad nutrition, malaria, it's a lot of local diseases, alone or in combination. Aids is a syndrome. ARVs, the drugs that fight it, are a conspiracy by Western drug companies to plunder sick people. And to poison Africans. ARVs – so goes the line – are more dangerous than the disease itself, which may not be the disease they say it is anyway. Koosie believes he can lick this thing without drugs. If he eats the right food and believes the right people. He's incredibly determined to do the right thing.'

Loyalty was what Koosie had always had. For Koosie, the Movement was not just his family, it was his church, it was his supreme guide. It had happened, this conversion, shortly before the shooting of Big Lou. In Koosie's religious scheme of things, the tiny killer who shot Big Lou was some sort of divine messenger sent to reinforce that faith. It was a faith he would die for, or kill for. He held his own life cheap when the divine adjudicator demanded obedience. Oh, yes, Koosie was loyal. Pristine. And I might have said dangerous, bone-headed, lamentable, principled and deranged; almost as crazy as all the other oafs who had ruled over us. Though I didn't say so.

We pulled up at a red light. On the traffic island sat a small tow truck with a logo on the driver's door that read: 'Harry's Cash and Carry'.

Cindy said: 'See that stubby little blue pick-up swinging a hook, parked on the traffic island. They call them happy hookers. Those pick-ups work the streets, just like girls on the game. Except these vultures are after road-kill. They listen in on police radio frequencies to catch news of a smash and head for the carnage. First come, first served. There are fights. They pay the cops kickbacks for early warning. But sometimes business is slow so be careful at crossings like this when it's wet. And after dark. Because when business is slow, the happy hookers like to sweeten the odds: they may reset the lights, or spread oil on the road after rain.'

'Nice guys.'

'It's a job.'

'I'll remember.'

'Good. Might save your life.'

I said: 'What's going to happen to Koosie?'

'Without the ARVs he'll die.'

'And this new doctor he talked to us about? The one who isn't killing him?'

'He's seeing a traditional healer. A *sangoma*. She's giving him some sort of special *muti* and he swears it's doing him good.'

I was unsure of what sort of response was required, or fitting, in the face of so much dying. Saving one's life was pretty problematical right now. The value placed upon any individual existence seemed to be not only sharply diminished but caring about it at all seemed to smack of intolerable elitism.

Soweto itself was marked by it; everywhere in the country was marked by it. The Pieterson memorial stood for heroic death, freely faced; the Mandela house remembered the death of children by torture; Koosie, thin, elegant, angry, smiling, wanted to dodge death by – what? Syndrome? But, then, what Koosie feared more than death was unbelief. Salvation lay in cleaving to the party line; in a land where the line was long ago shot to ribbons, and the party was a fractious band of avaricious fat cats fighting for position and power, Koosie remained a true believer. A kind of saint.

The Land Rover drifted along, through Craighall, Sandton, and on towards Four Ways and Lone Hill and Sheerhaven. I went with the flow, serenaded by the day's dark blues:

Crowds Stone Suspect
Uncle Rapes 6-yr-old
SA Tops Travel Poll
Gold Up
Eleven Cows Hacked with Pangas
Gold Down
Drugs Don't Cut Aids – Minister …

30

I wasn't in Forest Town much after that. It was too sad; just me and the wraith of my mother and an ectoplasmic Noddy, who went on living in the back-yard room and haunting the garden: remote, shadowy and unapproachable.

When I did go back to the house, it was with Benny, carrying his tennis racket. He loved looking at the pictures of the animals my mother had shot, and the mounted kudu heads, the leopard-skin rugs; he loved the picture of my mother with Baldy the grey parrot on her shoulder. He was sentenced to look always for things that made sense to him in a world where making sense was an ordeal. He was impervious to change and fiercely dependent on routine. And so we did the same things, in the same order, each time we visited my house. After turning all the lights on and off in precise patterns, we looked at photographs. I had to tell him in exactly the same words the story of how Baldy learned swearwords from the Flying Dutchmen who came to clean the house, when Koosie and I were boys. He was particularly fascinated by the pictures of Bara and Buti, the rainforest pygmies, and hearing how they stalked, and ate, old Baldy.

The way Bara was shown sticking his tongue out fascinated Benny. He always stuck his tongue out of his rather small round mouth, just as he was always smoothing the soft straight hair over the fold of skin at the back of his neck with small square hands on which his small fingers had just one joint, instead of the usual two.

'What does parrot taste like?' Benny would ask, holding his racket to his face and pressing the strings against his lips. With the racket strings breaking up into fleshy cubes the soft skin of his face, he looked like some odd little animal imprisoned in a hutch.

'Like fire-crackers and old shoes,' I always said.

'Do his feathers stick in your throat?'

'For a week and a half, at least.'

Cindy told me that he was so cemented into routines that Benny would take a trip with his classmates from the Sunbeam Shelter but when they got to the park or the cinema, or the museum, Benny stayed right where he was. Only when the bus was back at the Shelter would he agree to leave his seat, and then only in the correct order. He went last of all.

I took to spending the rest of my time in Sheerhaven, as a kind of honorary resident. The guards at the gate no longer asked my business; they knew the car, and they nodded me through. And once inside the walls, under the great silver sewer in the sky, I felt I'd migrated to some strange, quiet country. Maybe that is what it was, and it made a sort of sense: after all, if people lived parallel lives, they needed parallel worlds in which to live them. The rich no longer needed to move to other countries. They could build their own.

And there was Cindy. I hadn't decided what to do yet, and she didn't ask, and I was grateful. I had bequests to deliver; I still had to find Papadop and I had to see Queen Bama, and until I'd done what I'd undertaken to do, I was content to stay.

Being with Cindy was a bit like being at some non-stop late-night party where you feel, despite the fact that you're having a great time, that for some reason you can't quite put your finger on – perhaps it's your age, or the decor or the music – something doesn't quite fit.

On the other hand, what did? This was Jo'burg. Nothing fitted.

And then there was Koosie.

'You and Koosie are as close as that.' Cindy snipped her forefinger and index finger together. 'And yet you're at daggers drawn.'

'Maybe it comes of being almost brothers once.'

'He needs you now.'

'No, he doesn't need me. But I think he needs you. I think you remind him of my mother.'

She looked pleased. 'Really? That's a lovely thing to say.'

I didn't pay much attention then. Later on, I wished I'd thought harder about what I'd said, and why I'd said it.

'He was your friend first. Will you come with me?'

It was true enough. But what I did not say and she would not have understood was that the friendship had foundered long ago. After Koosie's conversion to the Cause, and to the anger I had first seen, but not understood, when Big Lou was shot.

'He won't thank me.'

She came over and kissed me. 'You're weird. D'you know that?'

'I know it.'

'So will you come?'

•

We got into a routine. Three days a week we'd drive from Sheerhaven, drop Benny at the Shelter and head on out to Soweto, and stay maybe an hour. We did not so much talk as listen because Koosie was growing weaker, he was in pain and it made him short-tempered and insistent, about everything. He was still losing weight and he complained of headaches. He insisted he was getting better, that he was responding well to the *muti* he'd got from the traditional healer. She was seeing him each morning and she was working marvels. He would be better soon. We never saw the healer but we saw her roots and powders beside his bed.

A few weeks later he was suffering hot and swollen feet. Increasingly often he wasn't up before noon. We went late in the day, and we cut the visiting time to thirty minutes. He tired so easily and he would nod off in the middle of a sentence ...

Then suddenly, without any sort of preamble, he announced that he was on new medication. And he had another 'health adviser'.

It was a strange term to use.

'What happened to the traditional healer?' Cindy asked.

Koosie shrugged his thin shoulders as if he could not be bothered to think back.

'She's not around any more. She moved on.'

'And the medicine she gave you, the special *muti*?' Cindy asked.

'I stopped taking that. It didn't agree with me.'

One morning, we found him sitting at his kitchen table drinking tea with a visitor, a sturdy, quiet, pale woman called Millie Loubser. She came from Brakpan, on the outskirts of town, and ran a garden-care business with her sons, when she wasn't helping people with Koosie's symptoms. It was hard to believe that a man like Koosie would be content to swallow large pink capsules from a bottle marked 'Celestial Solution', but swallow them he did. They were boosting his immune system, as Millie Loubser promised they would; he could feel it.

'She's a miracle worker.'

Koosie indeed looked good; he seemed stronger, he was almost his old self again, and he owed it all to her and her treatment.

'She turned up, like a gift from God. I opened the door and there she was. She looked at me, deeply, oh, so deeply, like she saw into my soul, and she said: "Do you want to live?" And I said yes.'

Millie Loubser diagnosed him as suffering from what she called 'immune imbalance', leaning into the syllables as if they were the name of some pop song or dance movement. Imm—une Imm—balance ...

'He's stronger every day, thank the Lord. I prayed for him to be spared, to live his life in and for the Lord. I've had patients far worse than this gentleman, and they're healthy today.'

As we were driving home Cindy said: 'The woman is a bloody fraud.'

She was, too; but what were we to do about it? Koosie believed in this pleasant charlatan, and that was the end of it, for the moment.

'Look at me!' Koosie would say each day. 'Aren't I better?'

And for a while he was. He religiously took the capsules three times a day, after meals, until he could not longer keep his meals down.

Cindy challenged Loubser. 'What qualifications do you have for treating someone like Koosie?'

Millie Loubser gave her a sweet smile. 'I had a favourite sister and she died of cancer, and the pain I felt was terrible. I am treating over a hundred people today, they come to me because I help them.'

'At how much a throw?'

Millie Loubser was unperturbed. 'One hundred rand for a week's supply of Celestial Solution.'

'You are a fraud; you take dying people for a ride.'

'If I take anything, I take their suffering into my heart. I ask God to ease the pain of people like Dr Nkosi: I pray for him to be spared.'

'You charge him a hundred bucks for a pack of pills. You're a fucking shyster, a blooming harpy, a vampire ...'

Millie Loubser looked at the furious Cindy and said simply: 'I forgive you, girlie. In your anger and pain you know not what you say. I will pray for you, too.'

'Pray for me, and I'll kick your teeth in,' Cindy said.

Millie Loubser did not stay to have her teeth kicked in. Koosie suddenly stopped taking her pills and, like the traditional healer, Millie Loubser no longer came to the house.

'I feel better without her,' said Koosie.

It became an exercise in helplessness, a drive to the now familiar streets of Diepkloof, there to sit and watch the cruel decline of a vibrant man. It was made worse by having to see the disease killing him and to feel we were being forced to attend some sort of religious seance. But the alternative was to stop visiting. So we had learnt to reduce ourselves, in the face of Koosie's remorseless emaciation. Cindy wore no make-up, she chose clothes that hid her flesh, masked her evident health, that would not seem an insult to the stick-thin man with the shining eyes.

We were the visiting party, the sympathisers, the people who wanted to help but could not. Cindy was very affected by her feelings of helplessness.

Coming home from Soweto of an evening, we would pass Buffalo Belle's and, it seemed, there was trouble. Women in white cowboy boots and stetsons, wearing very short skirts and carrying placards – 'No To Foreign Sex-Workers' – lobbied motorists at the stoplights. Their breasts fell forward into the driver's window when they leaned into the car and asked you to sign their petition to keep the joint open.

It was not sex for sale that got everyone so worked up. It was the girls selling the sex, the émigré paperless whores from Bulgaria, Cambodia, Burma and Estonia. The girls about whom Mona-Lize became so exercised. Taking jobs away from perfectly good local tarts. What did a girl from, say, the Hmong hill tribes of Vietnam know about the libido of the home-grown male? About golf? Or rugby?

'Keep lust local,' said these angry girls. 'Keep pussy patriotic.'

It went on for some weeks. The papers began to pick up on these protests – if rather gingerly – in headlines like 'Fourways Sex-Workers Forum on the March'. Headlines were always wordier when political correctness kicked in, and never did it kick in faster than in matters of sex.

Why not 'Whores Get Mad!'?

Too close to the bone; too un-South African.

We were travelling between the dying man and the protest-ing girls. I was struck again by the mischievous, if not malicious, juxtaposition of tragedy and comedy that South

African street life did so effortlessly. Cindy called Millie Loubser a joke. Yes, she was, if you could bear to laugh. And it did not stop there. We moved daily from the bedside of a dying man to the bordellos of the northern reaches and home to eerily, superbly sterile Sheerhaven. It was all perfectly ordinary. All in a day's drive.

In the following month, Koosie was in hospital twice: he had a bout of meningitis, and he also developed pneumonia. But he wasn't daunted; indeed, he put up with these illnesses almost cheerfully, with a sense of relief. They were identifiable, proven, curable; and he recovered.

That is to say he did not die. He came home from hospital, his bones poking up against his skin. He stared at us with hot eyes. They had given him a catheter; he was wearing nappies and he had full-time nursing care.

Dr Toodt was Dutch. She simply turned up, just as the others had done.

Dr Toodt said: 'I am a medical doctor, a trained chemist, and a researcher with many years of experience. I plan to treat this patient with micro-nutrients. I am here at the request of the Ministry of Health. They sent me and they trust me; and they know I can help Comrade Nkosi.'

To be 'sent', to be 'trusted', to be 'known': the sacred trinity of success.

She had an open, square face with strong, well-defined bones, and a very square jaw; and best of all, she was qualified. It seemed she specialised in cases of Koosie's sort. He was suffering from severe dietary deficiencies that had undermined his immune system.

Angela Toodt had developed a dietary supplement called the

African Antidote; it was composed of carrot, garlic, beetroot, lemon juice, yoghurt, banana, and *mielie-meal*, bolstered by various anti-oxidants, as well as grape seeds, lychee flesh, and extracts of the African potato. She was sure of everything. 'I belong to Africa,' she told us when Cindy asked about life in Holland, and I had the impression that what she really meant was that Africa belonged to her.

We were getting like Koosie, clutching at straws, and, for a while, we were very pleased to see Dr Toodt at his bedside.

Koosie took the medicine, when he could keep it down, and sometimes he seemed to brighten, and then he would call me to his bedside, obsessed with finding the missing Cuban. Our earlier argument over what was 'legal' was forgotten. In his increasingly confused mind, it was as if finding the Cuban would not only repair the damage done by his rejection of my mother when she went to see him but, somehow, by regularis-ing the refugee medic, he would be making a kind of recompense that might count well with those spirits in whose power it was to see him live or die.

'Time for your treatment, Dr Nkosi,' said Angela Toodt.

Cindy confronted her one morning.

'Why don't you put him on antiretrovirals?'

Angela Toodt looked at her calmly, as if this was a question she had been expecting and which it was possible, but only just, to answer with a modicum of civility.

'He doesn't need them, he doesn't want them, he would not take them if I gave them to him.'

It was chilling, watching this determined woman keeping African indigenous healing, Western science and the exigen-cies of Leninist discipline all in some sort of balance. She stood not just for the powers of the land but for health and sense and political probity: a woman who espoused by the belief that micro-nutrients, potato, garlic and lots of vitamins were making Koosie much better when, plainly, Koosie was dying.

We knew it, and he knew it.

'Find him,' Koosie would beg, 'and I'll fix it. Then he doesn't have to live his life as someone else. He can be himself again.'

'Koosie, I'll try. But please don't worry.'

Cindy also felt I should find Raoul. He had been the last man with whom my mother associated. Curious, how the Cuban worked on people. Schevitz had been just as insistent I should do something about him.

Koosie was comatose for long periods now. Cindy sat with him, holding his hand; I'd walk up and down the street. Dr Toodt continued to administer her diet of micro-nutrients and vitamins intravenously, and she saw an improvement.

She sent off regular blood samples for testing and confronted the results with grim equanimity. Koosie's immune system was now so weak it was prey to any passing opportunist infection.

We were watching death by ideology. Koosie was dying, persisting in saying that he was not ill, in line with party dogma. Both the physician and the dying patient were driven by principle, and Cindy and I were powerless to do anything but look on, excluded as we had been from what the principal actors considered the miraculous 'African Antidote'.

Cindy again challenged Angela Toodt. 'If you had what he has, would you take antiretrovirals?'

'I would not. They are toxic and they do not work.'

'The virus is killing him!'

'There is no virus,' said Angela Toodt.

But there were, nonetheless, signs of resistance from the patient himself. Not from Koosie the party member, but from Koosie the human being. He found it harder and harder to keep going, and this somewhat irked Dr Toodt who, though she never said so, gave the impression that he was not really trying hard enough; and what he was not trying hard enough to achieve had touched a metaphysical plane. It was no longer a question of illness: it was a matter of faith. Koosie was barely alive. Even Dr Toodt knew it. What mattered now was that he should achieve a good death.

We would return from Soweto to Sheerhaven wretched and depressed.

Then, one evening, the protesting cow-girls were gone, the sprawling ranchero stood dull and lifeless, the neon lariat on the roof was cold, a large lock hung on the gates. Instead, we saw police cars and a hovering helicopter. We were too exhausted to do more than note it in passing and wonder what was going on.

The answer came on the evening news. Belle's had been raided by the Aliens Investigation Unit. The cameras showed a group of women herded like frightened sheep into the street. They wouldn't show their faces: crouching on the pavement in the TV lights, legs bare, holding their handbags over their heads like hats. I remembered seeing on one of the last marches of the Fourways Sex-Workers Forum outside Buffalo Belle's, aimed at exposing the foreign competition, how they lifted their skimpy shirts to show, pinned to their panties coloured like the national flag, the slogan: 'Proudly South African!' The foreigners were a mixed bag: they came from Bangkok, Bucharest, Moscow. According to the report, the girls had been charged and then released on bail into the care of the medical officer serving the establishment and who was, it seemed, the only bona fide South African in the place.

There was a shot of him: he smiled a little bashfully at the camera; he wore a grey safari suit and large spectacles. He looked very convincing, and you would have said he was typically South African, if you hadn't once met him in another incarnation, in another life, when he lived in the back-yard room of your house, danced the mambo with your mother and was called Dr Raoul Mendoza.

I never knew whether it would have made Koosie feel better to know we'd found my mother's Cuban. Probably not. He was too weak by then to have done much about it and, anyway, I wondered what anyone could have done about it. Koosie's analysis of the position as he'd given it to my mother was correct. If you bought his line on legality, it mattered to Koosie that Raoul would be who he was. But why? Who in their right minds wanted to be who they were? Dr Mendoza was dead; long live Dr du Toit, physician to a group of foreign female refugees, who wanted as much as he did to be anyone in the world but themselves.

Our Cuban had been transformed into something so close to the real thing no one would ever be able to tell the difference. From where I stood it looked to me like Raoul was fine. Hell, he was better adapted and adjusted than I was. Dr Cornelius du Toit no doubt had all the features that testified to his new estate: the BMW, a gun safe, a swimming pool, and plenty of staff, behind a tall wall where he talked rugby and threw another chop on the barbecue with all the assurance of one born to braai.

·

The next day, when we went back to Diepkloof, the house was empty, Koosie was gone and so was Dr Toodt. We went over to the hospital and there they told us Dr Nkosi had died during the night.

Cindy said to me: 'Dr Toodt would have written the death certificate, wouldn't she?'

'She would.'

'What's the bet it says meningitis or pneumonia? Poor Koosie. She gets to say what he died of, she gets to tidy it up.'

I saw what she meant. How he died or why he died were beside the point. It was not the virus that killed him. He would have been struck down by a confirmed, observable, legitimate disease: malaria or TB or pneumonia, or 'acquired immuno-suppression'. His would have been a good end. Dr Toodt would have made sure of that. Yes, poor Koosie. Not only fictional lives, you also got imaginary deaths. Someone, some-where a long way away once said history was written by the winners. Not here it wasn't; here it was written by whoever made out the death certificates.

The Party arranged his funeral. We drove to the marquee, pitched on a football field. There were flags and speeches and songs; there were invocations of Koosie's past and his service to the cause and the struggle, there was praise for his loyalty, and his courage. There was no word spoken of his illness, and it was possible that many of those present were under the impression that he had not died at all but that he'd gone into quiet retirement, beside the sea perhaps, or somewhere in the country.

Then we followed the hearse to the graveyard and Koosie was laid to rest, and then six young men on motorbikes did a series of wheelies beside the grave, revving the big machines and kicking up clouds of red dust that made some of the guests cough and splutter, though they took it in good part and joined in the applause for the motorbike riders.

Back at the marquee, the sit-down meal was catered by La Rochelle Fine French Foods, the funeral DJ played Kwaito hits, and soon the party was swinging.

Cindy said: 'It's more like a wedding, isn't it?'

She was right: what started as a funeral became a kind of party. I kept remembering how, when we were boys together, brothers together, Koosie had taken me on Sunday afternoons into the hollow centre of the empty city to watch the gorgeous brides and grooms perched up on the back seats of the big Lincoln Continentals. What they were doing, in the face of blind immovable stupidity, was showing a bit of flash, having a bit of fun. I had the feeling Koosie might have liked the send-off he got.

Cindy said, 'I think maybe it's like a party because it happens so often. Because of the kill rate of the virus, because there are just so many funerals. People must spend almost every Saturday in a graveyard. Watching family and friends being buried. You can only take so much grief. So you begin to jazz things up. Like making a good show of it. Going out with a bang. Because that's the best you can do.'

Maybe so. But it was strange. The funeral wasn't just a party. Matters of status were involved. It had a kind of glossy format. It felt almost – if you forgot for the moment why you were there – like a religious revival. Koosie wasn't dead, he was elsewhere; there was no death, there was only dancing; there was no virus, there was only vitamin deficiency. So you took the tablets, took your partner, took courage, and danced at the edge of the grave till you dropped.

So we danced, too, Cindy and I.

'It's a pretty weird party, even so.'

'Weird is where we begin,' said Cindy.

31

To Queen Bama: her knitting patterns, her collection of needles, in bamboo, metal, rosewood; her crochet hooks; her magnetic case for metal needles and her big pencil box for wooden and plastic needles; her wools, remnants of yarns – merino, silk, and several balls of 10-ply wool in bright yellow and cerise, once destined to become a huge and serpentine scarf. All the other bits and bobs a knitter needs were in a small linen bag that closed with a bone button: things like needle-sizers, shawl closures, scissors and thimbles. In an old tin that had once held golden syrup she kept bobbins, buttons, block-ing pins, stitch holders and a box of plastic point protectors in lime green and flesh pink, with which she always carefully capped her metal needles.

I was carrying all this out to the car when Noddy came to me. He faced me, his manner polite, distant.

'I have a woman who may stay with me.'

'Good,' I said. 'Very good.'

'I'm telling you because it's your room and I must know if that's good with you.'

'You can have whoever you like.'

I was really pleased; maybe a girlfriend would make things easier. The man facing me in his blue overall, with the ridiculous job title he'd stitched in red across his back, was not Noddy, as I knew him. I missed my friend and I wanted him back.

I found my way to Lebalola country using the map in the pamphlet about the pleasures of the Platinum Province, handed to me by the Rain Queen's praise-singer at my mother's funeral. I had never been to visit Queen Bama *in situ* before, and all I had to go on was my mother's account of her first visit, sixty years earlier. On that occasion the Queen sat on her yellowwood throne, wearing a leopard-skin cloak, in front of her Great Place, flanked by courtiers and counsellors.

Her Great Place was situated on a hill known as Heaven's Tip and it was not particularly impressive. It looked like many hillsides in the Magaliesberg, a lunar loneliness, scattered with rusty boulders and dusty green scrub. I parked and walked up the hill. I found the village in the last of the light. Maybe thirty huts around a baked-earth compound, empty but for a few thin dogs and a couple of dripping stand-taps. Some of the huts had TV aerials above their thatched roofs. In the smoky evening among the huts, without a clue where to go, I heard her calling me.

'Welcome, Alexander, son of Kathleen, to the land of the Lebalola, to the country of Queen Bamadodi.'

I had thought I'd remembered the Rain Queen in every detail. A big woman, almost as tall as my mother, with an easy step. The little gnome who called to me, sitting on the stoop of an orange brick bungalow with a corrugated-iron roof, seemed a long way from the powerful woman I remembered; except, perhaps, for a smouldering, melancholy anger. She wore no cloak trimmed with leopard-skin; she was sitting in a Lay-Z-Boy recliner chair of what looked like yellow leatherette, rather patched. There was no court; there was no praise-singer; there was only, from somewhere behind us in one of the huts, a radio pumping out rap music.

Queen Bama said: 'We are in mourning for those who have gone. You cry for your mother who has gone to the Lord, and I cry for my daughter; she died a few days ago.'

I didn't know what to say.

'I had three daughters; two have died already. Before. And yesterday the last who was my eldest, she also died.'

She waited a moment and then she said: 'If the Queen has no daughters, as I have now no daughters, another girl has to be chosen.'

I didn't ask the question but she felt it in the air between us.

'But what will she find, the new Queen of the Lebalola, the one who comes after me? What kingdom will she come into?'

Around us, pressing close, the night was velvet, smelling of dust and dung and Africa. The rest of the people of the village, it seemed, were in front of the box, watching the usual Hollywood shoot-ups. Queen Bama stiffened in her Lay-Z-Boy recliner at the sound of repeated gunfire.

'Once, we took water from the river and we kept water in the calabash. Once, it was precious, it came from the sky, and we knew what it was to thirst. Then those boys, the new boys, from the government, they came here, and they said: "We will change things, we will give water to a million people, we will send water into the taps and people will drink and wash."

'And I chased them away with a sjambok; I hit them and hit them some more. But now, see, they have done what they said. We have a pipe and tap where once we had only the river below the hill. Oh, they were very happy! They laughed and said: "Yes, Queen Bama, things have changed and we have changed them."

'And again I took my sjambok then and I ran at them and I beat them and beat them till they cried and they ran away and they were shouting: "You may beat us, Queen Bama, but we are right."

She leaned over and spat on the ground. 'They are dogs. They are fools, they are liars. They put in their pipes and their taps and they say this is better. Where does it come from, the water that flows in the taps? From heaven! And where will it come from when the heavens give no more?'

There was no feast that night. Queen Bama and I ate a little chicken and rice from a tin, and she poured me a very strong brandy with a little water, and then I slept in a hut with two plastic chairs and a skinny metal bed.

In the morning, when I went to say goodbye, she was sitting in her Lay-Z-Boy, holding a heavy knobkerrie, and on the stoop in front of her were several rows of what looked like large bedsocks, or the soft nose-cones of woollen rockets, or very big tea-cosies, some with a pink or green tassels at their tips. Queen Bama took up a knobkerrie and began turning over the items at her feet.

'What are these, Queen Bama?'

She got up from her chair and with her knobkerrie she lifted up a woollen tower, knitted in pink and peppermint zigzags, crowned by a bright green pom-pom.

'Have you not heard, Alexander? Do they not have it far away? In places overseas? The slimming sickness that men have brought to my people; as men bring dangerous things. The sickness that took away the daughters of Bamadodi?'

'The doctors came from the hospital and they showed us little socks. And they said: "Women of Lebalola, these socks guard against the sickness. Show your men. When they come to you, show them how they must wear them."

'And we said: "Yes, these socks are well to wear but see how small they are. They fit on a finger." And so they told us to make big, big ones of wool and to take them to all the villages to show people.'

She held up the knobkerrie with its knitted candy-coloured condom bright in the early morning sun. Even here, in the large-scale production of teaching materials to be used in combating the Aids virus, the natural genius of the Lebalola knitters had reproduced on woollen condoms the patterns painted on the walls of their mud huts: the zigzags of lightning, the bright metal blue of the highveld sky and the black and grey undulating lines of the laden rainclouds.

I knew then how Queen Bama's daughters had died; I knew the sickness was rife amongst the Lebalola.

Queen Bama looked at me. 'What are we going to do?'

She asked me, just as she had once asked my mother, but I couldn't answer, like my mother, 'Search me, Bama,' and reach for the mint-green Royal Doulton teapot and the date loaf. And we couldn't hug each other and shake our heads, women together, appalled by the cruelty of the world. I wasn't my mother, I was only my mother's son.

Tears ran down her cheeks and into the dust; and the next thing I was crying, too.

She stopped first. She sniffed, straightened her shoulders, shuffled her feet, rocked her hips, and then she danced.

She had been the relief of my childhood. She had flown in the face of all the lethal cannons of customary boredom aimed at me. She did not – magnificently did not – do anything that everywhere passed for being 'normal'. She had always been – gloriously, stubbornly, madly – herself. The Bama I had known since I was a boy, and this was why I had always loved her. What she stood for was full rivers, irrigation, fat cows and dams aslop with chocolate water. What she knew was that much of Africa was desert and the desert was gaining. Queen Bama knew that water was more than H_2O; she knew there were cycles, seasons, rhythms, and unless they were observed with love and respect, they would die; and when they died, more of Africa would die, of disrespect, of neglect, of thirst.

I had to smile, and seeing this she danced harder, and I was with her, all the way. I even laughed. So did she, though it was more like a groan. We laughed, it was terrible, yes, but what were the alternatives? The woollen towers, castles, hoods and sheaths standing erect? The loss of those we loved; the mocking young men? The implacable virus?

Or the Rain Queen, on a dry summer evening, dancing a preferred world?

This wasn't a repeat performance of her triumphs in our garden: the sky remained blue and the confident note of the birds said rain wasn't coming. But she wasn't dancing for rain. She was dancing for me. For herself. Shaking her stick with its woollen hood and its ridiculous pom-pom at the empty sky.

'Young dogs,' said Queen Bama. 'I made them run.'

I was glad she had beaten her tormentors. It was an entirely splendid thing to have done. She was always splendid in her clear-sightedness. If the young men prevailed then all the trees in Africa, and then all the trees in the world, would be cut down, and in their place the young men would bring us beach umbrellas; they would be our forests.

She got things running. That was what she was for. She was for storms, for endless ooze, for the not-dry, for the unstuck, for the flow.

I drove down the hillside; the ancient rusty red rocks baked in the morning sun, the scrubby bushes were bunched like fists. Nothing had changed for thousands of years, but everything had altered. I'd seen the Rain Queen in full flood. No single thing I'd done had so cheered me since I stepped off the plane and went to my mother's bedside. Things were looking up.

When I arrived back at the gates of Sheerhaven the guards did not wave me through. I was handed a note. It was from Cindy and said simply:

'Gone to hospital. Ask security how to get there. Come quickly!'

32

She was in the waiting room, sitting in the corner, her arms folded and her face very white, her head pressed back against the wall, barely breathing. When I asked her what had happened, she told me; but she told me like she didn't believe it, like she was begging me to say it wasn't so, that there had been some mistake, that she was talking nonsense.

'Benny's in the theatre. They're operating now.'

'Operating?'

'To try and get the bullet out.'

Then she lay down, put her head in my lap and tried not to sob too much or too loudly. It was awful. I had no clear idea what had happened. Benny seemed too young and too small to have anything to do with bullets. But 'bullet' was what she said, and since it was all I had to go on, I said to myself, to stop thinking the worst, that if Benny had been in some sort of shooting, then at least he was in very good hands. No doctors outside a war zone had seen more gunshot wounds than the medics who held the line in this city, and who had Benny on the operating table.

We sat in the little waiting room for what seemed like hours until the surgeon came out and said faintly, warmly, 'We've removed the bullet, Mrs September. We're all in the laps of the gods now. You can see him for a few minutes.'

They had Benny rigged up to lots of monitors, his round smooth face faintly flushed on the pillow, his left side swathed in a dressing. Cindy bent over and kissed him and stroked his hair. But then they were busy around him again, and we had to go back to the waiting room.

Cindy didn't cry but she did tremble now and then, and said often, and without conviction: 'There's nothing to do but wait.'

Even that was too consoling. We had not waited more than an hour when they came to tell us they were very sorry.

We walked back into the ward and he looked just the same, except he was no longer rigged up and the people around him were gone. He was very small and very alone.

I held Cindy's hands; they were like ice.

'Poor, poor little boy,' she said.

This was something Cindy knew, something she had prepared for. She carried a gun, she knew the risks, she rehearsed in her mind again and again exactly the sort of scenario that had turned horribly real. She had taught me her rules of the road for staying alive and – it was hard but it had to be faced – she had taken some dark sardonic pleasure in the very brutality this town so feared, and secretly liked, condemned and extolled; she shared in the belief that Jo'burg was more than just bad: it was magnificently lethal.

But nothing had prepared her for this.

They said she should sleep in the hospital that night but she wouldn't. She was shaking; the idea of sleeping under the same roof as Benny filled her with horror. At the same time, she could not leave him. And yet she refused to go back to Sheerhaven, and her empty house. Could not stay. Could not go.

I said maybe it would be better if she came home with me,

and she said yes. As if this lifted from her a great weight, as if this was not a desertion of her beloved child but an awful compromise that she could live with, when she did not care whether she lived or not.

'I think I'll feel better somewhere else.'

It was not so much a statement as a prayer.

When we got back I knew she had been right: my house was cold and almost indifferent. There was relief in that. Having stood empty for some months, it had that slightly reproachful air neglected houses give out when their owners go missing. But it was nothing to her, and it was vacant, though a faint light burnt behind Noddy's window in the room in the back yard, and I wondered, briefly, if his woman had arrived.

I put her in my mother's room, beneath the gaze of Dr Schweitzer and Hemingway. Lions, kudu, okapi, dik-dik, springbuck, bongos – shot long ago and mounted on the dark wooden walls – looked down with liquid eyes. I helped her out of her clothes and found one of my mother's nightdresses, in white cotton. It was too big and made her look very small and very vulnerable and even paler than she was.

I gave her the sedative the doctor had said she should have, and she swallowed the capsules like a child. And then she asked me:

'What am I going to do now?'

It sounded like a sensible question, and any sort of sense was desirable in a world broken in madness. But it wasn't a question I could answer. It also assumed things could be done; it assumed an 'I' who functioned; it assumed a modicum of sense, and of security; it assumed a moment, a present, a 'now' in which one might *want* to do something; and I was not sure about any of that. A small boy had been shot to death and the world had not stopped in its turning, or cried out.

I lifted the blankets and helped her into bed.

'I'll need things from … the other place.' She could not bring herself to mention the name of Sheerhaven.

'Later. Leave it till later.'

'Yeah, later.' She nodded and closed her eyes. 'No hurry now, is there?'

Later was no better, no relief. Later was just when we knew what had happened. Later we traced the route the bus took that day, wondering again and again at the wild stupidity of it. We gave it a form, a beginning, middle, end … even though what had happened had no sense or form. What it did have was a grim logic: the thing Cindy knew about, guarded herself against, constantly talked of, fantasised over and had been so clever to avoid, suddenly sought her out, homed in and struck her like a grief-seeking missile.

Later we went over it, moment by moment, name by name. Cindy could think of nothing else, as if in explication some consolation might be found. The conventional wisdom at such times was that talking somehow helped. But it made things worse. And yet we went on talking and it never got any better.

The story we shaped was brief, unexceptional and without mercy.

The kids from Sunbeam Shelter had climbed that morning into their bus for one of their weekly outings, this time to the Zoo. It was a white Mercedes minibus that carried the exhortation, painted in big blue letters across the sliding door, 'Be Happy – Africa!' It had been specially adapted to carry wheelchairs, and had been donated by a spice merchant who blazoned his wares in tongues of forked flame along the side of the bus: 'Peck's Pimento – The Pepper Peter Piper Picked!'

In the roomy blue leather recesses of the bus rode four children, and one teacher named Muriel Makanya, who was in the rear seat. A six-year-old called Sammie leaned against Muriel's broad brown bosom. He had had polio and wore iron callipers on both legs, and a heavy boot. In the seat ahead of Sammie and Muriel sat Annie. She had been born blind, and was singing to herself. One seat ahead of her sat Benny in his chosen place. In the front of the bus, close to the door because it was always difficult to get her out of the vehicle, a paraplegic girl called Precious was in her wheelchair, which was anchored in the aisle, directly behind the driver, Josephus.

The bus was sailing down Jan Smuts Avenue, which dips steeply as it passes through Forest Town, and motorists usually put on speed as they approached the dip, in a Gadarene charge to the bottom of the hill.

Everyone on the bus was absorbed and happy, each with his own thoughts or his own game or his own song.

Up in the front, Precious was singing, 'We're off to see the Wild West Show, the elephant and the kangaroo-oo-oo-oo ...' helped by Josephus, the driver, one hand on the wheel while he conducted with the other.

Annie was listening to Benny who was calling out, as he always did when they made these trips: 'There's a car and there's another car and there's a bus, and there's a lamppost.'

Hardly riveting stuff, but Annie was riveted.

Muriel was singing to Sammie a Zulu lullaby about a baboon that stole a baby and ran off: '*Thula, Mama, Thula ...*'

I knew every inch of the route they took on that bright high-veld morning. I'd made the trip to the Zoo a thousand times: with my mother, with Koosie, with Nzong, the leopard boy, and later with Noddy. The kids would have passed my house in Forest Town and two blocks further down the bus turned right and set off down broad and tree-rich Saxonwold Drive, which curves around the southern edge of the Zoo, making for the entrance that lies close by.

It was then that a small saloon car – Josephus thought it was an Opel Corsa – moved to the middle of the road dead ahead of the bus, slowed suddenly, and stopped. Josephus had to brake hard and, as he did so, a large blue truck drew in tight behind and trapped the Mercedes. Two men got out of the Opel, guns in hand, and told Josephus to open the door, which he did, and they climbed into the bus.

What you had next was the typical, deeply insane encounter that pretty much passed for normal in this part of the world. The guys with guns had no other ambition that to hijack the vehicle. To them it wasn't a bus, it was a prize, it was a Mercedes, and they assumed that this glitzy high-powered cost-a-bomb bus was filled with cost-a-bomb people: sleek white male golfers, or rugby players, or salesmen, or rich stupid tourists in South Africa to see animals, and thus, all of them, not just easy game but deserving victims, folks who had too much anyway and got it from folks who had too little, and were suitable targets for a little bit of retributive Robin Hoodery.

But, instead, as Muriel Makanya the teacher, hugging the whimpering Sammie to her chest, told the two hijackers loudly, fiercely: 'These are special children, with special needs, and they can't just get off, like you say, just because you say get off!' Her voice trembling between fury and fear as she stared straight at the round black eyes of the men's pistols.

And as if to emphasise how special these children were, one of them, a little black girl strapped in a wheelchair, continued to sing, 'Never mind the weather, so long as we're together, we're off to see the Wild West Show', even though Josephus the driver was no longer conducting and was standing trembling on the pavement with a gun to his head.

The gunman on the bus realised this was not, then, your normal hijacking, where people did what you told them to do or they got shot. This one you had to work for. So he pocketed his weapon, reached forward and lifted the wheelchair containing Precious, and backed down the steps with his heavy burden, put the wheelchair down on the pavement while Precious sang through it all, of the elephant 'and the kangaroo-oo-oo …'

Now the aisle was clear, and the man got back on the bus, pointed his gun at Muriel and said: 'Off!'

Muriel carried Sammie slowly down the aisle, and his dangling steel callipers clanged on the seats in the hot silence.

'Is this the Zoo, Muriel?' Sammie said, and Muriel said: 'Yes, Sammie, this is the Zoo, this is where we get off.'

Hearing this, blind Annie obediently got up out of her seat and, guided by the sounds of Sammie's callipers hitting the metal floor, she came down the aisle to the exit. Josephus, moving very slowly so as not to give the impression to the nervous hijackers that he was threatening them in any way, helped her down the stops on to the pavement.

That left just Benny, sitting a long way back in his seat, watching but not moving.

This relative success in disposing of most of these unexpected problems had done the gunman's nerves no good. He was
faced by a small boy with a moony grin, staring back at him, as
if he had just recognised his best friend.

'Get off.'

'Hullo,' said Benny.

'Get off!' said the gunman, into whose barked repetition of
this phrase there had crept a note of raw panic. And his panic
sharpened when his partner climbed behind the wheel and
started up the engine.

'Let's go!' yelled the driver.

'Get off!' the gunman yelled again. He was almost in tears
now.

'Hullo, Baldy,' said Benny.

The gunman was not bald. But, then, Benny wasn't thinking
of him, he was almost certainly thinking of my mother's grey
parrot, the one that Bara and Buti had eaten, the bird that
tasted of old shoes. No, the man was not bald and he did not
look like a bird, so who knows what the connection was in
Benny's highly original mind. Maybe he thought the gunman
sounded like a parrot. Whatever it was, Muriel Makanya, who
saw it all, was perfectly clear that it was now that the gunman
came down the aisle and began pulling Benny out of his seat.

That was not a good idea: nothing ever moved Benny from
his place. He changed in an instant from a smiling boy into a
kicking, scratching ball of fury. He fought the gunman every
step of the way, screaming and grabbing at any rail or strap,
anything that prevented the gunman from getting him to the
door of the bus, which had begun to pull away from the kerb.

'Leave the boy!' Muriel banged on the window, terrified that
they were taking Benny with them. But a moment later he fell,

or was tossed, on to the pavement, and the Mercedes accelerated and vanished around the curve of Saxonwold Drive. Neither Muriel nor Josephus could be sure whether it was before or after Benny fell that they heard the shot.

The cops picked up Benny's killers inside an hour, standing beside the road, hitching. Bloody useless as hijackers, they had stalled the bus, and were no better at thumbing a lift. Their names were Unathi and Brightman, and they were both sixteen years old. Street kids, hustlers. Unathi, it turned out, was HIV positive and Brightman had a crack habit. They were also orphans, or at any rate without parents. Inept, deprived kids who didn't steal the bus because they wanted it but because there was a commission out on a good new Mercedes from the men who supplied customers in Mozambique, which was often the way it was done. Hijack by appointment, it was called in the trade. The hijackers claimed they had thrown Benny down the steps because he was slow. Not because they wished to kill him. They had dumped their pistols before the cops got them. Both denied shooting the boy; both were charged with murder.

33

Cindy would not go back to Sheerhaven, and she asked if I would mind if she looked through my mother's wardrobe to see if there was something 'more' she could wear. I have never forgotten that 'more'. She rummaged around and managed to find some stuff that just about fitted her, and she altered pants and blouses on my mother's old black Singer machine.

I suppose I'd just assumed her stay at my place was temporary and that eventually she'd want to go home to Sheerhaven. But it soon became clear that, as far as she was concerned, she didn't live there any more. She found herself on the other side of some ditch she did not know she'd jumped, shaken but alive, and hating herself for it. What had been her immediate past, like last week, yesterday, a few hours before, suddenly accelerated, so that what had been actually very close to her, just yesterday, felt like ages ago and faded as she watched. It was not the lightness of being that brought nausea, it was the feeling that all her belonging and belief, in that place and that time, with all the indications that this love for this person was real and lasting, were false. She'd woken up and found what had been closest to her, most precious to her, was rushing away at the speed of light. She did not only feel sad and weak, she felt betrayed; but she had the horrible feeling that she was, somehow, also the traitor.

In the time when she first stayed with me, after what we simply referred to as 'it', I hoped she might recuperate; as if she were a patient getting over a very painful operation, learning to get out of bed and walk a bit. She was so skittish, so fragile and tremulous. I told myself what you always say in the circumstances: that she had been shockingly wounded; that she wasn't herself; that she would get better. I waited for a sign that something of her raw suffering had eased a bit.

She asked me to make the funeral arrangements.

'At Rosebank Church. Like your mom.'

So that is what we did. Father Phil conducted the service. Doves made the arrangements. Cindy altered an old dress-suit of my mother's and looked very like an undertaker herself. She and I were alone in the front pew because she had refused even to tell her ex-husband about Benny. All the kids from the Shelter came along and that was good. And Precious, representing the kids who had been on the bus with Benny, laid a wreath of lily of the valley on the tiny casket on the altar steps. But we were a small congregation, easily outnumbered by the reporters who turned up.

There was a kid with a stiff wave of gelled hair, in a white suit, and a blonde in black, and several guys in jeans, with cellphones, and I knew they were having trouble working out what demeanour to affect, and what the fuck to do with their cellphones. I felt rather sorry for them, blinking rather shyly in the bright bars of green and pink lights thrown through the windows of Rosebank Church. They had been sent by their papers to cover the obsequies of the young victim whose passing has been recorded in headlines like 'Slow Boy Blown Away' or 'Sick Kid Slain' and 'Thugs Plug Toddler'. The papers were facing an impossible task. Expected to register, and condemn, and celebrate the violent cavalcade they paraded past the horrified eyes of the their readers: the rapes and muggings, hijackings and bank heists. And catering to what was pretty much the other urgent need set in the South African soul: the desire to see sporting opponents getting their faces kicked in, to read about bloody murder, big tits and good batting, and not necessarily in that order. But expected to keep paying at least lip service to the usual pieties about peace and harmony and pots of gold at both ends of the rainbow.

Benny, then, was big news. Even in a country where more people were killed by their neighbours than any other place on earth – except maybe Guatemala – where murder, so went the dark joke, was just a way of life. Where death by gunshot was democratic and almost equally available to all, whether you lived in a walled villa in a gated suburb or a wooden shack in a squatter camp. Where most murders rated less space than the stock exchange prices, Benny's death – the boy who was too slow to move – propelled his story into that terrible book of mythic murders, right up there alongside accounts of men who believed raping babies was a cure for Aids; or the farmer who dragged his workers behind his truck until the skin peeled off their bones; or the six men locked in the freezer van, whose scrabbling nails bleeding on the icy steel door so haunted my mother and Queen Bama...

One Sunday paper went so far as to split its front page. On the left was a picture of school kids visiting Jo'burg for a sports competition, grinning young guys in face-paint, beneath the banner headline: 'A Feast of Schoolboy Rugby'.

The right-hand half of the page showed the abandoned

white Mercedes minibus, under the headline: 'Sick Boy Tossed From Bus'.

There were angry editorials about the inhumanity of people who would drag a disabled child from a vehicle and, when he would not move fast enough, shoot him dead. There were sermons preached against our propensity to kill; there were anguished questions asked about a people who, in the first flush of their freedom from a murderous tyranny, seemed bent on destroying each other, more wantonly, more cruelly, and more frequently than ever.

Another Sunday paper, in that peculiarly sticky-sweet prose that characterised officially approved public debate, compared Benny with Elvis Presley. The argument was complicated: much in the way blacks and whites could enjoy Presley's music, as a symbol of their shared emotions, he being famously described a 'white Negro', so the nation might come together by seeing the murder of Benny both as a crime – shocking and savage and reprehensible – yet also as a lesson, and an opportunity. Whites were forever whining about crime and yet, to some, their complaints were really a kind of coded race hatred, because blacks were robbed, raped and killed far more often than anyone else. However, Benny straddled the race divide. The child of a mixed marriage, he was neither white nor black but both, or, as one columnist put it, stretching wildly for accuracy, 'pale-black'. This put his fate into a broader, and more desirable, context. It showed that inexplicable cruelty could happen to anyone, 'irrespective of colour, class, creed, gender or disability'... The lesson of Benny, the editorialists declared, was that we must 'pull together, sink our differences, level the playing field, and consult all relevant structures, stake-holders and role players ...' Benny, it was said, must be seen as a bridge.

To my alarm, Cindy seemed to take heart from this self-serving crap.

'Maybe he *can* be a bridge?'

I said, 'Why stop at Benny the bridge, why not the book of Benny? Why not the entire fucking Bible of Benny?'

She was hurt. 'But, Alex, Benny the bridge, it's only a metaphor; it speaks for what we can't say. It's really rather touching.'

Benny – the metaphor.

At Cindy's request, Benny's ashes were interred alongside my mother's, in the wall of the Garden of Remembrance at Rosebank Church. Later, we went back to the house in Forest Town – my house, my mother's house – as if this for her was the most natural thing in the world. As if she were coming home.

34

Although Cindy in no way resembled my mother, there were links, and they grew all the more evident in the weeks we lived side by side in the house in Forest Town. I didn't feel it was mimicry; it was a more a form of crusading approval, with something reckless about it.

'Your mother was number one. I really admired her. To the uttermost, to the nth degree.'

Cindy was trying on one of my mother's blue turbans.

'I mean, this is a woman who knew what she wanted; this is a woman who didn't let anyone give her uphill, hey? Who didn't take any bullshit—'

'I think you have to wind the turban the other way.'

'Show me.'

She stood in front of the mirror while I wound the bright blue sash around her small pale forehead, higher and higher, until she looked rather like Nefertiti.

I said: 'Cindy, I don't know about this mix and match business.'

'Oh, why not, hey? I'm only trying a few things.'

'I know, but it's a bit like walking into a charity shop and trying on the hats.'

'Whajamean?' Her anguished query rose to a note of high

keening: *me-e-e-ennnn?* 'Your mom wouldn't have minded. Your mom was a most generous person.'

Cindy had begun to wear more and more items from my mother's wardrobe: a yellow cardigan, a white blouse, a pair of old dungarees. She looked rather interesting in faded khaki bush jackets, jodhpurs, old jeans, velvet smoking jackets. All were rather mannish and gave her an elfin appeal; a little girl dressing up in her dad's clothes.

She wore her own shoes but that was because my mother had such big feet, just as she had very large hands. I got the feeling that she wasn't so much trying to wear her clothes as much as trying my mother on, getting the feel of her. There was, of course, a terrific disparity: my mother had been almost a foot taller, and much broader. Cindy could not wear her flying boots, and she could not have handled any of her heavy guns; she did not fly. Yet what she could do was to select samples, much as someone prospecting for gold takes samples of rock and tests it for signs of the auriferous seam that says: 'Here be riches.'

Cindy sat for hours carefully cleaning the glass frames that held the maps of Livingstone's travels. She marvelled at the photographs of Schweitzer and Bror Blixen; of Hemingway in shorts and sweatshirt, gloved up, facing my mother in her breast-protector. She pored over the weighty, leather-backed albums of black and white snaps showing my old lady stalking leopard, taxi-ing down the runway of some long-ago bush strip in some unnamed African colony, rafting rapids, fording rivers, posing beside the huge and wide-eyed head of a dead buffalo, picnicking, drinking, camping; my mother smiling, beside men of every type and height and moustache and rifle.

She was like some sort of refugee, someone in transit. It was not that she went backwards or forwards; no, I'd say she was going round and round, sinking deeper and deeper into her new role. There were parallels for this sort of biological camouflage. A little creature like the rabbit flea, being small and needy, has learnt that the price of staying alive in a lethal world is to bury itself in some bigger, warmer, body, and so it has adapted accordingly. The rabbit flea has surrendered its reproductive cycle to its host. The hormones of the rabbit govern the season when its invader has babies. The little bloodsucker gets pregnant only when mummy bunny gets broody.

That is what Cindy did, though she did it in such subtle ways that it took me some time to realise what was going on. She got broody, she took on things, she took things *in*; and she was full of something I did not see until it had grown too large to stop. I don't blame myself for not seeing what was going on; I don't think Cindy did either.

Perhaps, too, it was also a form of distraction, this dressing up in someone else's clothes. By shedding her former life and becoming someone else, something of the horror of Benny's death was eased in Cindy. She never spoke of him but by moving all the time deeper into my mother's wardrobe, someone who had known – and hugged – Benny, as she had known and hugged all the kids in the Shelter, was perhaps a way of clothing her wound in borrowed dressings. She seemed to be reaching into the immense amplitude that was my mother. The individual bits of clothing were not important: she used them as charms, or fetishes. Or relics.

There was also something bloody ridiculous about it. Here was this tiny Jo'burg kugel waltzing around in cardigans, turbans, bush-hats and the silk scarves my mother liked to knot at her throat when she took off for somewhere fun, like

Tanganyika. But I wasn't going to question it. She had gone through something so terrible there was nothing to say, and no comfort to be given. Benny was dead, in a way she had almost predicted. Her worst terror had come to call. It made her vulnerable and, yes, in its dreadful finality, and in her endurance, it made her unreachable.

We were lovers no longer, we were not sleeping together, we were merely occupying my mother's house; we might have been lodgers leading adjacent lives or some couple who had long since stopped coupling. We ate together, we talked, and we co-existed. I got the breakfast and later I went walking. She read my mother's books; she watched the old ciné films of the Waturi pygmies. At night she wanted stories about my mother, her life and her lovers. She began to tidy and dust and make some order in the accumulated souvenirs of a lifetime. Like the costume museum across the road, where the Bernberg sisters had lived.

My mother became the subject of our suppertime conversations; Cindy would look up over the angel fish, or the pasta, and say:

'Tell me about her time with Hemingway; tell me what she thought of Schweitzer; tell me about the leopard men...'

Cindy picked up my mother's old pipe, and stuck it between her teeth.

'Tell me what tobacco she smoked.'

'It was called Boxer tobacco. Strong black stuff. It came in a white cotton bag, with a drawstring neck.'

'Will you buy me some, hey?'

I found a bag of Boxer, showed her how to fill the pipe, lit it for her and watched her blow creamy smoke around the room.

'I puff but I can't inhale. No way!'

'Just as well, that stuff's lethal. Cindy, why are you walking around in my ma's kit?'

She blew smoke at Livingstone's maps on the wall. 'I like to feel close, that's why. You don't seem to miss her.'

I didn't like the question, or the tone. Cindy could dress herself up as much as she liked, but I wasn't going to partner her to the fancy-dress ball.

'Of course I miss her.'

'Oh, *ja*, how much?

'I don't know how to answer that.'

'Well, do you miss her more now that she's not here any more?'

'Listen; in the first place, I missed her even when she was here, when she was alive.'

She took the pipe from her mouth and slowly knocked out the tobacco in a back mahogany ashtray, carved to resemble an elephant carrying a maharajah. Then she spat out a few crumbs of tobacco that had travelled down the stem of the pipe, and made a face at the bitter burning on the tip of her tongue.

'There is something I'd better tell you. I'm going back to work.'

'Back to selling houses?'

She shook her head. 'No. I've signed up at the Sunbeam Shelter. Don't look so amazed. I start tomorrow morning.' She enjoyed my astonishment. Watching me steadily, her green eyes limpid in her clever, pretty face, under the great crown of turban. 'I wanted to do something for Benny. I reckoned this is what he knew, the school – and the kids.'

She said it with the utmost simplicity. Why then did I feel it was an excessive movement towards making things right? Making them … 'pristine'. There is, of course, nothing to be said when someone tells you that they have been moved by love and devotion to give themselves over to good works.

So she began working again at Sunbeam Shelter, setting off each morning in the old Land Rover, riding up the hill to the big house. I wondered if she was hugging the kids but I didn't want to ask: I had an idea what she'd say.

Cindy, once so irreverent, so deliciously wry, had gone the way of the heart. Some terrifying power had taken Benny from her. How was she to soften her anguish? She would not rail, she would submit. She was reaching out and taking into herself that which had swallowed up her son. She was repositioning herself for her life after Benny; in the house of my mother; in the role – dare I say it – of my mother, setting out to embrace 'Africa'.

Something, incidentally, that my mother never did. She took it by the throat, yes, but she never, ever saw Africa as morally improving. For the simple reason that she saw no reason for moral improvement, because things, and that included herself and her world, were quite perfect as they were, thank you very much. Yet when she died she tore a hole in our lives, and it was that loss which Cindy had found a way of repairing.

It was increasingly odd. Exactly who were these people living in my house? Cindy was someone else, Noddy was certainly someone else. Only I was the same and that was no great help. It was clear that I lacked a crucial ability: the gift of change. Others shuffled off their skins and became new people; it was like living in a fairy-tale, where I was the only grown-up, the only non-believer. It was not that I didn't aspire to the same magic – I did – but I simply could not see how to make it happen.

Noddy's friend who came to live in his room turned out to be a languorous young woman called Nonsuma, and he appeared to have as little as possible to do with her. Mostly, she sat outside Noddy's room in the sun, or she did a bit of washing and hung it on the line very slowly. I got the feeling Nonsuma didn't mean anything in herself, she was just another milestone on his road to perdition. Very soon she began to put on weight, and she made Noddy look even smaller.

He had always looked tiny but solid; now he looked just tiny. The only confidence he allowed himself now was at the week-end when he headed into the townships, spry and glittering in his golden suit and the rainbow wave of the feather in his hat.

And then, from one day to the next, Noddy and Nonsuma were gone.

But he had left behind every last thing he owned: his old grey flannels, his Gstaad T-shirt, his blue overall, his old dark blue Sunday suit and his golden shebeen suit. His building society book was there, still in its red rubber bands, and it showed Noddy's savings: he was several thousand bucks in credit. The letter his brother had written him, telling him the terrible news about Beauty: everything that went to make him the man he had been left with me. To me. Everything of himself, except his true self, and his hat. The hat was gone, too, along with its owner.

I packed all his gear in his suitcases: cardboard in a tartan pattern and cheap locks, which he had used when he travelled between his gardens in Jo'burg and his farm and family in Matabeleland. You never know, I thought, he might come back. But I wasn't counting on it.

•

I spent a lot of time in the afternoons wandering around the Zoo. I liked the polar bear. There had always been a polar bear when I was a kid, and he had seemed normal, just another of the many exotic species behind bars. Even though he was thousands of miles from where he lived, he belonged, because he was in the Zoo. That great, shaggy, rather dusty creature lived in a cage and reminded me of a giant furry phantom. They sprayed him with water from time to time to alleviate the heat from sharp highveld sun, and his cage always stank of fish. He struck me as lonely. He would push his paws through the bars and hang on for dear life. Or that's the way it looked. The new guy was in a glassed-in arctic habitat, at the right temperature, and he would stand quietly with his arms wrapped around his waist, like a man trying to warm up.

Remembering that bear, I had an explanation of my mother's extreme attachment to the children at Sunbeam Shelter. It wasn't about hugging them. It was herself she was warming. She was ill, she felt in danger of being swept away, and she needed someone to hold on to, so she put her arms around the kids. Maybe, like the polar bear, her situation was absurd. After a lifetime of doing and flying and being in Africa, she had come, as had her friend Queen Bama, to the recognition that she had got it all wrong, and everywhere about her she saw dissolution, the terrible onrush of time. A hurricane had torn past her and she took hold of whatever might save her from being blown away.

One day I was in the garden, looking at the lavender. The sky was that uncertain gold you see only on the highveld. It was about five in the afternoon and the grass, which I had recently mown, smelt of the shaded afternoons of my boyhood when the touch of grass on your bare soles spelt freedom and relief.

I heard the plane very low overhead. It was a Cessna and it circled over the house a couple of times, then soared up into the sky and then came in low over the telephone wires, and the birds sprang up, complaining.

When Cindy got in that evening she sat back in my mother's old leather chair, she put her feet up and I saw she was wearing a new pair of flying boots. Those at least were her own.

'I thought I'd surprise you. Did you know who it was?'

'Instantly. When did you get your licence?'

'I've been learning for weeks now. Today I made my first solo flight as a qualified pilot and I decided on a fly past to mark the event. Did you think of your mom?'

'In fact, no. If I was reminded of anyone, it was of a guy called Bob Mistry. D'you ever hear of him?'

She shook her head. 'Tell me.'

'Mistry was in the Congo in the old days, a journalist working for UPI. He had two things going for him: he could fly and he could use a film camera. That's what got him to the Congo where my ma met him. Mistry was amongst the first TV reporters in the Congo when it blew up in the sixties. He covered the rapes, the killings, the assassination of Patrice Lumumba. She took Bob Mistry hunting okapi with her, and she introduced him to her Wambuti friends. He wasn't a bad shot but what worked against Bob in the bush was his extreme fastidiousness. He was a dapper man, he loved wearing white, and he had a sleek brown moustache, neat little feet, pert little buttocks. He was so sleek and he combed his black hair over his head in a wave, like it was built of shellac. He looked to me a bit like an intelligent seal in a suit. Anyway, Mistry was crazy about my mother, and she liked him, I think.'

'Did she love him?'

Again the question. Really strange, that question. Delivered by a woman wearing my mother's yellow cardigan, smoking my mother's pipe, sitting in my mother's chair.

'I've tried to explain this before. I'm not sure if she ever loved anyone. A lot of men loved her, and a lot of them she devoured.'

'Go on.'

'When she'd finished hunting okapi, she'd done the Congo for a bit, and she'd done Bob Mistry. Only he didn't understand. He dropped everything and came down to Jo'burg. Now, my ma, when in another place, had no time and precious little recollection of what or whom she'd left behind. She didn't just go off the man, she couldn't quite remember who he was. But he kept turning up: at parties and picnics and airfields. Everywhere she looked, there was Mistry, with his white shoes and his shining moustache, pleading to be reunited, and appalled that my mother didn't seem to know, or care, who the hell he was. She lost patience – she never had much – and she told him if he kept pestering her, she'd kick his balls in. Mistry was pretty downcast, and that's why he did something so completely odd I've still not quite worked out why he chose it. So potentially messy. It was so out of character in such a prissy, contained man.'

She looked triumphant: 'He tried to kill himself?'

'Not quite. In fact, he tried to kill her. You looked surprised. But it was a smart move on his part. You see, if he'd tried to kill himself, my old lady would not have been very impressed. But trying to wipe her out, that was the sort of thing that gave her a lift. And then there was the way he set about it. Bob called up late one night and I took the call: she wouldn't speak to him. I told him what she said, which was to drop dead. Mistry sounded quite pleased, something I found puzzling. I realised later that the call had been a blind: he was making sure she was home. What Bob did then was to get seriously drunk, climb into his Cessna – rather like the one you were flying – and take off, leaving no flight plan. In those days my ma and I were living on the top floor of a three-storey block of flats called Fawn Glen, in Parkwood. Mistry flew over the building at around three in the morning when we were fast asleep; he took a bead on our flat, and flew his plane smack into the top storey.'

'Are you serious?'

'Totally. I've often thought of him since those planes smashed into the Twin Towers in New York. Our block was a lot smaller and a lot tougher. Those thirties blocks were built to last and, anyway, being pretty pissed, Mistry hit the wrong fucking flat. The one right next door. He didn't knock down the building, he didn't harm us, but he did kill the elderly couple next door, and himself.

'What did she say, your mom? Was she impressed?'

'Up to a point. She liked the fact he'd got off his arse and tried to wipe her out, but she thought him an idiot for missing the target.'

'Why are you telling me, Alex? Is there some kind of moral point here? Is it because I buzzed you? Is it because maybe you think I want to do to you what Mistry wanted to do to your mother?'

It was my turn to shake my head.

'This isn't a story, this is a factual account of something that really happened. That's why it sounds so weird. Bob Mistry's failure to kill my mother isn't really what it's about. It is about the people he did kill. It turned out that the elderly couple next door were old friends of Mistry's. The guy had been the bureau chief at UPI when he was starting out: Bob Mistry killed the man who made his career.'

'And what conclusion do you draw from this?'

'None. I don't do conclusions, and I don't do morals. It was just something that happened, and I'm aghast at the oddity of life, and death.' I looked at her. 'I don't do mothers either.'

'Tell me, Alex, tell me truly. Did you love Kathleen?'

'I think I did, when I didn't want to bump her off. A bit like Bob Mistry.'

'Bump her off?'

'Push her over a cliff. Something like that. Look, it's precisely because I did love her that there were times I'd have cheerfully strangled her. I loved her the way I love the southeaster that cuts your ears off, I loved her like I do the lightning that kills people on the highveld. I loved her the way I love diving very deep into clear water and lying there down at the bottom till my lungs are about to pop and I can feel myself passing out, but it's so big and peaceful and cool down there I don't want to surface ever, but I know if I don't come up for air, I'll die. That's how I loved her, like you love something that is big and wonderful and appalling; but often, very, very often, you just wish it would fucking well stop!'

'Why do you think your mother hugged the kids?'

'I don't know.'

'I told you what I think. I think it was an outpouring of love, she couldn't help herself. You're so suspicious of love you can't see it.'

'I think you're dead wrong. It assumes she had some sort of feeling for kids. Let me tell you that she was wholly lacking in maternal feelings. If I had to compare her with any other animal, any other species, I'd go for the cheetah. The cheetah makes sure she looks after her brood for just as long as she has to, until the cubs are functioning, and then she's off. Another mate, another litter, another life. Never looks back.'

35

On my mother's desk, between the pictures of Schweitzer and Hemingway, there now appeared photos of two young black boys, unsmiling. I knew who they were, I had been at the trial, I had heard them sentenced to twenty years. Unathi, wearing a white T-shirt, and Brightman in a black turtle-neck sweater.

Also new was the headed notepaper on her desk, heavy white bond with the embossed letterhead: 'The Benny September Memorial Trust'. Its directors were Cindy September and Jacob Schevitz.

This was a perfectly logical continuation of Cindy's new role – my mother's house, her gear, and now her lawyer. I don't think Cindy and I said more than good morning to each other after that. I went to see Schevitz and he told me what was going on.

'The Benny September Memorial Trust is dedicated to helping kids like Unathi and Brightman to realise their full potential as citizens of the new South Africa.' He saw my face and sighed. 'Hey, Alex, lay off. It's not my idea, this foundation. All I'm doing is setting it up for her.'

I think Schevitz probably found her visit even more perplexing than the time my ma hit him with her Cuban. Cindy was wearing a pair of my old lady's jodhpurs, a pink silk blouse, and her eyes were lovely. And, then, too, he felt he had failed my mother and he did not want to fail Cindy.

She told him: 'I think of them.'

He had not given her an easy ride. 'Why do you think of them?'

'Because they're so young!'

'Old enough to hijack a school bus, old enough to carry guns, old enough to use them.'

'Yes, but you know their history. Aids orphans, left to fend for themselves, then the move to Jo'burg, then the need to keep body and soul together.'

'Yes, then the guns, then the killing...'

'I know. But their faces haunt me. Where do you think they are? Can I go and visit them?' Cindy had asked him.

Schevitz told me this pretty matter-of-factly. 'Before you go off pop, let me tell you it also worries the hell out of me. But it's her choice; she wants it like this. Imagine, you commemorate the brutal killing of your only son by trying to help his killers. And whether you or I agree or not, it is, well, remarkable.'

'Yeah. Remarkable. Maybe we could start blaming Benny for being the boy he was, on the wrong bus at the wrong time, and being so slow, and so these guys were forced to shoot him. Maybe that's the next step, Schevvy: getting Benny back, to stand up and say he's really sorry, to apologise to these poor killers for being so unhelpful. Maybe that would be most remarkable of all; maybe since Benny can't say it himself, being dead and all, you could say it for him, stand up and say: "Unathi and Brightman are innocent, OK; and Benny's to blame."'

Schevitz said: 'Look, the love and tenderness thing towards these guys, the selflessness thing, is a bit much. I told her that. But you gotta think of the alternatives. You could say she was a shining example of forgiveness.'

'You could say that Benny was innocent kid who got murdered – and he deserved better than this crap.'

Schevitz stuck it out. 'You could say that she is taking an impossible situation, one that's full of pain and suffering, and changing it.'

'Go on say it: transforming it.'

'I didn't say that, you did.'

'You're right. I'm sorry I said that. It was a low blow.'

It was true. The old Schevitz had never gone in for that sort of crap, though it seemed he was skirting pretty close to it now. Transformation, the old Schevitz had once remarked, was about changing yesterday's blood into tomorrow's Mercedes Benz. But that had been before he fell into the arms of Cindy, and into the sticky, stifling web of culturally acceptable newspeak about what 'role players' and 'stakeholders' were 'bringing to the party' …

Schevitz said: 'She's the one who lost her kid; frankly, Alex, she's entitled to do any damn thing she wants about that. You haven't any business being less forgiving than her. Or angrier than her. And anyway, what are the alternatives? To be stuck in bitterness or to move on?'

'It's not about alternatives. Alternatives are exactly what are not available under what we might call the Cindy scenario. Alternatives imply choice and different versions and the hope of freedom; none of same are on offer here. There is only the authorised version of some very horrible facts. Those facts are now going to be shoved around till they come out looking different. What we have here is maybe the only story of this country: forms of force passing themselves off as freedom. The kind of freedom that says if you don't let me do what's good for you, I'll shove your face in.'

'Alex, I can see why you don't stay here. You've got nothing good to say about the place.'

'Fuck you, Schevvy.'

'OK, Alex. Let's leave it there, OK?'

Schevitz was a good guy, an honest guy, and he had never gone in for bullshit on a vast scale. Now he was ashamed, but I saw something else and it hit me like a locomotive. Schevitz was along for the ride. To ease what remorse he clearly felt at not helping my ma when he had the chance. But also because, after years of bitterness in the political wilderness, he was back where he had once been happy, fighting the good fight, being of service. I do not mean he championed the little killers of a small boy who didn't move fast enough: Schevitz might be making a fool of himself for love, perhaps, but he was no sentimentalist. No, the old dream had hooked Schevitz one more time, as it had done years before when he fought the good fight against the bastards who ran our world. After years of being out of it, a ridiculous old white liberal put out to grass, suddenly Schevitz had a cause again. The Benny September Memorial Trust ... Cindy's new deal.

And who could gainsay her? After all, as Schevitz had pointed out, it was her suffering, her child, her idea to make contact with his killers, her choice to forgive. Her right to do so. It didn't matter how it looked to me or to anybody else. It wasn't really our business. What was more, her way was consonant with so much that was morally uplifting as well as politically desirable in a country in which hatred between whites and blacks was always and everywhere. The way she had put aside her own anguish by bringing hope and consolation to those who did not deserve it was magnificent.

Why, then, did I find it so appalling? Noble, perhaps, but even so I recoiled before Cindy's selflessness. I also saw that what Cindy felt was not really perverse. If she had made herself over from the poor girl out of Blaukrans into the northern suburbs Jo'burg princess, she could do it again, and change herself into this saintly figure of forgiveness.

Brightman and Unathi were held in a detention centre for juveniles in the Limpopo Province, near a town called Polakwane. There was an airport at Polakwane and whenever she got permission, she and Schevitz flew to see 'the boys'. Cindy bought them books and baked them cakes and wrote them long letters on lilac paper in her sloping hand. She announced her five-year plan to rehabilitate them with the same degree of enthusiasm and passion that she'd once taught me the rules for staying alive on the road, or given me the low-down on Jo'burg as it really was.

That Cindy no longer existed; she had been too unserious, too flighty, too much of the 'old South Africa'. The new Cindy was earnest, repetitive, long-winded, well meaning and deeply, even fatally, confused. But she had the great gift of being able to believe every word she said, which meant she was perfectly suited to the times.

Her five-year plan was to win permission to visit 'the boys' once a month, and 'to win their trust'. That desire was nauseating, she knew it, but she didn't care to hide it, she simply repeated it when I winced. There was also an appeal in preparation. Next, in the fullness of time, she hoped to persuade the authorities to allow Unathi and Brightman out on parole so they could come home with her.

She had no doubt where home was, and I faced hard decisions. What was left of the place that had once been mine, of the mother who had given birth to me, and of the stories that she had told me, and what they said about who I was, who she was? Because the longer the 'new' Cindy lived there, the more the 'old' life was covered in the exciting revised customs and plans of the incomers. Cindy was colonising the space, and doing it for the best of motives.

I was living, then, in my mother's house, with someone who seemed increasingly to be not her double but her successor; and the more fully she filled that role, the more pointless staying on seemed to be. I felt what I guess my mother had been feeling in a world of brutal change.

The question now was: what was I to do? I knew I could go back to what was an ephemeral but useful job: the supply of cooler air in overheated spaces. Indeed, the more I thought about it, the more useful a job seemed it to be, in its modesty, its ability to clean, wash, steady the air we breathed.

The new Cindy not only had right on her side, she had the future on her side. And I was a hopeless reactionary. Because I preferred the house as it was; I preferred Noddy and Queen Bama; I preferred the leopard men and the Wambuti pygmies to this new version of events. And as sure as hell I preferred my mother to Cindy's version of her.

And yet both repelled me: my mother's high indifference to everything she flew over; and Cindy in emotional meltdown. When I considered what Cindy had melted down from, the smart cookie who flogged real estate, whose life revolved around big bucks, the right BMW, cash in the bank and a pistol in the glove compartment, to the Mother Teresa of the juvenile correctional facilities ...

Worse, I had to face the fact that she was on to something; she was immersing herself in the way things were, and had to be. And you did that or you stayed out in the cold.

It wasn't about humility or acceptance, not really. It was about what it was always about: it was about winning, it was about power; it was about moral elevation; and as soon as anyone claimed the high moral ground in Africa – you could put money on this – the more certainly and more cruelly it pressed down on the heads of the poor. What had Cindy found in the cupboard of my mother but the entire fucking outfit suitable for the high moral ground, after some slight adaptation, right down to the boots and right up to the fucking hat, or should I say turban?

There seemed nothing to keep me any longer, and very little chance of ever working out the two crucial mysteries that plagued me: why my mother hugged those kids; and why it was that Noddy still meant so much when he had finished with me. Why I still felt he pointed towards something vital, if only I could work out what the hell it was. I told myself, relieved to find some excuse for staying on, that I could not leave just yet. I had two last bequests still unfulfilled. The mambo music was meant to go to Raoul Mendoza. Having seen what it took to turn him into a happy, well-settled South African, I saw no need to blow his cover.

And then there was Papadop.

36

To Papadop went her Livingstone relics: these included one of the explorer's own route maps, tracing his prodigious treks to and fro across sub-Saharan Africa; a sketch of the Victoria Falls, with Livingstone's careful measurements in his clear hand: '1860 yards wide – 310 feet deep …' As if accuracy of this sort was a way of affixing certainty to a bewildering encounter with an Africa so resistant to good sense, so ungrateful to missionaries, explorers, soldiers, traders, visionaries. And yet so responsive, then as now, to the gimcracks and gewgaws given by invaders to chiefs and head honchos, those absurd big men whose role has been to soak and suppress their people, and to shaft their continent.

Also among her relics was a brass-bound mirror Livingstone had given to a chief in Ujiji, whose grandson in turn had given it to my mother, taking it from a glass cabinet in which he kept other memorabilia of the doctor: razors, beads, several iron spoons, one copper jug, a brass tray, a single-bladed penknife, a snuff box imprinted with the head of Queen Victoria, and a red and blue accordion that wheezed a bit but still worked. The chief had kept Livingstone's mirror in a cabinet of curiosities in order to study, she told me, 'in a state of permanent perplexity', the habits and customs of the early white invaders.

It was the perfect emblem of that invasion. Whoever looked into Livingstone's mirror found the face they wanted: their own.

There was also a sepia print of the old mango tree, which was said to mark the spot where Livingstone and Stanley met in Ujiji in 1871. Beneath it was a big stone identifying the site as 'The White Man's Tree'.

There was Livingstone's famous cap, with the blue crown and red band, which my ma had always insisted was the very one he tipped to Stanley. But then again, Livingstone's caps were not all that rare. He had lots of them made for him by Starkey's of Bond Street. It was an essential prop in a long career, as distinct a trade mark as Charlie Chaplin's bowler. Behind the legend of the missionary, the liberator of slaves, the explorer, geographer, the namer of mountains and waterfalls, the dour Scot who came to personify Africa to all the Anglo-Saxon world, was the other Livingstone, the mendicant trouper, proud, stubborn, cruelly uncaring of his wife and children, an actor never upstaged, with a fine line in hats.

I'd seen another of these caps displayed by the Royal Geographical Society in London; they swore theirs was one Livingstone doffed to Stanley. Questions of authenticity go to the heart of things in the long and violent poker game that is Africa. Who's faking it, and who's lying to whom? Those were the only questions worth asking.

I called Papadop's number in Mount Darwin, and I got someone on the line whose voice I didn't know.

'Papadopolous, he is not here.'

'When will he be back?'

There was a pause. 'Never.'

'Never?'

'He is not coming back.'

'Do you mean he's moved?'

'Yes.'

'Do you know where he's moved to?'

'No.'

'And what has happened to his place?'

'It is not his place; it is my place now.'

I got it then. I had heard of the seizure of white-owned farms by hopped-up young men claiming to be old soldiers of the liberation wars they were far too young to have fought. But somehow I never thought of Papadop as a farmer. He had stopped farming long ago, when he went into selling agricultural machinery. He owned land in Mount Darwin, stretching all the way to the river, where he had his fishing shack, but it never crossed my mind that someone would take his home, his land. And besides, Papadop was no ordinary white settler: he was a Zimbabwean citizen; a member of the ruling party; he spoke the language; he had been for years comrade mayor of the town.

I missed Noddy all over again. He was someone I could have talked to about this. For most people, Zimbabwe barely existed, or, if it did, it was that little place 'up north', formerly known as Rhodesia, famous for the Victoria Falls and bugger all else, run by a despot who kept stealing farms and locking up anyone who stepped out of line. Much as the crazy white despot who'd run Rhodesia had done, with the same support from our old 'white-is-right' gang of desperadoes as the current tyrant got from our new 'black-is-better' regime. And for much the same reasons: the big bully up north might be a bastard, but he was our bastard; he wasn't just kin, he was skin-kin.

I phoned everyone I could think of in Zim. The so-called war vets were on the rampage, some guy called Hitler Hunzvi was wrecking farms, people were dying. No one knew anything about Mount Darwin. Papadop seemed to have disappeared without trace.

Then I got lucky. I called one of the commercial farmers' unions which tried to keep track of their dispossessed members, and they gave me a lead. Word was he was no longer in Zim at all. It was thought he was across the border, living near a little town in north-eastern Mozambique called Chimoio. Getting there was not easy. I would need to fly from Jo'burg to Beira on the east coast, rent a car and head out into the country.

Beira airport was small and comfortable and the first thing I noticed was the marked lack of aggression. Everyone smiled. It was worrying. I paid seven dollars airport tax, I got my passport stamped and then I rented a small Toyota. When I told the girl I was heading for Chimoio, she smiled and said gently: 'Try to stay on marked routes all the time: there are uncleared land-mines up that way.'

I left behind the muddy, sludgy sea off Beira. The road was empty and fleecy clouds hung low in a coppery-blue sky. Travelling in this way always frees the mind. I was alone in a landscape of dark green bush and rich red earth and here and there a small, bourgeois, poignant Portuguese villa, stuck in the past, tin roof, paint-flaked shutters and shady veranda. Abandoned, suddenly, when independence came in 1975. Anywhere else these empty houses of the old Portuguese set-tlers would have been vandalised, or cannibalised, or turned into precarious squats. But they waited among the banana plants and the thorn trees, forlorn, deserted on the far shore of a vanished world.

After the Portuguese fled, civil war began: another of those cruel local wars, fought by proxies of the bigger powers. After sixteen years of fighting, a million dead, six million displaced, and most Mozambicans were living on under a dollar a day.

There would be landmines, said the car-hire girl. Of course! There must be landmines. But landmines did not compete in kill rate with a human carrying a Kalashnikov, and what was so extraordinary, on the road out of Beira, in a country ruined by strife, and as poor as any on earth, for someone fresh out of Jo'burg, was the deep peace and easy air of the place. Looking at the map, I saw that if I had kept travelling on up the coast from Beira I would have come to Quelimane, the port where Livingstone setttled for a while and became British consul. And here I was, on yet another bloody missionary venture into the interior, carrying in my pack some of the very trinkets Livingstone had handed out on his wanderings in this country. Except that Livingstone was there when the show began, when Africa opened like a brilliant and lavish production dedicated to 'commerce and Christianity and the suppression of slavery'. It was the greatest show on earth and Livingstone the first of its impresarios.

I was there to search for survivors, for whoever was left when the show closed and the circus headed out of town. A lost tribe of one.

Chimoio was sleepy and dusty. An old helicopter, probably brought down in the war, sat in someone's back yard like some giant toy. The bar in the middle of town was admirably named the Plymouth Arms. It was simply and ruggedly built: a concrete floor under a corrugated-iron roof, and a generous, shady stoop. A huge Union flag was painted on the back wall.

It was run by a Mozambican called Cecelia who wore denim hot pants and saw to it the booze kept flowing to her thirsty customers, half a dozen very large white men in khaki shorts who were knocking it back like there was no tomorrow.

I ordered a beer and asked Cecelia about Papadop.

Her English was pretty, oiled with the soft liquids of her own Portuguese. 'I know him. Big, dark, crazy old man. I know him. He comes here for a drink, for ice. He calls everyone "bastards".'

'Yeah, that sounds about right. Where do I find him?'

She sketched directions on the back of a paper napkin.

'Fifteen, maybe twenty kilometres. Hard country. Stay on the track and you'll find him. Look for a tent on a hill.'

She caught the look in my eyes and waved a hand at the men drinking behind me. 'Zimbos.'

'Zimbos?'

Cecelia's smile showed white, even teeth. 'Yeah. In Chimoio we have got Zimbos, Ports and Pongos, but Zimbos are …' She lifted a finger like a pistol and trained it on her right temple.

'Why's that, Cecelia?'

'Because they come here from Zim with …' she joined thumb and forefinger in a neat O '… *nada em tudo*: nothing. And they kill themselves.'

'How do they kill themselves?'

'It's the malaria. Or too much work.' She flicked her dark eyes towards the big men at their table that was carpeted in litre bottles of lager. 'Or too much of mine. If they wish to kill themselves, for me it is better when they do it with mine.'

She had a point.

The sweltering land I drove through was lush, but empty. Fine farming country, yet left alone, aching to sprout. Everywhere there was this feeling of something waiting to happen. Fifteen kilometres out of town, I spotted a tent on the crest of a hill. I had to manoeuvre up a track so rocky I left the car and walked the rest of the way.

He was sitting on a stone outside his tent, old Rhodesian army issue, with his back to me, staring out towards the low hills on the horizon. In the gentle valley below him was an enormous and beautiful field of young tobacco plants.

I said: 'How you doing, Papadop?'

He turned and stared, then he got up slowly, wiping sweat from his forehead with the brim of his floppy khaki hat.

'Bloody hell – Alex!'

For the next few hours we sat outside his tent and drank brandies and Cokes, and he told me in his flat, rhythmic drawl the story of how his world had fallen to pieces.

'I got this first Section 5 – like a warning, notice, order, whatever the fuck it's called – it said my farm was listed. Listed for expropriation. I was being evicted. I thought, they can't be serious. I hadn't farmed that land in twenty years. I'm not a farmer; I buy and sell machinery. I tore up the letter and had a word to the party boss in Darwin and he said I had nothing to worry about, an old comrade like me. Three months later, I got another Section 5. This time I went to see a lawyer in Harare and he said we would lodge an objection to the eviction order. Weekend after that, I went fishing, stayed a few days at the shack, and when I got back I found my land had been pegged, divided up, and there were people settled all over the place. About forty families camped on my land. I told the bastards to get off. They told me to get lost – and if I didn't clear off they'd kill me. "Come and try," I said. A month later I got another order – a Section 7 – it said I had forty-five days to vacate. So I went back to the lawyer and he went to court to try and stop it. I also went to see the DA, another old friend, and I asked for help. The DA looked into my eyes and said he'd do anything he could. I knew he meant it and I also knew he couldn't do a bloody thing. Next morning the guys camped on my land stole my tractors, and my borehole pump. They told me again to leave or they'd take me out. I don't want to sound like I had it so hard. Everyone was getting invaded, beaten, robbed. I mean, at least I wasn't murdered. But I was alone and if I'd been taken out no one would have noticed. Other farmers had rigged up a support network; they kept in touch by radio, phone; they had patrols; they had family. Hell, I didn't even have a security fence. What for? I was home, wasn't I? But these guys had pangas, and they weren't kidding. "I can't just pack up and leave. It's been forty years," I said. "Go, or die," they said. I went to the cops and told them I was being threatened; they were very polite and said they'd come over and take care of it. But they never pitched.

'A few nights later, the squatters lit fires in the garden; they were dancing and singing. My own staff took off; they were too scared to stay. I tried to phone the cops but the line was cut. I sat up with a shotgun, but the guys in the garden knew I'd fall asleep sooner or later. Frankly, I was fucked. So, around midnight, I packed up some food, some clothes, my passport, some booze and loaded the Nissan *bakkie*. And then I waited. When first light came and I knew the bastards would be getting some kip, I opened the barn doors, climbed into the *bakkie* and put my foot flat on the floor. I hit the farm gate at about forty k's and tore right through it before they could rub the sleep out of their eyes. You know, Alex, when I landed in Darwin, back in 1963, I was carrying more than when I fucking left.' Papadop laughed. 'Bloody funny, isn't it, hey?'

'Not really.'

'*Ja*, well, no, maybe not; that's why I'm laughing. What else can you do?' Papadop poured us more brandy. 'Sorry about no ice in the Coke. I always stock up on ice at the Plymouth Arms when I go into town, but I got nothing to keep it bloody cold, you see, except a cool-bag. As soon as I earn some bucks from that ...' he waved towards his field of tobacco '... a fridge is first on my list.'

I reckoned it was a long list. He had next to nothing: his tent, a sleeping bag, a shaving mirror, a few clothes and an old Nissan truck. Yet the man exuded a kind of weary relief. Anywhere was better than home was the way he put it. 'I been in Moz five months now, and I'm winning.' By scrounging what he needed from neighbours he'd planted his first tobacco crop. He had been down with malaria a couple of times, 'It's bloody endemic here. But they got good Chinese *muti* at the hospital. Couple of shots, and you sweat it out. Shit, man, I tell you malaria's manageable; Mugabe isn't. I love it here. I go down on my knees and thank God for my lease.'

'You don't own this land?'

Papadop enjoyed explaining: it appealed to his sense of the ridiculous. There were some verbal adjustments that needed to be made. Mozambique clung poignantly to old Marxist ideas, and all land belonged to the state. New farmers, said Papadop, could not buy land but they could lease a patch for fifty years.

He was seventy-four, his black hair streaked with grey, but he was full of plans. The soil was rich, the rains good, water plentiful, and the local labour force was 'wonderful'.

'They'd steal the milk outa your coffee if you didn't keep an eye on them, but really nice people.'

He spoke no Portuguese but his Shona was better than his English.

'After all, we're just down the fucking road from Zim. Head on up the road and you're *en route* for Harare. All the guys in these parts speak or understand Shona.'

There were around two dozen Zimbos farming around Chimoio, said Papadop.

'The woman over at the Plymouth Arms, she talked of Ports and Pongos. Who are they?'

'Ports are Portuguese who've come back to Mozambique to farm, or whatever. Pongos are Brits who turn up, as Brits do, in odd places like this. We've even got a few Boers here from South Africa. But it's us Zimbos or ex-Zimbos who're making stuff grow. Or putting in some dairy herds, or farming flowers.'

It made a kind of twisted sense. Mozambique needed skilled technicians, which farmers were, and the old colonist bosses needed a leg-up. Put them together and bingo! Except that the Zimbos were not colonists, they were – or they had been – citizens. Until suddenly they weren't. They were homeless, stateless, unmentionable.

'I'm not allowed to call myself a "farmer" 'cause that has, well, layers of meaning. Back in Zim, it means settler, and settler means white. So here I'm not a farmer; they call us "investors". But it's being white, that's the bugger, Alex. It really is.'

Being white in Zim endangered your health; all it did in Moz, said Papadop, was to cramp your mobility a bit. Official thinking had it that hard-drinking Zimbos in the bush would gang together and begin behaving badly. And it might look like the bad old days. So the Mozambicans had taken a leaf from old ethno-fascist South Africa which always believed tribe trumped all other considerations: it was a wheeze called 'influx control' that Mozambique used to limit the numbers of white Zimbos in any one area.

However, these restrictions aside, the visitors might plough, sow, reap and sell to their hearts' content.

And it worked. Zimbos, Pongos, Brits, Ports and Boers raised cattle, fish and flowers. They swapped tractors, begged capital, sold themselves to the big tobacco companies; they hustled, schemed and grafted. They got legless at Cecelia's pub. They lived under tents, in shacks, they took over deserted Portuguese villas, they camped in caravans or in half-built ranches on remote hills.

It was admirable, and it was weird; they were doing what their great-grandparents had done, making a home in Africa. They were boisterous, big-mouthed and rude: in a word, they were pioneers. All over again.

In Africa, what passed as a new dawn was as often as not just the old dawn repackaged. I remembered how Papadop had hated the old racial divisions as practised down south, the boxed-in mind and manners of the apartheid state; how he'd settled in a free country, Southern Rhodesia, and acclimatised. Then did it all again in a free country called Zimbabwe. And now here he was, once again, on a hillside in Marxist Mozambique ...

'Right back where I fucking well began: the bastards!'

'What or who do you feel you are now, Papadop?'

'Buggered if I know. When I came to South Africa I was a

Greek; then I moved to Darwin and I was Rhodesian; then I was a Zimbabwean. I thought I'd die a Zimbabwean.' He chuckled. 'Come to think of it, I damn nearly did!'

'So what'll you do?'

He scratched his head and reached for the brandy. 'Keep going.'

'Forward?'

'No, Alex. Not forward. There is no forward for me. Keep on, that's all. It's over for me. But here I can at least pretend.'

'Pretend what?'

'Pretend to be liked, pretend to be home. When I first came to Africa there was British Nyasaland, German South West Africa, Portuguese Zambesia, Northern and Southern Rhodesia, French Equatorial Africa; the Spanish Sahara, Belgian Congo, Italians in Abyssinia, Germans in Cameroon. Some guys even dreamt of a new Israel – in Uganda. That was the time of the visitors: Asians, Chinese, Russians, Lebanese diamond dealers, Belgian priests, French colonials, British polo players, Ports, Germans, Rhodies ... Zimbos. Odds and sods from the world over. Where are they now? Or, where are we?' He showed his good, strong teeth. 'I think it's over, the whole adventure. Finished. And soon it will reach down south.'

'It's started. There are South African expats from Detroit to Vancouver. You even get them in Greece. Could you go back to being Greek?'

He laughed again and shook his head, 'Man, I can't even remember being Greek. My trouble is I love Africa, and that's a very bad mistake because she does not love me.'

'But you're still here, Papadop.'

He shook his head. 'Some of me, maybe. Pretending to belong, pretending to be a pioneer. Can't be done. It doesn't really work. It could work, maybe, if I came at it from some utterly strange direction. Maybe you gotta die, and come back as someone else? Even then, I'd stay very, very close to the ground, so I didn't cast a big shadow. Look at me. Look where I am now. A little patch of rented land, a few tobacco plants. I'm not really a farmer, not a Zimbo, not a settler. If I went up the road an hour or two I'd hit the Zim border. I can just about see from here the land I left, but it isn't home any more. And I think maybe it never was.'

He did not suggest I stay and I would not have wished it. I'd found him, I'd done what I'd wanted, he was still alive, and that was good to know. He walked me down to my car, and I gave him the stuff.

'My ma wanted you to have these.'

Papadop examined the map showing Livingstone's journey from coast to coast; he laughed at the rusty sound of the accordion; Livingstone's cap fascinated him. He kept turning it around in his hands. But he also looked a bit perplexed. He rubbed his jaw in the way I always remembered and which, for some reason, I found very moving.

'Bloody hell, man, is it the very thing?'

'She thought so.'

'It's not that I'm not very grateful, Alex boy, but I don't know quite what to do with them. You see how I live.' He waved his hands at the tent, his camp fire, the empty land that reached to the smudgy hills on the horizon.

I said: 'Yeah, I see.' He hugged me and I climbed into the car.

I couldn't turn the Toyota so I backed slowly down the hill. He watched me; a bulky man on a hillside in Mozambique, waving me on encouragingly with the cap until I'd bounced and scraped my way to the road. When I looked back he'd put on the cap and was watching me. It suited him, that cap; you could say it fitted.

After their famous meeting under the old mango tree, Livingstone went on to die a hero and a saint, and Stanley went on to seriously fuck up the Congo. Both were vividly remembered. Papadop was not going to be remembered. Except by me. Perhaps that was the real sign of change. Whites who came to Africa once strove for remembrance; now all they ask is to be forgotten and forgiven. Or ignored. Like Jimmy Li Fu in far-away Malaysia, thanking God that the government tolerated him, and did not send him 'home'.

I drove down Jan Smuts Avenue, and parked outside the house. I unlocked the security gate. The lights in the house were on and I heard music from the living room. It was '*Mambo Italiano*', then '*Freeway Mambo*', and then, as I stood there in the garden, it was '*Besame Mucho*', and I heard a man say, '*Hecho muy bien, Seendie!*'

I knew many things all at once.

The last of my mother's lovers had found each other. Or at least a way of life that suited the circumstances. In my mother's house that very finished South African, Dr Cornelius du Toit, could pretend for a while to be a refugee again, a Latino on the lam, daring, wild, exciting. And Cindy could pretend to be my mother.

My mother had felt the wind blowing and held on to the kids. Papadop, too. The kids made a pretty insubstantial anchor and so did Papadop's ridiculous lease but nonetheless he clung to it, in his tent, on the rich red hillside of a foreign land. Hung on for dear life.

The music stopped and started again. Again, I knew the tune. They were dancing now to '*La Faroana*', and I heard Raoul clap, and snap his fingers, and call out when she got going: '*Mambo, qué rico el mambo!*'

I knew, too, that this latest development left me free to leave. But I kept walking.

You gotta die, and come back again as someone else ...

So what changed?

As you might expect, everything and not much. I still went to the Zoo and stood in front of the gorilla. I remembered that Alexander Barnes, who roamed across the Congo with his 'kine', and whose jerky films of the Waturi pygmies, those 'forest dwarfs', lit up my boyhood, had a particular weakness for shooting any animal at all, but killing gorillas was amongst his favourite forms of slaughter. He gave my mother a picture of a rare Kivu gorilla he had shot in the Virunga Mountains. The gorilla looked alive, seated on the grass, his eyes open, his mouth gaping, his arms raised above his head: you needed to look carefully to see they were roped by the wrists to an overhead branch. Next to the rare gorilla was his servant, identified on the photograph as 'the boy Swalim'. He was a man of about forty, a tiny figure in a buttoned white tunic, sitting beside the great ape, to give a sense of human scale.

I went most days to the Bernberg Museum, though it opened now for just three mornings a week. It was a sign of the times. The present Jo'burg City Council was not the one to which the sisters left their house. The new council was strapped for cash. It had other priorities. A museum of European fashion did not accord with the spirit of the new council, which wanted to put its money into break-dancing.

People who wanted old Eurocentric stuff, like couture and ballet, could pay for it themselves.

To begin with I think Cindy was a little perplexed to find me among the flower-beds, mowing the lawn, weeding. But she got over it. After all, everything was sort of back to normal. My mother's house again had an owner, and a gardener in the back room. After a few weeks no one looked at me twice.

One evening, about six months later, I was in the garden. The light softened and lay gently on the grass, the colours that had burnt out in the midday sun came flooding back and everything turned gentle and flowed and I could forget Jo'burg was flat stony veld set about with mine-dumps. I had the sprinkler going on the lawn, the grass smelt of water and earth, when looping over the electrified fence topping the security walls came the evening paper. It landed with a thud in the concrete path: the Johannesburg *Star*. I could read the headline: 'Jo'burg to Get a Thousand More Cops!' Lying beside the paper was Noddy's hat. The feather caught the sun, all its rainbow colours shimmering.

I kept the handsome Tyrolean hat on the hook on the wall in his old room, waiting for him. Sometimes I used to go and look at it, so silly, so lost. A hat without a head. I knew what it was to exist cut off from the vital reality that makes us make sense to ourselves. Without the person of Noddy to give this hat a body, an Africa to carry it off in, it remained marooned. Something similar was facing me. Get ahead of the game, or fuck off out of here, said the voice of sharp Jo'burg wisdom. Grab hold of things, or get lost.

Cindy knew that. Almost every day there was a new move.

She was on her way: Dr du Toit came at night, moonlighting, literally. Upstanding general practitioner of impeccable credentials by day, mambo dancer by moonlight, and the man who taught her the difficult rhythms of that most tricky dance. Cindy perhaps taught him those things he most needed to understand: like the meaning of *ubuntu*; and empowerment and stakeholders and what a role player was.

So I did as Papadop suggested: I kept my head down, kept myself to myself. I wasn't an air-conditioning salesman, I wasn't a white South African, I wasn't a gun owner, I wasn't interested in politics, or the price of gold, and I had no intention of making myself known to anyone.

I have very little in my room. A bed, a hat, a box. The box is the one we always believed once held the skull of Mrs Ples. I like to think of her as one of the first in these parts to have got the hang of things, to have known she was transitional, destined to pass away, but who give rise to some hair-raising descendants, alarming super-hominids of which Jo'burgers are still the primal example. It all began here; what a sobering thought. My mother had been quite right: this town doesn't have a history, it has a police record. Or would, if only there were some cosmic cops around. As it is, I'd take Cindy's advice: 'If stopped by the police, do not stop ...'

I kept an eye on Cindy, in the way we like to think the spirits of the departed keep watch over the living world. At least, I liked to think so. Cindy said this haunting freaked her out, but I had to correct her. I was no ghost, I was simply the gardener, I lived in the room assigned to the gardener.

I didn't shout the odds. Neither did I assume too much authority, even on my chosen patch; after all, my knowledge was minimal, the little I'd picked up from Noddy. I had to teach myself a lot before I could tell the difference between a poor man's orchid (Schizanthus) and a cupid's dart (Catananche). But I knew how to lift dahlia tubers without breaking their necks. And I bought wilt-resistant snapdragons.